continued . . .

Berkley Sensation books by Julia London

MATERIAL GIRL
BEAUTY QUEEN
MISS FORTUNE

Miss Fortune

JULIA LONDON

BERKLEY SENSATION, NEW YORK

THE BERKLEY PUBLISHING GROUP
Published by the Penguin Group
Penguin Group (USA) Inc.
375 Hudson Street, New York, New York 10014, USA
Penguin Group (Canada), 10 Alcorn Avenue, Toronto, Ontario M4V 3B2, Canada
(a division of Pearson Penguin Canada Inc.)
Penguin Books Ltd., 80 Strand, London WC2R 0RL, England
Penguin Group Ireland, 25 St. Stephen's Green, Dublin 2, Ireland (a division of Penguin Books Ltd.)
Penguin Group (Australia), 250 Camberwell Road, Camberwell, Victoria 3124, Australia
(a division of Pearson Australia Group Pty. Ltd.)
Penguin Books India Pvt. Ltd., 11 Community Centre, Panchsheel Park, New Delhi—110 017,
India
Penguin Group (NZ), Cnr. Airborne and Rosedale Roads, Albany, Auckland 1310, New Zealand
(a division of Pearson New Zealand Ltd.)
Penguin Books (South Africa) (Pty.) Ltd., 24 Sturdee Avenue, Rosebank, Johannesburg 2196,
South Africa

Penguin Books Ltd., Registered Offices: 80 Strand, London WC2R 0RL, England

This is a work of fiction. Names, characters, places, and incidents either are the product of the author's imagination or are used fictitiously, and any resemblance to actual persons, living or dead, business establishments, events, or locales is entirely coincidental.

MISS FORTUNE

A Berkley Sensation Book / published by arrangement with the author

PRINTING HISTORY
Berkley Sensation edition / November 2004

Copyright © 2004 by Julie London.
Cover design by Rita Frangie.
Cover photo by Chad Baker/Ryan McVay for Getty Images.
Interior text design by Kristin del Rosario.

ISBN: 0-425-19917-7

BERKLEY® SENSATION
Berkley Sensation Books are published by The Berkley Publishing Group,
a division of Penguin Group (USA) Inc.,
375 Hudson Street, New York, New York 10014.
BERKLEY SENSATION and the "B" design
are trademarks belonging to Penguin Group (USA) Inc.

PRINTED IN THE UNITED STATES OF AMERICA

10 9 8 7 6 5 4 3 2 1

FORKLIFT ACCIDENT DAMAGES PRICELESS ARTIFACTS

By Mary Finnegan

NEWPORT, Aug. 21—A priceless Revolutionary-era hutch, inlaid with gold and ivory, as well as some china bowls and plates, on loan to the Rhode Island Historical Preservation Society (RIHPS) from the Hamblen family, were damaged beyond repair last week when a forklift, involved in the repair of the foundation of the historical Botwick House in Newport, Rhode Island, collided with an exterior wall.

An assistant curator, Professor Myron Tidwell, 38, said that in the course of repairing the foundation, the forklift gears jammed and the front loader hit the wall, damaging the contents inside. "We are assessing the incident now," Professor Tidwell said. "If we find the driver was at fault, we will take appropriate action, but at the moment, it looks like a tragic accident and a loss to America of precious pre–Revolutionary War artifacts.

"The loss value of the hutch and china could very well be in the thousands. The damage to the structure could likewise be very costly. We are quantifying the claim," Tidwell said. The RIHPS insures its structures and their contents.

Chapter One

✦ ✦ ✦

New York City

THEY were seated in two overstuffed chairs that put their heads below that of the marriage therapist across from them, who, with his legs comfortably crossed, drummed idly on the armrest as he peered down at his notes.

Aaron Lear thought this guy probably liked this setup, lording himself over all the poor slobs who couldn't make their relationships with even their underwear work.

Daniel (the therapist preferred the use of first names) was wearing a custom-made suit and square matchbox glasses. He had a dozen or more certificates framed and hung on the wall behind him, and boxes of tissue on every conceivable surface.

Frankly, Aaron hated him and his psycho-crap and how he looked down his nose and asked them to describe their feelings. Honestly, he couldn't say which was worse—enduring the pain and sickness and overwhelming disappointment of having to undergo chemo and radiation again for a cancer that had come back with a vengeance? Or that he had to share his feelings?

Either way, it all led to the same, mortal conclusion, and he preferred not to sit around pondering the inevitability of his life coming to an end. Shit, he was a year away from being sixty years old and still had too much to do.

Granted, in the last two years he had seen his oldest two daughters find love and contentment, which was his most pressing pre-death desire. But he still had another daughter who needed him, the most hapless of his girls, his baby, Rachel. She hadn't found her way in life. How could he go before he had seen her through to . . . something?

And of course there was Bonnie, the love of his life, the mother of his children, the woman he had treated like shit for more than thirty years, which, incidentally, was why they were sitting here waiting for Daniel the Overpriced Therapist to review some notes.

Actually, Aaron still thought it pretty remarkable they had reconciled. The day he had strapped on a pair of balls and gone to Los Angeles to beg her to give him one more chance he didn't deserve, he'd seen her face and knew at once he'd do anything. He'd seen the beautiful blue eyes that still glistened after all these years, the shiny dark hair with just a hint of gray . . . and the unforgiving set of her jaw.

That was the moment he'd known she'd not allow him back into her life, would not sully one more day with him. Frankly, he'd been more certain of that than he had been that the cancer had returned.

But somehow—perhaps through divine intervention, who knew?—Bonnie had let him in one last time. But with concessions. A host of them he couldn't really recall right now except for the pompous ass seated across from them.

The pompous ass must have felt his despising vibes, because he looked up, smiled at Aaron, and said, "We did some *good* work Monday! We learned about our mutual feelings surrounding the first separation, didn't we?"

Bonnie nodded. Aaron just glared at him.

"Now Bonnie, when we met on Monday, you indicated you were agitated about a recent event, do you recall?" Daniel asked.

"Yes, I do," Bonnie said primly. She was sitting ramrod straight, her hands folded in her lap, looking gorgeous with her dark hair cropped short and wild, just like he saw in the magazines he read when he was getting chemo.

"Would you care to talk a little about that?" Daniel prompted.

She sighed, looked at Aaron. "I guess its old news now. It was just that our daughter Rachel had been up to care for Aaron while I went back to Los Angeles to take care of a few things—"

"Because your primary home is in Los Angeles, correct? And you've come to New York to be with your husband during a difficult time," Daniel said, a little heavy on the forlorn.

"That's right." Bonnie nodded, just as forlornly. "Anyway, Rachel did not want to come to New York. She's trying to finish her degree, you see—"

"That's not why she didn't want to come, Bonnie, and you know it," Aaron said.

"*Aaron,*" Daniel said gently. "Remember our rules—no one talks over their partner. Everyone has a chance to speak. When Bonnie finishes, you'll have your turn to speak."

Bonnie sat a little straighter. "It is true that Rachel has had a difficult time finishing school and moving on with her life," Bonnie conceded. "She has been a doctoral candidate for a couple of years now."

Daniel chuckled. "I can attest to the fact that taking a couple of years to finish a doctorate may not be as strange as it sounds."

God, what an idiot, Aaron thought with disgust.

"Yes, well . . . Rachel has been dating this man—a professor—and hasn't really shown any inclination to finish her doctorate and get on with her life."

"Can you give me some examples of her disinclination?"

Aaron damn sure could, but Bonnie always got to go first.

"Okay, for example, she travels to England frequently to find a topic for her dissertation—her degree is in ancient British history, we think. But she says there are so many interesting ideas that she hasn't been able to land on a topic yet."

"And you think that is . . . ? What, untrue?"

"Hell yes we think it's untrue!" Aaron interjected.

"*Aaron* thinks it is untrue," Bonnie corrected him. "But I don't. Rachel is bright and articulate and has a heart of gold. She just doesn't understand where she fits in to this world, and she never really has. And when she has to land on something as defining as a dissertation topic, she can't find her answer."

"And why is that, do you think?" Daniel asked. Bonnie shrugged. Daniel nodded, wrote something down on his notepad. "How exactly did Rachel's indecision lead to your recent agitation with Aaron?"

Bonnie snorted and looked out the window. "Aaron wouldn't leave her alone. The whole time I was gone, he kept badgering her about her useless degree, and her useless boyfriend, and her *weight,* of all things! By the time I got back from L.A., Rachel had fled back to Providence."

"That was very upsetting for you, wasn't it, Bonnie?"

"Yes! He *swore* he wouldn't do that!" she said, pinning Aaron with a heated look.

"But I didn't swear I would let my daughter flounder!" Aaron shot back at her.

"Aaron, remember our rule," Daniel reminded him once more with a smile.

Aaron came very close to telling him to go fuck his rules, but bit his tongue because he had promised Bonnie he would do this counseling, even if it killed him.

Daniel kept smiling. "Let's talk a moment about the promises we think we hear. Bonnie, what did you hear Aaron promise you?"

"That he would change," she said, shooting him another look. "And that he would attend marriage counseling with me, that he'd go to church and *listen,* and that he would stop berating our daughters for every little thing. He's been doing that all their lives, always thinking he knows best, and he practically alienated our oldest, Robin, from us for good because he was always *pushing,* and then there was Rebecca—that poor girl had just suffered through a difficult time with her divorce, and Aaron was so certain he had to *teach* her something instead of letting her figure it out on her own, and now with Rachel . . . I'm just worried that he will push her away, too, and of all our daughters, I think Rachel is the one who really needs us the most."

"When the hell do *I* get to talk?" Aaron demanded.

"You may talk now," Daniel said cheerfully.

"Okay, here is what happened," Aaron said, sitting up a little straighter. "First of all, this guy Rachel's been hanging around the last couple of years is *never* going to support her. In fact, she's been loaning money to that loser, which means she's been loaning him *my* money! And she can't even see the irony in that! She's like, 'Dad, he really needs it more than me.' Bullshit! And speaking of irony, here's my second point," he said, pausing to take a breath. "I told her when I first got sick that she had one year to finish her degree. I said, 'Either shit or get off the pot, but you have to figure out how to make your own way in this world, because dear old Dad ain't going to be around to make it for you.' Come on, Bonnie, you backed me up on that," he reminded her.

Bonnie looked at her lap and nodded.

"So I told Rach that the money train she'd been living off of for thirty or so years was leaving the station. And you know what? She had *more* than a year! She had almost *two,* for Chrissakes, and she *still* hasn't finished her degree!"

"And how does it make you feel when Rachel doesn't do what you ask?"

Was this joker kidding? "Well, *Daniel,* it makes me *angry,* and before you give me that smirk, I'll add that you have no idea how maddening it is to see your own flesh and blood just twisting in the wind! And you know what the shit of it is? Of all our girls, Rachel is the most creative, and may even be the brightest, but there she goes, spinning her wheels in a dead-end graduate field with a dead-end guy. Aimless!" he said, throwing up his hands. "Totally aimless!"

"You don't understand her, Aaron, and you never have!" Bonnie exclaimed, and Aaron wondered why *she* got to talk during *his* time. "Rachel is a pretty girl, but she's not a beauty like her sisters."

"What do looks have to do with it?" Aaron demanded. "You ask me, Rachel is more attractive than her sisters. She's got that all-American rosy-cheek look and that long dark curly hair she ties up on her head," he said, gesturing at his head in a tie-up way. "Her problem is she doesn't want to go where life is leading her."

"Not where *life* is leading her," Bonnie said. "Where *you're* leading her."

Oddly enough, that remark stopped Aaron cold, and he stared at Bonnie for a long moment.

"How does that make you feel, Aaron?" Daniel asked quietly.

"It makes me feel like Bonnie doesn't understand me. It's not *me* that's leading her; it's that useless degree and that useless boyfriend. That's real nice, ain't it? After ten years of higher education, what have we got to show for it?"

"Go with that," Daniel urged him. "Go with your feelings. How are you feeling?"

"Ashamed," he said flatly, ignoring Bonnie's gasp. "Ashamed that we didn't do better by her. Sorry that I don't have the time to go back and fix it all. Yet I have to do *something* because that girl is still relying on me—I asked her, 'What are you going to do when I die?' and all she could do was cry. It's like talking to a goddamn wall."

"I'd like to suggest a couple of things here, Aaron," Daniel said, templing his fingers. "First of all, it is possible that Rachel is quite happy in what she is doing. She may not aspire to the same things you aspire to for her."

"Obviously!" he snorted, folding his arms over his chest.

"Your message is a good one, however. You want her to learn to provide for herself, to be an adult, am I right?"

"Yes! That is exactly what I am trying to do, but oh no, I'm the *monster*," he said, mimicking quotation marks at Bonnie.

"Perhaps, then, since your usual way of communicating with Rachel doesn't appear to be working, you might try a different approach," Daniel said smoothly. "If you feel like you are talking to a brick wall, then change the way you are talking."

"How the hell can I be any plainer?"

"What do you think would happen if you were kind to Rachel?" Daniel asked.

Aaron blinked. "Come again?"

"Think about being kind to Rachel. Try seeing the situation from her shoes."

Aaron frowned. "I don't know what you mean."

"Well, let me try this," Daniel said, exchanging a look with Bonnie. "If I'm Rachel, I'm around thirty years old, I've been in school for a long time. Maybe so long I don't even remember what the real world looks like anymore. And maybe I like my professor boyfriend because he doesn't push me; he just lets me be who I am. And maybe, when someone suggests I step outside my comfortable world into the real world, it makes me nervous, and I do things to maintain a sense of comfort, like overeat."

Aaron was already shaking his head at the mumbo jumbo. "Why in God's name would she be afraid to step out into the real world?"

"Because," Bonnie said softly, "every time she has, she stood in the shadow of two very accomplished and beautiful older sisters, and she is criticized for the way she looks, and for the things that interest her, and essentially, for who she is. In Providence, she's not criticized, she's accepted for who she is. She's safe. Out there, she's not."

Aaron felt a little dip in his belly.

"So I'm going to suggest some communication exercises you can do over the weekend," Daniel began, and reached for a pair of booklets.

Aaron closed his eyes, thought that he just might vomit.

Chapter Two

✦ ✦ ✦

Providence, Rhode Island
Two weeks later

THE whole thing started with a bottle of wine and a heated debate over which spell to use.

Dagne Delaney, Rachel's best friend, was over for dinner when Rachel said she thought Dagne's spell sounded like some kid's jump rope rhyme, and suggested, seeing as how Dagne was brand-new to the witchcraft thing, that perhaps she needed a little more study before they did something really stupid.

Dagne, predictably, did not appreciate Rachel's suggestion in the least.

But Rachel wasn't into the white magic thing. In all fairness, she'd tried to explain to Dagne more than once that she really did think this witch deal was sort of out there.

But when Dagne was starting off on some grand adventure, she tended not to hear very well. Unless, of course, you said you thought her spell sucked, and then she'd hear each word, memorize them, and repeat them back with a hurtful look like you had criticized her shoes or something. Judas Priest.

In spite of Dagne being slender, strawberry blond, and

pretty—the sort of gal pal Rachel typically avoided—they had met at Brown University a few years ago when they were both students of history, and quickly discovered a shared fascination for all manner of funky things.

Rachel was still a student of history (or as her father said, a PERPETUAL student of history), but Dagne got bored with it, decided she couldn't afford it on her hair stylist income, and come to think of it, she was way more interested in hairstyling than history. And even though she'd gone on to be more interested in massage therapy than hairstyling, she and Rachel had remained fast friends.

Which was why Dagne was in her house now, bugging her about witchcraft. This particular thing had started when Rachel returned from New York and after the worst fight with Dad she'd ever had. She had made the mistake of studying her astrology chart to see what was up and concluded that the planets were pushing her to make some changes. When she showed the chart to Dagne, her brown eyes sort of bugged out, and she said, "Girl, you have *got* to make some *changes*."

And then she'd shown up tonight, fully prepared to make Rachel's changes for her. After dinner, of course, which Rachel was still in the midst of preparing.

Dagne helped herself to a glass of wine and asked, "So what have you come up with?"

"Nothing," Rachel sighed, tossing the salad.

Dagne paused to swipe a chunk of red bell pepper from the salad Rachel was making. "Hey, cool bowl," she remarked.

Yes, cool bowl. Very pretty bowl. Cut glass, gilded rim, hand-painted scenes of a lovely French countryside painted around the bottom. "A gift from Myron," Rachel said. "They must be having a sale at the museum gift shop."

Myron used to be her boyfriend. Now he was her friend and a part-time assistant curator with the Rhode Island Historical Preservation Society. He had a habit of bringing her gifts from the museum gift shops instead of the money he owed her.

"So I've been thinking about this," Dagne said earnestly. "Did you notice that Mars and Mercury are in retrograde? That makes everything *soooo* obvious. I mean, it's like *impossible* to try and move forward with your life with that going on, right?"

Who could argue the retrograde theory?

"Everything is pointing toward reassessment. Whatever you thought your plan was? Rethink it."

Rachel snorted as she added slivers of portabella mushrooms to the salad. "*What* plan? I don't have a plan! My internship just ended, I hardly have enough to pay the utilities and phone bill, and my dad is *so* not going to help me out."

"That's the other thing," Dagne said cheerfully. "Jupiter is getting close to the sun, which, of course, will affect your income, so by the end of the month, you should be flush." This she announced as if it was a done deal, no questions asked. All Rachel had to do was wake up at the end of the month and *presto!* Money.

"*Flush?*" Rachel said accusingly, and carried a bowl of salad to the dining room.

"*Flush,*" Dagne said emphatically. "Listen to your cosmic meter, Rachel."

Frankly, Rachel sometimes wondered if she shouldn't listen to anything or anyone but Dagne. She returned to the kitchen, grabbed the wine and their glasses, and brought those to the dining room while Dagne grabbed her canvas bag and the tofu lasagna.

"There's actually some good news in my horoscope," Rachel said as she pushed the salad toward Dagne. "When Mars comes out of retrograde at the end of the month, it should kick some butt in my tenth house, which means . . . drum roll, please . . . new job!" She lifted salad tongs in triumph, then handed them to Dagne.

"Really," she continued. "I believe that once Mars and Mercury wake up, things are going to start happening for me—new job, new money, new life. I just have to make a couple of other teeny-tiny adjustments."

"Like better money management!"

Dagne declared it so adamantly that Rachel looked at her in surprise. Dagne raised her brows, silently daring Rachel to argue. Oh sure, like Dagne was a wiz at money management, which she was so not!

"I *mean* . . . you should stop giving it away," Dagne clarified.

Rachel laughed. "I don't give it all away!"

"Well, you're always loaning money to friends," she said, and the Wiz at Money Management should know, since she had borrowed money from Rachel in the past. "But now that you're completely on your own, you're going to have to take care of yourself first."

"Fine," Rachel said with a shrug. "Better money management. But the big thing is, I need to lose some weight."

Dagne winced a little, looked at the salad bowl again. "That's really a beautiful bowl," she said. "It's amazing how antiquey they can make these copies look."

Wow. Apparently she *did* need to lose some weight. "You don't have to act like you haven't noticed," Rachel said petulantly.

"*I* think you look terrific!" Dagne insisted. "Full figures are all the rage! But you know . . . it never hurts to drop a couple of lbs before you start a new project."

Ouch. That bad. So much for trotting out the double-fudge brownies for dessert. But it wasn't like her weight was anything new. Her dad mentioned it every other breath, Grandma kept sending diet books, Mom tiptoed around the subject like she thought Rachel might crumple into a crying heap.

All right, it was true. She'd steadily put on a few pounds each year until she was now about twenty pounds . . . okay, twenty-five . . . over what she ought to weigh. It wouldn't be so bad if she didn't have two older sisters, Robin and Rebecca, who were both pencil thin and beautiful. Why stop there? They were beautiful and rich in their own right and married to wonderful men and had beautiful children surrounding them.

And here sat Rachel, their fat-ass little sister whose eyes were too far apart and her hair too wild to be stylish and her feet too big for really cool strappy high heels, dammit!

"I'm sorry," Dagne said.

"Don't be," Rachel said sincerely. "I need something like finding a new job to plant the boot in my butt and make me do it. I'll just have to stop buying the junk food Myron likes."

Dagne frowned at that, picked up her fork, and stabbed her lasagna. "As to *that*," she said sternly, "you should know that Venus and Neptune are on a collision course, and when those two worlds collide, look out, because you just might find the love of your life, and his name is *so* not Myron!"

"I know his name isn't *Myron*."

"Are you sure? I mean, the guy eats you out of house and home, he's always borrowing your stuff *and* your money, and what do you get out of it?"

Rachel could feel her face flaming. "We're *friends*," she said, and hid behind a good slug of wine.

"You're *his* friend. Myron just takes."

"That's not true. He's been very supportive of my education when no one else would be, and he's been a real trooper when it comes to Dad. I mean, he picked me up at the train station when I got back from the two-week trip through hell, and he couldn't have been more understanding. And look at all the stuff he's given me."

"I just think it's weird to be friends with a guy who dumped you."

"He didn't dump me! It was mutual!" Rachel insisted. "And he's just a *friend*. What's wrong with that? It's not like men are banging down the door, Dagne."

"They would if you'd let them," she said, and that was the moment the debate started, because Dagne instantly flashed a bright smile. "And when I'm through with you, girl, they'll be lined up around the block!"

Rachel instantly knew what she was up to and immediately started waving a hand at her. "No way! That witch thingy is your deal, not mine."

"What have you got to lose?" Dagne asked cheerfully.

"No," Rachel said.

"Come on," Dagne pleaded.

"NO!"

And on it went through dinner and another glass of wine, until Rachel was feeling pretty groovy and agreeable.

Dagne picked up the big canvas bag she carried everywhere she went and pulled some items from it, including a pink, leather-bound spell book (purchased on eBay, Dagne proudly proclaimed, and seemed not to appreciate the irony of someone hocking her spell book); a silver chalice; a leather string tied to an amulet that looked, from where Rachel was sitting, like a peace sign; and several candles of varying sizes. "We really should be outside, you know, calling on Mother Nature and all that, but it's too damn cold tonight," she explained, and pulled out a clump of dirt. "I'm pretty sure it doesn't matter."

"What are you *doing?*" Rachel asked as Dagne arranged her things on the dining room table.

"Making your spell, hello! A little magic to bring you peace and prosperity."

"Can you do one for a knight in shining armor?" Rachel asked, all chipper now. "That would be way cool. Make him tall. With dark hair. And available."

Dagne frowned at her lack of seriousness. "We can do a spell for *love,* but you have to be serious or it won't work. White magic is all about belief."

Rachel stifled another giggle. "Okay," she said, and held up her hand. "I'm serious. I *beeee-lieeeeeve.*" Except that she couldn't possibly believe it and burst into another fit of giggles.

"Rachel!"

"All right, all right," she said, and as it was obvious that Dagne was getting perturbed, she tried very hard to wipe the smirk from her face.

Dagne arranged the candles according to size, from the tallest to the shortest. She then instructed Rachel to get another bottle of wine (Rachel voiced her doubts about adding another bottle of wine to the mix, but Dagne insisted), and poured a generous amount of wine into a chalice that still had the Big Lots tag stuck to the bottom.

Dagne laid the leather string in a line below the candles, reached into her canvas bag, pulled out a tiny brass incense holder, a stick of incense, and lit it. "Air," she said in a loud whisper, "is for change and lightness and freedom."

"I'm all for that," Rachel said cheerfully.

"Sssh!" Dagne hissed, then poured some wine for herself and stood back, motioned for Rachel to come around to the side of the table. "Now. Are you *serious?*"

"I am. I really am," Rachel said, nodding emphatically at Dagne's dubious expression.

"You better be," Dagne said, and handed Rachel a fireplace lighter. "First, we'll do the weight-loss spell. Light the candles from tall to short, and say this as you do it: *As the moon wanes, so shall I decrease.*"

Rachel took the lighter and looked at the candles. "That's it?"

"That's it. The rest is up to you."

How fortunate for Dagne that Rachel had had just enough wine to make her pliable and think this was all sort of illicit fun. She picked up the lighter, lit the tallest candle. "As the moon wanes," she said soft and low as she began lighting the five candles, "so shall I decrease." She finished lighting the candles and looked at Dagne.

Dagne glanced at the spell book, shrugged, and took the lighter, put it back in her canvas bag. "Now for the next one. *Prosperity.*" She handed the chalice of wine to Rachel, then picked up the clump of dirt.

"What *is* that?" Rachel asked.

"Earth. You crumble this in your wine, and you say:

Add this earth to my wine, and prosperity shall I find. And then you drink."

"Wait, wait—are you saying I have to drink dirt?"

"Do you want a job?" Dagne shot back.

Rachel sighed, took the clump of dirt, and with a frown for Dagne, repeated solemnly, "Add this earth to my wine, and prosperity shall I find," as she crumbled the dirt clod into her wine. When she did not immediately pick up the chalice, Dagne poked her, and reluctantly, and grimacing, Rachel picked it up, held her breath, and drank it as quickly as she could.

Hey . . . it was kind of tasty! She smacked her lips, shoved the chalice back across the table toward a beaming Dagne.

"Okay!" Now Dagne took the leather string and amulet, which, on closer inspection, really was a tiny pewter peace sign. "You have to make three knots. And this is what you say: *As these knots I do entwine, find the heart to link to mine—*"

"Oh please—"

"Just do it, Rachel." Dagne sighed wearily.

Rachel frowned, picked up the leather string, and tied a loose knot. "As these knots I do entwine," she said, tying another one, "find the heart to link to mine." She finished with the third, twirled the little peace sign around her finger and off again, and handed the string back to Dagne. "So what, he'll come knocking any minute? How do I look?"

"No, wait," Dagne said, with a thoughtful frown. "That's not right."

"What's not right? I tied three knots like you said."

"No, the *spell*," Dagne said as she reached for her spell book and began to flip through the pages.

"Maybe you forgot the part where we dance around the campfire," Rachel suggested.

"Would you stop?"

"No, really. Don't you dance around fire or something?"

Dagne sighed. "Just shut up, will you? I need to look something up."

Rachel fell into her chair, wished for the brownies.

"Aha! *This* is it!" Dagne said excitedly, jabbing her finger onto a page. "Do you have any rose petals?"

Rachel rolled her eyes. *"No."*

Dagne looked up and around, saw a bunch of alstromerias in a vase on the hutch. "Those will have to do," she muttered, and stood up, marched around the table, and pulled one out of the vase.

"Hey!"

"Just the one," Dagne said, and put the stem on the table, picked up the chalice, and went into the kitchen.

"What are you doing?" Rachel called after her.

"Cleaning this and adding purified water!" she called back, and appeared a moment later with the chalice in hand, the water magically purified, apparently. Anxiously motioning for Rachel to stand, she said, "The first spell was to *find* the guy. But you need one to *see* the guy. I mean, you can't really do anything if you don't know who it is, right?"

"Dagne—"

Dagne thrust the alstromeria at her. "Tear the petals into small pieces and put them in the water," she said, "and then say this before you drink it in one gulp—"

"With the petals?"

"You drank dirt, Rachel. Surely you can drink a flower. Tear them up, then say: *In the night I sleep and there shall I glean, he who steals my heart from his image in my dreams.*"

Her wine buzz was definitely wearing off, and Rachel shook her head. "The first one was better. Simple, to the point. This one isn't even proper English. And besides, I think you're going overboard."

"But they're different spells."

"I don't care. The first one will do the trick and I don't want to drink flowers."

"Come *on,* Rachel!"

"No. This is stupid and I am not going to glean anything from my dreams!"

"Yes, you are. I already put a dream spell on you. *Do* it," Dagne said, thrusting the flower stem at her.

"Make me," Rachel shot back, folding her arms across her middle.

Dagne groaned to the ceiling. "Thanks a lot, Rachel! Thanks a whole helluva lot! This is my first *real* attempt at beneficial magic and you are screwing everything up! Would it *kill* you to try a spell? Would it *kill* you to help me out?"

Oh *puh-leez*, the drama queen had arrived! *"Fine,"* Rachel snapped, and snatched the flower and the chalice, and ripped the petals of the alstromeria apart, put them in the water, and picked up the chalice, holding it before her. In a stage voice worthy of a Tony Award, she said dramatically, "In the *night* I *sleep* and there shall I *dream*—"

"Glean! Shall I *glean!"* Dagne corrected her. "Start over!"

"Could you be just a little bossier? In the night I sleep and there shall I GLEAN," she repeated loudly and clearly, "he who steals my heart from his image in my dreams." She tossed the water and the alstromeria petals down her throat, slapped down the chalice.

Dagne indicated she had a part of a flower on her lip; Rachel brushed it off and said, "That may have been the dumbest thing I've ever done. And that is saying a lot."

"Have another glass of wine," Dagne said blithely.

After that, she needed one.

Actually, they both had another glass of wine, and Rachel talked Dagne into showing her a pagan ritual dance. In spite of Dagne's best efforts to remain true to her newfound beliefs, they both dissolved into a pile of giggles in the middle of her living room floor.

At that point, they decided double fudge brownies were definitely in order.

When Dagne finally went home, Rachel was feeling lighter and happier than she had since her return from New

York. She brushed her teeth, put on her favorite flannel pajamas, and crawled into bed with a romance novel about Sir Adam Percy, an English knight.

And that night, Rachel had an extremely vivid dream of said knight, who, incidentally, looked a lot like Colin Farrell, rode a mean horse, and was very much in love with her.

Chapter Three

✦ ✦ ✦

THE next morning, Rachel awoke with an uncharacteristically enthusiastic mind-set about her new diet and exercise program. She showered, donned the requisite spandex for the gym, and checked her horoscope. *People who respect your power are in short supply. You may need to step up . . .*

Not exactly the auspicious beginning she was looking for, so she checked the other water signs, Pisces and Scorpio (*Focus on accepting your faults; recent financial risks might not get the return you hoped for*), and gave up on that idea, and checked her e-mail instead. There were two.

Subject: Grandpa's Irregularity
From: Lillian Stanton <lilandel@aol.com>
To: Rachel Ellen Lear <earthangel@hotmail.com>

Hi Little Angel! This is your grandma. Is it cold in
Providence yet it was 90 degrees yesterday and I

damn near had a heatstroke working in the garden.
Your grandpa hasn't been regular in two weeks and
if something doesn't unplug that pipe I might kill him.
You ain't never seen him so grumpy but I remember
at Blue Cross you told me about some natural something I could give him to help loosen him up. What
was the name of it again? Thanks, angel. Luv U.
Grandma. P.S. I almost forgot I am sending you this
seaweed diet from the Internet because I know how
much you like things like seaweed.

Rachel quickly dispatched a response to Grandma that
did not invite any discussion about Grandpa's problem, nor
did she correct Grandma's misinterpretation that a seaweed wrap was edible. The next e-mail was from her oldest sister, Robin.

Subject: Hey
From: <rmanning70@earthlink.net>
To: Rach <earthangel@hotmail.com>

Yo, whassup dawg? Ha HAAA. Coming home for
Christmas? Hope so. Listen, remember that night
out at Blue Cross when we drank the bottle of
tequila and you tried to explain the theory behind
the universe or something equally boring, and Bec
and I were laughing at you? Not to be confused
with all the other times we've laughed at you, but
the tequila night in particular. One thing you said
sorta stuck with me—the tantric sex thing, remember? I was just wondering if there's a website or a
video or someplace like that where inquiring
minds could go nose around. Some people in
Houston might be interested.

Subject: Re: Hey
FROM: <earthangel@hotmail.com>
To: <rmanning70@earthlink.net>

Hi Robbie. Dear God, could there be trouble in PARADISE? Didn't you say once that you had the best sex life of any woman under the sun? WHAT HAPPENED??? So what, you have a baby and the spark is suddenly gone? As in kaput, snuffed out, drowned? I'll look around and see if there is a website, but most of what I was TRYING to tell you came from books. I'm amazed anything stuck with you at all after all the tequila you drank. So why don't you and Jake just make a date for the library some evening? You may be delighted and titillated by what you find there.

Rachel, who thinks it's funny you need a little spice in the boudoir.

That was all her mail, and as nothing earth-shattering was happening in Texas, she grabbed her gym bag and made for the kitchen and a bottle of water before heading out.

She stuffed the bottled water into her gym bag, hoisted it onto her shoulder, and started for the back door . . . and instantly noticed the brownies from last night staring up at her from the breakfast bar, screaming her name. No, really, they were screaming, *Rachel, Rachel, you're going to the gym anyway, so what's one brownie?*

The brownies had a point. Surely she'd burn off any brownie calories in the first half hour. In fact, she could do the power Yogilates class to be extra sure . . . which really gave her license to eat two brownies, didn't it?

She managed to escape the kitchen before a third brownie jumped into her hand, and she paused at the back door, peering furtively out the little window to make sure her next-door neighbors weren't outside engaged in their obsessive-compulsive disorder behavior of excessive yard work. This was not something she was exaggerating—there really was something seriously wrong with the Valicielos. As in, Mr. Valicielo spent most afternoons trimming something—shrubs, grass, trees, even their ridiculously tiny dog. And when he ran out of things to trim, he mowed a new pattern in the lawn—crisscrosses, checkerboards, gridirons.

Likewise, Mrs. Valicielo was forever on her foam rubber knee pads, her enormous butt high in the air while she weeded the garden, although it was hard to see how a weed could possibly even root, much less bare its ugly head, as vigilant as she was with her trowel.

The Valicielos were so obsessed with that yard that when the elm in Rachel's backyard succumbed to root rot and fell over, landing squarely on top of the Valicielos's chain-link fence, she knew it was big trouble.

Yep, Mr. Valicielo was over within the hour, anxiously gripping and ungripping his gardening hat as he inquired as to when she might have the tree removed.

"As soon as I can, Mr. Valicielo," she said. "I don't have the money just now."

"Aha," he said, and looked at the tree laid across his fence again, wincing. "But it will ruin the fence. . . . There's gotta be *something* you can do."

Rachel looked at the tree. "I guess I could try and move it," she said, and the two of them did indeed try to move it. But they at last gave in and stood there, hands on hips, huffing with the exertion of having tried to move a tree that seemed much larger on its side than when it was standing up. "I won't leave it, I promise," she had wheezed. "I'll have it moved just as soon as I get paid."

Mr. Valicielo had looked at her like he thought that was a load of crap.

With good reason, as it turned out. It had been three weeks now, and Rachel still didn't have the money to have the tree removed. So she'd adopted the attitude of hide and watch, and when she was certain the Valicielos weren't around, she'd make a mad dash for her VW Beetle, tear out of the driveway as if she was fleeing the scene of a murder, and burn rubber all the way down Slater Avenue.

The only problem with her approach was that the Valicielos were just as determined to casually run into her and badger her about that tree. On more than one occasion, Mr. Valicielo had chased her down the drive and into the street.

Fortunately, this morning there was no sign of them, so Rachel tiptoed out to the yellow convertible Beetle, fired her up, and raced backward out of the drive. As she backed onto Slater Avenue, she noticed that while she'd been busy hiding, her neighbors (*Welcome to Our House!* a plaque on their door read, *Tony and Ermaline Valicielo*) had added two new plastic deer to accompany the five-hundred-head herd, the plastic giant frog, and the pinwheels on their perfectly manicured and festive lawn.

Rachel hit the gas and sped down the street, just in case one of them was looking out the window.

A quarter of an hour later, she bounced into the gym, carrying her extra-large café au lait. Lori, the gal at the desk, almost choked on her tomato juice when she saw Rachel. "God, I thought you had, like, *died* or something!" she exclaimed loudly.

Rachel laughed as she signed in.

"No, seriously, I thought I heard that!" Lori insisted.

All right already, so she'd missed a few weeks at the gym. "I've been out of town."

"For a whole *year?*"

That was so stupid. It hadn't been more than ten months, max, Rachel thought as she proceeded down the hall.

Her power Yogilates instructor—who had been Rachel's yoga instructor ten months ago—seemed a little confused, too, when she came into the studio. Her face scrunched up as she stared at Rachel. "Diane, right?"

"Rachel. I'm in your yoga class?"

The instructor blinked. "I haven't taught yoga in like . . . a *year,*" she said.

Well pardon her, was she the only one in Providence to have ever taken a little time off from the fitness program? Why didn't they just run something over to the paper and announce it had been A YEAR since Tubby Rachel Lear had been to the gym?

She walked to the very back corner of the room, where no one could possibly get in behind her, and rolled out her mat.

The class started out great. She remembered the moves and was feeling very rejuvenated. And then the power part began, and she was quickly so dizzy from not being able to breathe that her muscles felt like jelly. All she knew was that if the session didn't end soon, someone was going to have to call an ambulance.

When the session, at last, did end, one girl leaned over Rachel—who was lying on her mat, staring at the fluorescent lights above her. "Are you all right?" she asked, looking really concerned.

"Fine," Rachel wheezed, catching her breath and sitting up, marveling at how sadly out of shape she was. Well, no more. Rachel Lear was a new person!

She headed for the gym and the stationary bikes—just a little something to get the juices flowing. Her pace was leisurely, and she set her monitor to random hills.

She hadn't even gotten off the flat part and into the hills before a woman in gym pants and cropped top that showed off her flat belly got on the bike beside her. She looked impossibly bored as she punched some control buttons on the panel and began to cycle.

Rachel could not help noticing that when the woman leaned over, her stomach did not make little rolls. It was perfectly flat.

Gawd, she hated that woman.

Hated her so bad that in a fit of zealous bigotry, she punched "in-zone training plus" and began to pedal furiously, too. And in the space of maybe a minute, she was huffing like an old woman, sweat was trickling down between her breasts and over *her* roll and into the waistband of her spandex yoga pants, which now seemed ridiculously tight and unforgiving.

She glanced at the woman from the corner of her eye—who was on the same setting, but doing five million rpms faster than Rachel, and hadn't even broken a sweat.

Rachel suddenly stopped pedaling. "Whew!" she said, to signal to anyone who might be watching that she had just finished *her* ride through the Rocky Mountains, and swung off the bike like she did it every day.

It was nothing short of a miracle that her legs actually held her up and she didn't collapse into an enormous pile of sticky jelly goo. Rachel mopped her forehead and saun-tered—well, lurched, anyway—to the weight machines.

A full two hours after she'd entered the gym, and after several hundred pounds of lifting and squatting in various humiliating forms and fashions, still sweating and her hair going in five thousand directions in spite of the two tight coils she had wound it into, Rachel made her way out to the parking lot, Frankenstein style, one hand on the stitch in her side while images of steaming baths and candles danced in her mind's eye.

As she staggered to her car (she would have to have parked in the very last slot on the very last row), she no-ticed that the coffeehouse next to the gym had filled to ca-pacity with people who had nothing better to do on such a wet and dreary day. The place was so full that as she neared the end of the parking lot, she saw that someone had parked behind her, blocking her in. *Dammit!*

She groaned, debated what to do, and inadvertently caught sight of herself in the reflection of the back wind-shield. Her face was the exact shade of a fireplug. The *exact shade*. It wasn't enough that she was soaked and probably reeking—she had to herald her terribly out-of-shape body to the world with a fireplug face. Even worse, small corkscrews of hair around her face stuck out in every conceivable direction. She looked like she had stuck her finger into a light socket.

Time to call Dagne to come save her. Later, she could

get Dagne or Myron to bring her back for her car. Rachel fished in her bag for her brand-new T-Mobile cell phone . . . but it wasn't in her bag, and she remembered leaving it on the kitchen counter. Oooh, *fabulous.* A big fat splat of something landed on top of her head, and she glanced up, got hit in the eye by another fat raindrop. She looked around, saw the coffeehouse, and made a mad sort of half-hobbling, half-loping dash for it.

The place was jammed to the rafters with toned and beautiful bodies, all drinking coffee and poring over books and laptops and looking very stylish and hip. In a sort of ironic contrast, she looked a little like a Holstein cow in her black yoga pants and white tank. And what was up with always putting phones and toilets in the back of establishments? Was that some sort of national code?

Rachel sucked in her breath, lowered her eyes, and with her head down, marched through the crowd, hitting at least two people in the head and shoulders with her gym bag.

At the phone bank, she dug in her bag for change, and pulled out wads of money. Literally, wads of balled up bills—a ten, a fiver, three ones. But no change. Not a quarter, not a dime, not one lousy penny.

With a sigh of great irritation, Rachel glanced around. This was really just too much—where were all the fabulous things that were supposed to happen to her, according to Dagne and several horoscopes? The prosperity and happiness and all that crap? And man, it was so *warm* in there—someone needed to crack a window or something. Well anyway, one thing was certain—when she got hold of Dagne, she was going to let her know that her stupid spells weren't working for *shit*—

"I beg your pardon, but might I be of assistance?"

Rachel froze in the maniacal search of her bag, wondered if that question had been actually addressed to her, and slowly looked up . . . and up . . . at a very handsome man with a sexy British accent. He was smiling. His gorgeous blue-gray eyes sort of shimmered in a pool of dark lashes, and a strand of his thick chestnut hair actually fell over one eye. He was wearing a well-cut dark pinstripe suit and a long trench coat that looked very expensive, like he'd just walked off the set of a James Bond movie. A horrible swell of panic surged in Rachel—the guy was movie-star gorgeous and standing so close that he could probably *smell* her.

"You look as if you could use a hand, eh?" he asked, grinning lopsidedly as he fished in his pocket.

Dear God, she was gaping at him like she'd never seen a man before, and unthinkingly jerked backward, away from him, and almost killed herself, thank you, by impaling herself on the little box around the pay phone. But forget that, because she suddenly remembered the little wisps of hair sticking up all over her head and thought she might actually die of embarrassment. Just expire cold, right there.

"No, ah, no . . ." she managed to get out, smiling sheepishly. "No, thank you, but I've definitely got it," she said, and whirled around, her hand still shoved in her bag, frantically searching for a coin, *any* coin. JUST A COIN, DAMMIT!

"I've got a bit of change if you'd like," he continued, and Rachel, her back to him, shook her head, felt one of the tight coils of her hair start to come undone. "Thanks! I've got it!" she said to the wall.

He made a noise that sounded a little like a chuckle. Which meant, of course, that now the movie-star guy was laughing at her. How dare he laugh at her? She shot him a glance over her shoulder, but . . . he wasn't really laughing at all. He was just smiling, and really very warmly, showing some very white and very straight teeth for a Brit.

"I don't think you've got it at all, really," he said, holding out his hand. "I've some coins here," he said, opening the palm of his hand and studying the coins there. "Ah, here we are," he said cheerfully, and held up two quarters.

Rachel looked at the quarters and wondered, madly, if her face was still fireplug red, or please, God, had it calmed down a little, to maybe just cherry red?

He mistook her silence as refusal and said congenially,

"The thing is, you obviously haven't got the proper change and I'm really quite happy to help."

Okay, okay, now she got it—if a man who looked like him, all buff and handsome and wearing a suit, was talking to her, it was probably one of those reality TV things—

He cocked his head and dipped it a little bit to see her better, and Rachel instantly swiped the back of her arm across her forehead. "Right. Well, then, if you'd be so kind as to take the quarters and perhaps ring whomever you are ringing so the rest of us might have a go?" he asked, gesturing toward the phone. "I don't mean to impose, but I really need to make a call."

"Oh!" she said, and began frantically searching her bag again. "I'm sorry, I don't mean to hold you up, but I can't take your quarters because I *have* quarters, if I could just get to the bottom of my bag," she said, glancing at him from the corner of her eye. "Why don't you go ahead?"

"I couldn't possibly take your place in the queue," he said, looking at her bag. "You've quite a large bag there."

"Yes, it's very big, because I have lots of . . ." Well, junk, really. "Important stuff. Lots of it," she muttered.

Bonny Prince Charlie just stood there, smiling down at her, until it became apparent to even her that she was not going to magically produce two quarters, and she sighed.

"I rather thought you'd see it my way," he said happily, and leaned forward, his arm extended, coming right at her . . . *then around her!* To the phone, to be precise, which put him in dangerously close proximity to her sweaty self.

Rachel gasped with humiliation—there was no way he couldn't smell her now. "I wouldn't do that if I were you!" she cried, and tried to move, but managed to impale herself once more on the phone box. "Ow," she whimpered. "Ow, ow, ow."

"Mind the box," James Bond said with a chuckle, and blithely continued reaching around her, to the phone itself. "Before you go all barmy on me," he said, his voice pleasantly soft as his gaze flicked from her face to her appallingly red bosom, "I promise you may have the quarters.

I won't demand interest or the like," he said, his nose as yet unwrinkled, as he deposited one quarter. "But I wouldn't mind a bit if you determined you were so indebted to me that you might buy me a cup of tea with the five you dropped on the floor." He deposited the second quarter.

Rachel blinked, stole a glimpse at the floor without actually moving. There it was, a crumpled five-dollar bill at her feet. "Oh, man," she said, and slid down to her haunches to pick it up, then stood so quickly that she banged the top of her head into his arm, which was now holding the receiver out to her. "Oops. Sorry," she said, wincing again.

He smilingly offered the phone. "Quite all right. So then, I've only just arrived and it's rather dreary out, isn't it? I could use a spot of tea, how about you? Here you are . . . your call?"

All right, *now* she was mortified to the tips of her toes—was he playing some sort of mind game, asking her to tea? What in God's name was he doing in Providence, anyway? He should be in London, stepping off the tube with some dish, walking to some posh and trendy pub.

Rachel snatched the phone from his hand, punched Dagne's numbers into the phone, and silently begged her to pick up the goddamn phone. On the fourth ring, when she had decided that God was indeed smiting her and was not going to help her in the least because she had played around with witchcraft, Dagne picked up. "Hello?" she said sleepily.

"Dagne!" Rachel hissed, whirling around so that her back was to Prince Charming. "Come and get me!"

"Why? Where are you?" she asked through a yawn.

"At the gym—"

"Hey! You didn't waste any time—"

"Come and *get* me!" she said again. "If you're not here in five minutes—"

"Why? Where's your car? Wait a minute—does Myron have it? Because if Myron took your car—"

"No, no, it's here! But I'm blocked in and I really, really need to go."

"What's the hurry?"

"Dagne!" Rachel hissed.

"All *right*," Dagne said, obviously irritated. "I'll be there in a few. But this better be good!" She hung up.

Rachel put the receiver in the cradle, turned slowly toward the Brit, and pulled her gym bag around in front of her stomach. She flashed a self-conscious smile. "Thanks," she said. "That was really very decent of you. I appreciate the help."

"You're quite welcome. And now that you've successfully completed your ringing operation, what do you say to that cup of tea?"

If Dagne had put some sort of spell on her that made her attract handsome men, she was going to kill her. "Oh gee, I'm sorry, I really can't," she said quickly, stepping around him. "I've got a . . . a really important appointment I've got to get to. But, ah . . . thanks. Thanks so much." She flashed him another quick smile, clutched her bag closely to her body, and mowed her way out of the coffeehouse.

She got one last look at the to-die-for Brit as she pushed through the glass doors. He was standing at the phone, staring after her, a sort of bemused look on his face.

Seriously, she was going to *kill* Dagne.

Chapter Four

DAGNE was, predictably, very excited about Rachel's brush with royalty in a trench coat. *"See?"* she insisted. "Witchcraft *does* work."

"Did you put some sort of spell on me?" Rachel demanded as she emerged from Dagne's shower, wrapped in a towel.

"No! And why didn't you buy him a cup of tea?" she cried, punching Rachel in the arm.

"Are you nuts?" Rachel rubbed her arm where Dagne had punched her. "Did you *see* me? I was sweaty and red-faced and I must have stunk to high heaven!"

"Yeah . . . I see what you mean," Dagne said, wrinkling her nose.

"Oh thanks," Rachel muttered miserably. "Don't you have a spell for that? *Here's a drink so you won't stink,* something along those lines?"

"That's not nice," Dagne said, which prompted another argument about witchcraft that continued until *Trading Spaces* came on, at which point it was abruptly halted, as both couples hated their new rooms.

Afterward, when Rachel's hair had dried, Dagne

dropped her at her car with one last lecture about seizing opportunity when it presented itself. Sure, Dagne could say that. She was tall and willowy and strawberry blond. Bitch.

As Dagne drove off, Rachel glanced at the coffeehouse and wondered if he was still in there. Maybe having tea with some other unsuspecting cow. Or with a really pretty girl, thanking his lucky stars he hadn't roped himself into a tea date with a fireplug.

Whatever. She'd had her brush with gorgeous and shrugged it off, got in her car, and drove to the organic grocery store.

She returned to her house under the cloak of dusk so the Valicielos couldn't see her. As she turned into her drive, she saw Myron's faded red Geo Metro parked next to the house.

Great.

As she struggled through the kitchen door with two huge grocery bags, Myron waved at her from his seat at the breakfast bar, where he was having a sandwich. He was the kind of guy who did his food shopping in his friends' refrigerators.

"Hey," he said as Rachel fumbled the grocery bags onto the countertop.

"Hey," she said, and, getting the bags down, pushed the hair from her eyes. "What are you doing here?"

"Eating a sandwich," he said, holding up a disgustingly stuffed triple-decker salami (salami she had bought expressly because Myron said he loved it and wished she had some). "Where you been?"

"The gym."

"The *gym?*" He laughed as if that was the most hilarious thing he'd ever heard. "So hey, Pete Lancaster is doing a poetry reading tonight," he continued once he was through laughing. "You wanna go?"

"I can't. I have my weaving class tonight." She moved to put the milk away and noticed the brownie pan. An empty brownie pan, in which there previously had been four good-sized brownies left. "Dammit, Myron, you ate my brownies!" she exclaimed hotly.

Myron paused in his chewing and looked at the empty pan, surprised, then shrugged. "You didn't leave a note or anything," he said, flipped the long tail of his hair over his shoulder, and took another enormous bite of salami sandwich. "So what'd you get at the store?" he asked shamelessly.

"Food." She peevishly shoved her hand into the paper bag and began to withdraw the contents and put them away.

"Got any sodas?"

"In there," she said, gesturing toward the pantry, the same place she had kept the sodas for the two years she'd known Myron. She watched him get up off the stool, hitch up baggy corduroy slacks over his bony butt, and recalled Dad shouting at her about worthless Myron. Well, the joke was on Dad, hardy har har, because her love life was on the shelf.

Okay, so Dad and the rest of the family thought Myron Tidwell was her boyfriend. But Myron was not her boyfriend and he hadn't been in a very long time. Rachel had just never had the guts to tell Mom and Dad that it was over with Myron because there'd be a whole big thing about her never having boyfriends and all that.

She and Myron had been an item for two whole semesters, a personal best for her. He taught early colonial history. Rachel had taken his class and thought he was so cool then—he had long, thick hair he wore in a ponytail, cords, and crewneck sweaters, and was casually laid back when he talked.

One afternoon, Myron asked her to stay after class to talk about some of the little doodles she had drawn in her blue book—hearts, actually—and that had been the beginning of a teacher-student relationship that had evolved into a boyfriend-girlfriend thing. But the whole thing had sort of died on the vine when it became clear that their interests in life and relationships were not the same.

As in, he was not that interested.

Unfortunately, that happened *after* Rachel had waited the requisite amount of time to make sure she actually *had* a boyfriend and had proclaimed it proudly to her family. And as they had never really expected her to have a boyfriend (in fact, they'd been just a little *too* surprised by it) . . . Well, long story short, she and Myron had remained friends and she just never mentioned otherwise, preferring to go with the old *what they don't know won't hurt them* theory. It was easy to do—she was way up here in Rhode Island, they were way down there in Texas—

"So your dad called while you were out," Myron said, bent over deep into the pantry, looking for a cream soda.

That startled Rachel out of her thoughts fast enough. "Did you *talk* to him?"

"Hell no, just let the answering machine take it. He asked about your dissertation. Sounded like he had an attitude. Is he still giving you grief about it?"

"Among other things."

"Rachel, don't let him get to you. Here's the thing," Myron said, emerging at last with the cream soda, "your dad has only a high school education. He doesn't understand the concept of higher learning and how difficult or important a dissertation can be." He walked to the cabinet and fished out a glass, then reached for the fridge door for ice. "I mean, it's like my situation."

Frankly, everything was like Myron's situation if she let him talk long enough.

"If I don't get published in the right journals on the right topic in the right time frame, I'm never going to get tenure. And if I don't get tenure, my ass is out on the street, you know what I'm saying? But it's just not that easy—these academic things don't make sense to people like your dad, but they're really very important."

"My dissertation and your tenure aren't really the same thing, do you think?" Rachel suggested as he helped himself to a glass and a few cubes of ice (leaving one cube sliding helplessly around the tiled countertop until Rachel caught it and tossed it in the sink).

"You know what Dean Holcroft told me?" Myron continued, ignoring her question. "He said they'll be looking for something next fall. What he's saying is, if I don't have an article written and published by next fall—that's a little less than a *year*—then they're going to deny me tenure. Can you fucking believe that?" he demanded indignantly before pouring the cream soda.

"Sort of," she admitted, but again, Myron didn't seem to hear her—he was shaking his head at the injustice of it all. And while he waxed indignantly about an unfair system, there was a little thought in Rachel's head that Myron *had* been a professor of history for years now, and that he *had* been struggling through the very same scholarly article about pre-colonial America for as long as she had known him. Once she even suggested he find a new topic, and he had all but taken her head off.

When Myron finished his impassioned speech about the communist basis for tenure, he returned to his sandwich, moved aside the groceries that were in his way, and settled in to finish it off.

As Rachel put some apples in the fruit bowl, she noticed her new T-Mobile phone beside it. She picked it up to check for messages.

"Hey, *cool*. Can I see that?" Myron asked when he saw her phone. She handed him the cell phone, continued putting groceries away. "This is really cool. Where did you get it?"

"New York. Mom got it for me. She wants instant access."

"Now see, your mom understands you better than your dad, I think. She's back in New York, right? Taking care of Aaron? He actually sounded pretty good on the answering machine."

The comment gave her pause, and she looked out over the kitchen sink to her unkempt lawn below. "He's really sick," she said honestly. "The chemo and radiation have made him weak." So sick that all he could do, apparently, was lie around and think of ways to badger her after Mom had cajoled her into coming to New York while she went back to L.A. to take care of a few things.

It had been okay at first—still stressful, because Dad was always stressful, but not unbearable. In fact, Rachel was beginning to believe that she could handle the old man. It didn't get bad between them, really, until he asked her how much her graduate teaching position was paying. "It's not," Rachel had answered truthfully. "The professor took a post at UCLA and I lost my internship."

She could recall Dad on the couch, looking bone thin and exhausted and dumbfounded. "So . . . what are you doing for money?"

Gawd, she hated money. Which was sort of ironic, seeing as how she came from a family with loads of it. "I'm teaching a weaving class—"

"A *what* class?"

"A *weaving* class. You know, like tapestries and rugs and—"

"I know what the hell a *weaving* class is, Rachel. I just can't believe that is your solution to replacing my money. You think weaving is going to pay your bills?"

Well no, she never thought it was going to pay her bills, particularly since she had waived the fee for half the class—hey, times were hard and people needed a break. And even though a few could pay, their fees did not add up to enough to pay her utility bill, which, in September, had swooped into her mailbox, demanding one hundred and fifty dollars that she did not have.

At any rate, the conversation had deteriorated from there, and Dad had reminded her for the umpteenth time that he was pulling all support for her school, (a) because she had just turned thirty-one years old and was still in school and would never finish, (b) because she would never finish, she would never amount to anything, and (c) because she would never amount to anything, she would have to rely on the likes of Byron Tidwell to provide for

her, but hey, if she wanted to live under a bridge somewhere, that was okay.

Well, (a) she *would* finish school, even if Dad didn't believe her. She was searching through what seemed like a
haystack of hypotheses for a needle of a dissertation, and
that was all she had left. And (c) she wouldn't rely on
Myron, not Byron, for ·anything but friendship, because
like it or not, *he* understood her and accepted who she was
while Dad just wanted her to be someone else entirely—
like her sisters, Rebecca and Robin. She was never going
to be a Rebecca or a Robin. Which left (b), the part about
her never amounting to anything.

That was the part that had sent her, fists clenched
around a Big Grab bag of potato chips, on a train back to
Providence.

"Hey listen, I got something for you," Myron said,
pushing aside his empty plate. He got up, walked into the
adjoining dining room where he'd dumped his stuff, and
came back with a box.

"What is it?"

"Check it out," he said, and beamed like a little kid as
Rachel opened the box and pulled out a figurine of a dancing woman. She was wearing a blue dress with a pink sash
and was holding up one side of her gown as she twirled
about.

"It's beautiful," she said, holding it up, wondering
where in God's name she'd put something like that. "I saw
something very similar to this in a museum in England."
Which was where things like this belonged, really. In museums, not in bungalows.

Myron nodded eagerly. "This is a copy of a French
piece Lord Billingham brought from England to New York
in the eighteenth century. His was bone china and hand-
gilded." As an assistant curator, Myron got an employee
discount in the many gift shops of the Rhode Island
Historical Preservation Society, and recently had become
fond of buying reproductions.

"It's lovely, Myron," she said, putting it down again. "But you really shouldn't buy me gifts."

"Why not?" he asked with a quick, friendly buss to her temple. "I like to give you things."

Right. But what she would really like to get from him was the money he owed her. She could just never think of a polite way to ask for it, and tried to think of one as she watched Myron pick up his ancient canvas backpack.

But as no polite way came to her, another thought did. "Hey, I've got an idea," she said, putting the figurine down. "Do you think you could get me a job with the preservation society?"

Myron choked on a cough. "A *job?*" he asked incredulously as he slung his backpack over his shoulder. "Why do you want a *job?*" He said it like she was asking for a shot at leprosy.

"Because my dad is seriously cutting me off and I lost my internship, and I have a utility bill and a tree problem and about twenty bucks in the bank. It's serious, Myron— I'm out of salami. . . . So do you think you could get me one?"

Myron adjusted the backpack, looked at the kitchen door. "Well . . . *no.* No!" he exclaimed, obviously flustered. "You can't work at the preservation society, Rachel. I mean, you have to know what you are doing—"

"You can teach me!" she said brightly.

With a bark of laughter, he reached for the doorknob. "Please! I don't think so! It's not like it's on-the-job training, Rachel. You have to know about the history and the artwork. Besides, you don't want to work there—the pay's no good. So okay!" he said quickly before she could argue that some pay was better than none. "I'll check you later, okay?" And with a jaunty wave, he stepped through the back door and shut it soundly behind him.

Dipshit.

She looked again at the little figurine he had brought her, put it back in the box, and left it on the breakfast bar while she decided where to store it. In the meantime, she picked up Myron's dirty plate, noticed her new, multi-function T-Mobile phone was gone, and looked around for it. It was nowhere. Myron must have inadvertently put it in his backpack. *Gawd.*

She put the dirty dishes away, then tried to raise Myron on the T-Mobile.

He didn't answer, of course—probably didn't know he had it. Rachel finally gave up and flipped on her computer to check her e-mail before she had to go teach her weaving class.

Subject: Re: Re: Hey
From: <rmanning70@earthlink.net>
To: Rach <earthangel@hotmail.com>

F. Y. IIIIIII you moron, the zing in our sex life is helped along by experimentation across a broad spectrum, and if you EVER tell Jake I said that, I will kill you. Anyway, I just figured you and My-Ron are doing the tantric thing, so why can't we? Just send me the stinking book already, will you? Rob

Subject: Re: Re: Re: Hey
From: <earthangel@hotmail.com>
To: <manning70@earthlink.net>

First of all, Einstein, Tantra is not a sex manual. It's a way of thinking and believing and is all about the harmony of spirits. Do you even have a spirit, by the way? If you want EZ-read pictures, go get a copy of the Kama Sutra. That should give you some broad spectrum to talk about. And F.Y.IIIIIIII, Myron and I do not practice tantric ANYTHING. Our relationship is strictly platonic. I thought I told you that! I know I did!! If you'd get your

*mind out of the gutter you might remember some of the very
important stuff I tell you! Stop bugging me.*
Rachel

She hit the Send button and happened to notice the
time—she was going to be late. She grabbed up her purse
and headed for the corner grocer near class, cursing My-
Ron the whole way for eating all her brownies.

At the grocery, she grabbed a few things lest the night
clerk think that she had actually jumped in her car and driven down for something as singularly sinful and indulgent
as a brownie. She picked up enough trash bags to last
through the millennium, some laundry soap in the event
she took up laundry as opposed to sending it out, and an
extra-large box of super-duty tampons, as they were on
sale. With her finances in the shape they were in, that was
definitely not a product she wanted to take a chance on
running low.

With those items in her basket, she nonchalantly
strolled to the deli counter.

The counter was closed, but the deli guy had left a basket on the counter with the day's unsold products, nicely
wrapped and dated. Rachel rifled through the cookies and
brownies until she found an enormous double-chocolate
brownie that looked to be about as big as her head. She
shoved it down into her little basket, then walked briskly
to the front.

When she paid for her items, she walked outside,
paused next to the trash can to pull out the brownie, and
unwrapped it. She took one very large bite—after all, she
was running a little late and wouldn't have time to scarf it
all before class, but why not have a little taste?—and was
about to wrap it up again when she suddenly felt the presence of someone close by. She stopped mid-munch and
slowly turned her head.

There was a man in a suit standing before her, his hands
shoved deep in his trench coat, his grin nice and wide. He
startled her so badly that when Rachel tried to step out of

his way, she dropped her bag, and the tampons went shooting out across the walk, which, naturally, she couldn't catch because she had a giant brownie in her hand.

"What a happy coincidence," the Brit said cheerfully. And as he dipped down to retrieve her tampons, he smiled so warmly at her that he damn near melted her brownie.

Chapter Five

✦ ✦ ✦

RACHEL sprang into action, swooping down on the tampon box like a buzzard on roadkill, snatching it at the exact same time he wrapped his big hand around it. They looked at each other, the tampons between them. "I've got it," she said, and jerked it out of his hand. Only it took her *two* hands to grab it, the box was so enormous. He was surely thinking she had some sort of horrific problem and she quickly stood up, which caused her to make a little sound of pain when her legs barked at her.

"Are you quite all right?" bonny Prince Charlie asked, standing smoothly and effortlessly, holding her trash bags in one hand, the bag with the laundry soap in the other.

"Yes. Yes!" she said again, trying desperately to juggle tampons and the brownie.

"This is a little strange, isn't it?" he laughed.

Well, of course it was, and she could feel her face growing hot with complete and total humiliation for the *second* time that day. "Not really. They were having a sale," she said as she finally managed to balance the tampons between her arm and her chest, the brownie on top.

He glanced at the tampons. "Actually, I meant running

into one another again," he said, smiling, and before she had the opportunity to just die right there, he smoothly changed the subject. "You must live in the area, eh?"

Rachel looked at him fully then, noticed for the first time that he had the sexy shadow of a beard, and his hair was a little mussed, and wondered if he'd looked like that today at the coffeehouse. How could she have known, her face up against the wall as it was?

"Do you?"

"I'm sorry?" she asked, startled.

"Live in the area."

"Oh!" Rachel put her free hand to her nape. "Umm . . . well, as a matter of fact, I do. Do *you*?" she asked suspiciously.

He chuckled. "I've only recently arrived, and at present, I'm staying with friends nearby. I quite like the area, however. It's rather quaint, really, and the people are remarkably friendly."

So what was *that* supposed to mean? Was that some sort of dry-humored British joke? Was he making a dig at her? Okay, she hadn't been exactly *friendly*, but honestly, she'd been smelly and sweaty and—

"By the bye, I hope you will forgive my demanding a cup of tea earlier," he said, as if reading her mind. "I suppose that was a bit forward of me."

"Oh no!" she said instantly, blushing furiously. "No, I didn't think . . . I mean, I didn't, ah . . . I was really in a rush," she babbled, and noticed he still held her things in his hands. Very big hands to match his broad shoulders. Rachel couldn't help herself; she glanced at his feet. A healthy size—she could just hear Robin now, *"Big hands, big feet, big—"*

"Yes, well, I didn't want you to think the worst. But I've only been in the States a few days, and I was a bit hungry for a chat."

Why in God's name would he want to chat with her, *especially* having actually *seen* her this morning? "Ah," she said stupidly, nodding, and sheepishly peeked up at him.

"Could I, ah . . . just have that, please?" she asked, nodding at her items.

He glanced at the bag and chuckled sheepishly as he handed them to her. Only Rachel wasn't quite prepared to take it, what with the stupid tampons, so he politely held the bag open for her and stood patiently as she wrestled the box inside, followed by the brownie, which, she couldn't help notice, had been hopelessly mangled in her struggle to appear calm and collected.

"That's a pity," he said, peering with her into the bag at the brownie. He added the box of trash bags, then closed the grocery bag and handed it to her. As she took it from him, his fingers accidentally brushed her palm, and an amazing little shiver ran up her arm and directly into her groin. "Thanks. Thank you," she said, a little unnerved by that shiver, and awkwardly stepped around him.

He turned halfway around. "Should I suppose, then, that it won't do me the slightest bit of good to ask you for a drink?"

Okay, *what* was going *on* here? Guys like *him* did not ask chicks like *her* for drinks! She self-consciously pushed her braid over her shoulder and folded her arms over the bag as she tried to sort it out.

When she didn't answer, he sighed, shoved a hand through his hair. "Bloody marvelous, I've gone and done it again, haven't I? At least give me your name, will you? That way, the next time I'm so bloody forward, I might apologize properly."

He sounded so sincere that she couldn't help it; she smiled.

"Aha!" he said delightedly. "I'd made a small wager with myself that you did indeed have teeth. And do you perhaps have a name as well?"

"Of course I have teeth," she said, her smile deepening. "And the name is . . . Rachel."

"*Thank* you, Rachel!" he said with a bow, as if she'd done him an enormous favor. "I'm Flynn."

Flynn. How dashing. How *British*. She flashed another

self-conscious grin, and still clutching her bag, she began to walk toward her car.

"Ah . . . Rachel?" he said after her. She turned around, still smiling stupidly. "Would this mean that you are declining my offer of a drink?"

"Oh!" she said, laughing a little as her blush deepened. "Thanks . . . but I can't. I have class."

"Ah. And it wouldn't do to skive out of it, I suppose?" he asked with a gorgeous, dazzling, *GQ* smile. If *GQ* guys ever smiled. If they did, they would look just like Flynn.

In fact, that smile was so dazzling that she was somehow walking backward, smiling back, her bag clutched tightly against her as she laughingly shook her head. "I can't! I'm the teacher!" she said, and jarred herself right out of the clouds by stepping off the curb and stumbling backward into the parking lot before righting herself. All righty, then! If ever there was a cosmic sign, that was it— with a quick wave, she turned and hurried to her car.

FLYNN Oliver shook his head as he watched her get into her little yellow car and drive off. A smidge odd, that girl, but really rather pretty what with a bit of tidying up, wasn't she? Her eyes, which he'd not, apparently, appreciated fully this morning, were a teal blue, and in her woolen jumper and long black skirt, with her hair braided down her back, she looked exactly like what he'd always pictured an all-American girl to be. Rather charming, really.

With a shake of his head, he walked into the grocer. After a bit of wandering about, he picked up some kippers, sliced bread, and a six-pack of what Americans called beer, then headed for what was temporarily home.

As he passed through the lobby, he said good evening to the night clerk. "Hi, Mr. Oliver," the night clerk, a goth kid, said. "Do anything fun today?"

"Nothing that you'd find terribly exciting, I'm quite certain," he said with a wave, and got in the lift. It took him to the fifth floor and a small corporate apartment.

He pitched the keys to his rental car on the table, put down his bag, and shoved out of his trench coat and suit jacket before proceeding to the kitchenette and putting away the few things he'd bought to supplement the eggs and cheese he had purchased two days ago.

Beer in hand, Flynn loosened his tie and walked to the phone, pressed the little blinking light indicating there were messages.

"Flynn, darling!" Iris's voice, accompanied by music and voices in the background, pierced the quiet of his flat. "You naughty boy, I'm frightfully worried about you," she exclaimed. "Really, you haven't rung up in days, so do please ring us, will you, darling? Ta-ta, love."

Flynn rolled his eyes and took a swig of beer as the next message beeped.

"Yo, dude. Got one if you want to ride along." The deep male voice belonged to Joe, his American counterpart. "Give me a buzz if you're up for it."

Flynn instantly picked up the phone and dialed Joe's mobile.

"Yo," Joe said on the first ring.

"Flynn here."

"Hey, buddy, wanna ride?"

"That would be lovely, thanks."

"Dude! You have *got* to stop saying that!" Joe chastised him. "I'll pick you up in ten."

"Smashing," Flynn said, and clicked off. Without bothering to hear the rest of his messages, he went to change to dungarees.

Chapter Six

* ✳ *

RACHEL drove in something of a fog the short distance to the Rhode Island School of Design—her mind could not quite wrap around the idea that a guy who looked as good as Flynn would be talking to her. Twice. To Rachel Ellen Lear, the dough ball, the ugly duckling of the Lear sisters, the one they used to call Miss Fortune in high school.

Okay, well, she was a long way from high school, but still.

She walked into her class, her head still encased in fog, beaming at the seven of ten students who were still in attendance after four weeks. That was a pretty good sign, seeing as how she usually lost four or five by this point, when students realized that large-scale weaving was not easy. That always left her with the eccentric ones who had the sort of lives that lended them to weaving medieval tapestries.

Sandy, a middle-aged hypochondriac, was showing a pattern of what she was weaving on the loom. "Sandy, that's beautiful," Rachel said admiringly.

"Thanks!" Sandy said proudly. "I was hoping to get a

little further along before this class, but I have IBS, you know."

"IBS?" Mr. Gregory asked. He was an ancient old flamer who had expressed a desire to weave rugs and was doggedly cold in his determination to do it.

"Irritable Bowel Syndrome," Sandy said without an ounce of self-consciousness.

"Oh, dear," Mr. Gregory said, wrinkling his nose with distaste.

"Yeah, it's not pretty." Sandy laughed.

"But . . . didn't you say last week they thought it was a pelvic inflammation thing?" Lucy, one-half of Dave and Lucy, the All-Natural Couple, whispered loudly.

"I have *both*," Sandy said, nodding enthusiastically as she carefully folded the pattern. "That's probably why I had another flare-up of IBS. My doctor doesn't really know for sure."

Actually, if everyone just hung on, Sandy would list all her maladies before the end of the class. She was talented, but because of her raging hypochondria, Rachel had begun to keep ibuprofen and antacids in her purse for Sandy's major flare-ups.

"My sister had that," Lucy said, to which Dave rolled his eyes.

"IBS or pelvic inflammation?" Sandy asked, her eyes narrowing suspiciously, waiting to pounce on the first opportunity to top whatever Lucy's sister had.

"IBS," Lucy said.

"Do we *have* to talk about this?" Chantal demanded of Rachel as everyone began to find their seats. Chantal had signed up with her friend Tiffinnae, who owned a hair salon and wanted to make some cool stuff for the walls to complement her hair-weave designs. Chantal was along just for grins. She had not, as far as Rachel knew, actually touched the loom.

"We do have a lot of ground to cover tonight, so if everyone could take a seat?" Rachel suggested. "I'm going to talk about yarn," she said, wincing a little as she lifted her bag to put it on the table.

"Are you all right?" Sandy immediately asked. "Was that your shoulder? Because I had tendonitis once, and I have this cream—"

"Ah, no," Rachel said, quickly cutting her off. "I just overdid it at the gym today."

"Gym?" Tiffinnae said, sizing her up, one large girl to another.

"I'm a little out of shape."

"Oh, she ain't out of no shape," Chantal said, waving a hand as she strutted to the loom she shared with Tiffinnae. "She goin' cuz she got herself a *maaaan,*" she said in a singsong way, and instantly gained the class's undivided attention.

Rachel couldn't have been more surprised if Chantal had done a pirouette. "No, I don't! I really—"

"Yes, you do. I saw you smiling real pretty at him down at Oakley's Grocery," Chantal insisted as she smoothed the back of her hair. "I walked right past you and said hi and you couldn't even take your eyes off him to say nothing in return!"

"You walked *past* me?" Rachel exclaimed disbelievingly. The class suddenly erupted into laughter.

"Oh, come on, it's not what you think!" Rachel tried.

"And he be *fiiiiine,*" Chantal shouted over her, and exchanged a high five with Tiffinnae.

"Actually, I didn't know that man," Rachel tried again, but could feel a hot blush returning, full throttle, to her cheeks. It was a full minute before she could get the class focused on the fascinating world of looms and weaving in medieval times.

At the end of the class, when Sandy said she had to get home because of a flare-up of acid reflux, Tiffinnae and Chantal took their own sweet time packing up their things as everyone else filtered out, calling good night to Rachel. "I know when a girl's got her eye on a man," Chantal said loudly to Tiffinnae.

"Mmm-hmm," Tiffinnae responded.

"Miss Rachel's got *two* eyes on *that* man, all moon-eyed and smiley-faced!" She and Tiffinnae fell out laughing at Rachel's wide-eyed, puffed-cheek look, and waved a cheery good night as they pushed one another out the door.

Gawd.

There was only one person left in class, a kid named Jason, maybe nineteen, who preferred dressing in solid black and added eyeliner to his eyes to give him a really gothic look. "Ah, Miss Lear?" he said quietly, raising his hand in spite of there being no one else left in the classroom.

"Hey Jason, what's up?" she asked as she picked up her giant bunker-buster tote bag.

He shoved his hands into his enormous pockets. "Listen, I'm going to have to drop out," he said meekly.

"Drop out? But why? Is it Chantal? I can—"

"No, she's okay," he said, looking extremely chagrined. He cast his gaze to the floor. "I can't afford it," he said. "I borrowed the money from my mom to sign up, and she thought it was sort of stupid." The kid blanched when he said it, and instantly shook his head. "I don't mean your *class* is stupid, but she thought it was stupid for me to take it . . . Well, anyway, I really want to take this class. I didn't realize we'd have to pay for the yarn and stuff."

Even though it was clearly stated in the course materials, Rachel smiled. "Is *that* all, Jason? Don't worry about that. I've got extra yarn."

"Really?" he asked, sort of lifting his gaze to her waist. "I mean, are you sure?"

"Are you kidding?" She paused at the light switch. "I have tons," she lied as Jason gave her a skeptical look and preceded her out of the classroom.

She walked with Jason out to the parking lot while he told her how cool he thought medieval art was, and how (interestingly) he had a suit of armor at home, and how he really hoped to get to England one day, and in fact, had a bunch of travel brochures that maybe he'd bring to the next class, if that was all right.

Rachel told him that was all right.

THAT night, after the remainder of her humongous brownie had been devoured and her tampons safely tucked away, she picked up her romance novel and quickly lost herself in King Edward I's court.

As she drifted off to sleep, the novel still in hand, Rachel could see the hero atop his white steed, his hair flowing, his scabbard bouncing at his side as he raced across the barren moors.

Funny, she thought sleepily, how much that guy looked like Flynn . . . except for the scabbard. And the horse.

HER dreamy sleep was rudely awakened by the phone.

At the first ring, Rachel came out of bed with a start; the book went flying across the room, and every muscle in her body seized up in pain.

"Ow! Ow, ow, ow, ow . . ." she hissed as she threw the covers off of her. She glanced at the clock as she fumbled for the cordless. It was ten in the morning—how had she slept so long? She punched the Talk button. "Hello?" she said, and realized she could not straighten her neck.

"You *cannot* still be asleep!" Dagne exclaimed, surprised. "I thought you were going to the employment office today!"

"Ohmigod, I can't *move!*" Rachel cried, grimacing as she tried to move her leg.

"Well, hurry up and go so you can call me back. I may want to do something later, I don't know."

Begging the question of why she was calling at ten, for Chrissakes, but nevertheless, Rachel rubbed her neck and said, "Guess what. I saw him again."

"Who?"

"Him. The British guy."

Dagne gasped. Then squealed. "What *happened?*"

Rachel told her about the scene at the corner grocery, complete with brownie and tampons. At the end of it, Dagne said nothing. "Hello?" Rachel said into the phone.

"WHY DIDN'T YOU GET HIS NUMBER?" Dagne shrieked. "God, what is the *matter* with you, Rachel?"

"And what would I do with his number? Call him up and say hey, I have about ten bucks in the bank, but let's grab that coffee! Please! And besides, it wasn't anything—he was being nice," she said, really hoping Dagne would disagree.

Dagne obliged her by demanding, "Then why did he ask you for a drink, huh?"

"I don't know. You know how polite the British are—he probably thought he had to or something."

"You are so stupid," Dagne said disgustedly. "A good-looking guy—"

"And *hot.*"

"—*hot* guy asks you for a drink, and you think he is following some international protocol of manners for foreigners? How can you possibly be a candidate for a Ph.D. if you are that stupid?"

"Please. A Ph.D. doesn't necessarily mean a person is smart," Rachel said. "Look, I gotta get moving."

"You blew it, Rach. If you ever see him again—"

"Which I won't—"

"You might! And if you do, you better get his number or I'll . . . I'll put a hex on you!"

"Oh stop! I gotta go. I'll speak with you later," Rachel said. "Cheerio," she added in the fake British accent she had tried to perfect while in England the last time, and clicked off.

She struggled to her feet, determined the job hunt would have to come later. First things first—a hot shower so that she could move, a trip to the gym to work the kinks out, and *then* a job.

The hot shower helped, but still, she could barely get her gym clothes on and was still walking funny, holding her head at an odd angle, which is why she didn't see Mr. Valicielo standing at the foot of her fallen elm tree until it was too late. At the precise moment she was inching her way into her car (first one leg, then the careful lowering of the body, then the white-knuckled grip of the steering wheel as she dragged the other leg inside), she heard him shout her name.

"Damn," she muttered, and quickly fired up her VW and recklessly backed out of the drive, seeing as how she could not turn her head.

"Rachel!"

"Damndamndamndamn*damn*," she squealed as the back of her car bottomed out when she reached the street. She turned the steering wheel as fast as she could, whimpering in pain, and from the corner of her eye, she saw Mr. Valicielo running on short, stocky legs down the drive. At the end of it, he threw his rake at the back of her car, but could only heave it about three feet.

Rachel shot down Slater toward Laurel, and as she hurtled onto Laurel, she struggled to turn around to see where Mr. Valicielo was. But her reflexes were off terribly, as the slightest movement of her head sent a shooting pain down her side, and she was, therefore, a little slow straightening around again.

She saw the jogger at the very last second and swerved to the right to avoid hitting him. With every muscle screaming at that unpredicted movement, she flew around the jogger and away from Mr. Valicielo.

And as she drove down Laurel, her muscles momentarily under control, she thought she was really going to have to have her head checked, because she barely had a glimpse of the jogger and still thought that he looked just like Flynn.

Man, this guy was turning up everywhere.

At the gym, Lori at the desk was rubbing lotion onto her overly developed Popeye biceps when Rachel struggled to the desk to sign in. She nodded knowingly as Rachel winced when she picked up the pen. "Overdid it, huh?"

Rachel nodded slowly and painfully.

"Better warm up this time," Lori chided her. "You can't just jump in with both feet after a whole year, and remember, it's not like you were in such great shape even then."

"Thanks. Thanks for your help," Rachel said snidely, and tried to give her a look, but Lori had already gone back to her can of spinach, so she just hobbled on.

Her first stop was the stationary bike. She did a slow, easy, flat-line ride, and as her body began to loosen up, she pondered what in the hell she was going to do about that damn tree . . . until she realized she'd been thinking about the tree and Mr. Valicielo for almost forty-five minutes.

But *hey,* her legs actually felt a little stronger! She walked around in a circle for a moment to make sure they weren't going to buckle or anything, and convinced they weren't, she headed for the weight bench.

She was beginning to feel her cheerful self again, and was even achieving some weird endorphin high that caused her to actually contemplate an aerobics class. That might jump-start the ol' metabolism, maybe burn off that huge honking brownie she'd eaten last night.

She headed up front to check out the class schedules, mopping her face and neck with a towel, still trying to catch her breath after doing four sets of power squats. She rounded the corner, squinted at the front desk. Lori was leaning all the way across, smiling like a goon at some guy, flexing her biceps—

Wait. Wait just a damn minute—that could *not* be him! What the hell was going on? What sort of freaky cosmic disturbance was rearranging her reality? She hadn't had time to check her horoscope this morning, but she was pretty sure it didn't say some British guy would keep popping up like a jack-in-the-box everywhere she went!

But it was him, all right, having a lovely little chat with Lori. And then he turned slightly to pick up his gym bag and saw Rachel at the exact moment she realized she was staring at him. He opened his mouth; she turned abruptly—

"Rachel?"

Crap. This was really just too much. It was all Dagne's doing, she was certain. She'd probably screwed up the spell so this guy was only going to see her when she was in some humiliating circumstance, like sweating. Or stuffing brownies into her face.

"Rachel!" he said, smiling.

She tried not to look at the clingy gym pants he was wearing, but he was the kind of man it was hard to ignore in that regard. "Oh! Hi, Flynn!"

"You're popping up all over, aren't you!" he exclaimed cheerfully, forgetting, it seemed, that he was the one doing the popping. "You're a member, are you?"

Man, he was built—she could make out a broad chest beneath his T-shirt. He was trim, but muscular. "Yeah," she said carefully, and folded her arms, wincing a little as she silently thanked herself for choosing to wear these ridiculously shorty shorts that showcased her blubbery legs. And to add insult to injury, he was looking at them.

"This is smashing—we could have a bit of a run, if you're up for it."

"Ah, no, no . . . I was just leaving!" she said, self-consciously poking some wild hair behind her ears.

"Oh," he said, and he seemed, remarkably, disappointed as he lifted his gaze from her chunky legs to her face.

"Anyway, I don't really run."

"Don't you?"

"No, no . . ." she said, but was momentarily stymied by the glimpse of hair on his chest beneath his T-shirt, and thought that she'd really like a better look. But certainly not badly enough to actually try to run next to him, which prompted her to blurt, "It's really too . . . complicated." *Complicated?* Oh Jesus.

"What, the treadmill? I'll show you if you like."

"No, not *that,*" she said, as if that was a perfectly ridiculous suggestion. "I mean the, ah, workout schedules."

He looked confused.

So was she. "You know . . . I have to watch my ketones,

that sort of thing," she said, and wished she could crawl into a hole, for she had no idea what she was saying.

"Oh. Right you are. Ketones," he said.

"Okay, so have a good workout!" she said brightly, and punched him collegially on the shoulder as she took a step toward the ladies' room. But he put his hand on her sweaty arm, and she instantly swiped at his hand with her towel.

"Beg your pardon."

"No, not at all, it's just that . . . ah, were you going to say something?"

"Actually," he said with a charmingly lopsided smile, "I was going to say that you have some *crackin'* legs, if you don't mind."

She had what? *What?*

"What I mean by that—they're fantastic," he clarified with another knee-rattling grin.

Fantastic? He thought her legs were *fantastic?* "Oh. Well," she said, peering down to have a look. "Yeah, I work at it," she lied, and looked up, saw the glimmer in his eyes. "Okay! Really gotta go! Nice seeing you!" she said, and made a long jump into the ladies' locker room before he could stop her.

Her heart was racing a million miles a minute.

She stood just inside, trying to catch her breath. She could feel every inch of her skin his gaze had touched, like little bee stings. One thing was certain. She was *definitely* doing more squats tomorrow.

Rachel showered and dressed in black slacks and a black sweater over a white collared shirt, and braided her hair. In her bag, she found an old tube of Maybelline mascara and a little blush, and counted herself successful when she smudged the mascara on only one eye. Convinced she looked presentable, she slung her gym bag over one shoulder with only a little *ouch,* and her tote on the other, and opened the ladies' locker room door a crack. From there, she looked furtively about, saw no Brits anywhere, and made a beeline for the parking lot and her car.

• • •

AT the employment office, she filled out all the paperwork to request assistance in finding a job, then handed the paperwork to a woman who never made eye contact, and proceeded to pass the time waiting for an employment counselor to see her by perusing a list of jobs posted at the bulletin board.

Wanda Dennard called her name after a wait of almost an hour. She introduced herself, showed Rachel into a tiny cubicle, and invited her to sit while she looked over Rachel's paperwork.

Rachel sat. Wanda read. And read. And read so long that Rachel wondered if she maybe hadn't fallen asleep.

Wanda's desk was very neat. She had a half-dozen pictures of children around her desk, and her screen saver was a picture of a row of sleeping kittens. The binders on her shelves were obscured with various plastic green plants and one very odd-looking marble sculpture of some sort.

Rachel was trying to figure out what that sculpture was when Wanda looked up over her reading glasses. "You're way overqualified for our jobs," she said. "There's nothing here to fit you."

That was not what she wanted to hear. "But I need a job, I really do. I'll do anything," Rachel earnestly assured her, inching up on her orange plastic chair.

Wanda frowned, looked at her paperwork again, then sighed and punched a button on her computer, instantly bringing up a listing of jobs. "Let's see . . . there's a position for a short-order fry cook."

"Is there?" Rachel asked with a wince. "I'm not really overqualified for *that,* am I?" she asked with a laugh.

Wanda did not laugh. Wanda gave off another sigh that sounded like she thought this was going to be a very trying task. "Sacking specialist?"

"Sacking specialist?"

Wanda gave her a sidelong glance. "A grocery sacker."

A *grocery sacker?* Was this woman for real? Not that Rachel had anything against grocery sackers, of course not, but didn't those jobs usually go to teenage boys? She could just imagine herself on checkout nine between two sixteen-year-old boys who amused themselves by hurling lugies at her when the boss wasn't looking. Just the image made her shudder.

Wanda frowned. "I told you you're overqualified!"

"What about teaching jobs? Do you have anything like that? I really like teaching. Even an assistant position would be okay. Do you have that?"

"Oh, *sure*! Why didn't you say so?" Wanda said with a bright smile.

A ray of light! "Really?"

"No, not really! Are you crazy?" Wanda snapped. "This isn't a placement program at Brown, Miss Lear. We have the jobs that no one else will take. Now, if you want me to sit here and rattle off all the jobs no one else will take, I'll do it. But if you think you will be *underqualified* for them all, why don't you do us both a favor and just say so now and we can each get on with our lives?"

Wanda had no idea how badly Rachel wanted to do just that. And she came very, *very* close—but she had to go and think of her bank balance, and the utility bill, and the tree on Mr. Valicielo's fence, and then *Dad,* and smiled meekly. "I won't say that anymore, I promise."

Wanda rolled her eyes, sighed again, only a lot louder and longer, and turned back to the screen. "How do you feel about cleaning downtown offices at night?"

Frankly, not that great, but she forced a smile for Wanda's sake all the same.

Chapter Seven

＊ ✳ ＊

WHEN Rachel arrived home that afternoon—undetected by the Valicielos—she found a note from Dagne stuck in the door. *Hi. Stopped to find something. Call me later.*

Probably a toad's wart or something.

She let herself in the front door, dropped her tote bag in the living room, and still holding the referral sheet from the employment office, she walked into the kitchen—and shrieked.

Myron was sitting there, his head in his hands.

"Jesus, Myron! You scared me!" Rachel exclaimed, her hand and referral sheet clamped over her heart as she sagged against the countertop. "Couldn't you have said something when I came in?"

"Sorry," he said, without bothering to look up.

"I didn't see your car outside."

"A friend dropped me," Myron said, and lifted his head. He looked, Rachel thought, like he hadn't slept well in days. "Sorry I scared you." With a heavy sigh, he got up and walked to the fridge and opened it wide. He stood there for a long moment, his frown going deeper as his fingers impatiently drummed against the door. "You don't have much of anything, do you?"

Yes, well, she was having a bit of a financial crisis. Enough of one that she was screwing up the courage to ask him to repay the money he owed her.

"I thought you just went to the store a couple of days ago."

"Listen, Myron, I really need to ask you something."

"Okay, so ask," he said as he shut the fridge and headed for the pantry. He flung that door open and stood, hand on hip, studying the shelves.

"I am really, really broke—"

"Join the crowd," he snorted.

Right. Well, at least he had a job—*two*, actually. "Okay . . . so I'm really broke, and I was wondering if you might be able to, ah . . ." Man, this was harder than she thought. Why couldn't she just open her mouth and make the words come out? Myron looked over his shoulder. Rachel winced, said in a rush, "Maybe pay back the money you borrowed?"

His expression immediately went dark and sure enough, she felt like a bitch for even asking. "Not all of it," she quickly said. "Just some of it. Enough so I can get by. Like maybe . . . a hundred?" Okay, that was good. Some of what he'd borrowed couldn't be too hard for him.

But Myron said nothing, continued to stare at her, as if he could not believe she was asking him for even that.

"It would really be great if you could pay me just a hundred, or even fifty," she said, her voice noticeably weaker.

Myron sighed and stared at the floor for a moment. "Look, Rach, I know I owe you some money. But you could not have possibly chosen a worse time to ask me for it."

"I couldn't?"

"I've been dealing with some stuff that I wasn't going to burden you with, but since you asked, I guess I'll have to."

"What stuff?" As far as she knew, the only "stuff" Myron ever dealt with was his lack of tenure.

"Something happened at work. A forklift jammed and

damaged a pre-Revolutionary hutch and some china. So we filed a claim. But I guess the claim wasn't done right, so now the insurer has come down to investigate."

"Okay," Rachel said, still waiting for the "stuff" that stood in the way of him paying her back.

"*Okay?* That's all you're going to say? Rachel, *I* am the one who prepares the estimates of loss. I am the one who works with the insurance company. I have the whole administration crawling up my ass over some stupid forklift accident!"

"Why?"

"You just don't get it," Myron groaned, rolling his eyes dramatically. "The bottom line is a person can't just do their job anymore. The slightest thing goes wrong and everyone from the janitor on up is a *suspect,*" he said, making giant, invisible quotation marks with his fingers.

"Suspect!" Rachel exclaimed. "That sounds like there was a crime or something!"

"Whatever the word is," he said dismissively as he returned to the breakfast bar and fell onto a stool. "What I am trying to say is that bureaucracy can get so huge that there's nothing personal in a job anymore. They might as well line up a bunch of robots!" His face was beginning to turn curiously red.

"Okay . . . I didn't know you were having such a rough time at work."

"That's because I didn't want to bring you down," he said miserably, then exhaled a long and weary sigh again. "But you sort of forced my hand. Gawd, I feel like a beer. You wanna go get a beer?"

Hello? Had he heard anything she'd said? "I can't, Myron. I'm really broke."

Myron smiled then. "It's on me," he said, and stood, shoving his hands into his jeans. "Let's go down to Fratangelo's and see what's going on."

What she really wanted to know was why the forklift accident had anything to do with the money he owed her, but before she could ask, Myron asked, "What's that?"

She glanced down at the paper she was still clutching. "Oh! I went to the employment agency today. It's a job referral."

"A job. Really?" he said, his face brightening. "So you'll get yourself a job! There you go—problem solved!" he said happily.

"Not really. It's just a temp agency—part-time work."

Myron shrugged. "It'll at least give you grocery money."

Yeah, and if he'd repay the loan she'd made him, she could pay her utility bill. Which reminded her . . . "By the way, Myron—do you have my T-Mobile?" she asked.

"Oh yeah," he said, and laughed sheepishly. "I meant to bring that back. I don't know where my head's been! I'll bring it back, I promise," he said, and walked to the door. "Hurry up, will you? After what I've been through today, I could really use that beer."

FRATANGELO'S, near the Brown campus at the edge of the Blackstone neighborhood where Rachel lived, was a place Myron had always liked because of the cheap happy hour and even cheaper eats. Tonight, as usual, it was packed with an odd mix of the hip young urban crowd and the graduate student–professor crowd.

They had a seat at the bar and Myron ordered a couple of beers. He then proceeded the regular rant of his tenure problem—same song, louder refrain. "I just need time to research the theory I'm working on," he explained for at least the thousandth, millionth to the nth power time.

Rachel absently nodded—she had learned a long time ago it was best just to zone when Myron went down the gotta-get-tenure path. He rarely heard anything she said, and if he did, it typically made him mad. So as he continued to drone on about it, she let her gaze wander the crowded bar, saw Dave Stolanski, a permanent fixture at Fratangelo's. Dave had been in school almost as long as she had, which wasn't a particularly comforting thought.

Rachel frowned at her beer, then at Dave—but noticed someone behind him who looked an awful lot like Flynn.

She froze, the beer halfway to her mouth, squinting across the smoke-filled room.

"What are you looking at?" Myron asked, shifting his gaze in the direction she was looking. "Oh," he said, seeing Dave Stolanski. "Don't get your heart set on him, Rach. The guy's a loser. He's been in the program five years now and still hasn't made any progress toward finishing his doctorate."

Rachel gave him a withering look, but Myron took a swig of his beer, completely oblivious. "*I've* been in that long, too," she reminded him. "Does that make *me* a loser?"

Startled by the question, Myron quickly shook his head and tried to laugh it off. "No, of *course* not, Rachel! It's different with you!" He laughed again, only a little higher.

"How so?"

"Because!" he insisted nervously. "At least you're at dissertation, right? Dave's not even at dissertation!" he scoffed, waving a hand at Dave, who was intently studying something atop the bar. Myron took another long swig of beer, then held up two fingers to the barkeep to signal another round. "Listen, don't misunderstand. It took me a couple of years to get my dissertation out of the way, too. And you know, back then, I was the *bomb*. The profs loved me! They thought I was the greatest thing since sliced bread, and my work on pre-Revolutionary American history?" He paused to sigh loudly and shake his head. *"Golden."*

Rachel rolled her eyes, put down her beer. "I'm going to the ladies' room."

Thanks to Myron, all she could see as she made her way around the crowded bar was the word *loser.* And it was that word that prevented her from seeing Flynn at all until she turned down the little corridor that led to the bathrooms and practically collided with the hard wall of his chest.

Somehow, she managed to stop herself before doing

that, and stared for a moment at the Oxford shirt, the silk tie . . . the square chin, the sexy five o'clock shadow, and the dancing gray eyes framed in very thick and dark lashes. And when she had made it that far, he smiled and said, "Hello, Rachel."

Her pulse jumped up a couple of notches. "Ah . . . hey."

His smile was dazzling, all pearly white and gorgeous, just like in the James Bond movies, and he unabashedly let his gaze drift the length of her. "How fortunate—I *thought* it was you."

"You did?" she asked, still blinking up at him, still trying to reconcile that gorgeous smile with the fact that it was aimed directly at her. Again. *Again.*

"Yes, of course," he said with a laugh. "In case you haven't noticed, I've been working a bit to gain your attention."

"Where—*here?*" she asked, confused, and unthinkingly glanced over her shoulder into the crowded bar area. When she turned around, she started—Flynn had casually braced himself with an arm to the wall, one hand on his very trim waist, and had blocked her way to the ladies' room.

"Here, there, and everywhere, really. But I'm rather beginning to believe I'm invisible."

Oh nooooo, he wasn't invisible, he wasn't even *remotely* invisible. More like a peacock, gorgeous and impossible to miss, even in a crowd.

"It's been rather bruising to the ego, actually, so if you might possibly shake your head just a bit to indicate that I'm really not so invisible after all?"

Rachel shook her head just a bit.

He laughed low, a sound that tingled down her spine. "That's quite a load off," he said, and shifted closer. So close that she thought she could detect the pleasantly spicy scent of his Calvin Klein cologne. And he was still smiling at her, his gaze sort of dancing between her eyes, her lips, and her bosom. "So now that we've established that I'm not entirely invisible, perhaps we might move on to discussing what it will take to get you to agree to have a drink with me . . . unless, of course, it's too complicated. The ketones, or the schedule, you know."

She loved the way he said *schedule*. Okay. All right. Now there was a fire building in her belly and spreading to her limbs, to her face, and she smiled, her face practically splitting open with it. "A drink," she repeated, and wished to God she could make more use of her tongue than to repeat everything he said.

"A drink. A cocktail," he said, moving even closer, "a nightcap, or a belt, if you prefer, or even a cozy cup of tea . . . whatever you desire, if you'd only nod your head or otherwise indicate your consent that yes, it is indeed within the realm of possibility."

With a laugh, Rachel self-consciously folded her arms across her middle. He smiled softly, moved closer, and lifted his hand from his waist and touched a curl at her temple. Rachel froze, absolutely paralyzed by his touch. A real *man's* touch.

A fire-breathing dragon could not possibly have made her hotter than that single touch.

"Ah . . . you know?" she stammered, seeing as how he was very casually fingering the curl at her temple and that fire-breathing dragon was setting her shorts on full-blown inferno. "You, ah, really don't have to do this. I wasn't offended that day at the phone."

"Quite happy to hear that you weren't, yet I don't believe I am making myself entirely clear. I don't *have* to do this. I *want* to do this."

Okay, hats off to Dagne. She would never say a disparaging word about white magic again. *Never.* But still . . . this was so improbable, so unreal—men never looked at her like *that,* never stalked her for a drink, and she had never, *ever,* melted under the intensity of a man's gaze like she was melting this very minute. That, naturally, sent up all sorts of red flags, and she suddenly blurted, "Are you making a film?"

"Beg your pardon?"

"Or maybe a documentary? Like a reality show where

you maybe go around asking American women out to see what they'll say or do?"

"Clever idea, but not the case. And if it were, I'd be the bloke whose face was flashed across millions of tellies with the caption, *Horribly unsuccessful thus far*."

"So you really want to have a drink with me?" she asked as his hand dropped to the braid that hung over her shoulder, calmly feeling the weight of it. "Why me?"

He smiled, stooping a little so that he could look her directly in the eye, and she could see the glimmer of amusement in his. "Ah, Rachel, it's all quite simple, really. Where I come from, if a man is interested in getting to know a woman, he asks her out for a drink. It's quite a common practice around the world, actually. Are you not familiar with it?"

"That's an understatement," she muttered.

"Aha. So what, then, is the proper protocol on your planet?"

"Luck. Pure dumb luck."

"Hmm. Perhaps fun, but not entirely effective. So as it stands, and without much luck thus far, you really leave me no choice," he said, and took her braid fully in hand, using it to pull her a little closer, "than to declare straightaway that I find you terribly attractive. And as it would be frightfully inappropriate to jump your lovely bones in this horrid little corridor—not to mention that hardly being the most romantic gesture in the world, and fantastically presumptuous as well—I'm hoping for at least the chance to chat," he said, and let go of her braid. His hand drifted across her jawline, then down her neck.

"Ooh," she whispered.

"Rachel?"

Myron's voice was no less startling than a screech of tires, and startled Rachel so badly that she actually bumped into Flynn as she jerked around. "Myron!" Why did Myron have to choose *that* moment of all moments in the universe to show up? It made her feel angrily flustered, angry that he even existed.

Myron was staring at Flynn, and idiot that he was, unabashedly sizing him up. "What's going on here?"

"I ah . . . this is ah . . . Flynn."

"Flynn Oliver," Flynn said, extending his hand.

Myron reluctantly took Flynn's hand and dropped it quickly. "Is everything okay?" he asked Rachel, still staring at Flynn.

"Yes, of course!" she exclaimed a little heatedly.

"I just wondered if everything was all right. I mean, when you didn't come back—"

"I wasn't gone *that* long."

"Well, your beer is getting warm," Myron said. "Are you going to drink it?"

"I didn't realize," Flynn said politely, and stepped away from her, leaving a cold draft on her back. "I'm sorry to have interrupted your evening—it would seem I owe you another apology." He made a move to step around Myron.

"No, really, you don't owe me an apology!" Rachel exclaimed as she realized he was leaving. "I didn't . . . I mean, I'm not really—"

"Oh, sorry," Myron said as he moved out of Flynn's way and bumped up against Rachel.

Flynn smiled, let his gaze flick over her once more before lifting his hand. "Have a good evening." He turned and walked on, leaving her there with a moron.

As he disappeared into the crowd, Rachel sighed with great exasperation and shoved Myron away from her.

"What?" he demanded. "I thought that dude was bothering you!"

"He wasn't *bothering* me!"

"You mean you *liked* him?" the dolt asked, looking over his shoulder at Flynn's retreating back.

"Oh just . . . shut *up,* Myron!" she said hotly, and walked into the ladies' room, furious with herself for not having more guts.

•　　•　　•

FLYNN walked to the other side of the bar, nodded slyly at Joe, then proceeded to the parking lot, Joe following behind. He got in the passenger side of the car; Joe got in behind the wheel and started up his blue 1977 Camaro, revving the motor a couple of times as he liked to do.

"So?" Joe asked as he coasted through the parking lot toward the street.

"Apparently she's already hooked up," Flynn said.

"You mean you got *nothing?*"

"I wouldn't say *nothing,*" Flynn said. "I got a look."

"A look? What look?"

"A look," Flynn repeated, motioning vaguely with his hand. "You know . . . a bloody *look.*"

"Dude . . ." Joe sighed, shook his head. "You're going about this all wrong. You have to come on to her! Let her know you want in her pants. Rub up against her, like, let her know what you're working with. Women like that."

"Seems terribly doglike, doesn't it?"

Joe shrugged as he turned the Camaro onto the street. "Works for me," he said, and hit the gas.

Chapter Eight

✦ ✦ ✦

RACHEL'S night went from bad to worse, but all things being equal, the incident involving the police later went pretty well, considering Dagne was involved.

After Myron had chased Flynn away, Rachel called Glinda the Good Witch from Fratangelo's and convinced her to show up at her house a little later with some Chinese food and her spell book.

"For *real?*" Dagne asked, all excited.

"For real. I think. No, no, not for *real*, just . . . I don't know—"

"I'll meet you in an hour," Dagne said, and hung up before Rachel could talk herself out of it.

She finished her beer, left a sulky Myron, and went home, where she changed into black yoga pants and a hooded fleece jacket. When Dagne arrived a short time later, they laid out the Chinese food in the living room, lit a bunch of candles and a fire to keep the energy costs down, and sat on big floor pillows to dine on sweet and sour pork. It's hard to do witchcraft on an empty stomach.

By this point, of course, Rachel had lost all confidence

and had convinced herself that Flynn had to be put off by Myron at the very least.

As she told Dagne about it, Dagne's chopsticks froze midway to her mouth, a piece of pork dangling precariously over the coffee table, and she remained that way, wide-eyed, until Rachel finished the story.

"Is that all?" Dagne asked.

Rachel nodded.

Dagne suddenly shot her arms straight up in the air, miraculously holding on to the pork, and gave a shout of triumph before popping the bite into her mouth. "This is *fantastic!*"

"I wish," Rachel said, shaking her head. "But I think it's over," she said, staring into her container. "He thinks Myron and I are together."

"Are you *nuts?* Remember our spells? Don't you believe in *anything?*"

"I know this will come as a shock, Dagne, but I sort of have a hard time believing in witchcraft—even the good kind."

"Oh, sure," Dagne said, putting down her chopsticks with a *thwack.* "You can believe in astrology and parallel universes and past lives, but *noooo,* can't believe in a little magic, can you?" She folded her arms across her middle, pouting. "Spirituality is *so far* out of the realm of possibility, isn't it!"

"It's not that I don't believe in the possibility," Rachel patiently tried to explain, "but I think it's more likely that he got a good look at Ben and Jerry back here," she said, patting her butt, "*and* Myron, and then wondered what drugs he was on."

"God, Rachel!" Dagne said angrily. "Why do you always have to put yourself down?"

"Hey! When it comes to guys, I know of what I speak."

"Bullshit!" Dagne said low.

"Okay, let's start with high school," Rachel said, jabbing at Dagne in the air with her chopsticks. "Did I ever tell you that guys used to call me Miss Fortune? Get it?

Lots of money, but what a misfortune that I was a fat one. And then, when I was a senior, this *god* asked me out. I mean, he was hot and the most popular guy in school, and he was asking *me,* tubby drama student with frizzy hair, out on a date! And the first date was great—we went to a carnival. He won me a big teddy bear, and then took me home, does *not* kiss me good night, but casually asks if my sister Rebecca was home for the summer. You remember Bec? The beauty queen? Tall and thin and gorgeous and sleek hair? Then our second date, he comes over to pick me up, and didn't even get past the *gate* before he was asking if Rebecca was there. Well, long story short, the guy was only interested in Rebecca, and he was using me to get to her. And *that,* Dagne, was just the beginning of a long line of complete disasters!"

God, even though it had been fifteen years, it still stung like hell.

"What has that got to do with Flynn?" Dagne demanded.

"Everything!" Rachel shot back. "The point is, guys like him are usually after something else, like, say, my *sister.* And even if you argue that's not the deal with Flynn, then I will argue that the situation is actually even worse, because now he thinks Myron is my *boyfriend.*"

"He used to be."

"Are you ever going to let me forget it?"

"No," Dagne said immediately. "So anyway, what if Flynn thinks Myron the leech is your boyfriend? You'll set the record straight. And listen, *everyone* had a bad experience or two in high school! Are you going to let that guide the rest of your life? Jesus, George Steinbrenner talked me into taking off my shirt in front of the entire football team, and I did it, but do you think I sit around moping about it now?"

The moment the words were out of Dagne's mouth, she made a tiny gasp of surprise, and she and Rachel sat there, staring at each other, until an unspoken agreement passed that they would leave that admission for another time.

"Not *that* George Steinbrenner," Dagne hastily clarified, and picked up her chopsticks. "All I'm saying is that you need to have a little faith. Lookit, I did a spell on Glenn and he called. I did a couple of spells on you and you got a job and you've got a cool guy interested in you, so—"

"*Glenn* called you?" Rachel interrupted, dumbfounded. "I thought you didn't like Glenn!"

Dagne shrugged. "I was practicing something. So come on, just try believing for a week, and I really mean, *just* a week, and I promise, Flynn will find you again, and he *will* be interested in you, and he will *not* be afraid of your enormous butt *or* Myron."

Rachel laughed. "Okay," she said, "I am willing to concede something witchcrafty may be going on here. But need I remind you that not all your spells are working? The weight-loss spell doesn't work for shit, thank you, and I don't have a *real* job yet."

"I never said a *real* job," Dagne said cheerfully.

"So . . . if I *believe* . . . do you think . . . I mean, is it possible . . ." Rachel stopped there, couldn't believe such ludicrous thoughts were about to turn into words and come out of her mouth.

"What?"

"Is it possible to do a spell that would make me . . . you know, less . . . *tongue-tied* or something?" Rachel blurted, gesturing impatiently at her mouth, and then slapped her hand against her forehead as her own words filtered into her consciousness. "*Gawd,* I am so pathetic! Listen to me, asking you to cast some spell that will make me less of a geek!"

"You're not a geek, Rach."

"Yes I am!" she insisted, burying her face in her arms folded on the coffee table. "I'm *so* not used to guys, especially drop-dead gorgeous guys, and I don't know what to say, and all I want is for once, just *once,* to be, I don't know . . . sexy."

"You *are* sexy," Dagne insisted, and bonked Rachel on

the top of her head with her chopsticks. "Anyway, this guy is already under your spell, and it's only a matter of when he'll find you, and he will be crazy about you. *You*, Rachel."

"That's so nice," she said with a smile. "But I am hardly convinced. Come on, please?"

Dagne sighed, pulled the heavy spell book from her canvas bag. "You're such work, you know that? Living in some high school drama and worried about a perfectly fine ass. Of course you're sexy, Rachel! You think you have to look like your sisters to be desirable, and that's so maddeningly dumb for someone so smart that it just makes me want to *scream*. Look at you! Open your eyes! In fact, *look* at your eyes! You have gorgeous blue-green eyes, and all that black heroine hair, and you are very shapely! Do you know how many women would kill for that shape? *I* wish I had your curves—but okay," she said, holding up a hand as Rachel opened her mouth to argue, "if you want a spell to make you desirable, we'll do one."

"Finally!" Rachel said cheerfully, and got up, removed all the Chinese food containers as Dagne searched the spell book.

After a half hour, she said "Aha!" and began jabbing her finger at one musty, pink page. "Got it. The spell should encompass his senses. So, for example, scent. Every time he smells a certain scent, he'll want you." She looked up, her eyes shining. "We *have* to be outside this time. This one is all about the moon. Do you have gardenia oil?"

Rachel laughed. "No. Does anyone have gardenia oil?"

"Rose oil?"

"No."

"Come on, you have to have something that smells really good, something natural."

Rachel thought a moment, suggested slowly, "I have Mexican vanilla."

Dagne thought about it. "Okay, let's use that," she said, and sprang to her feet, headed for the kitchen.

Rachel was right behind her.

They managed to find substitutes for everything Dagne said they needed—and Dagne assured her, with what Rachel thought was false bravado, that it was *quite* all right to substitute in spell work. Skeptical, Rachel nonetheless stomped outside with Dagne, behind the garage, where the elm tree lay across Mr. Valicielo's fence. And they even managed to complete one spell—the scent spell—before the police arrived, called by Mr. Valicielo, naturally, who was convinced someone was sneaking around wanting to steal his backyard gnomes.

The two cops who came—cute guys—looked at Dagne like she was a freak when she explained she was casting a spell.

The blond one told them both to stop casting spells and go inside and quit bothering the neighbors. Fortunately, Dagne did not argue, because they were both freezing to death. But, Dagne noted cheerfully, all was not lost. If everything went according to plan, Rachel would wake up sexy.

And vanilla, apparently.

The spell-casting made Rachel sleepy, and she slept soundly, with the curious scent of vanilla all around her, while a dream of a Flynn Knight romped round her mind.

Only this time, he was naked.

WHILE Rachel was dreaming of him naked, Flynn opened the door to his corporate apartment, walked inside and dumped his trench coat, and headed straight for the fridge. He grabbed a kitchen towel, opened the freezer compartment, and filled it with several ice cubes. Then he got a beer and walked over to the cheap, fake leather couch and lay down, his head propped on one arm folded slung behind him. He took a swig of beer, then put the towel with the ice on his left eye.

Ouch. That really stung.

He knew the moment he laid eyes on that dodgy water-

front pub there would be trouble; he could tell by the way
all the blokes had sneered at him and Joe when they had
entered the establishment. Nevertheless, he never dreamed
that the situation would actually result in fisticuffs.

He couldn't help himself—he smiled broadly. And immediately winced at the pain it caused his bruised eye.

He'd really sent that sad bastard sailing across the table,
hadn't he? That was a bloody good cut he'd got off, and
furthermore, he was quite pleased to note that not one of
those sodding nancy boys had gotten as much as a lick on
him. In fact it was the bartender who, in an effort to break
up the fight, had knocked Flynn across the face with the
bar stool.

All in all, he'd had a rather jolly good time of it.

He was still grinning at the ceiling when the phone
rang. He glanced at the clock—three in the morning,
which, unfortunately, could only mean one thing.

With a sigh, he pushed himself up and reached for the
phone. "Hello."

"Flynn, darling, is that you?"

Funny how sharp Iris's voice could sound, even from
across the pond.

"Yes, Iris. Who exactly were you expecting?"

"Oh, darling, don't be naff, please! I've been trying to
get you for ages!"

"And now you have me," he said, gingerly pressing the
towel and ice to his eye.

"Are you quite all right? When you didn't ring back, I
began to suspect the worst."

"I'm fine. I've just been frightfully busy."

"Have you? You really mustn't overwork yourself."

"Mmm."

"I've been frightfully busy myself," she said with a bit
of a laugh. "Eileen Fiskmark-Jones had a lovely gathering
just this last weekend, and I must have gone daft, because
I promised to help her put it all on. She held it at the Royal
Fitzhugh Hotel on Regent Street. You know the one, where
Charles and Camilla had their spring fling last year?"

Flynn rolled his eyes.

"You simply could not imagine all the trouble we had with the caterer! Firstly, they were to have served duck, but what did they come with? Cornish game hens! Can you imagine?"

"The horror," he muttered.

"Quite," Iris said, missing the sarcasm in his voice. "And then, as if that weren't tragedy enough, the flowers didn't arrive until a quarter to. Eileen was simply beside herself."

"Eileen is always beside herself, Iris. She's barmy."

"Oh Flynn, America's made you cheeky!"

"Has it? I'm a bit knackered, that's all. It is three o'clock here. In the *morning*."

"Aren't you the least interested in how the whole do turned out?" Iris asked, her voice taking on a familiar whine.

Flynn sighed. "How did it turn out, Iris?"

"It was smashing, of course. Honestly, when Eileen and I put our heads together, everything goes tickety-boo!"

"Was Paul Haversham at this do?" Flynn asked calmly. "Because I know everything goes *tickety-boo* when you and he take off your pants, too."

"Dear God, that's ugly." She sighed irritably. "Why must you always be so cross?"

"Oh, I don't know, Iris. Perhaps because you are my fiancée and you cheated on me? That might make a man a bit cross."

She sighed again, only louder. "It was a *fling,* nothing more! Are you intent on punishing me for the rest of our lives? I told you I'm frightfully sorry for it, and frankly, I cannot understand why you won't accept my apology! Really, Flynn, you were gone for *weeks,* off to Monaco, then to Lithuania . . . what was I to do?"

"You were to keep your knickers on," Flynn said coldly, and lowered the ice from his eye, ignoring her little gasp of hurt. "If there is nothing else, I'd really like to get some sleep," he said, and quietly clicked off before she could object.

He tossed the phone aside, lay back on the couch and closed his eyes, and felt the fatigue wash over him. His mind raced with various images—Iris's pale and delicate face, which he had once thought was so bloody beautiful . . . and oddly, the smiling, pretty face of Rachel. There was certainly a look of honesty there in her smile and in her eyes . . . a look that Iris did not possess, nor could she, apparently, manufacture.

As Flynn drifted off to sleep on that couch, the image of Rachel in his mind's eye, that long thick braid of hair over her shoulder, those lovely blue-green eyes, he thought he smelled something a little curious. *What was it?*

Vanilla?

Interesting. It reminded him of his mother's butter rum cake.

FLYNN was still dreaming of butter rum cake when Aaron and Bonnie departed the marriage therapist's office. They'd canceled the last two appointments because Aaron was feeling too ill from the chemotherapy. At least that was the lie Bonnie told the therapist.

The truth was he had refused to do his homework. He had never bargained for homework when he signed up for marriage counseling, and it wasn't until a tearful Bonnie started to pack a bag that he gave in, sat down, and did it.

And as he predicted, things hadn't gone exactly well this morning. Bonnie was hardly speaking to him now, but he wondered what the hell she expected when that fucking therapist had given them their "marital" workbooks at the last session. He'd known instantly they were headed for disaster.

The first exercise was what Daniel called "amazingly simple." Aaron was supposed to list three things about Bonnie that he loved, and how each "thing" made him feel, and then he was to list three things he did *not* love and how those things made him feel.

The first part had been easy. He loved her smiling laughter, loved the way she adored her children, and the way she worked so hard to make their marriage work. Bonnie had, naturally, beamed like a ray of sunshine as he had listed those things, along with how they made him feel. Happy. Content. Loved.

And then there were the three things he did not love. He listed: her obsession with her looks, harping on him, and snoring. The snoring wasn't even real—he'd just thrown it in there because he couldn't think of anything else, and thought it was so innocuous that Bonnie would gloss right over it.

Bonnie did not gloss right over it. Bonnie didn't gloss over anything, except the obsession with her looks, which was the one thing he thought would make her really mad. But oh no, she and Daniel agreed that it was a woman's curse in life, which left plenty of room for Bonnie to get mad about the harping and the snoring.

After Daniel had Bonnie reveal and relate (this dude *loved* making up catchphrases) her feelings about Aaron's list (and what the hell was the point, again?), it was Bonnie's turn to list the three things *she* loved about *him*: generous spirit (not that he really had one, but he'd take it), his fierce love of his daughters (damn straight), and the way his eyes crinkled when he laughed (actually, he thought they were lines from chemo, but he didn't have the heart to tell her). The things she did not love about him were: his illness (that was so safe to list that Aaron almost cried foul and accused her of cheating), his moments of self-pity (well, okay, he hated them, too), and the fact that he could not seem to understand her (it wasn't like he didn't try!).

And now, here they sat, side by side in his Lincoln town car, stuck in crosstown traffic on the way to Presbyterian Hospital, where he'd undergo his umpteenth round of chemo. Neither of them had said a word since they left the therapist's office. Aaron was too afraid. Bonnie was too mad.

But as they turned onto Madison Avenue, she sighed,

tapped her hand against the window. "I only *harped* on you about calling Rachel."

"But even when I called Rachel, it still wasn't enough for you," he said, keeping his gaze straight ahead.

"That's right—because you left her your typical message, that she'd better be doing things your way, or there would be hell to pay. What happened to nice, Aaron? What happened to trying a new approach with her?"

All right, so he hadn't exactly been eloquent in his message. But he'd been really sick that day.

"I know you were feeling really sick that day, so I can't help wonder why you'd choose that time to call her. It's like you *wanted* to be in the worst possible frame of mind."

Wow. Preemptive strike. A *good* preemptive strike. "I don't know," he said. "I never feel good anymore, so I'm not sure when a good time would be."

"Here you go with the self-pity defense," she said irritably.

"And here you go harping again," he said. "Wasn't that the whole point of today's session? Try not to push each other's buttons?"

"I'm not *harping,* Aaron. I am just trying to get you to hear me. If you want to get through to Rachel, try being nice instead of being an ass."

Aaron leaned his head back against the headrest, closed his eyes, wondered if he even had it in him anymore to be nice or if they'd zapped that along with the cancer cells.

"And there is one other thing—I do *not* snore."

"Oh Bonnie," he sighed. "Of course you don't snore!"

"Then why the hell did you say I did?"

"I just needed something to say, that's all."

"Oh that's just great! God, Aaron, this will never work if you don't take it seriously!"

It wasn't going to work if he pitched headfirst off the top of Presbyterian Hospital, either, he thought petulantly, and crossing his arms over his chest, he glared out the window for the rest of the drive.

Chapter Nine

✦ ✦ ✦

Subject: What's going on?
From: Rebecca Parrish <reparrish72@aol.com>
To: Rach <earthangel@hotmail.com>

Hi Rachel. I hadn't heard from you in a while, and
Mom said you and Dad had a fight and you haven't
talked to him since then. Is everything okay? Don't let
him get to you, because he really is just a dumb lamb
in sheep's clothing for the most part.

BTW, I got an e-mail from Robbie, and she said that
you said that your relationship with Myron was strictly
platonic? Is that TRUE? I didn't know that! Why didn't
I know that? I demand details! Rebecca

P.S. The herbs you sent for Grayson's allergies worked
GREAT. Can you get some more?

Subject: Re: What's going on?
From: <earthangel@hotmail.com>
To: <reparrish72@aol.com>

Hey Bec. Glad Gray is doing better, and yes, I can get some more. I'll check my connection (ha ha haaaa). I will try and find a place in Texas that mixes this particular combination of herbs, tho. As for Dad, I don't know what he is other than a real asshole sometimes, but what else is new. Most of the time, we get along. But there are times he can really piss me off.

As for Myron, I did so tell you and Robin that it was "getting" to a platonic state that night we were drinking tequila at the ranch!!!! Why can't y'all EVER remember anything I say???? But I don't want to talk about it, because there is nothing to talk about. We had a thing. Now we're friends. End of really very boring story. Gotta run. Say hi to Matt and Gray for me!

Rachel . . . who, BTW, met a guy. Sort of. Actually, Dagne and I used a little witchcraft to conjure him up, but he is SOOO cute! More later . . .

Rachel had a ton of stuff to do the next day, so of course it would be raining.

Her first stop was Turbo Temps, where the employment agency had sent her. With a little luck—and okay, a little magic—Rachel hoped to get some sort of part-time gig. She pulled into a parking spot, found her umbrella, then opened the door, wrestling with the umbrella and the door while she tried to squeeze between her Bug and the SUV next to her, but stepped into a puddle in the course of it and flooded her boot.

Clutching a soggy referral sheet, she reached the inside of Turbo Temps, where a woman immediately barked at her to put her umbrella in the can. She did that, and then squished back to the counter and handed the woman her referral sheet.

The woman took it, grimacing, and made a huge show of straightening it out.

"I'm really sorry," Rachel said. "It's raining out."

The woman looked up at her like she didn't believe her, then reviewed the referral sheet, the copy of Rachel's résumé attached to it, and without a word, turned and punched a couple of buttons on her computer. An old dot-matrix printer began rattling behind her, during which time she stared at the computer screen. When the thing finally stopped printing, she swiveled around, extracted it from the printer, and handed it to Rachel. "Call before showing up," she said.

Rachel took the paper and looked at it. *Baumgartner Medical,* it read under the word *Client. Transcribing medical transcripts from draft to final form. Requirements: Typing, 50 wpms, use of computer and word-processing software.*

Rachel glanced up at the clerk. She was staring intently at her computer screen, but said, "That's all we have today. Baumgartner will give you a paper to bring back here for payment. If you want to get paid, don't leave the job without getting that paper. And make sure someone signs it!"

The only good thing about her visit to Turbo Temps was that when she came out, the rain had let up a little. Rachel threw the papers into the backseat and headed over to Providence Fabrics. Because the cops had busted the coven (yes, her sense of humor was still intact) they hadn't done the sight spell. So Dagne, in a great show of faith, left her pink spell book with Rachel. "I've gotta do some stuff on eBay tomorrow," she said. Honestly, Dagne spent so much time on eBay that it was a wonder they hadn't given her an honorary page or something. "Try it yourself!" she had cheerfully urged Rachel.

Rachel had at first laughed it off, but the more she thought about it, the more she thought, why not? She was doing all the work anyway—Dagne just stood around handing her stuff to drink and then telling her what to recite. And besides, she'd seen another weight-loss spell in there that she really wanted to try.

At the fabric store, she looked for the perfect swath of lavender. She figured it needed to be velvet or brocade—something weighty and therefore, meaningful. And on the next to the last aisle, she found what she was looking for. It was silk chenille and a beautiful shade of lavender. It was very expensive, too . . . so Rachel didn't even look at her credit card as she handed it to the clerk. Can't see it, can't feel it.

A quarter of an hour later, she left the store with three yards of the silk chenille and enough lavender silk fringe to trim it. She figured she had enough to not only cast a spell, but to make a shawl, too.

From there, Rachel headed for campus and the Brown University Library, where she spent the remainder of that soggy afternoon holed up at a desk with several books around her, working on dissertation theories.

Darkness had fallen when she returned home. There was a note from Dagne stuck in her door—*Came by to pick up some stuff*—and Rachel panicked for a moment, thinking "stuff" equaled the spell book. But it was exactly where she'd left it, on the kitchen bar, a couple of pages dog-eared. So she made herself a box of macaroni and cheese (not exactly healthy, but she really didn't have much else, as it was obvious Myron had been by, too), then wandered into the living room, flicked on the TV, and then promptly got up and left it on, off to find her Pilates book.

She returned to the living room a little later dressed in yoga clothes, her hair knotted into what Dagne called her Mickey Mouse look—two knots atop her head—and her yoga mat. And while Korean TV played in the background—some sort of variety show with Asian subtitles (the need for which fascinated her)—she worked through her Pilates book until her muscles screamed at her.

Now she was ready for a few spells.

Dagne said atmosphere was very important, so she

wandered around her house and gathered up all the candles she could find.

Once she had the candles lit and placed around the room to create the right atmosphere, she flipped off Korean TV, opened the spell book to one of the pages she had marked, took the lavender silk chenille and Dagne's magic amulet, and placed them together. And then she rounded up a saucer, a pair of scissors, and some matches.

She read the spell several times, thought if Grandma knew what she was doing, she'd have a double coronary on the spot.

But she was, she knew, attracted to this guy big time, and she supposed she was willing to walk the extra mile . . . albeit an extremely bizarre mile.

And in fact, the whole thing was so stupid to the intellectual side of her that she read the spell once more, wondered if the position of the moon or whatever really mattered like the spell book said, remembered all the things Dagne told her she had to do, and at last stood, let her hair down (atmosphere), draped the length of chenille on the floor, and cut an inch across the bottom. She picked up the chenille from the floor and draped it around her shoulders. Then she took a match, lit it, and held it to the piece of chenille she'd cut. When it caught fire, she dropped it into the saucer, held the saucer up before her, and said solemnly, "From these ashes smoke will rise, and lift my color to his eyes."

She put the saucer down, picked up the amulet, and began to swing it above the saucer as she walked in a circle. "The color of me shall my true love see," she said, her voice rising and falling like she had heard on the WB's *Charmed,* "and instantly know his desire for me."

She paused there, watched the last of the chenille burn and tried not to wrinkle her nose, because it really stunk. Then circled again, chanting the same spell two more times. Once she'd done three recitations, she put the amulet down, and as Dagne had instructed her, she stood above the burned fabric and waved her hands in a circular, witchy way, dissipating the smoke.

After a few moments of that, it was over.

Rachel stood, hands on hips, and stared down at the plate. Was it her, or were all these spells a little anticlimactic? It would be cool if lightning would flash, or a clap of thunder would rattle her bungalow. But so far in her experience, there was only a mess to clean up.

She cleaned up this mess, then gathered up the spell book and moved to her bedroom, laid the spell book on her bed, and returned to the living room for her candles. She brought a half-dozen to the master bath, another half-dozen for her bedroom, then started running the water for her bath. She undressed, added bubble bath, decided there wasn't enough light in the bathroom, and looked out the door, into her room for the miniature twin torchères Myron had given her. How odd . . . they weren't in her room.

Rachel wrapped a bath sheet around her and did a quick search of her house for the torchères, but still couldn't find them. She supposed she had put them upstairs in the guest room and shrugged it off. She had enough candles, and besides, her tub was filling.

She hurried back to her bath, turned off the water, and studied her last spell. This was the one for insurance, the shot at losing her butt, otherwise known as Ben and Jerry.

OUTSIDE, on Slater, the rain had deteriorated into a heavy mist and fog was rolling in. Parked outside her house, below the limbs of an old sycamore tree that badly needed trimming, Flynn watched the windows of Rachel's little house.

He'd thought to go to the door to present himself, and was working on a plausible explanation, but he had noticed that Rachel was the sort to leave her blinds open, and there she was, lying on the floor, doing some sort of strange thing with her legs, while on the telly, images of singing Asians flashed across.

Naturally, he'd not wanted to disturb her in the middle of whatever it was she was doing, but he really didn't want to sit out in the car like some pervert, either.

While he was debating it, however, Rachel suddenly popped up, turned off the telly, and disappeared into the back. Flynn got out of his hired car, put on his trench coat . . . but then she had reappeared, carrying an enormous book of some sort, put it down, disappeared again, and just as quickly reappeared with an armful of candles. Something told him to wait. Something told him to get back into the car.

He watched, fascinated, as she lit the candles, let down what looked to be a mane of gorgeous, wavy hair from that odd poodle-ear arrangement, and opened that enormous book. She knelt in front of it, studying it for what seemed an eternity, and, he thought, she laughed once or twice.

Suddenly, she was up on her feet.

He couldn't quite make out what she was doing, and she disappeared from his sight for a moment, stooping to the floor—but after a moment, she stood again, with a cloth draped across her shoulders. And then she lit something, another cloth, it looked like, dropped it onto a plate, and began to move in a circle, swinging something over it.

Flynn drew a long and soft breath. Perhaps he'd been running on fumes so long that he'd lost his mind, but then again, he could swear the bird was doing some sort of witchcraft.

He was so fascinated by it, in fact, that when she had finished her strange little dance and moved to the back part of the house, he did, too, stealing into the darkened area between houses.

Certainly he knew what he was doing was not only lewd but unlawful, and really, he could lose his job and be booted back across the pond were he caught. He knew all that, but the man in him was far too intrigued to pay much mind to the laws of this country, and standing between the neighbor's rubbish bins as he was, he watched her emerge in a towel from a candlelit bathroom, watched her with that large book again, watched her do some sort of dance around two of those candles, her lovely back exposed, before disappearing into the bath again.

At that point, Flynn regained some of his senses—precious few, really, but enough to make him move back to his car.

He sat in the driver's seat, staring blindly at the windshield, imagining her, naked, in her bath, doing some sort of witchcrafty thing.

That had been remarkable. *That* had conjured up all sorts of images of Wiccan-like sex (whatever Wiccan-like sex might be, but at the moment he was beyond randy and ready to entertain any number of theories). *That* had cast this enticing young woman in a whole new light.

A light that was, strangely, a lovely shade of lavender.

AN hour later, Flynn met Joe at the coffeehouse where the locals liked to read poetry. Joe was seated in the very back, in the shadows. So deeply shadowed, in fact, that Flynn had a difficult time finding him. He sat, asked the girl who followed him for a cup of hot tea, then turned and smiled at Joe.

"Any luck?" he asked.

Flynn shook his head.

Joe groaned. "You're starting to make me think I'm gonna have to do it for you, pal."

Flynn laughed, straightened his tie. "The day I need *you* to *do it for me* is the day I will bloody well kill myself, thank you."

Joe laughed, clapped him cheerfully on the back. "If it comes to that, you have my word we'll ship you home in one piece—at least no more than two. Scout's honor, dude."

Chapter Ten

✦ ✦ ✦

RACHEL was beginning to get a little depressed.

It wasn't her temporary job, which, incidentally, was *not* typing medical transcripts as she had been led to believe, but in fact, a backlog of autopsy reports (*DOB 8-16-39. Subject a fully developed Black adult male. Legs unremarkable. Arms unremarkable. Torso unremarkable . . .*).

It was enough to depress anyone, and while reading about people's unremarkable body parts was not exactly ego-boosting, it wasn't that which had Rachel down. And it wasn't her weight-loss program, either, which, if anyone was interested, wasn't working for shit, regardless of her trips to the gym and general state of poverty. All right, it had only been a couple of weeks or so. But *still.*

Nor was it the fact that she had just received her utility bill, which was now officially forty-five days delinquent. That came to $175 plus fines and penalties.

It was that Flynn had disappeared. As in, off the face of the earth. As in, one day, she was seeing him all over the place and the next day it was like he never existed. Which, Rachel thought, was not exactly out of the realm of possibility. In spite of Dagne's assurances to the contrary, she was nearing the end of her one-week experiment in *really believing,* and no Flynn.

It was more likely, given her thirty-one years of experience thus far, that Flynn, just like she'd feared, really had been horrified, and worse, he really did think Myron was her boyfriend. Okay, all right, so Myron had been her boyfriend once, but he wasn't her boyfriend *now,* and seeing him through Flynn's eyes, well . . . she thought she might as well crack open the cookie dough and mainline it, because Flynn wasn't coming back.

Except that, thanks to her new status as pauper, she didn't have any cookie dough.

She checked her horoscope in the paper instead. *Some ideas seem new and interesting but are better left unexplored.*

Great. That made her feel so much better about the witchcraft thing. *Not.*

With a sigh of resignation, Rachel tossed the horoscope aside and went to dress for her weaving class.

She donned a black, ankle-length skirt and a tight-fitting, low-cut gray sweater that made her look thin, she thought, bound her hair up in a massive knot at her nape, put on the amethyst earrings she had picked up on the Isle of Skye during a research trip that had quickly gone nowhere, and her brand-new Donald J. Pilner embroidered boots.

Okay, so she'd charged brand-new, extremely expensive boots at a point she was desperate for money. But she had the autopsy job, and if push came to shove, she could borrow the money from Robin or Rebecca. At least, she hoped she could. But she really *needed* those boots to make her feel better.

Then she draped the lavender shawl she had made Saturday around her shoulders. At least her dabble in witchcraft wasn't a complete loss—she had a beautiful shawl to show for it. But she wasn't giving up. Not yet, anyway. And in an act of semi-desperation, she dabbed a little Mexican vanilla behind one ear. Really stupid, but it wasn't like anyone was going to be sniffing around and asking if her perfume came in a bottle with the Pillsbury Doughboy on the label. Besides, she found the smell of vanilla to be very calming.

When she arrived at class with the box of yarns she would discuss, most of her students were already gathered. Sandy was regaling a very shocked-looking Mr. Gregory with her latest bout of diverticulitis, Chantal and Tiffinnae were arguing about the progress Tiffinnae had made on their weaving thus far, which was pretty close to none, given their penchant for talking and bothering others who were trying to weave, and Jason was sitting quietly with a stack of what Rachel supposed was travel brochures—she made a mental note to mention them to the class.

She said hi, walked to the front of the class, and put down her box. There was a message taped to the chalkboard for her—it was from a school secretary and it said Dave and Lucy were running late, and one new student had signed up for class.

"Woo-*hoo,* girl!" Chantal said as Rachel read the note. "Don't *you* got it going on!" Rachel looked up. Chantal was mimicking some sort of bird walk, going round in a little circle, dipping her head as she admired Rachel's shawl.

"You like it?" Rachel asked proudly, and very theatrically tossed one end over her shoulder. "I made it this weekend."

"You *made* that?" Tiffinnae exclaimed.

"I mean, I sewed the edges and the fringe."

"What is that? Silk?" Tiffinnae asked.

"Chenille," Rachel said. "I'm going to talk a little bit about it and all the different threads and yarns and how they've evolved through the years."

Neither Tiffinnae nor Chantal looked very thrilled by the prospect, and Mr. Gregory actually groaned—at her or Sandy, she couldn't tell.

Rachel arranged her visual aids and notes, and while she was reviewing her remarks, she heard the door open and glanced up; it was Dave and Lucy. She smiled, gave a little wave at the same time she looked away.

When at last she was ready, she glanced up at the classroom clock, saw that it was time to begin, and took her place behind the podium. Only then did she look up, smiling at the class . . . and felt the hard leap of her heart.

It *worked!*

It was nothing short of a miracle that she stopped herself from dancing a little end zone dance. Hot damn, there he was, sitting in the back row next to Jason, wearing a navy blazer and a starched white button-down shirt tucked into a pair of jeans. On his feet was a pair of very European-looking boots. His hair, nice and thick, just brushed the top of his collar, and his smile, which was brilliantly white, made his skin look bronzed. No, really— *bronzed.* And even more interesting, he appeared, at least from where she was standing, to have a black eye.

"Looks like we got us some new blood," Chantal observed.

He must have come in behind Dave and Lucy, but never mind that; the whole class was looking at her, then looking at Flynn.

"Ah!" Rachel exclaimed brightly, silently cursing the little shake in her voice, not to mention the brilliance of her vocabulary.

Chantal twisted in her chair (as best she could, seeing as how she was a couple of sizes larger than the chair) and peered at Flynn. "What's *your* name?"

"Flynn," he said cheerfully, leaning forward on his desk. "Flynn Oliver."

"Where'd you get that shiner?"

"Beg your pardon?"

"The black eye, she means," Tiffinnae helpfully clarified.

"Ah. A bit of a contretemps, I'm afraid."

Chantal blinked and looked at Tiffinnae. Both of them looked at Mr. Gregory, who shrugged. Then Chantal asked, "You from England?"

"Yes, as a matter of fact." As Chantal kept staring,

Flynn cleared his throat a little. "Ah . . . London, actually. But I, ah . . . was born . . . reared, as it were . . . in ah, in Butler Cropwell."

Dave, perhaps feeling a little sorry for Flynn, jumped right into the opening. "Is there some rule where the new guy gets the third degree?" he asked laughingly, and glanced over his shoulder at Flynn. "I'm Dave. This is my wife, Lucy."

"How do you do," Flynn said politely, and Chantal and Tiffinnae dipped their heads together to snicker.

"That's Chantal and Tiffinnae," Dave continued, taking on the role of host. "And Sandy and Mr. Gregory. And that's Jason sitting next to you," he said.

Flynn looked at Jason, who did not look up from his intent study of the table next to the loom.

"So you've decided to tackle weaving?" Dave continued with a laugh.

"If it's quite all right with the instructor, yes."

Everyone looked at Rachel. "Of course!" she said, a tad too enthusiastically. "Welcome to our class!" But wait . . . what *was* he doing here? As in, how could he have possibly known she taught a weaving—right, right . . . she had told him she taught a class the night of the tampons. Not a weaving class, but . . . but everyone was staring at her. "All righty, then!" she said, and looked down at her notes, shook her head a little. With a smile plastered on her face, Rachel lifted her head. "Before we get to work on the looms, I'm going to talk a little more about yarns."

Sandy instantly responded by sitting up in her seat, pen and paper ready to take notes. Flynn settled back, that ever-present smile on his lips.

"Last week, we talked about the origins of weaving, and how far back we could trace it."

Mr. Gregory's hand shot up. He was very enthusiastic about history, Rachel had learned. "Yes, Mr. Gregory?"

"You said no one actually knows when the process began, given that few remnants survive, but that there is evidence of cloth being made as early as seven to eight thousand B.C., and that the earliest evidence of large tapestries being woven in Europe is just before the twelfth century, of which, by the way, you promised a picture."

Damn, he was good. "I have it right here," she said, and fished a picture of a tapestry out of her box and handed it to Chantal, motioning for her to send it around. "So who knows what tapestries were typically used for in medieval Europe?"

"Rugs?" Dave tossed out.

"No, but close," Rachel said.

"Furniture coverings?" Sandy guessed.

"Smaller tapestries were used over furniture at times. But I'm talking about the large tapestries that depicted romance and gothic themes—there was a more common use for them."

The students stared at her blankly. Rachel glanced at Flynn. "Ah . . . perhaps our new student knows the answer?"

That suggestion seemed to surprise Flynn. He sat up a little straighter and glanced around. "Tapestry?" he repeated.

Rachel nodded.

"Right. Of course. They were . . . bed coverings."

"Well . . ." Rachel winced inwardly at having put him on the spot. "I suppose they *could* have been. But they were actually wall hangings. Weavers would create these gigantically thick tapestries to hang along the walls of big old castles to keep drafts out of the rooms."

"How we supposed to know that! None of us ever been in a castle!" Chantal groused, and glanced at Flynn over her shoulder. "You ever been to a castle?"

"Ah . . . actually, my mum took me to visit Windsor Castle when I was a lad."

"Windsor. That's where the queen lives," Tiffinnae informed them all.

"No she doesn't, she lives in Buckingham!" Mr. Gregory said with a sniff of disdain.

"Actually," Rachel said, "I believe she travels between

Buckingham and Windsor, and even up to Balmoral in Scotland, and a few other places. Is that right, Flynn?"

Now everyone was looking at him, and Flynn flashed a perfectly charming smile. "Ah . . . actually, I haven't had access to her itinerary, so I can't really say for certain."

"You sure you English?" Chantal demanded.

"Excellent question. I shall inquire of my parents once more."

That earned a laugh from everyone in the room—except Jason, naturally.

"Perhaps if I talked a little about tapestries," Rachel suggested, and launched into her notes.

By the end of her talk, when it was apparent everyone had had their fill of looms and yarns, Rachel gave them time to work on their projects before the end of class. Dave and Lucy quickly took Flynn under their wing—Rachel even spied him weaving a little as she helped Jason, who, she was sorry to see, had retained absolutely nothing from last week.

"Man, am I glad this is over!" Chantal announced to the room at large when the clock struck nine. "I been smelling cookies the whole time and I'm damn close to gnawing my left arm off."

"I smelled them too," Sandy said, nodding. "I can smell it a mile away because I'm allergic to chocolate."

With a roll of his eyes, Mr. Gregory sighed heavily as he strolled out the door. Dave and Lucy were right behind him, Lucy sadly shaking her head and remarking how unfortunate it was that Sandy had so many problems. Sandy, close on their heels, enthusiastically agreed, and was beginning a discourse on yet another of her illnesses for Lucy's benefit.

And of course Chantal and Tiffinnae were taking their own sweet time, stealing glimpses of Rachel while making *yum-yum* sounds at Flynn. When they had at last gathered their things, Chantal warned Rachel, "Now don't go doing nothing I wouldn't do!" And with that, she and Tiffinnae exited stage left, falling over each other with loud laughter.

Rachel could only hope that her face wasn't glowing siren red like it felt at the moment, and glanced uncertainly at Flynn.

Oh Christ, she'd forgotten Jason, who reluctantly got to his feet and picked up his stack of travel brochures. *Damn.* She'd been so rattled by Flynn's surprise appearance that she'd forgotten that, too.

For a moment, he stood awkwardly, looking at Flynn from the corner of his eye, nervously handling his brochures.

"Jason, I'm so sorry!" Rachel exclaimed, and walked back to where he was standing, shifting the brochures from one hand to another. "I meant to ask you to show the brochures to class. Can I see them?"

Jason looked sidelong at Flynn and shrugged. "Nah . . . that's okay."

"No, really. I'd love to see them. Please?" she asked, putting a hand on his arm. But Jason couldn't take his eyes off Flynn, and unthinkingly, Rachel looked beseechingly at him.

Flynn instantly seemed to understand and came to his feet, peering curiously at the brochures Jason held. "What have you got there, travel pamphlets? I'd love a peek, if you'd not mind. I'm constantly racking the old noggin for an idea of where to go on holiday."

Rachel smiled gratefully.

Jason looked at Rachel and said, "Okay." And he proceeded to spread them out on the top of the table. "These are for England and Ireland," he said, pointing to brochures that said *Ireland, 2000!* and *1999 Self-Drive Tours of England: The Cotswalds.* "I really like these because they have good pictures," he said, opening one and showing them a lovely photo of a thatched-roof house somewhere in England. "And these," he said, picking up three more, "are for Spain. I got 'em a couple of years ago, but I don't think I really want to go there. Anyway, there's some pretty cool buildings . . ."

As Jason talked, Rachel took a seat on the end of the table, watching him. She'd only spoken to Jason a couple of times, but she knew there was something not quite right about him. She had a sense that he was a boy in a young man's body, someone who perhaps dreamed of great adventure but did not have the capacity or courage to seize it.

But what truly astounded her was the look of genuine compassion on Flynn's face. He listened to Jason, asked questions, made comments about the brochures.

A smile slowly spread across her lips. A gorgeous, *nice* man.

When Jason was through with his brochures, he sort of stuffed them under his arm, looked at his feet. "Okay. I guess I'll go now. Next week I'll bring my books."

Rachel had no idea what books he meant, but nodded all the same. "That would be great."

Jason glanced at Rachel, and with the barest hint of a smile, he walked out of the room, head down, without looking at Flynn.

When he had slipped out the door, Rachel turned a bright smile to Flynn. "Thanks," she said. "You didn't have to do that."

"Do what? I really *do* like looking at brochures."

"And what about weaving? Are you really interested in that?"

He laughed sheepishly, thrust a hand through his hair, dislodging one thick strand that fell over his eye. "Truthfully?"

"Truthfully."

"I'm not entirely certain it's my cup of tea . . . but I will admit to a certain perverse fascination with all this talk of warp and woof . . . and I'm completely bewitched with warp and woof instructors."

"Oh, yeah?"

"Absolutely. I have squads of dirty magazines and videos featuring warp and woof instructors and their looms."

Oh God, here went the red siren face again, and Rachel laughed, rubbed the nape of her neck. "So . . . how did you find me?"

"Rachel!" he laughingly protested as he reached for the corner of her shawl and felt the weight of it. "You can't possibly ask me to give away my secrets! I consider myself quite lucky that I found at least one place from which you can't easily flee or hook up with some other guy to avoid me altogether without causing talk," he said with a grin. "And I should hope that you'd reward my diligent efforts to find you by agreeing to a coffee."

Rachel smiled; Flynn glanced at the corner of the lavender shawl he held between finger and thumb. "That's really stunning, you know," he said, lifting his gaze to her eyes. "Just . . . a stunning color. It's marvelous on you. Frankly, *you're* stunning."

She blushed so furiously she forgot to be excited that her color spell had obviously worked.

"So, then, will you allow me to buy you a cup of coffee?"

"Okay," she said, feeling remarkably lighter than air, suddenly skinny and beautiful and real.

"And perhaps a bit of cake," he said, standing up and taking her hand in his. "I've had a craving for butter rum cake for a few days now. Isn't that odd?"

He had no idea how odd.

Chapter Eleven

✦ ✶ ✦

RACHEL suggested a coffeehouse that featured would-be poets, a place Flynn knew quite well. He kept that to himself, however, and with a smile agreed to meet her there.

Naturally, the usual coterie of poets was there—Flynn recognized a few, and one could spot them a mile away— they congregated like a flock of penguins around the bar, all atwitter as they waited for their café au laits to be steamed.

Flynn escorted Rachel to a secluded corner table he also knew very well, bought a fu-fu coffee for her, a hot tea for him, and a large cinnamon bun to share. As she went about the task of cutting up the enormous bun with a little plastic knife, he said, "Funny, but I wouldn't have guessed you a teacher."

Her astounding blue-green eyes sparkled charmingly as she smiled at him. "Maybe that's because I'm *not* a teacher."

"Beg your pardon?"

"Weaving aside," she said gaily, "which I'm only doing to earn a little extra money . . . except that I haven't earned even a dime, because the cost of renting space at the design school and all the materials have skyrocketed, and I can't bring myself to charge more than I do for the course." She laughed a little self-consciously. "That was probably in the too-much-information category."

"If you're not really a teacher, then you ought to be," he said sincerely. "You're quite good." Actually, he'd been very impressed with her ability to engage such an eclectic group of people, particularly with something as horrendously boring as weaving.

"So what would you have guessed me to be?" she asked as she resumed the sawing of the world's largest cinnamon bun.

"Hmmm . . . excellent question. You've been so bloody mysterious . . . I had you pegged as a mass murderer at first, but then you were too kind to Chantal, who one might guess is a likely candidate for mass murder," he opined.

"Mmm, no," Rachel said thoughtfully, shaking her head. "Chantal's too loud for just the casual sort of murder. She'd require something completely diabolical."

"Quite right," he said. "And I hadn't pegged you as the diabolical type."

"No?" she asked, looking slightly disappointed.

"No. Clever, but not diabolical."

"Ah," she said with a nod, her eyes sparkling.

"So, clearly not a mass murderer. What about . . . sorceress?" he asked.

Rachel snapped the plastic knife in the bun, and clutching the bottom half of the knife, she blinked up at him. *"Seriously?"*

He grinned, shrugged a little, and fished the other half of the knife from the bun. "Why? *Are* you?"

"I'm *not* a sorceress," she said in all seriousness.

"Is that true, or are you afraid to admit it?" he asked laughingly.

"No, really, I just—" She suddenly stopped, bit her lower lip, and looked at the cinnamon bun. "I just *love* cinnamon buns. I'll be right back," she said, and popped up before he could stop her.

She returned a moment later, a new plastic knife in hand, and picked up with a vengeance where she'd left off on the cinnamon bun.

"If you are not, in truth, a sorceress," Flynn asked, amused by how intent she was on the bun, "then what do you do?"

She stopped sawing on the bun, perhaps because she'd divided it into equal parts of eight, and set aside the plastic knife. She clasped her hands together on the table. "I'm, ah . . . a student."

"Are you! What type?"

Rachel picked up her coffee and looked around the room and muttered something unintelligible.

"Beg your pardon?" he asked, leaning forward to hear her as he helped himself to the bun.

She sighed irritably and glanced at him from the corner of her eye. "Of history!" she said, a little louder.

"Really? How impressive," he said, taking another bite of what was, surprisingly, an extremely delicious cinnamon bun. Full of . . . something like vanilla, he thought.

"Not really," she said with a snort. "It will probably floor you to know that I've been in a doctorate program for almost four years."

Flynn looked up to see if she was joking. She did not, however, appear to be joking, and in fact, shook her head to indicate she definitely was not. "Any plans to finish?"

"Yes!" she cried heavenward, but caught herself and smiled. "Sorry. A little history there," she said with a laugh. "So what about *you?* What are you doing in the States?"

"Consultant," he said.

"Oh! What sort?"

"Computers."

"Really?" she asked, her brow wrinkling a bit. "And was it a computer that gave you the black eye?"

Flynn had forgotten about that nasty little bruise, and unconsciously touched his eye.

"I think . . . you're *really* a James Bond type of guy on some exciting international case," she said.

"Actually, I was involved in a local homicide investigation. I ran into a spot of trouble at a dodgy pub on the pier."

She laughed. "And then jumped in your cigarette boat and sped away, right?"

"No. Just an ordinary motorcar."

"Okay, so how did you really manage to get that black eye?"

"Honestly," he said, holding up his scout hand. "A bloke at the pier."

Rachel's pretty smile got prettier; she cocked her head to one side. "Okay . . . so you won't tell me. That of course leads me to believe it was a lover's spat."

"I should certainly hope not," he said with a laugh.

"So what sort of international computer consultant are you, anyway?"

"Software development—banks, mostly."

"U.S. banks?"

"Mmm," he said, and helped himself to more of that terribly decadent and astoundingly delicious cinnamon bun. "My turn. What sort of history do you study? American, I presume?"

She laughed heartily. Flynn liked that; an honest laugh. "What's funny?" he asked, smiling.

"I really have no idea," she said, smiling broadly, and sighed heavenward. "Okay. I study British history," she admitted with a grin. "Medieval stuff."

"Really?" he asked, unfazed, but wondered how in God's name a woman as lovely as Rachel could pick up something so dreadfully dull. "How did you settle on that fascinating subject?"

She laughed again, a sort of bubbly laugh that was surprisingly silky and as pleasing to the ears as her smile was to the eyes. "Because . . . I don't know. It's . . . *romantic,*" she said. "Especially the medieval period. You know, knights and damsels in distress and all that," she said. Her cheeks, he noticed, had turned appealingly pink.

Still, he had a hard time seeing her buried in some musty old book. "So you think that it's romantic that old Henry off'd the heads of his five damsels, eh?"

"Well . . . *technically,* Henry VIII was not a medieval king. And it was only two."

"Two?"

"Two heads he off'd. Of six wives."

Now it was Flynn's turn to laugh. "There you are, you've discovered my secret—I'm frightfully ignorant of my heritage." With a smile, he pushed the plate of bun toward her, of which, he noticed with chagrin, he'd eaten two-thirds. "But I'm curious—what do you plan to do with this Ph.D. in British history?"

"You and my father!" she said with a sheepish little laugh. "Congratulations, for you have just posed the sixty-four-million-dollar question, and one I can't really answer, except to say, at present, it doesn't look like much."

"That bad, eh?"

"That bad," she said with a winsome smile.

"What of your boyfriend?" Flynn asked, looking at her pointedly. The color seemed to drain from her face, and she became all wide-eyed. "The chap with the hair," he reminded her.

"He's not my *boyfriend.*"

"Isn't he, really?"

"No! He's just a friend! You didn't really think . . ."

"I did."

"Oh *no,*" she insisted again, so emphatically that he wanted to laugh. "No, no no, *noooo.*"

"Then if he's *not* your boyfriend, that can only mean one thing," he said, glancing at her from the corner of his eye.

"What?"

"That you are . . ." He looked around them, then leaned closer. "Quite unattached."

Her cheeks went pinker. "Well. Not to *him* anyway."

Flynn shifted a little closer, his gaze on her luscious lips. "Another chap, then?"

She laughed again, tossing her head back and showing the smooth curve of her slender neck. "You might as well know. I'm very attached to chocolate."

"Chocolate? Is he still about? I thought he was dead and gone," he said in all seriousness, but he could feel himself being pulled in by her effervescent smile, and he couldn't help but recall her as she had been that damp night alone in her house, twirling about, and then later, with nothing but a towel wrapped around her, the smooth shape of her back bared to him. In the wake of that memory, he scooted his chair closer.

"Oh no, he's very much alive," she said, nodding. "I'm surprised you haven't seen him. He follows me everywhere—he's in my milk, in my brownies, in my cake," she said as Flynn reached for her hand, covering it with his, letting his fingers slide up her wrist, then wrap around it, so that he could feel the delicate bones.

"And what of your pudding?" he asked, studying her hand. "Is he there as well?"

"Absolutely, he's there, too," she said, her eyes sparkling as she turned her wrist in his hand. "And he sneaks in my purse when I'm not looking and wraps himself in bright red and silver tinfoils so that I can't resist him."

The lights flickered, indicating one of the poets would begin soon.

"That's really a very clever idea," Flynn murmured. "I'll have to give it a go."

Her laugh sounded different somehow, and when he glanced up, the smile had gone from her face. She lifted her gaze from his hand on her wrist and said, "I can't do this."

"Can't do what?" he asked, leaning over to take in the fragrance of her hair.

"I can't pretend—it's not right."

Flynn froze for a moment, thought he was going to hear

some sort of confession. He slowly moved back, so that he could see her face.

"Can't pretend? Are you pretending?"

"I mean . . . I should really tell you that you are here with me now under false pretense," she said, releasing her breath in a rush.

"How can that be?" he asked, his finger caressing the inside of her wrist. "I believe I asked you here."

"I know you did, but that's because . . ." She paused, looked surreptitiously about, and Flynn's heart began to beat a little faster.

"Because?"

She turned her gaze to him again, winced a little. "Because I . . . I put a spell on you," she said quite low, just as someone took the stage and the crowd began to applaud.

Flynn's hand stilled on her wrist, and in the midst of that applause, he looked deep into her lovely eyes. "I beg your pardon?"

Rachel glanced around again, leaned a little closer. "When you said I was a sorceress, I thought you knew. I'm not *really* one, I just tried it, and I . . . I put a *spell* on you," she said in a horrified whisper.

Flynn waited a moment or two for the punch line before asking, "You aren't joking, are you?"

"Unfortunately, no." She sighed sadly. "It's really true. If you think about it, the two times we've seen each other, I was really a mess, and normally, guys like you wouldn't ask girls like me for coffee."

He'd been with her up until that statement, willing to play along, but that didn't make the slightest bit of sense. "Why wouldn't I?" he asked, truly confused. "Because I'm British?"

"British?" she echoed incredulously and suddenly laughed.

"And what makes you think I've only seen you twice?" he asked, moving his hand a little higher, to the crook of her elbow. "How do you know that I haven't seen you a million times and wished for just this moment?"

Rachel blinked. Her mouth opened. Then closed. Then opened again. "You saw me before that day by the . . . phone thing?"

"Actually, I'd seen you on campus. Which, incidentally, is how I discovered your weaving class."

"Campus," she repeated weakly, her gaze falling to his mouth again and stirring something deep inside him.

"I've been doing a bit of work there, and I saw you one day. Several times, actually. Enough that I wanted to meet you. Granted, the day I met you at the phone was a coincidence, but it seemed like every time I found you after that, you were rushing off and away from me. I had no choice but to take matters into my own hands."

"No," Rachel murmured. "No way. I put a spell on you!"

He was suddenly struck with the image of her doing that strange little dance in her living room, and felt his blood start to rush hot. The whole notion was terribly seductive somehow, and he couldn't quite suppress his grin. "It is true that I'm completely under your spell," he said as he leaned into her again, his nostrils filling with the curious scent of vanilla and cinnamon buns, his lips just a hairsbreadth from her lips.

"*Ahem*. . . . If I could have everyone's attention," the man on stage said dispassionately. "Our first poet tonight is Marianne Breck."

Flynn touched his lips to Rachel's, felt a spark ignite.

Marianne cleared her throat. "What is love? It is *red, red, red*. What is hate? It is *white, white, white!*"

Rachel made a little sound deep in her throat, a soft sigh of some sort, and the spark in Flynn was instantly fanned into a flame. As Marianne droned on about how red and white she was, Flynn could feel the red of his own body, red desire, spreading through him with the quickness of light. He moved his hand from Rachel's wrist to her neck, felt the earring she wore bouncing against his knuckles, felt the rapid beat of her pulse, the warmth of her skin. His other hand found her waist and then the small of her back and he held her there, so that he could explore lips that were full and succulent, softly delectable.

He drew her bottom lip between his teeth, gingerly tested the soft pliability of it, then slipped his tongue into her sweet mouth. She opened up beneath him like a bloody flower, tilting her head to accommodate him.

Frankly, that kiss surprised Flynn. He'd not intended this to happen, had not intended to do much of anything but talk . . . but the memory of her strange little pagan dance and of her wrapped in that towel, along with the oddly invigorating scent of vanilla and her assertion that she had cast a spell on him spurred him into territory he'd not intended to enter.

At the moment, it hardly seemed to matter, as his body was too interested in her mouth, the baby softness of the skin at her neck, and the velvet lobe of her ear, and Flynn imagined that mane of hair tumbling down around them as they made wild, pagan love.

"My love is *red,* my hate is *white!*" Marianne insisted from the stage. *"But what color is my soul?"*

Who cares? Flynn thought in the midst of thundering applause and whistles for Marianne's rather bland color scheme. But with the applause, he felt Rachel pull away, and reluctantly lifted his head.

She blinked up at him, her lips curved into a wonderfully Cheshire little smile of pleasure. "Okay," she said, her hand lifting to brush aside the lock of hair on his brow. "You cannot tell me *that* wasn't the result of a spell."

Flynn grinned. "Let's get out of here, shall we?" He stood, helped Rachel from her chair, and escorted her out as Marianne trotted out another appallingly bad bit of poetry. *"Water runs swift, the moon sinks low . . ."*

They walked out onto the sidewalk, and Rachel paused to adjust her shawl around her shoulders. She turned a brilliant smile to him, one that was shrouded in lavender and lovely, soft light. "Thanks. Thanks so much for asking me for coffee, Flynn."

"What—you're going?" he asked, surprised by his disappointment.

"I really should. I have to get up and go to work," she said, and laughed a little. "I mean, such that it is. I wouldn't call it work, really, but still, I should strive not to screw it up." She took a step toward the car park, looked at him to see if he was coming.

This was definitely not how he wanted the evening to end, but he reluctantly stepped up beside her, and together, they walked down the sidewalk toward the tiny car park. But just before they reached it, Rachel stopped and turned, pressed her back against the brick wall of the coffeehouse and peered up at Flynn. "How . . . I mean, may I ask . . . how, ah, how long are you in the States?"

"Indefinitely," Flynn said.

"Oh." She glanced at the car park, drew her bottom lip between her teeth for a moment. "Do you think . . . I mean, are you planning . . . ?"

Her voice trailed off; she bit her lip again. Flynn stepped close to her, lifted her face to his. "I'd really like to see you again, Rachel Lear," he said sincerely. "If that's quite all right with you."

She seemed to consider it for a moment, but then Flynn saw the light of a smile in her eyes. "Maybe," she said. "But I'll have to speak with chocolate first. He has all my attention, you know. And then, of course, I really should consult the spell book."

"If I may, I'd like to go on record as not really caring for eyes of newts, if you please."

"Oh! Oh *no*," she said, and laid a hand lightly on his chest, tapped one finger. "No newt eyes, okay . . . but I hope you're okay with newt tongues."

"What, you think me a complete rube? Of course I'm quite all right with tongues. It's just the eyes." Flynn grinned, covered her hand with his. "Then shall I ring you up?"

"Yes, please," she said, and the brilliant light in her eyes spilled over to her whole face. "I'll just jot down the number," she said, already fumbling around in her big tote bag. And while she rummaged around for a pen or paper, Flynn honestly couldn't help himself—he dipped his head again, kissed the delightful curve of her neck.

Rachel let out a contented sigh and stopped rummaging about her bag. Flynn took that to mean carry on, and he straddled her legs with his, put his hands on her waist as his lips moved across her skin, along the line of her jaw, to her mouth. Her enormous bag hit him in the foot when she dropped it to lace her arms around his neck, and they stood there, making out like two teenagers, until someone pulled out of the car park and honked at them.

Flynn stepped back, chuckling a little, and picked up her bag.

He made sure she was safely tucked away in her car before leaving, and kissed her once more. "Cheers," he said, with a little wave, and walked away, her number in his pocket, a happy jaunt to his step.

He got in his rental, pulled out, and moved down the street, his mind sort of numb and his body uncomfortably hard, and really looking quite forward to their next encounter.

BEHIND him, Rachel watched him speed off, and released a long, blissful sigh. The spells had worked. He thought she, Rachel Lear, was *sexy*. He wanted to see her again! The most magnificent guy in the whole wide world wanted to see *her*. Rachel Lear. *Again!*

With a squeal of happiness, Rachel turned in the opposite direction and puttered home, having completely forgotten that she had earlier wondered how he had learned of her weaving class, as it was her own doing and not associated with Brown University.

Chapter Twelve

✦ ✶ ✦

WHEN Myron showed up for work at the Rhode Island Historical Preservation Society curator offices Wednesday morning, the head curator, Darwin Richter, stopped by his cube with a bespectacled gentleman who was wearing a Windbreaker and jeans.

"I'd like you to meet Detective Keating," Darwin said. "He's from the Rhode Island State Police and he's been looking into the spate of thefts we've had."

"Oh!" Myron said, coming instantly to his feet.

"This is Professor Tidwell," Darwin explained to the detective. "He's the one who knows our catalog backwards and forwards. He prepares all our insurance claims."

"Yeah, I read about that forklift accident," the detective said. "Weird that it happened when these thefts happened, huh?"

"Yeah," Myron said, and timidly stuck out his hand.

Detective Keating flashed a warm grin and grabbed his hand, shook it so hard that Myron feared something tore in his shoulder. "Good to meet you, Professor," the detective said cheerfully. "Mr. Richter here says you'll be able to help us make sense of all this stuff," he said, pointing at a file he held.

"Yes! Of course!" Myron quickly assured him. "Anything I can do to help!"

"Yeah," the detective sighed, shaking his head. "When someone steals from a museum, he's got to be scum."

"Ab-so-*lute*-ly!" Myron quickly agreed.

"I mean, you need money, you hold up a bank or something, right? You don't take from a museum! That just hurts everyone!"

"I couldn't agree more," Myron said, folding his arms across his chest. Darwin also shook his head, as if offended by the very suggestion someone would steal from a museum.

"I wonder why they do it," the detective continued. "It's not exactly easy to fence this stuff, is it?"

"I guess some people still feel disenfranchised," Myron opined, positioning himself on the corner of the desk in his cubicle. "They see stately homes from a bygone era, figure that society owes them somehow, and think there's no harm in taking a trinket here or there."

"Right," the detective said thoughtfully. "But it's really more than trinkets, wouldn't you say? From what Mr. Richter was telling me here, some of these things might look pretty ordinary, but in actuality, are really very valuable. You know that—you did the insurance work. But I wouldn't think the average Joe would know how valuable they were."

Myron shrugged. "I think you underestimate the average Joe, detective. Many art thieves are highly educated people."

The detective nodded, seemed to ponder that for a moment, his gaze intent on Myron. And then he cocked his head to one side and asked, "Do you think we're dealing with art thieves, Professor?"

A strange heat filled Myron's collar, and he quickly laughed and stood up. "Who knows? I'm just theorizing, that's all. So when do you want to start looking at the catalogs?" he asked.

The detective smiled. "Now, if that's all right with you."

"You bet," Myron said. "Maybe we could go down to the library. There's a lot of ground to cover and my desk is really small."

"That would be great," the detective said, and smiled in a way that made Myron flush hotly.

Chapter Thirteen

* * *

GREAT, it was middle school all over again, like *anyone* needed to go back there, and especially not Miss Fortune.

Yet after that toe-curling kiss, Rachel could hardly hear the autopsies being piped into her head over the Dictaphone for all her thoughts shouting at her. So she typed fast and furious so that she could rush home to see if he called.

So what if that was a little on the juvenile side? She was certain that sophisticated women like her sisters had, at least once, anyway, lived and breathed each moment wondering if some guy had called back during the day—and even if they hadn't, she couldn't help it! She could not seem to think of anything but Flynn. Flynn Bond, the complete anti-Myron.

When she finished up for the day (having typed an astounding twelve autopsy reports), she drove straight home, did not pass Go, did not collect two hundred dollars, and even waved at Mr. Valicielo as she pulled into the drive. And again, as she stepped out of her car, when Mr. Valicielo instantly appeared beside her, rake in hand, she cheerfully assured him that she'd do something about that tree.

"This is hurting my fence," he said for the umpteenth time. "I'll have to pay to have my fence repaired!"

"No you won't, Mr. Valicielo," she brightly assured him, "because I have a job! I mean, it's only a temporary one, but still, I should earn enough to move the tree before long, and if the fence needs to be repaired, I'll do that, too."

Mr. Valicielo gripped his rake so tightly that his knuckles went white and he looked back to the fallen tree. Reluctantly, he nodded. "Okay," he said. "Okay."

Rachel patted him on the back before bouncing up the porch stairs to her kitchen door.

Once inside, she dropped her bag and made a beeline for the answering machine, certain there would be a blinking light . . . but there was no blinking light!

No blinking light.

Rachel gaped at the answering machine. How could that be? She'd been so *certain*. They had really hit it off, hadn't they? She'd given him her number; he'd said he would call her. And that *kiss!* Her toes had curled, goddammit! A small kernel of fear—not the scary kind of fear, but the kind of fear that comes with realizing that you are an absolutely clueless moron—sprouted in her belly.

Rachel glared at the phone. Okay. All right. This was ridiculous. She was just being her usual insecure self. Flynn hadn't called because she was working; she'd told him she'd be working. So he'd call tonight! Crisis averted!

An hour later, when the phone rang, Rachel almost killed herself getting to it. "Hello?" she asked breathlessly, grimacing at how teenaged-anxious she sounded.

"Hey!" Dagne said.

"Hey, Dagne," Rachel sighed, the teenager gone right out of her. "What's up?"

"I have to come over," Dagne said. "We've got to do another spell."

"We do?"

"Yes! The mistake I made with Glenn is *waaaay* out of control. He won't leave me alone! I'll be over later, okay?"

"Fine. Whatever," Rachel said, but Dagne had already hung up. She put the phone back in the cradle and glared at it. "Not. Funny," she told it, and went back to her dissertation work at the dining room table.

A couple of hours later, when her eyes were beginning to blur, she searched her pantry for something diety to eat, and finding nothing, gave in and made herself some pancakes. But with each flip of the cake, she glanced at the clock, noted he *still* hadn't called. And then, to make herself as miserable as she possibly knew how, she made a game of trying to remember every single word he'd said last night.

This was stupid.

Pancakes and schoolwork were not working, so Rachel stacked the dirty dishes in the sink and went upstairs to take a hot bath.

As usual, she placed candles around her old clawfoot tub, found her current romance novel, and placed it next to the tub. Just as she was dipping her toe in the steaming water, the phone rang.

"Dammit!" she shouted, and fumbled with a bathsheet that she managed to get partially around her as she dashed into the bedroom to pick up the phone on the fourth ring. *"Yes, hello?"* she all but shouted into the phone.

"Rachel, it's your father."

Oh. *God.* She closed her eyes, drew a long, fortifying breath. "Hi, Dad."

"How are you?"

"I'm . . . fine," she said, instantly suspicious. "Why?"

"What do you mean, *why?* I'm your father and I am calling to see how my baby girl is doing."

Since when? And he didn't have to be so gruff about it, did he? "Okay. I'm doing fine," she said, tightening her towel around her. "How are you?"

"Good."

"Feeling better?"

"I don't know if you can feel better with chemo, to tell you the truth. So listen, kiddo," he said, before she could comment on the chemo, "your mom and I were talking, and I've been thinking . . . I don't like the way we left things when you left New York."

Jesus, this was about her leaving in a huff. Why now? Why why why why *now?* "I shouldn't have left like that," she said, knowing it was better to give in than to argue.

"Well . . . I guess I had it coming," he admitted, surprising the holy hell out of her. "But I've been thinking . . . I'd really like to come to Providence and see you."

Her blood stopped pumping there for a minute. "W-what?" she stammered, but her mind was screaming *No! NO, NO!* "Dad!" she said, laughing nervously. "You don't need to do that! I mean, you've got chemo, right?"

"Not for much longer. I could come in a couple of weeks or so."

That sprung her right off the bed and into a full pace around her room. "But . . . but you said you were going back to the ranch to recuperate after it was over. You don't want to come to Providence! It's cold and wet—"

"But I *do* want to come to Providence, baby girl. We need to talk about what you are going to do. I want to help you plan it out. I'm starting to realize that your reluctance to enter the real world has a lot to do with your insecurities and perhaps your inexperience, and I think if we plan this together—"

"I am not reluctant!" she cried, feeling desperate now, as she had never heard her dad talk so . . . so therapeutically. "I just need to finish my dissertation!"

"I need to see that bungalow anyway," he said, talking over her, "because when you *do* move on, which you'll have to do if you want a real job, then I'll need to sell that house."

"Sell my house?" she repeated weakly.

"Well, sure! You're not going to stay at Brown forever, Rachel. In fact, you're going to get your butt *out* of Brown and get on with your life," he said, his voice taking on a familiar and overbearing tone.

"I know, but—"

"Speaking of jobs, what have you done?"

"Actually Dad," she said, feeling her heart start to pump again, "I got a job! Not a *big* one, but enough to pay the bills."

"*Really?*" he asked, sounding extremely skeptical.

"Really!" she lied. "You don't have to worry about me, Dad! I understood what you said and I took it to heart!"

"That's great, Rachel. That's really . . . *great*. And what about your degree? Did you land on a dissertation topic?"

"I'm working on it!" she said, trying to sound upbeat and optimistic.

Dad didn't say anything for a moment. "Why didn't you call to tell me about the job? What *sort* of job did you get?" he asked, his voice full of suspicion now.

"Ah . . . well, it's just a temporary one."

"Not that weaving gig! That's not a job, Rachel! And by the way, are you still paying for all the materials out of your own pocket?"

Christ. "Not the weaving class, Dad!" she exclaimed, as if that was the most ridiculous thing he'd ever said. "Data entry!"

"Data entry? What *sort* of data entry?"

"Data entry! You know . . . entering data. Facts and figures, that sort of thing."

"I hope you're not talking about a cash register somewhere," he said sternly. "I meant for you to get a job, but I didn't mean for you to take all the money I have spent on your education and go to McDonald's with it!"

"Dad, please!" she scoffed. "So anyway, how's Mom?"

He sighed, recognizing her dodge for what it was. "All right. All right for now, Rachel. Now listen, I'll be through with this chemo in a few weeks. I'll come out then, and we can discuss your situation like two adults."

Right. *Sure* they could. Just like they always had. And while they were having this adult conversation, perhaps aliens would land and take over Washington.

"Rachel?"

"Let's just wait and see how you are feeling, okay, Dad? Listen, is Mom there?"

Dad muttered something, but called Mom to the phone and said a terse good-bye.

"Hi, honey!" Mom sang brightly.

"Mom, was this your idea?"

"What?"

"What? To send Dad to Providence, that's what! Because if it was, I'd like to ask you not to help me! I don't want him to come to Providence! All he'll do is find fault with the way I've done *everything!*"

"Not this time, honey. Dad is in therapy and he is working to make amends for past wrongs," Mom said patiently.

"Oh jeez! Can't he make amends to Robbie and Bec?"

"He is. And he's making some remarkable progress . . ."

A door opened downstairs; Rachel tightened the towel around her and padded out of her room to the top of the stairs, squatted down, saw the tail of Myron's car through the dining room window as Mom droned on about Dad's remarkable progress toward being an actual human being.

"That's great, it really is, and I'm so glad he is attending sessions with you," Rachel said, waving at Myron as he passed by the stairs on the first floor. "But does he have to come *here?*"

"He's your father, Rachel. You and he need to talk about what happened in New York."

"Nothing happened! He was his usual, hypercritical self, and I just got fed up! We don't need to talk about it! Dad was being Dad, and there's nothing left to say—"

"Rachel," Mom said in the voice she generally used when she was asserting her maternal authority, "Aaron is making a yeoman's effort to change the way he behaves toward his daughters. I would think the least you could do is allow him to come to see you, the daughter he sired with *his* sperm, in the house *he* bought so that you'd have a place to live while you pursued an education *he* financed. Is that really asking so much?"

Oh, for God's sake! Rachel groaned; below her, she

could hear Myron banging around the kitchen. "All right. Just give me plenty of notice, okay?"

"We will."

"In the meantime, Mom . . . I need to ask you a favor," Rachel said gingerly. "I got a job—a temporary job—"

"Really?" she said, obviously and inordinately pleased. "Doing what?"

Rachel swallowed down a groan. "Actually, it's a temp agency. Right now I am typing autopsy reports. There's a bit of a backlog."

"Eewee—"

"I know, I know," Rachel said, cutting her off. "But I don't get paid for two weeks, and I have this really humongous utility bill . . ."

Now it was Mom's turn to sigh. "What about the money Myron owes you?"

"Well," Rachel said, jumping a little as the sound of something glass shattering on the kitchen floor reached her, "he doesn't really have it, either."

"Why not? Doesn't he have *two* jobs?"

"Mom, please? I asked him, but Myron said he was in a bind, and he's really going through some bad stuff at work right now. Could you just loan me the money this time?"

"All right, Rachel. But I really wish you'd get serious about finding a *real* job, and preferably something that hasn't anything to do with dead people. Why don't you start looking in a big metropolitan area, like New York or Boston or Chicago? Maybe you could get a job in a museum. And you could live someplace nice and fashionable where there are good jobs for girls with your background and lots of nice young men who have good professions."

"Right," Rachel said as Myron appeared on the bottom step, sandwich in hand, her T-Mobile phone in the other, which he waved at her before tossing onto a chair. "I'll think about it, I really will. But will you help me out?"

"How much?" Mom asked.

"One seventy-five."

"Oh dear. All right, I'll put it in the mail. By the way,

why don't you ever answer the T-Mobile I gave you?" she asked. "I've called it a half-dozen times and you never answer."

"Really? I guess I haven't heard it. No phones allowed in the morgue," she said as Myron ascended the stairs, munching determinedly on his sandwich and practically stepping on top of her as he passed. "I'll adjust the ringer."

"Please do. All right, honey, we'll talk to you soon."

Rachel hung up the phone just as Myron disappeared into the guest room. She got up, adjusted her towel, and followed him, watched him open the closet door.

"Myron?"

Myron paused, looked at her in the door, sort of squinting.

"You almost stepped on me coming up the stairs."

He blinked. "Hey! I brought your phone. It's really *cool*, man!"

Rachel's eyes narrowed. "Are you stoned?" she demanded.

"Maybe a little," he said, and looked in the closet.

Was there really such thing as a little stoned? Seemed to her that when Myron was a little stoned, he was wasted. Period. "What are you looking for?" she demanded as he took a huge bite of sandwich.

"Ah dummoh," he said through the mouthful of bologna and closed the closet door, walked to the opposite end of the room, and looked at the nightstand. "Di ah eve iss ooo-ooo?"

"What?" she snapped irritably. "I can't understand a word you're saying! Didn't anyone ever tell you not to talk with your mouth full?"

That made Myron laugh uproariously. But then he stopped abruptly when he almost choked on his sandwich, and swallowed it in one huge gulp. "Did I give this to you?"

"What?"

"The nightstand thingy," he said, motioning at the table with the last half of his sandwich.

"No."

"Oh." He stared at the nightstand some more. Rachel sighed irritably and turned away. If he was going to do a lot of staring at furniture, she was going to go take her bath. "See you later, Myron. Don't let the door hit you on the butt when you leave!"

"Wow," Myron said, nodding. "That's harsh."

Whatever. Rachel left Myron standing in the guest room.

Her bath water was tepid now, so she drained the tub while she messed with her hair—trying new knots, because God knew she hadn't tried every hair knot known to woman—and finally resorted to winding two big lumps on top of her head, Mickey Mouse style, as per usual.

She started her bath again, and when she was content with the temperature, she plugged it, stood, and started to shut the door—but jumped a good foot in the air because Myron was standing in the door, his hands in his pockets, his eyes bloodshot from the pot.

"Jesus, Myron! Can't you *knock?*"

"I did!" he protested. "But you were upstairs on the phone and didn't hear me."

"I meant *now*—never mind. If you'll excuse me, I'm going to take a bath."

"Sure," he said, nodding. But he didn't move.

"Okay! If you'll just back up and let me shut the—"

"So listen, Rachel. I've been doing some painting again."

It was all Rachel could do to keep from groaning. Myron went through periods during which he fancied himself a painter.

"Is it okay if I put some of them here? I don't have room in my apartment."

"Sure, Myron. Just put them in the basement, will you? Nothing on the walls."

"The *basement?* You want me to put my paintings in the basement?"

"Yes," she said, resolutely. The last time she'd let him bring paintings over, he had taken it upon himself to hang a few. She wasn't a great decorator, but they had been too awful even for her.

"Great," he groused. "I go to the trouble to paint for you and that is the thanks I get?"

Oh right, like he cared what she thought of his paintings. "No, the thanks you get is a place to store them. Ta-ta, Myron!" she called, and waved him out of the bathroom. "Come back when you're not stoned," she added as she started to swing the bathroom door shut.

Muttering under his breath, Myron backed up, banged into the doorjamb, and grabbed it to steady himself on the way out. But then he stopped, looked over his shoulder at her. "What about the other paintings? What did you do with them?" he demanded.

"Oh those!" she said. "I threw them away." And with that, she shut the door.

On the other side of the door, she heard Myron laugh. And then gasp, *That's* hilarious!"

She locked the door, lit her candles, and crawled into the steaming water to read what her medieval knight was up to today. Saving the woman he loved from a burning castle, apparently. Wouldn't it be nice if he could come around and save her from the bungalow?

After reading awhile, Rachel closed her eyes, felt the hot water and bubbles sliding over her body. She saw Flynn's face peering down at her in her mind's eye, only he had long, shoulder-length wavy hair. And he was wearing leather. *Lots* of leather. And there was deep concern etched into the fine lines around his gray eyes, that lock of hair falling across his brow . . .

A muffled but persistent knock on her front door brought her up with a splash and a toppling of at least one candle as the book went flying across the bathroom.

She sat for a moment, straining to hear. It couldn't be Dagne—she'd walk on in. If it wasn't Dagne, and it wasn't Myron . . .

Flynn.

She heard the second round of raps on the door more

clearly and managed to get out of the tub and throw the towel around her, but her hands were wet, and she wrestled with the doorknob for a moment before the thing finally came open. Flying across her bed, she panicked at the sound of another series of knocks, and vaulted down the stairs, skidded across the polished oak floor, almost slamming into the front door, which she managed to throw open at the same time she grabbed for her towel before it slipped from her body.

Chapter Fourteen

✦ ✦ ✦

"WHAT?" Dagne demanded on the other side of the screen door when Rachel groaned.

"Why didn't you just come in?"

"I can't find my key." She adjusted the heavy stick thing she was holding.

Rachel peered at the thing. "What is that?"

"It's a coatrack. I got it off eBay," Dagne said proudly, adjusting it again. "But it's really heavy."

Rachel pushed the screen door open and stepped aside, let Dagne struggle through with her big wooden coatrack, which she managed to get inside by taking only an inch of skin from one of Rachel's shins. Rachel closed the screen door, grabbed the front door, and was shutting it when she saw a sporty blue car drive by that looked vaguely familiar. But not so familiar that she was willing to stand there and freeze to death and figure out whose it was, so she shut the door.

"Why don't you have any clothes on?" Dagne asked, standing there with her ridiculous coatrack.

"Because, Dagne, I was taking a bath. What do you think? And why did you bring a coatrack here?"

"It's for you," Dagne said, beaming. "I bought it for dirt cheap from eBay and figured you could use it. I don't have room for it in my apartment." She put the coatrack next to the door, stood back to admire it.

"I'm going to ask a crazy question here . . . but why do you buy things you don't need?" Rachel asked, looking at the coatrack.

"Who says I don't? I'd keep it, but it's too big for my place." She walked into the living room and tossed aside her coat. "It smells funny in here," she said thoughtfully. "Has Myron been here?"

"Yeah—he brought my phone. Listen, I'm going to go get dressed."

"Wait!" Dagne cried. "Did he call?"

With one foot on the stairs, Rachel glanced over her shoulder at Dagne. "No," she said, feeling absurdly disappointed, like she'd just missed winning the lottery by one number. "Nothing. Not even a message." Those words tasted bitterly familiar in her mouth, and without waiting for Dagne's response, she ran up the stairs to dress.

She returned a few minutes later in a mock turtleneck and a pair of faded overalls. Dagne was sitting on the couch going through her spell book, having helped herself to a glass of wine, some crackers, and the last of the cheese. Rachel didn't get paid for another week. She sure hoped she could make a box of mac and cheese and saltine crackers last that long.

"So listen," Dagne said, flipping through the pages of the spell book as if they were a fashion magazine, "don't be too upset that he didn't call."

"I'm not upset—who said I was upset?"

"You didn't say it, but you looked it."

"Whatever," Rachel said. "I just saw him last night. If he calls, he calls. If he doesn't, no skin off my nose. I can take him or leave him, really." And that was such an enormous lie that Rachel couldn't even look at Dagne.

Dagne kept flipping through the pages of her spell book. After a moment, she said, "I read in *Cosmo* that they did this study of who are the sexiest people, as in nations? And the Hungarians were the sexiest, can you believe it? I would have guessed Spaniards."

"Spaniards?"

"Like Antonio Banderas," Dagne said with a dreamy sigh. "Anyway, the Hungarians have sex like a million times a week. And then it was the Russians, and the Americans were up there, too. But guess where the British were?"

"I don't know—where?"

"Almost at the bottom. Just above Iraq."

Rachel laughed.

"I'm serious, Rach. The British are not a sexy people. You might be better off if he never calls. He probably didn't call because he doesn't think like most guys."

"Huh?" Rachel asked as she walked into the kitchen to get herself a wineglass.

"I mean, most guys think about sex all the time, something like once every seven seconds—"

"No way!"

"Yes, it's true! They reported it in *Men's Health* magazine. But Flynn is British, so he probably doesn't think about it all that much, maybe something like once every seven days. Therefore, he doesn't call."

She said it as if she had some scientifically controlled study to back it up.

"So . . . you think that (a), that kiss was just a fluke, and (b), his interest in me was just about sex?" Rachel asked, reappearing with an empty wineglass. "Because (a), that kiss was fabulous, maybe the best kiss I've ever had in my life, and (b), if it *was* only about sex, I should be insulted, but I'm not. I'm okay with just sex. Just sex is great! Actually, just sex would be beyond fantastic. But I don't see how a basically British guy, and therefore a basically sexless guy, could kiss like that."

"Good point," Dagne said in all seriousness. "Okay, so

maybe he's not sexless, just really repressed. They're *all* repressed over there. I mean, look at the queen. Can you see the queen doing it?"

"Don't!" Rachel protested. "That's like imagining Grandma and Grandpa—*eeew,* gross! Besides, there are lots of Brits probably sitting around their flats sipping tea right now trying to imagine the president doing it, and therefore, using your example, they've probably come to the conclusion that Americans are sexless, too."

"Ah. But *Cosmo* has the study to back up *my* example," Dagne politely corrected her.

"Oh, *that's* right. *Cosmo,*" Rachel said, and nodded thoughtfully as she poured a glass of wine. "Here's a different theory for you to chew on," she said, lifting her glass to toast Dagne. "Maybe *he* didn't think the kiss was all that great, and maybe he didn't call because he's not that interested, which is really okay, because I have enough on my plate trying to figure out how to pay my bills around here without worrying if some temporary British guy is going to call me or not," she said, and sat on a floor pillow across from Dagne.

"First, don't worry about your bills," Dagne said, waving a hand at her. "Things are going to work out for you. You'll see," she added with a confident nod.

"Oh right," Rachel said with a roll of her eyes. "Well, that's great. I'll pay all my bills and die a lonely old woman."

"Oh God, here we go," Dagne exclaimed to the ceiling.

"Well, what would you think if it were you?" Rachel challenged her. "I mean, we have this absolutely amazing kiss, and he gets my number, says he is going to call, and doesn't! What am I supposed to think?"

"How about this—that maybe he really did like the kiss, so much that it scared him, and he's not sure how to act on those feelings, so he pours himself into his work—what is his work, anyway?"

"Computers."

"He pours himself into computers and tries not to think

of you because he knows he is really drawn to you—witchcraft, *hello*!" she shouted, jabbing her hands to the ceiling. "Of *course* he's drawn to you! But he's afraid because if he starts anything, he won't be able to finish it because he has to go back to England. Did you think of that?"

"No," Rachel said truthfully. "We had one night out—it wasn't like he had to declare the rest of his life or anything. What's wrong with having a little fling while he's in town? And what about my class? He signed up for my weaving class, dammit!"

"There you go!" Dagne said brightly. "You'll definitely see him at class next week!"

"But that's a whole *weeeeek*!" Rachel moaned, and laid her forehead on the coffee table. "If he's going to call, he has to do it before next week! I can't wait that long, I'll be a basket case by then, and I'll make a fool of myself at class, and we're in the middle of *looms*!"

"Not to worry," Dagne said, reaching across the table and patting Rachel on the head. "We'll do a little spell."

"Jesus, Dagne, is that your answer to everything?"

"It's a lot better than moping," she said, lifting her chin a little. "Anyway, I have *got* to do something about Glenn!" Dagne snorted, and muttered, "*So* stupid! You should never play around with magic."

"Excuse me, but what do you think you're doing on a fairly routine basis here? So, anyway, what happened?"

Dagne sighed. "Okay, here it is. I wanted to do a spell on Ricky Bayless. Remember him?"

"The greatest sex of your life? That Ricky Bayless?"

"*That* Ricky Bayless," Dagne said. "Man, the guy was good—he did things I didn't even know you could *do*! So anyway, I was going to do a spell on him, but I wanted to make sure it was right, so I practiced it. And . . . and I sort of used Glenn instead of Ricky. And then the next thing you know, I run into Glenn down at the hair place—you know, where his sister works?—and he's all smiles and goo-goo-eyed."

"That's because he's always had a crush on you,"

Rachel reminded her. "That's why you quit going to his sister's place."

"But she's so much cheaper than anyone else! Well anyway, apparently the spell worked, because he was so gaga. 'How have you been, Dagne?'" she mimicked him, making huge moon eyes. "'I've been thinking a lot about you, Dagne.'" She laughed. "And now he keeps calling since I invited him over—"

"You *what?*" Rachel cried. "Why did you invite him over?"

"Because he was sort of cute that day, and besides, I *had* to! How was I going to break the spell? The only problem was, I couldn't break it without the spell book, and now he won't leave me alone! I *have* to do a spell that drives him away before he makes me completely bonkers," she said, and looked down at the book, tapped on a page. "Do you think we could get Mr. Valicielo's cat to pee into a cup?"

"Oh please no, God," Rachel groaned, and dropped her forehead to the coffee table again. Only this time, she banged it against the table. Three times.

That night, when Dagne finally gathered her spell things to go home (having been astoundingly unsuccessful in finding the right ingredients, or substitutes, for her spell), Rachel walked with her to the door. "I'll call you tomorrow," she said as Dagne walked down the steps of the porch.

"Okay!" Dagne said.

"Bye!" Rachel called as Dagne loped to her car, then glanced at her watch—a little past one in the morning. She glanced up again to make sure Dagne was in her car, and from the corner of her eye, she saw the blue car turn onto the next street. Odd, she thought, but it looked like the one she had seen earlier. Where had she seen that car before?

With a shrug, she waved to Dagne, closed the door, and headed to bed.

•   •   •

FLYNN was awakened the next afternoon by the ring of the telephone, and stumbled out of bed to retrieve it. "Hello," he mumbled into the phone through a yawn.

"Flynn, darling?"

"Hi, Mum," he said, sleepily scratching his bare chest.

"Have you been *sleeping?*" his mother asked, sounding terribly offended.

"I've had quite a lot of work—all day yesterday and well into the night."

"Oh Flynn, I don't think this particular assignment is very good for you. You sound absolutely ill."

"Thanks, Mum, but I'm fine. Really," he said, standing and stifling another yawn. "How's Dad?" he asked as he stumbled into the kitchen for a glass of water.

"Oh, he's quite all right. He hung tartan curtains in the guest rooms all morning, and this afternoon, he nearly took off a finger hanging that sign that says a hundred thousand welcomes in Gaelic. You know, whatever it is the Scots say."

Flynn lowered his glass, stared straight ahead for a moment before asking, *"Why?"*

"Why? Because the Americans and Japanese love that sort of thing," Mum explained matter-of-factly, as if it was perfectly natural to own a B and B in Butler Cropwell, otherwise known as smack-in-the-bloody-middle-of-jolly-old-England, and dress the place up as if it were a B and B in the Scottish Highlands.

"I didn't tell you, but we had some rather important people come through last week," Mum said.

"Did you?"

"The Winston party. From *America,*" she said, as if it were a palace instead of a country. "They are part of the Winston tobacco family, fourth cousins once removed. That's rather exciting, isn't it?"

Actually, Flynn thought his socks were a bit more exciting, but his mother reveled in such things. "Smashing."

"We've really got a reputation, what with our ties and all," she sniffed.

Mum meant, of course, their aristocratic ties—the ties he'd been hearing about all his bloody life, owing chiefly to a very distant relation to the Duke of Alnwick on his mother's side, the cousin of a cousin of a second cousin, something like that. Which meant, therefore, that they, the lowly Olivers, were in line for the throne . . . should there be a nuclear war that left absolutely no one else in England.

"Flynn, love," his mother said, then paused to sigh wearily.

Flynn braced himself for what he knew was coming.

"I know you are quite cross with Iris, but the poor dear has been pining since you left. Don't you think you could just ring her up and speak to her?"

Iris had not pined for him in two years, but his mother was far too naïve to understand a woman of Iris's nerve. "If I've time, perhaps."

"You can very well make the time and you know it."

"Yes, I suppose I do. But I'm really astoundingly busy at present."

"Oh, darling, Iris is frightfully upset about your misunderstanding," she purred.

What a lovely way to put an unpleasant turn of events—a man comes home early from a business trip and discovers his fiancée in bed with another man. Both wearing dressing gowns, mind you, and both having a bit of a post-coital smoke. What part, exactly, had he misunderstood? "It was hardly a misunderstanding, Mother," Flynn said. "Delicately put, Iris was shagging another man in my absence."

"She didn't mean to! You were away so long and she rather forgot herself!" Mum insisted. "It won't happen again."

Flynn removed the phone from his ear and stared at it for a moment, wondered which puffy little cloud his mother had descended from, and put the thing back to his ear. "How can you be so sure?"

"She gave me her word!" Mum said earnestly. "I hardly think she'd lie at this point, do you?"

Of course he did! But it was hardly a debate he wanted to wage with his mother of all people, so Flynn did what he typically did in these situations with his mother. He lied. "All right, Mum. I'll give her a ring."

"*Thank* you, darling! She'll be thrilled! Now. When are you coming home? We've been invited to the Farmingham Fall gala. It's rather important that we all attend, as they are our cousins after all."

"They are not our cousins," Flynn said calmly. "They are only distantly related through several questionable liaisons."

"That's not true!" his mother cried hurtfully. "We are related through the Duke of Alnwick. How I wish you'd take it more seriously, Flynn! Something horrible and catastrophic could happen and we could very well be called to Buckingham!"

"Mum," Flynn said patiently, "even if we were related to the Farminghams in some believable or even traceable way, we are roughly 1,536th in line to the throne. We will *not* be called to Buckingham, with the possible exception to hoover their bloody floors!"

"Oh!" Mum exclaimed crossly. "I shan't listen to this at all! Now please come home before the yuletide holidays because I will not allow the Olivers to snub the Farminghams. Do I make myself quite clear?"

"Exceedingly," he said. "And if there's nothing else, I really must get to work."

"All right, then, darling. And don't forget Iris. She's very sad."

"Good-bye, Mum. Hello to Dad for me."

"Hugs and kisses, sweetie. Ta-ta!" she trilled and hung up.

Flynn hung up the phone and shuffled off to the shower, where he seriously contemplated getting a new number. Perhaps at a maximum security loony bin or someplace likewise exotic and far away from England.

Chapter Fifteen

✦ ✦

RACHEL'S mood did not improve the next day.

Three days of maniacal typing had yielded a whopping $108.33 after all the tax and FICA were removed. It wasn't even enough to cover the utility bill—thank God Mom's check had arrived for that.

Which meant, after depositing the stupid check, she had exactly $163.13 in her account to pay for phone and cable (which she was cutting just as soon as they saw the last episode of this season's *Trading Spaces*), and to fill an empty pantry.

So, to review: It was a *good* thing Flynn had not called the last couple of days, because she was really too busy squeezing blood from a turnip to even *think* about going out with him.

Standing in the Turbo Temp office front, Rachel shoved the check into her satchel and turned around, walked back to the counter. The girl who had handed her the check was still sitting there, chewing a huge wad of bubble gum as she stared at the computer screen. She did not look up when Rachel reappeared at the counter.

Rachel waited politely for the girl to at least notice her,

which she would not do. Even moving around a little, from one foot to the other, got no reaction. So Rachel very carefully poked the little bell ringer.

The girl looked up. "Yeah?"

"Ah . . . I don't suppose you have another job in there?"

"It's Thursday already."

"Right." Yes, indeed it *was* Thursday already, but for the life of her Rachel couldn't see what that had to do with the price of tea. "So is there anything else you might have?"

"What I mean is, until next week, there won't be anything." This, she said without even looking at the computer. But she did blow a big pink bubble.

Man, Rachel was tempted to pop that thing, but asked instead, "Could you just look? Maybe there's a day thing I could do until next week."

The girl acted as if she'd just been asked to get her toothbrush and soap and get after Mt. Rushmore. With a very loud sigh, she pulled herself around to the computer and punched a couple of buttons. She sighed again for good measure as the thing loaded. Several boxes popped up on the screen that Rachel couldn't quite make out. The girl stared intently, then said, "Got nothing this week."

"Nothing?"

"Nothing. Like I said—come back Monday."

Dejected, Rachel turned to go.

"Unless . . ."

She whipped back around. "Unless?"

"There's this big party in the Blackstone neighborhood. One of those mansions over there. The caterer could use some help."

"Okay!"

"No, not okay. Your quals don't match up. I'm not allowed to send you out if your quals don't match up."

"I beg your pardon, my what doesn't match up?"

"Your *quals*. Qual-i-fi-ca-tions," she articulated scornfully. "'Course, I don't have anyone else to do it."

"What exactly do you not have someone to do? Because

I am sure I could do it, whatever it is," Rachel said, anxiously leaning over the counter to see what the girl was looking at. But the girl didn't care for that and gave Rachel a look from the corner of her eye as she angled the monitor away from Rachel.

"The thing is, even if you can do it, I'm not allowed to send you to the job site if your quals don't match."

"What do I have to do to make my quals match?"

The girl fixed a look on her that gave Rachel the distinct impression she thought she was dealing with a moron. "They *have* to be *on* your résumé. Here—" She punched a button and swiveled around to the printer, retrieved a paper when it finished printing, and handed it to Rachel.

Caterer's assistant. Ability to help serve food and drinks to party of 50–100 persons. Knowledge of meal courses, including appetizers, entrees, and desserts. Knowledge of cocktails and wines. Physical requirements: Ability to lift up to 25 pounds. Black attire required, including shoes. Apron will be provided.

Rachel looked at the girl. "Are you saying I'm not qualified for *this*?"

"It don't say so on your résumé!" she reiterated, a little too adamantly. "Your quals don't say food service."

Rachel looked at the paper again. "How much do they pay?"

The girl glanced at the screen. "Hundred for Saturday night. About six hours of work."

"So," Rachel said, drumming her fingers on the counter, "what would it take to get *food service* added to my *quals?*"

With a slight shrug, the girl blew a bubble and popped it, then said, "A ten ought to do it."

She had to resist the urge to wrap ten fingers around her skinny throat and dug in her bag, unwrapped a wad consisting of a five and four ones, found four quarters in the bottom, and pushed it all across the counter to the girl. "Add *food service* to my quals, will you?" she asked, and still clutching the paper, she marched out the door.

• • •

HER phone did not ring that night either, dammit!
   She did, however, get some e-mail.

Subject: Re: What's going on?
From: Rebecca Parrish <reparrish72@aol.com>
To: Rach <earthangel@hotmail.com>
CC: Robbie <rmanning70@earthlink.net>

WHAT GUY!?!?!? You can't drop a little tidbit like that
and just leave it hanging! And I assume you are KID-
DING when you say you and Dagne used witchcraft
because I KNOW you wouldn't get into something so
going-to-hell as witchcraft, RIGHT, RACHEL???

So anyway, what's he like? Is he nice? What does he
look like? Have you actually gone out on a date, or are
you angling for one? Where did you meet him? Does
he know you're rich? You know that's the first thing
Mom and Dad will want to know. Write back and tell
us what's going on!

By the way . . . Mom called the other day and seems to
think I should talk to you about finishing school and
getting a job. So, here is me telling you to finish school
and get a job. :)

Bec, who's dying to know about the GUY!

Subject: Re: [FWD: Re: What's going on?]
From: <rmanning70@houston.rr.com>
To: Rach <earthangel@hotmail.com>
CC: Rebecca Parrish <reparrish72@aol.com>

First of all, what KIND of witchcraft? If it's the weird kind, you're dead. Do you have any idea what Grandma would do? I'm tempted to call her just for the entertainment value alone. Okay, so who is this guy? Why can't you ever just send an e-mail with all the information instead of making us jump through five million hoops to find out what's going on?

Okay, back to me. I checked out the link you sent on (let me get this right) TAN-TRA, and it didn't have any pictures. Come on, don't you have a book or something? Maybe a video? That would actually be better because Jake and I aren't big readers. Rob.

Subject: RE: RE: [FWD: Re: What's going on?]
From: Rebecca Parrish <reparrish72@aol.com>
To: Robbie <rmanning70@houston.rr.com>
CC: Rach <earthangel@hotmail.com>

Oh right, I meant to ask you about that tantric thing. Can Matt and I get a book, too? But not a video. I would die if a video like that showed up and Grayson plugged it into the TV. Anyway, I don't think it's legal to send that kind of video through the mail. Bec

Subject: RE: RE: [FWD: Re: What's going on?]
From: <earthangel@hotmail.com>
To: <reparrish72@aol.com>
CC: <rmanning70@earthlink.net>

News Flash—maybe one of the reasons I don't send long e-mails is because of the response I get from my older sis-

ters (e.g., please see thread below). First—okay, you guys, let me try this again. TANTRA is an eastern mystical science and it's all about understating the universe you live in. It is not a sex manual, for God's sake. If you really want to get into it, you're supposed to study how to connect with the universe and become more complete in ALL aspects of your life, not just the bedroom, you sex-starved dolts. But okay, part of that connection is an awareness and release of sexual energy. So if y'all will promise to at least read about the mystical science of Tantra, I will send you a little pocket companion book I have that talks about the sexual energy part and how to release it. Do you promise????? I'm not sending it unless you say you promise.

So as for the guy, it's really nothing. I was just filling up the white space on the screen so I wouldn't be accused of not giving enough info. Really, he's not that spectacular or anything, and I'm not sure I'm interested. It's too much trouble at this point, anyway. I mean, I have to get a job and finish school. I really don't have time for a relationship right now. Speaking of jobs, I have to go. TTFN. . . . Rachel

P.S. And it's WHITE magic, although I am sure I will have to explain that, too. :)

When she finished answering nosey e-mails from her sister, Rachel went to bed, and lay there, staring at the ceiling for a long time.

The next day, she tackled the clutter of her house. Sort of. She was actually looking for the little gift book on tantric sex someone had given her so she could send it to the maniacs in Texas, but she couldn't find it, which forced her to dig through the clutter and tidy up.

It was easy for her house to become cluttered; it was very small for one thing, and she had a bit of a pack-rat habit. There were lots of things she recognized she had kept too long, but could not bring herself to throw away—like the ferns and ivies and herbal baskets that hung in sev-

eral corners of her house. Most of them had lived past their
prime, but Rachel refused to give up on living things and
would diligently nurse them back to life after long winters.
She did, however, rearrange them.

And there were the many hand-woven, thick wool rugs
scattered about the wood floors, all from her weaving
classes, and most of them projects abandoned by her less-
industrious students that she had finished. There were so
many of them that they almost formed a carpet.

She had a lot of furniture (and wind chimes), too, the result of one overly enthusiastic spending spree in search of
feng shui. In her one living area were two overstuffed
couches, an armchair, and a huge ottoman. There was also
a large wood frame on which was her latest needlework
project—a copy of a fourteenth-century French tapestry.
Reduced in size, naturally. Which accounted for the sheets
of paper and the calculator nearby as she figured propor-
tions from the original.

And of course, on every conceivable surface, there were
books. Stacks and stacks of them, some read, some intended to be read. School books, reference materials, old
dusty-paged tomes of medieval history and ancient lan-
guages. There were stacks of fiction books, too, which
Rachel knew she would never get around to reading as
much as she would like to, but was loath to give away, just
in case something catastrophic happened, like she had a
horrible accident that required an extensive period of recu-
peration during which she'd be confined to bed and could
do nothing but read. God forbid she should come up short
on books if *that* happened.

So she just kept moving the stacks around, dusting over
them and around them and adding to them every time she
came within a five-mile radius of anyplace that sold books.

There were also the odds and ends that kept ending up
in her house. Some were her own doing—every time she
went to England, she'd come back with a bagful of trinkets, most of which she could never remember why she
bought.

She found lots of stuff, too—like the four hand-painted teacups and saucers, which she was certain had come from Myron, but couldn't remember having received from him. And now, on the dining room hutch her mother had insisted she have, a new collection of little thick-glassed bottles and bowls, all thanks to her dabbling in Dagne's witchcraft.

That was where she found the book on tantric sex for some odd reason, and as it was small enough to lose again, she stuck it in her bag so she wouldn't forget to mail it.

That was where she found her horoscope chart, too, and checked to see if Mars was still in retrograde or *what* the hell the problem was. Her study of the chart, however, was not illuminating. Go figure.

And as she tossed that onto a new stack, she noticed the spell book Dagne had brought into her life. *Wicked Good: A Witch's Guide to Effective Spells for Women.*

Rachel picked it up, intending to put it away, but the heavy book somehow slipped between her fingers and fell onto the hardwood floor with a *thud*. She picked it up by the spine, and the book started to slip again, so she caught it underneath with her other arm . . . and noticed that it had fallen on the page of Seduction Spells.

"Isn't *that* rich," she said with a frown, not happy at all to be reminded of Flynn, the Loser Who Had Not Called. She moved to close the book and put it away, but her eye caught tiny print on the bottom of a table of contents that guided the reader to enchanting spells of seduction and everlasting love.

"That's weird," she muttered. It was something she had not heretofore noticed, and she'd damn sure looked at the page enough times. The print was so tiny and the daylight was fading so fast that Rachel had to lift the book to her face and squint to read it.

Warning! Spells cannot be used to enslave another being! To hold someone against their will is wrong! If you are guilty of using one of these

powerful spells to entice love that is not meant to
be, the spell will only be temporary, and may
cause more heartache than good!

She lifted her head, blinked down at the page. How in
the hell had she missed *that* warning? It seemed pretty important, and really, having spent the last several weeks
honing her spell-casting abilities, one would think she
might have *noticed* an important disclaimer like that!

Christ, no wonder Flynn hadn't called!

She had used her goddess powers to entice someone
who didn't want to be enticed, and in return, she'd gotten
majorly worked up over a kiss that was going nowhere!
"How stupid *am* I?" she cried, and slapped the spell book
shut, slammed it down on the hutch, and glared at it, furious.

Oh yeah, she was furious, all right. Furious that she'd
made a fool of herself over some stranger, had believed it
was kismet, had even made the fatal mistake of mentioning it to her sisters, dammit! And she was furious for being
so naïve and stupid and *trusting* of a woman she knew better than to trust! She was furious with Dagne, too, and held
her totally responsible for this mess, because she was the
one who had forced Rachel into this stupid *stupid* witchcraft business to begin with.

But then again, who was the idiot who had been dumb
enough to believe *anything* Dagne Delaney had to say, and
worse, had actually cast all those ridiculous spells?

"Her name is *Rachel*! And don't forget the spells with
the actual dancing, you dolt. *Augh!*" she shrieked at the
book. "Gawd, I am so through with this crap!" she said angrily, and whipped around to find a box to put all the
witchcraft junk in, because that was definitely the *one* box
she would toss out to the street—

But her sleeve caught the hutch and the spell book and
sent it flying across the dining room. It sailed wide of the
hutch and landed, spine up, pages down, beneath the arch
that separated the dining room from the living room.

Only . . . the funny thing was, Rachel didn't remember hitting it, exactly. In fact, she was pretty certain she hadn't touched the book. Just the hutch.

Shit. A cold shiver ran down her spine, and she slowly turned and looked at the hutch. Nothing else was disturbed. This was a little too spooky for her, and she glanced at the spell book again, wondered how it had defied physics to land spine up again, its pages bunched and folded beneath the heavy cardboard covers.

"This isn't creepy!" she scoffed aloud, hugging herself. "Because this stuff isn't real! It's bullshit, like everything else Dagne does!"

So why, then, did she hear a tiny little voice in her head that sounded exactly like Dagne telling her if she believed, it was real?

"No. This is so ridiculous!" But she took a step toward the spell book. And another. Was she imagining things, or had it grown unusually cold in here? And another step, and another, until she was suddenly running in little-girl steps to the book, which she snatched up quickly and held to her chest as she ran into the living room and threw herself on the couch, burying her face in the pillows.

But after a moment, when she realized she really couldn't breathe, she slowly pushed herself up, peeled the spell book from her chest, and looked down at the pages to where it had fallen open. It was a spell of personal growth and prosperity.

Physical and emotional prosperity will come when you are ready to receive it. To prepare yourself, you will need . . .

Now that was a classic example of serendipity if ever she'd seen one, and she was not so practical as to turn her back on it. So Rachel pushed herself up, shoved her hair behind her ears, and began to read how to prepare herself for physical and emotional prosperity.

Chapter Sixteen

* * *

THE address for the Saturday soiree was near Blackstone Avenue, a swank area of town full of mansions and old money and old people with enough history in town to throw massive parties where hundreds might attend. This one was set in an old colonial mansion, which was painted yellow and sat back from the street on a grassy hill behind a tall wrought iron fence.

Rachel motored up the long, circular drive, and was immediately met out front of the large portico by a man dressed in an old-style footman's uniform, complete with white-haired wig and queue. "Yes?" he asked tersely when Rachel rolled down her window.

"I'm supposed to meet the caterer."

"The *caterer* was told to have all staff park on the street!" he said, pointing with his big, white, cartoonish gloved hands toward the gate. "Once you've done so, you may find your crew just up the drive there," he said, and pointed toward the service drive.

"Thanks!" Rachel called out the window as he stalked away. "Jerk," she muttered beneath her breath as she motored on around the drive and onto the street.

Naturally, she had to park fourteen thousand miles away, and it was freezing out, and she was really PMS-ing, as in, retaining water like the proverbial sea cow. She didn't have anything but her lavender shawl, so her teeth were chattering by the time she reached the top of the hill. She skirted around the end of the house so as not to run into Paul Revere, Doorman, and trudged on the path that led to the servants' entrance (she knew exactly what the path was, having spent her formative years in Houston in a house of similar size, where they'd had an actual guard posted at their gate for reasons that seemed more ridiculous the older she got).

It was amazing, given her foul state of mind and the fact that her teeth were chattering, that she even heard the mewling sound. But she did hear it, and stopped in her tracks. There it was, very faint. She looked around, toward the hedges, and then to the bushes that lined the exterior of the garage. She heard it again, only louder this time, and as she neared the edge of the four-car garage, she saw the cat.

A cat that was, inexplicably, chained to a tree. Granted, there was a little kitty shanty there, and a bowl of water, but the cat was chained to a tree. In her thirty-one years, Rachel had never seen a chained cat. She didn't even know it was possible to *chain* a cat.

And the cat obviously didn't like it; she meowed at Rachel, who immediately moved to pet it, but the poor thing was so traumatized that it jumped away, aiming for her little kitty jail. Only the feline fell short because of the weight of the chain. Rachel moved very slowly, singing *Kitty, kitty, kitty* . . . until she at last got close enough to pet it.

That was, as it turned out, a huge mistake, because the cat was really frightened and let out a cat screech that echoed throughout the entire neighborhood.

"We're not going to stand for this," Rachel assured the cat. "We'll think of something. Just give me a few minutes."

And she did have every intention of doing something,

but the sudden sound of pots and pans being clanged together startled her, and she turned to see a woman's head pop out from behind the door leading to the kitchen.

Rachel instantly jumped up; the woman's hair was in disarray, and there was what looked like fingerprints on her blouse. "Are you the help?" she asked quickly.

"Yes. My name—"

"Get rid of that shawl and hurry up. This is a *nightmare!*" she exclaimed, and disappeared again.

Rachel moved quickly; she followed the woman into a small sort of mudroom off the kitchen, saw hooks with coats on them, and hung her bag, then her shawl over the bag, and was straightening her clothing and hair when the woman shouted, "Hurry *up* . . . what's your name?"

"Rachel!"

"Rachel! Hurry the hell up! We're already a half hour behind schedule!"

Rachel hurried the hell up, and stepped through that interior door into a madhouse. Men and women were rushing around an industrial-sized kitchen, checking pots and pans, carrying trays, and barely avoiding collisions with one another. The woman was standing at a small desk with a sheaf of papers in one hand, a Diet Coke in the other. She took one look at Rachel, up and down, and shook her head. "I said *skirt!* What sort of moron shows up to cocktail in *pants?*"

"I ah, I . . . the temp agency said black attire."

"Jesus Christ!" The woman slammed the Diet Coke down onto the desk, spun around, and rifled through several clothes hanging from hooks next to her. She finally pulled out a skirt that looked five sizes too small and thrust it at Rachel as she glanced at her feet. "Oh *great,* boots with heels?" she cried angrily. "What the hell do I care? If your feet are killing you at the end of the night, it's not my fault!" she snapped. "There's a toilet at the end of the kitchen. Go change!"

Rachel looked at the skirt, then at the woman, who looked as if she might come apart at the seams at any moment, glaring fiercely and daring Rachel to argue, which Rachel was not stupid enough to do. She just clutched the skirt tightly to her, said thanks, and ran.

Unfortunately, it took her several minutes to maneuver into that skirt, and it didn't help matters that she was as bloated as a stuck pig. In the end, she had to settle for zipping only. The button was not going in the buttonhole, no way, no how.

She at last emerged, poured into the skirt so tight that she could hardly breathe. Thank God she had on a long sweater that covered any unsightly bulging and knee-high boots. Her hair was braided down her back, and having done some whimsical spell casting on her personal behalf, she'd felt a little festive—she'd threaded gold filigree through her hair to give it a sort of medieval look.

As long as she didn't have to bend or sit, she was okay.

The woman was instantly at her side, pulling her pants from her grip and shoving an apron at her, which she gestured for Rachel to put on. It was white and said across the bodice, *Queen Mary's Catering,* and was embroidered with tiny little ships around the lettering.

The woman waited impatiently for Rachel to tie the apron, then shoved a beverage tray into her hand. "I'm Mary. If you have any questions about *anything,* you find me. Do *not* bother the hostess! You're serving drinks. Now go!" she said, and fairly pushed Rachel through a swinging door, which she stumbled through, seeing as how she could hardly move her legs in that skirt. Once she was certain she wouldn't topple over, she paused and had a look around.

She was not prepared for the room that greeted her.

On the other side of that swinging door was a large room, perhaps a ballroom at one point. A thick oriental carpet covered the floor. The crown molding along the ceiling was papier-mâché in the old style, with flying baby cherubs forming a ring around the room and around the huge candelabra that hung from the middle. There was a small jazz quartet at the far end of the room, seated at the edge of a portable dance floor that couldn't have been larger than about eight feet. There was a full bar manned by two bartenders directly across from the enormous hearth, and a smattering of tables built for two.

The hosts had gone to great expense to decorate with a Thanksgiving theme—cornucopias overflowing with fruits and grains were in the corners, and two cornucopias on the bar were pouring what looked like champagne. In addition, funky but elaborate paper and feathered turkeys graced the tabletops, as well as a huge one in front of the fireplace.

Moreover, many of the guests were wearing pilgrim hats.

Her perusal of the room was interrupted by the arrival of Mary again, who came barging through the swinging door with something that smelled divine. "What are you waiting for?" she hissed at Rachel's back. "Get out there!"

Rachel stumbled into the midst of the partygoers and asked the first couple she came to, "Drink?"

"Darling, I thought you'd never arrive!" the woman laughed. "I'll have a Manhattan, but please tell the bartender that I want just a *dash* of vermouth, and in fact, I'd really prefer it if he'd dash just a *little* more bitters than vermouth," she said, holding up her fingers to indicate how much more.

"Sure!" Rachel said, even as she was trying to commit to memory what the woman had just said.

"I'll have an Italian Nut. Lots of ice," the man added.

"An Italian Nut?" Rachel echoed.

"Yes. An Italian Nut," he said with a completely straight face.

"Got it!" Rachel said with a smile, and headed for the bar, knowing, even at this early stage, that one hundred dollars was not going to be nearly enough for this evening, because she recognized all the signs of a blow-out, as she had been forced to attend parties like this when she was a teenager.

When she reached the bar, she smiled and said to one of the bartenders, "I need a Manhattan, with a dash of vermouth. And she asked if you would dash more bitters than vermouth."

"Gotcha," he said, and started making the drink.

"And an Italian Nut," she said carefully.

"Oh man!" He laughed. "These people got more money than brains, huh? You'll have heard it all by the time this is over, sweetheart. I'm Mike, by the way."

"Rachel," she said with a smile.

"Looking good, Rachel!" he said with another wink, and handed her the two drinks.

The remark surprised her so completely that she almost withdrew the tray before he could set them on there. She blinked up at him to see if he was making fun of her. But he just smiled. Rachel smiled, too. And kept smiling as she reached the couple with their drinks.

FLYNN was napping peacefully when Joe shoved him awake by bouncing his head against the car window. Flynn's eyes flew open with a curse. "Bollocks! What did you do that for?" he asked as he rubbed his head where it had collided with the window.

"He's here," Joe said.

"Of course he is. Couldn't arrive a little late and let a bloke have a bit of a kip, could he, now?"

Joe laughed. "Dude. You act like you've never had to work a couple of full days before. Don't you have to pull extra shifts from time to time over there?"

"Lest you forget, I am actually doing *two* jobs. The one I'm paid quite handsomely to perform, thank you, and then, of course, *your* job," Flynn said through a yawn as he straightened his tie. "Naturally, I am quite indebted to you for the opportunity, but that does not make me particularly adept at napping in a car, of all places. So which one is he?" he asked, squinting through the windshield.

Joe handed him the binoculars. "Tall guy, black suit." Flynn looked through the binoculars. A tall man in a black suit was hugging a trim woman in a tight skirt and high heels. As he watched, the woman reared back, said something, then went up on her tiptoes to kiss him. Their prime suspect tightened his arm around her waist and held her to him, kissed her for what seemed awfully long for a man who had just buried his wife, and, presumably, his wife's dog, as that little bugger had also had the bloody bad misfortune to have been murdered.

"Ready?" Joe asked as Flynn lowered the binoculars.

"Quite."

Joe clapped him on the shoulder. "You know where to find me," he said with a grin. Flynn opened the car door, and as he stepped out, Joe leaned over and said, "Hey, bring me something back, will ya? Like a turkey sandwich, something like that. And oh yeah . . . a piece of pumpkin pie."

"Righto," Flynn said cheerfully, and slammed the door shut, knowing full well—as he was certain Joe knew—that he had no intention of lugging any sort of food item back from this posh little Thanksgiving gathering. It was most decidedly not his style to diddle food.

With the invitation they had secured (through "channels" Joe said), he walked up the drive to the front steps, where a footman in an Indian suit opened the door for him. He stepped inside the marbled foyer and was instantly greeted by Mr. Edward Feizel (of Feizel, Goldman, and Bernstein), and presumably, Mr. Feizel's wife, both of whom looked exactly like the file photos Joe had shown him.

The Feizels were hosting a holiday party for their more lucrative clients and consorts, which, apparently, they did with annual regularity. It was, by all accounts, quite a smashing do.

Feizel squinted up at Flynn, a blank look in his eye as he searched his memory banks. Flynn handed him the invitation, and with one look at it, Mr. Feizel immediately nodded. "Aha! Honey, it's the guy I told you about. Mr. Oliver, is that right?" he asked, extending his hand.

"Thank you, Mr. Feizel," Flynn said, shaking his hand, then extending it to the missus. "Good evening, madam, and thank you for allowing me to attend."

"Oh," she said, touching her ear as she smiled up at him with big brown eyes. "You're *quite* welcome!"

Feizel's eyes widened slightly. "You're British? Shit!" he exclaimed, and leaned into Flynn to whisper, "I didn't know Wasserman was in that *kind* of dutch!"

Flynn leaned into Feizel and said pleasantly, "Actually, we're not entirely certain Mr. Wasserman is involved in any sort of dutch, so it's probably best to keep it all rather hush-hush."

"Right, right," Feizel said, lifting a finger to his thick lips to show how hush-hush he intended to keep it. "But between you and me, Ollie, I never much liked the bastard." He clapped Flynn on the back. "The party is just through there," he said, nodding at a pair of double open doors that led into what looked like a ballroom. "Help yourself to food and booze and have a happy Thanksgiving."

"Thank you for coming," Mrs. Feizel said, still smiling like she'd eaten a canary.

"Ah, but thank *you,*" Flynn said, and with a subtle wink for the missus, shoved his hands into his pockets and strolled into the party.

It was packed already, with half the guests milling around in some sort of ridiculous-looking pilgrim hats, the very same sort of hat that a maid tried to put on Flynn's head. He politely declined, walked farther into the room, and had a look around, thought to himself that Joe would crap if he knew what beauties were milling about inside. There were plenty of them, all wearing tight dresses and sweaters that showed their rather curveless frames to their best advantage.

And there were plenty of chaps, too, dressed mostly in dark suits that made it impossible to distinguish one from the other. Fortunately, Wasserman's height made it quite easy to spot him, and he was, remarkably, already in deep conversation with another woman.

There was plenty of time for Wasserman, Flynn figured, and he was a bit ravenous, so he walked to the buffet, helped himself to a plate full of grilled shrimp and little pastry cups with something mushy in them, as well as a cup of the black shit Americans called coffee.

He was just polishing off the last of the shrimp when a woman behind him said, "How very boring of you."

Flynn turned to see who had said it and was pleasantly surprised—she had long blond hair that hung straight past her shoulders, a skinny black dress that barely covered her bum and dipped almost to her navel. She was holding a martini in long slender fingers and sucking on the olive. He smiled, held up the coffee. "It's rather chilly out."

She pulled the olive from her lips, dipped it into the martini, and slowly put it in her mouth again. "I don't think we've met. I'm Marlene Reston."

"Charlie Windsor," he said, extending his hand.

The use of the crown prince Charles's name did not register anywhere in the pretty blonde's head, judging by her blank expression. She flipped her hair to one side before putting her hand in his, and blatantly trailed her fingers slowly across his palm.

"It's a pleasure, Charlie," she said with a wink. "Are you with FG and B?"

"In a manner of speaking . . . they are associated with our firm on the other side of the pond," he said, smiling as she skimmed his palm again.

"I'm not with them, either," she said, now stirring her martini with the olive. "I'm an associate. They like to invite us to these things to remind us what we're missing by not working at their firm."

"And are you missing this?"

She shrugged a little as she looked around. "I don't know. Maybe. But I can't stand the thought of having to sleep with one of the toads who run the place. So . . . did you come alone?" she asked, moving, almost imperceptibly, closer to him.

"Yes, actually," Flynn said, sipping his coffee. "My fiancée is in London."

"*Tsk, tsk,* Charlie! Partying alone and so far from home!" she playfully admonished him, and looked up at him through a pair of very thick and very long false eyelashes. "That's really very naughty of you." She smiled saucily, and honestly, Flynn felt his wanker give him a bit of a nudge.

All right, what was a poor chap to do? He was a guy after all, and a guy who, regrettably, had not had any sort of carnal relations in quite some time, and the sort of smile she was pointing at him now was designed to catch his attention. And besides, there was plenty of time for surveillance work, wasn't there?

Flynn smiled wickedly. "It is quite naughty, isn't it? I really ought to be punished for it. What do you suppose my punishment should be?"

"*Ooh,* I don't know," she purred, licking at that damn olive again. "Do you like spankings?"

"Adore them," he said, and grinned, a little lopsidedly, as he moved closer to Marlene . . . but a movement in his peripheral vision caught his eye, and he turned his head before he could stop himself, still smiling—

And saw Rachel standing there in an apron, gaping at him. For a moment, she didn't move, but then she suddenly turned away and disappeared into the crowd.

Blast it, this wasn't very good then, was it?

FROM Rachel's perspective, it was disastrous. She wanted to die, right there, in the middle of that fancy house with all those fancy skinny beautiful people around her—let them deal with *that* while they wore their stupid pilgrim hats—a beached whale right in the middle of them. She could just imagine the scene, all gathered around her, cocktails in hand, peering down with looks of horror. "Do you think the poor thing is *dead?*" one would ask—

"Excuse me, miss? I'd like a scotch and water, neat," a man said.

Rachel snapped out of it, nodded curtly to the man, and walked to the bar, asked Mike for a scotch and water, neat. He poured the drink, looking at Rachel the whole time. "You all right, kid? You look a little flushed," he said.

"Do I?" she asked, absently putting a hand to her face. Which was flaming, naturally, because even though Flynn was the jerk, *she* was the one who felt like a moron. And here she was in a skirt that was literally exploding off her and a stupid apron, of all things! Not exactly the sexy image she wanted to put out there, was it? Mike was still looking at her, however, and she quickly shook her head. "Nah, I'm fine. Just one too many turkeys in here."

He laughed, handed her the drink. "Come see me if you need a little pick-me-up," he said with a wink. "I've got access to all kinds of good booze."

She smiled gratefully, put the drink on her tray, turned around—and almost collided with Flynn.

He had the presence of mind to jump back, and once he was assured she wasn't going to pour a drink all over him, he relaxed and smiled. "Rachel?"

Think, you idiot! her mind screamed. "Oh!" she said, looking very surprised. "Flynn? Is that you?"

"I didn't know you'd be here tonight!"

That was obvious. What, he hadn't thought she'd be invited to some posh party in the swankest part of town? Even to serve drinks? Perhaps she had failed to mention that she was dead flat broke and on the verge of selling her blood to buy food.

"Yep," she said, a little loudly. "I'm here!" And she laughed . . . unfortunately, it came out more like a horse's whinny.

He smiled, seemed to wait for her to say more.

She was *so* not going to say more, because she knew what it would be, something completely pathetic like, *Why didn't you call me?* And as she had no desire to make an even bigger fool of herself, she smiled brightly, said,

"Okay! Good to see you!" and stepped around him, tried to waddle off.

"Wait!" he said, before she could take a step, and of course she couldn't help herself. Rachel turned around.

He was looking at her hair. "I beg your pardon, but I thought I saw glitter in your hair."

She gripped the tray. "As a matter of fact," she said, pasting the bright smile to her face, regretting ever having put it in her hair, "it's stardust."

"Stardust?"

"Yes, stardust. You can get it at this little shop . . ." Wait. Scratch that. No need to mention the witchcraft stuff again. "It's to bring me good luck." And what a lucky batch she managed to get her hands on! PMS, a skirt so tight it was cutting off all feeling from the waist down, and now Flynn at a posh party where she was a lowly serving wench!

"Oh." He stood there, and Rachel could almost see the wheels turning, could almost hear him think, *How in the bloody hell do I get my arse out of this one?* "It's really quite . . . fetching," he said.

"I *know,*" Rachel responded, smarty-like, and turned around, marched away, hoping to high heaven Flynn at least had the good sense to look away from her butt.

She delivered the scotch and water, heard some elderly woman tell the man she was so sorry about his loss, and thought, judging by his expression, that the loss must have been a stock or something, and kept walking, right through the swinging door and into the kitchen where she put her tray down. "Anyone have a smoke?" she asked.

One of the girls nodded and fished it out of her skirt pocket. "Don't let Queen Mary catch you, or she'll can you on the spot," she warned as she handed Rachel a lighter.

Rachel nodded, walked to the back of the kitchen, swiping up a few grilled shrimp as she went, and snuck out to the little area between the garage and the work quarters. She popped a shrimp into her mouth, leaned down to where Fraidy Cat was sitting at the end of her chain, and placed two shrimp in front of her. "Hurry up," she said to the cat, and lit the cigarette, felt the nicotine rush through her limbs as she watched the cat sniff carefully around the shrimp.

She heard the crunch of feet on the drive before he spoke, and she closed her eyes, imagined what he'd say. *I'm so sorry. I'm an idiot. I adore you, and it frightened me . . .* Or the more likely, *Uh, pardon, but could you move your car? You're blocking me, and Blondie and I are going to go have a quick shag.*

The feet stopped behind her. She took another drag off the cigarette, waited for him to say something that would crush her. But instead, he said, "Hey, is everything okay?"

All right, that was a decent beginning, better than she would have guessed, maybe a seven on a scale of ten. There was only one little problem. It wasn't Flynn.

It was Mike, the bartender.

Chapter Seventeen

* * *

MIKE was smiling, so she figured she hadn't been fired for sneaking out for a smoke. "I'm fine," she said, holding up the cigarette. "Just having a smoke."

"Mind if I join you?" he asked, taking a pack out of his breast pocket and lighting one up, and therein answering the burning question of what, exactly, he was doing out here. And in fact, up on a small patio, there were several party guests huddled together, also having a smoke.

Mike laughed. "Help down by the garbage cans. Guests this way." He looked around; saw the cat munching on shrimp. "What's that around its neck?"

"A chain."

"A chain? What's that, their watch cat?" He laughed loudly at his own joke, but turned away from the poor cat and dragged on his smoke.

Rachel didn't think it was particularly funny. She thought it was downright cruel.

"Anyone see you come out?" he asked, looking toward the service door.

"I don't think so."

"So, Rachel," he said, exhaling smoke. "Rachel, Rachel."

"That's me!" she said in a singsong voice.

"Do you live in Providence?"

She nodded.

"Get out much?"

What did that mean? Was she acting weird, or something? Okay, she couldn't breathe, thanks to the skirt and the PMS, but still—

"Like out to clubs," he helpfully clarified.

"Oh. Not a lot. I'm in school."

"Aren't we all."

"You, too? Brown?"

He snorted. "Nah. Rhode Island Community College. Business Administration. You go to Brown? What are you studying?"

Okey-doke, here they went. Rachel inhaled and felt nauseated. That was the thing about smoking. The idea was always better than the real thing. "History," she said.

"Wow. Gonna be a professor, I guess."

"I guess," she said. At the rate things were going, she'd probably end up typing routine autopsy reports or something likewise fabulously successful and awe-inspiring.

"Let me ask you something," Mike said, glancing at his wristwatch. "You ever take a break from those books long enough to go out for a drink?"

Get. *Out!* Was he really asking her for a *date*? Couldn't he see that she was poured into this skirt? Man, she was sold on the benefits of witchcraft already! With a grin, she turned toward him. "Sometimes. Why?"

"Why?" he asked with a lopsided grin. "Because I thought maybe you'd go have a drink with me. Is that possible? Or do you have 'em lined up around the corner and can't be bothered?"

Now she laughed. "Yeah, I can be bothered," she said, and tossed down her smoke, ground it out with the pointy heel of her boot, then smiled at Mike from the corner of her eye. "For the right guy." *Hey,* did she just say that? Could she be *flirting*?

Mike grinned, let his gaze slide down her body and back. "Where do I put in my application for the right guy?"

Rachel smiled. "I think we can consider the application filed," she said, and thought maybe there was something in the make-me-sexy-and-hurry spell. Okay, okay, it hadn't worked on Flynn, but, still, Mike was no slouch! He was nice-looking enough, and he had a really nice smile, and nice pale blue eyes, and okay, maybe she could see herself dating this guy, and stepped, surprisingly—like *way* surprisingly—a little closer to him—

That was when she saw Flynn, standing on the patio with the other guests. Only he wasn't smoking. With his hands in his pockets, and his head down, he was looking at her. Well, actually, to be perfectly clear . . . he was looking at her flirt with Mike. And he was not smiling his usual charming smile. In fact, he was looking a little grim up there.

"That's great," Mike said. "Look, I really gotta get back in there. But I'll catch you before you leave and get your number, all right?"

"Sure! I'd really like that," she said brightly. Too brightly. So brightly that it rang false. Gawd, what was she *saying?* She hardly even knew this guy! Wasn't the usual protocol to at least have a conversation with a guy before you went out with him? That was a problem with these spells, she was discovering. She didn't quite know how to act when they started working.

"Okay!" he said, and smiled. "So . . . I'd love to stand out here and freeze my ass off with you all night, but I really have to work," he said, and reached out to touch her hand.

"I guess I should, too," she said, and stole a glimpse at Flynn. Only Flynn wasn't up there looking down at her anymore. He was looking at the blonde hanging off his shoulder.

"You coming?" Mike asked, and Rachel jerked her gaze to him, smiled brightly, and joined him to sneak back inside.

Okay, all right, Rachel told herself as she picked up her tray and some sushi-looking thing and went back into the party room; she shouldn't have looked up there. She should have let well enough alone, and she *damn* sure should have looked at her horoscope before she came tonight.

Right. But here she was looking for Flynn again, whom she instantly spotted, with his blonde of course, yukking it up with the tall man whose pet had died and some other woman who was pencil-thin and beautiful. Nothing like a bunch of pencil-thin beauties to bring a woman squeezed into a skirt two sizes too small crashing back to earth.

"Excuse me, miss!" some woman shouted at her before she could get too caught up in Flynn's world. "Can we get some *drinks* please?"

Why, of course. Now that the woman had helpfully reduced her down to servant again, all was right with the world.

FROM across the room, standing with Marlene and Phil Wasserman and some woman whose name he did not catch, Flynn watched Rachel from the corner of his eye. He figured, being a veteran of females, which he could certainly claim to be, that he had made a rather bad mistake in not ringing her after that astonishing little kiss they had shared. Unfortunately, ringing her up was not something he'd really had time to do until right around the moment he saw her lovely face staring at him from across the room tonight.

Not that he had forgotten Rachel, God no. Nor that bloody amazing kiss.

He was really rather intrigued by her, more and more all the time. Not all girls went about with stardust in their hair, did they? And she looked, he had to admit, terribly curvaceous in that black sweater and short little skirt and high-heeled, knee-high boots.

Oh no, he'd had every intention of ringing her, and was

looking quite forward to an evening with a woman who actually thought of things beyond what royal would be where on any given occasion. It was just that between the two rather involved situations he was currently engaged in, time had, unfortunately, gotten away from him. He'd meant to find a moment to explain it all to her, but then he'd seen her with that American bloke having a fag, and thought it was perhaps too late.

And really, he told himself, as he listened to Phil Wasserman speak reverently of his dead wife, that was perhaps just as well, for inevitably it would end—and end disastrously, wouldn't it? He risked finding himself a bit too intrigued with her, and eventually, he'd have to tell her his true reason for being in America.

That would not go well. Not at all. And then he'd actually have to return to England and leave things at sixes and sevens. He really fancied her far too much to create a complete mess of things.

Yes, eventually, anything he started would come to a crushing end, which was why Flynn forced himself to stop seeking Rachel out in that room. Nor did he look at Marlene, who was tragically lacking in any curves at all, and instead focused his attention on Wasserman, his reason for being here at all.

But try as he might, he really couldn't keep himself from stealing glimpses of Rachel as he sort of trailed along after Wasserman, because she was really a bit of all right. Quite dishy and very sexy with that gold in her hair, and frankly, he could count her bum among the best he'd ever had the good fortune to view. Round and bouncy, the sort a man could imagine really grabbing on to as he . . .

What in the bloody hell was the *matter* with him? He was *working,* for God's sake! And he was not the sort of bloke who was easily confounded by a bird!

Besides, Rachel seemed to be enjoying herself at the bar with her sodding bartender. Even if he wanted to have a word with her, he couldn't really, not with the ever-present Marlene, who was, it seemed, quite pissed after imbibing a lorry load of martinis. *Quite* pissed, as in plastered, and falling down, making-moon-eyes-and-suggesting-lewd-things-to-him drunk. He had absolutely no idea how to get rid of her.

When he at last convinced Marlene to have a seat at one of the little tables and tried to get her to have a bite, she refused, shaking her head in a slow-motioned drunken way, with her hair sort of flying dramatically across her eyes and whatnot. Flynn had every desire to leave her there, but frankly, he was far too much the gentleman to do it properly.

Shoving a hand through his hair, he looked desperately around for someone who might help. Naturally, his gaze fell on Rachel, who was, as luck would have it, only a few feet away.

"Rachel!" he called out to her as she delivered drinks to a very disorderly quartet of attorneys.

She looked over her shoulder at him, and he could swear her eyes went soft for a moment before cooling off to perfect cubes of ice. She cocked her tray high and walked to where he stood with a smile rather forcefully smashed onto her face. *"Drink?"* she drawled.

"Ah, no. I rather think not—there's been quite enough served here as it is. I hate to be a bother, but would you mind terribly locating Mr. Feizel? I'm afraid his guest has had one too many."

"I have *not,* Charlie!" Marlene insisted, stabbing her elbow onto the little table to steady herself and almost toppling the thing over.

Rachel looked at Marlene. "Charlie?"

"Long story," Flynn quickly interjected.

"Go on," Marlene said to Rachel, waving a loose wrist at her. "Be a sweetie and go get me a martini," she said, before covering her face with both hands.

Rachel and Flynn exchanged a look.

"I'd really rather you not," he said. "Do you think you might find Mr. Feizel?"

"I'll get him right away." She walked away without another word.

She returned a moment later with Mr. Feizel, who gave Marlene one look and sighed. "Dammit, Marlene, you did this last year!"

"Did what?" she asked, smiling sloppily at him.

He sighed with exasperation and looked at Flynn. "She *did* do this last year. We let her sleep it off upstairs and she stayed two days. I can't let her do that again—my wife would kill me."

"Yeah, well, I don't *want* to stay here!" Marlene said defiantly and tried to fold her arms against her tiny little waist, but couldn't keep her balance and slid into the table.

"Come on, Ollie, would you mind?" Mr. Feizel asked him, his dark eyes pleading.

"Me?" Flynn exclaimed, surprised. "I hardly know her, Mr. Feizel. I just thought that you might—"

"The thing about Marlene is she's really a brilliant attorney."

"The best! No one wins more cases than me!" Marlene shouted, jabbing her chest with her finger.

"But she and gin don't mix. If you'll just drive your car up, I'll help you get her inside of it."

"I don't *have* a car," Flynn objected, then noticed Rachel, standing behind Mr. Feizel, lift a curious brow at that.

"Come on, man!" Feizel pleaded, ignoring his protests. "Take her home, have a little fun." He made a crude gesture with his tongue in his cheek just in case Flynn wasn't quite following his meaning.

"Dear God," Flynn said.

"Char-*leee,* I wanna go home now. I really wanna go home," Marlene began to whine, working her way to her feet as Rachel stepped out of the way.

Quite a few people were turning around now and, from the look of it, were enjoying Marlene's slide into oblivion. It was the last sort of notoriety that Flynn needed, and it seemed that the proverbial handwriting was on the sodding wall. *"Bugger!"* he muttered irritably.

Marlene laughed as she moved to slide her arm around his neck. "I love the way you *talk,* Charlie!" she said, then hiccupped.

He sighed, put his arm around her waist, and pulled her into his side, forcing her to stand up, but her limbs were like those of a rag doll.

"Thanks, Ollie. We owe you one," Mr. Feizel said, and with a friendly pat on the arm, he wandered off, leaving Rachel there, holding her service tray.

There was nothing he could say that could possibly improve the situation now, but he looked at Rachel as Marlene waved happily at someone across the room. "I meant to ring," he said.

"Did you, Charlie?"

Flynn winced slightly. "I'd rather like a chance to explain—"

"By all means, Ollie, explain away."

To hell with it, then. He tried, but she had her knickers in a wad, and he had a sot hanging off his bloody arm. "I would. I *will.* But now does not seem a very convenient time for it— Cheers, then," he said irritably, and without another look at her, he dragged Marlene across the room and from the party altogether, rolling his eyes at some of the more colorful things the Americans shouted at him.

He dragged Marlene's almost useless body onto the drive (although she was still lucid enough to laugh at how inoperable her feet were). "What's the matter, Charlie?" she asked, looking up at him, her head balanced precariously on a roly-poly neck.

"If you must know, I'm a bit brassed off at Rachel."

"Who?"

"After all, it's only been two bloody days," he said, making Marlene move. "There is not, as far as I am aware, some rule about the time frame in which one must ring a girl after a kiss, and I did not, to the best of my recollection, say, *I'll ring you in the morning,* or *I'll ring you within forty-eight hours.* I said I would ring, and I fully intended to ring, but I hadn't gotten round to it quite yet, that's all."

"I'm *freezing!* Where's my coat?" Marlene demanded, confused.

"Your coat?" Flynn asked absently as he pulled her down the walk.

"I want my coat!" she wailed.

With a sigh, Flynn stopped just at the end of the house, propped Marlene up against the wall, shrugged out of his coat, draped it round her bony shoulders, and hauled her back into his side. "You're really quite a piece of work, Marlene."

"I just *love* the way you talk!" Marlene giggled.

Flynn pushed on, and at the end of the drive, he saw Joe get out of the driver's seat and stand behind the open door, staring in disbelief as Flynn dragged Marlene to the car.

"Hi!" Marlene said, laughing as she tried to wave. "Who are you?"

"He's a mate who's to give us a lift," Flynn said, and opened the door to the backseat.

"You have got to be kidding me!" Joe exclaimed as he pushed Marlene into the backseat head first.

"Frankly, I'd give all that I had to say that I was," Flynn avowed earnestly as he made certain all of her body parts were inside. He shut the door, braced himself on the car, and looked at Joe. "But unfortunately, I cannot."

Joe groaned. "So what are we going to tell her?"

"Just what I said—that you're a mate who's come to give us a lift."

Joe planted his hands on his hips and thought about it, dipping once to see her, sprawled across the backseat. "Okay," he said at last. "As long as she stays half conscious back there. We just can't let her see any of the equipment in the front." He looked at Flynn again. "So where are we taking your girl, here, dude?"

Right. *Where?* "Bloody rotten hell," Flynn groaned.

●　　●　　●

FORTUNATELY, although Marlene couldn't remember where she was, she could remember her address, but was passed out cold by the time they reached it. A quick search through her purse and Joe found keys. It took the combined efforts of Flynn and Joe to drag Marlene into her upscale condo and deposit her carcass on the couch. When they were quite satisfied she'd not expire, Joe (being the sort of chap that he was) wiped down all the surfaces with a kitchen towel, and they slipped out, leaving a snoring Marlene behind.

Once they had cleared Marlene's neighborhood, Joe asked Flynn what he'd learned about Wasserman.

"Quite friendly, that one. Likes to chat it up," he said. "But I don't believe he's our man."

Joe snorted. "Bullshit. Of course he is. Think about it—he's the first guy to arrive on the scene. There's no evidence of forced entry—"

"It was four o'clock in the afternoon. She might have left the door open at that hour," Flynn interjected.

"Okay, but what about the dog?" Joe shot back. "She's found stabbed to death in the master bedroom, *her* dog is found stabbed to death in the master bedroom, but *his* dog is just roaming free in the kitchen? And don't forget, no one heard the dogs bark all afternoon, so the dogs probably knew the perp. So who does that leave, Sherlock? Her mother and her husband, and her mother has an alibi. Her husband doesn't."

"I haven't quite worked it out," Flynn said truthfully. "But you can't dismiss the fact that a paroled armed robber with a history of assault is suspected in two recent robberies in the area."

"All right . . . but what about the visit we paid to the waterfront? That guy has an alibi a mile long that says he wasn't anywhere near the area that day. Thought that black eye convinced you of that."

"Hardly. If not him, perhaps someone like him."

"Okay, so say it was your robber theory," Joe continued. "The dogs would have *barked,* dude. And no one heard a dog bark all afternoon. It was Wasserman, I am telling you. So now our task is to figure out *why* Wasserman might want his wife dead. And if you ask me, going to a shindig like this not two weeks after burying her is not cool."

"He was actually quite reverent of her memory this evening."

"Uh-huh. And the chicks hanging all over him?"

"Merely passing along their condolences to a bereaved, yet wealthy chap," he said with a grin.

Joe looked at Flynn sidelong as he pulled into the parking lot where Flynn had left his rental. "You really believe it wasn't him?"

"I really believe it."

Joe sighed, shook his head. "This is the problem with the U.K., you know. Not enough homicides to give you guys some instincts!"

Flynn laughed, opened the passenger door. "See you tomorrow, eh?"

"Wouldn't miss it," Joe said.

Flynn got out, waited until Joe drove away before getting in his car.

Then, instead of pointing his car home, he drove in the direction of the Feizel mansion to have the last word with Rachel Lear.

When he arrived back at the mansion, the party was clearly winding down. Several happy guests were on the drive, laughing and screeching at one another as they attempted to find their automobiles. The two footmen were ushering them into the nearest vehicle they could and directing traffic.

Flynn parked at the bottom of the drive and walked up to the house. He did not go in the front door, however, but kept walking straight on, into the shadowy drive that led up to the service entrance.

He heard Rachel's laugh as he rounded a flower bed, then saw her near the garage in the company of the bartender. They were laughing, talking low. Flynn stopped, stepped back, beneath the shadow of a tree. He couldn't quite make out what they were saying, but he got the distinct impression that the chap wanted Rachel to come along with him. After some giggling and nattering on, she gestured behind her, to the mansion. After a few moments, the chap walked on, shoving his hands into his Members Only jacket as he strolled down the drive.

Splendid, Flynn thought. He stepped out of the trees, looked back to where they'd been standing. Rachel was there, walking just outside the service entrance with something draped over her arm. But instead of proceeding down the drive, she paused near the rubbish bins, had a quick look around, shoved the thing on her arm into her bag, had *another* quick look around, then stepped behind the bins . . . and knelt down, out of his sight.

What in God's name is she about?

Flynn couldn't stand it. He moved in that direction, but he heard her voice and stopped again.

"Stop it," she was saying. But to *whom*? "You want to live like this for the rest of your life? Then *stop* it."

The shrill sound of an angry mewling cat startled Flynn, and it got louder and louder as he stood there. At least he thought it was a cat—it might also have been a shrieking banshee.

Then Rachel suddenly screeched, and the animal howled, and a horrible noise of chains and breaking glass and God knew what else could be heard as she suddenly appeared from behind the rubbish bin and began running down the drive.

Flynn stepped in her path. Rachel shrieked again, clamped a hand over her mouth once she recognized him, grabbed his arm, and very nervously glanced over her shoulder. "What are *you* doing here?" she demanded in a very hot whisper.

"One might ask the same of you."

"I'm—"

She was interrupted by a sudden flood of light everywhere, the sound of a door swinging open, and a male voice calling, "Boots?"

Boots?

But Rachel was suddenly and wildly waving her hands at Flynn, gesturing for him to run, and she obviously meant it, for *she* was running. Flynn looked back, saw the shoulder of a man. "What the hell?" the man exclaimed, and Flynn did what Rachel suggested.

He ran.

Chapter Eighteen

HE caught her just past the garage, and with a firm grip on her elbow, forced her to run to his car faster than he would have thought possible in those high-heeled boots. Opening the passenger door, he shoved her inside, then rushed around to the driver's seat, turned over the ignition, and threw the auto into gear before he asked, "*Why* are we running?"

"Because I just did something I shouldn't have done!" she exclaimed breathlessly, twisting in her seat to peer behind them as he drove around the circle drive and down again.

"What?"

"I just broke the law, okay? At least I *think* I broke the law, but I'm not really sure." She turned round to face front again, but scooched down into the seat so that her knees were jammed up against the dash.

"You broke the *law?*" he said in disbelief as he waited for the electronic gate to slowly slide open. She must have done, for she looked dangerously close to tears. And then there was the blood on her hands. Streaks of it.

"I *had* to!" she said frantically. "You wouldn't believe what those people do! Is anyone following us?"

Flynn looked in the rearview. "No—"

"Good! Okay, okay, turn left," she insisted as he carried on through the gate. "Turn left, turn left—*left*!"

Flynn jerked a hard left and sped down the street until he came upon a stop sign. He hit the brakes hard, got hold of his senses. "Whatever you think you've done, Rachel, it will be much easier to face it than to run from it," he said sternly. "Tell me what you've done and I'll help you."

"I set their cat free. Come on, let's go," she said, gesturing for him to drive on.

"You did what?" he asked again as he peered at the blood on her hands.

"Those people chain their cat to a *tree!* Can you believe that? Of course I had to let it go!"

He still wasn't certain she hadn't perhaps pick-axed someone to death as the blood on her hands would indicate. "Let me see if I have this—you set their pet cat free?"

"Yes!" she said defiantly. "Yes, I did! It's not right to keep a cat chained! It goes entirely against their nature! I couldn't stand to see it, so I let it go. In fact, if you'd really like to know, I was going to *steal* it, but the damn thing had a different idea," she said, looking at her hands for the first time. "Oh my God," she said.

"You're bleeding rather badly."

"The cat had some *claws*," she said with wonder.

"Most felines do." He put the car in gear, turned right, heading for Blackstone Boulevard.

"Wait—my car is back there. Where are you going? And why are you *here?*"

"We must clean your hands. No telling what sort of ugly kitty germs you have there, and as to why I'm here, I am asking myself the very same thing."

"But my car is just around the corner and you can just drop me there—"

"I rather think not," he said calmly. "I have something that should do the trick."

"Where?" she asked, her voice full of suspicion.

"My place."

"*Your* place! I can't go to your place!"

"And why not? Have you committed to trawling the city and freeing more cats tonight?"

"No! It's just that . . . Don't you have a blonde waiting for you somewhere, Charlie?"

"Actually, I prefer Flynn instead of Charlie, and if you must know, I can hardly be held responsible when a drunken woman attaches herself to me and refuses to let go."

Rachel did not look convinced.

"Honestly, Rachel, I intend to bandage your hand. I'm not the sort to bring a girl home under false pretense and shag her," he said firmly, although the thought of shagging her did indeed cross his mind and had crossed his mind several times. And was it a cruel hoax of his imagination, or did she seem slightly disappointed by that declaration?

Rachel wasn't disappointed, exactly. She was absolutely *mortified*.

First, the thought of shagging the English guy had crossed her mind plenty of times, but that little premenstrual water retention problem she was having was out of control, building up like a dam in her, and if she didn't get out of this skirt soon, she was certain the dam would, literally, break. And she couldn't put her pants back on because she had wadded them up and stuffed them in her bag in order to free the cat. She'd look like a bag lady if she tried it.

Second, in the event the dam *did* break, she was wholly unprepared for it, in spite of owning an enormous box of tampons that took up half her bathroom. Honestly, she could have sworn she put a couple in her giant bag, but for the life of her, she couldn't find any in there.

And third, she was starving, because Mary the caterer had stated, pretty emphatically, that the food was bought and paid for by the Feizels, and as *they* hadn't invited anyone to eat it, *she* certainly wasn't going to invite them to it.

The upshot was that Rachel had hardly had a bite today,

save a couple of shrimp, and was starving so badly that her stomach was making really weird and frighteningly gluttonous noises that Flynn couldn't hear over the car's engine, but would most *definitely* hear at his place. "I can't," she said again, sliding back up to a sitting position to get some oxygen to her brain.

"Of course you can."

"I really *can't*."

"I won't accept no as an answer, at least not until we've got you properly cleaned up. And then, naturally, I'll need to contact the authorities and report you," he said, all stodgy and British.

Rachel gaped at him.

He flashed her one of his gut-sinking grins. "Not really. I rather imagine they'd think you were completely off your trolley and trot you off to some sort of institution straightaway."

"Or they might issue a citation against the Feizels; did you ever think of that? I'm of half a mind to call the humane society," she insisted.

"Yes, why don't you? And then you can explain to them that while you feared for the poor puss's safety, you set it free in the wilds of Providence and haven't the slightest idea where they might pick it up."

"Good point," she said reluctantly.

"Frankly, I don't quite understand," he said, turning a corner, "why you didn't simply put a spell on the poor thing—you know, bewitch it a bit?" he said, and put a finger to his nose and wiggled it, Samantha Stevens style.

"I suppose that's your attempt at being funny?"

"Can't really say for certain what that was," he said cheerfully, and turned into the parking lot of Corporate Suites, Inc.

"*Now* where are we going?"

"This is home, for the time being." He turned off the car, grabbed her bag and the door handle at the same time.

"*Home?* I thought you said you were staying with friends!" she said suspiciously.

"I did," he said with a wink and popped out, walked briskly around the front of the car to her side, and opened her door. "Come on, then." He offered her his hand.

Rachel reluctantly took it—yep, big and warm, just like she remembered. His fingers closed around her hand, and by some miracle of science, he managed to pop her out of his car.

"Have you got a coat?" he asked once she was standing at the side of the car, looking up and down her body.

"Not with me," she said, pulling her lavender shawl around her. Flynn clucked his opinion of her lack of preparedness, shut the door, opened the backseat door, reached in, and withdrew the trench coat she had seen him wear. Without a word, he draped it around her shoulders, then pulled it together under her chin. "There you are."

Yes, there she was, in an awfully nice coat, made of some sort of silky but sturdy trench-coaty fabric and lined with cashmere.

But the best news of all was that it *engulfed* her.

Still smiling, Flynn put his arm around Rachel's waist, took her bag, and slung it over his shoulder. "What in the hell have you got in here?" he asked as he pulled her into his side to lead her to the entrance of the corporate suites. "Rather feels like a lorry-load of bricks."

It was nice being at his side like that, wearing his coat, and even nicer being pressed against a hot guy. She didn't think she'd ever been pressed up against such a firm and masculine body, and enjoyed it so much that she was reaching the happy point where she didn't care if her skirt exploded off her or not.

They entered the foyer; some kid behind the counter looked up and smiled, his eyes going wide when he saw Rachel. "Hel-*loh*, Mr. Oliver!" he said cheerfully.

"Cheers," Flynn said, and proceeded to lead Rachel across the standard-issue hotel foyer to the elevator. Inside, he punched five and looked up at the floor display. And the whole time he was holding Rachel against him, as if it were the most natural thing to do. It *felt* natural.

When at last they came to the door of his apartment, she asked him who it belonged to.

"My company," he said, and pushed the door open, gave Rachel a nudge across the threshold.

The place looked like a sort of sterile bachelor pad—small and really plastic. A tiny kitchen, completely equipped in miniature appliances, was off to the right, with a nice little bar separating the kitchen from the even smaller dining area.

The living area had a couch and two chairs, a run-of-the-mill coffee table, which was covered with newspapers and work papers and a John Grisham novel. There was also an end table with a huge mauve lamp that matched the mauve frames of the really blah seaside pictures on one wall.

On one chair was an assortment of laundry—either there to go out or having just come in, she couldn't really tell. But she could tell with just a casual glance that he was a boxer as opposed to a brief man.

"Doesn't exactly have a homey feel to it, does it?" he quipped as he tossed his keys onto the dining table, where a stack of mail, several files, and a laptop resided. He put her bag next to his laptop. "Make yourself at home, will you, while I fetch the instruments of my torture," he said and disappeared into a darkened door that she assumed was the bedroom.

Rachel walked further into the room, reluctantly draped his trench coat across the back of a chair at the table where he'd left her bag, and stood there, afraid to sit.

"Come on then, let's have a look."

She turned toward the sound of his voice. He was holding a bottle of something and some cotton balls. "Madam, your surgery awaits," he said, bowing a little, and stepped aside so that she could enter the kitchen.

Rachel gathered her shawl about her and picked up her bag.

He ushered her to the sink, took her bag from her hand. "Must have something frightfully important in that very large container vessel you have there, seeing as you won't let it out of your sight," he said as he put it on the counter behind her. Then he turned on the tap water, picked up a little sample bottle of Anti-Bacterial Dial, and, taking her hand in his, put a little soap in her palm, then put it under the warm water.

"Ouch!" she said as the soap hit the deep scratches the ungrateful cat had left.

"Rather nasty, really," he opined as his fingers began to move on her, gently sudsing the wounds, taking care to clean the deeper scratches, then turning her hand over and washing the back side in the same, delicate manner. Each time his finger moved against her skin, Rachel could feel the electricity of it firing up her arm and into her chest.

His hands were magical—strong, yet gentle, and *huge*. Her hand looked so small in his. She suddenly pictured those big hands on her breasts . . . and remembered herself, jerked her gaze up. He was calmly rinsing the soap from her hand; he had a wonderfully handsome profile—very Anglican, with a thin, straight nose, a strong chin, a strong brow—

"Now the other, if you please," he said, gesturing for her left hand, and wordlessly repeated the same process, shaking his head when he saw a really deep scratch that ran up her wrist, and that sexy strand of hair fell over his eye.

But the caress of his fingers on her wrist was almost her undoing, and now she was seeing images slide past, images of that very same hand, purposeful and commanding, on other parts of her body—

"Am I hurting you?" he asked quietly, glancing at her with a hint of a smile on his lips.

"N-no," she stammered as he rinsed her left hand.

"I'd like to see the cat, frankly," he quipped as he took a dish towel that looked as if it had never been used and pressed it gently against her skin.

As he dried her hands, he looked at her through thick, sandy brown lashes, let his gaze wander her face, smiling softly at the gold in her hair. "You're rather surprising, Rachel Lear," he said quietly. "What with all the witchcraft and weaving and catering and cat-liberating. One can't be entirely certain what will come next."

"The same could be said of *you,* you know. One minute you're Flynn, then you're Charlie, then you're Ollie."

"All quite good blokes, actually," he said with a wink. "This might sting a bit," he said, pulling a bottle of iodine from his trouser pocket.

"It's *iodine?*" She laughed. "What sort of man lives in a corporate apartment, has never used the kitchen, and carries a bottle of iodine?"

"A resourceful one, thank you," he said, smiling, and dabbed some on the first scratch. Rachel sucked a breath. "My mum always said that one must be fully prepared for all eventualities. She was the sort to make certain that our names were indelibly marked in our knickers."

Rachel laughed as he dabbed more iodine on her cuts.

"I'd cringe every time I saw her with a Sharpie in hand," he said as he turned her hand over and began to coat the scratches on her palm.

"I bet you have peanut butter and water on hand in the event of a blackout, right?"

"Kippers, actually," he said dryly. "And I'll have you know that I've certainly used this kitchen on more than one occasion to dry my socks. The oven is perfectly suited for them, having just the right dimensions."

Rachel laughed again, hardly noticing that he had finished one hand and started the other.

"Do you have a father?" she asked, wincing a little as he coated the scratch on her wrist.

"By that do you mean am I the product of some science experiment gone awry, or is he living?"

"Living."

"Indeed he is. He's a putterer, my dear old dad, always on the prowl to mend something around the house and never getting it quite right. And what of your parents?"

"I don't think my mom owns a Sharpie, but she's always had plenty of peanut butter on hand," she said, laughing a little. "And my dad, he's . . ." She stopped there, uncertain what to say. An asshole? Dying? Threatening to come to Providence? "He's not very handy when it comes to the house," she said quickly, and glanced at her hands, now stained hideously purple with iodine. "Wow. It looks worse now than before."

"There's one last thing," Flynn said, and took her right hand, held it in his palm as he examined five small but deep scratches on the back of her hand. He lifted her hand, leaned over, and touched his lips to her fingers. "It's always recommended to seal the cuts with a kiss, or, in the case of a prodigious use of iodine, as close to the cuts as one can possibly get." He kissed her palm. And then her wrist, his mouth casually surrounding her pulse, his lips lingering like gossamer clouds on her skin.

A conflagration of pure lust erupted in her, searing her from top to bottom. She sucked in a cool breath, and Flynn lifted his head, gave her a languidly scorching smile as he took her other hand and turned it over, to the scratch on her wrist.

"All those passions bubbling in you," he said softly. "Cats and history and art. One can't help but wonder how a woman like yourself releases the steam of it all."

"A woman like me can't help but wonder the same thing," she said with a crooked little grin as she gazed at his gorgeous, lush mouth.

"I had every intention of ringing you up, you know," he muttered softly. "But time ran away from me."

"Ooh," she breathed, as he pressed his lips to a soft patch of skin directly above the scratch on her wrist.

"I've been rather swamped with work lately, working long hours," he added, before touching his lips to another spot on her wrist, and lingering there, his mouth warm and wet.

"Oooh . . ." she whispered as he slowly and calmly and, hell, so *expertly* moved his lips up her wrist, to her arm and her elbow, lightly drawing the flesh in between his teeth, nibbling her skin as if it was some delicacy. "But I'll not make the same mistake again."

Rachel just stood there, rooted to her spot, her mind gone to mush, aware of nothing but his mouth and his body.

He kept moving, up the bunched fabric of the sweater she had pushed up over her elbow, his breath seeping hot through the sweater, moving up, until his mouth was at her neck.

"Oh Jesus," she whispered as she bent her head to one side to accommodate him. He laughed somewhere deep in his chest and slowly devoured her neck, caressing the skin with his lips and tongue. His hands landed on her waist and pulled her to him; she could feel the start of an impressive erection in his trousers and thought, with a violent shiver, that all the passions bubbling inside her might burst prematurely, all over his pristine kitchen.

"You smell wonderful," he whispered as he casually moved to her earlobe, taking it in between his teeth. "A bit like vanilla."

This cannot be happening. This can so *not be happening,* she thought wildly as she leaned her head to the side and back, silently willing him to cover every inch of her with his mouth. *Every* inch of her, and she didn't give a damn how bloated she was, for at the moment she felt incredibly sexy.

He drew her earlobe into his mouth, as well as her dangling earring, while his tongue languidly flicked about her lobe. His hands moved slowly up her sides, to the sides of her breasts and gently pressed against them, and around them, cupping them.

A sigh of pure longing escaped her, and Flynn moved his mouth from her ear, letting the earring fall from his mouth and swing, wet, against her skin, as his lips left a warm, damp trail across the skin of her cheek. "Did you know," he murmured, "that in some cultures, a kiss is considered an exchange of souls?"

"Aah," she whispered as his tongue flicked into the corner of her lips, leaving a stunning sensation behind.

"And did you know that there are those who believe the

scent of a woman's skin is more arousing than the touch of it?" he asked, nipping her bottom lip.

Rachel never had the chance to answer, because his tongue slid inside her mouth. She knew nothing after that, only that her hands had found his neck and shoulders, and that his hands had slipped beneath her sweater, sliding over her bare skin, to her breasts, pressing and kneading in rhythm to his lips and tongue. She felt herself on a slippery slope, only moments away from sliding onto the kitchen floor and taking him down with her, to be on top of her. His attentions to her body had turned molten in her groin; there was a wetness building between her legs that made her ache with desire, and her skin felt almost as if it was shimmering beneath her clothing.

Flynn eased her back against the countertop and remarkably, slipped one hand beneath her tight skirt as he continued to kiss her. He easily pushed her skirt up, until his hand was on her hip. His fingers sank into her flesh so that he was gripping her, holding her against his cock, moving suggestively against her while the intensity of his kiss deepened.

Rachel hadn't longed for a man, hadn't craved a man's touch this bad since . . . since *ever*. She hooked one leg around him, pushed against his erection as she pushed her breast into his hand.

Flynn moaned into her mouth, and he suddenly grabbed her by both hips, lifted her off the floor as if she weighed nothing, and pushed her back against the counter as he pushed himself between her legs so that she could feel his erection sliding up and down and around her sex.

Rachel's arms went around his neck, her hands sank into his gorgeous hair, and she wished to heaven he'd unhook her bra.

But Flynn lazily lifted his head, brushed a long strand of curly hair away that had been caught between their mouths. "I believe it's yours," he said, and kissed her forehead.

"Mine," she echoed dreamily as he let go her hips and let her legs ease toward the floor.

"Your mobile," he said, and she realized that the Vivaldi she was hearing in her head was actually in her bag.

Her eyes flew open—no one had ever called her on that phone, and she imagined her mother. *Dad.* Something had happened to Dad—she jerked around frantically fumbled for it, yanking it from her bag. She punched more than one button before she found the one that answered.

"Hello?" she said breathlessly, heard the voice on the other end, and felt her heart sink like a rock.

Chapter Nineteen

+ * +

"RACHEL?" Myron said, his voice full of concern.

How embarrassing. She could just die—and *why* was he calling her, anyway? Why, of all the times he could have called her, the months and weeks and years, did it have to be *now?* "Uh . . . yeah. Hey," she said quietly, and self-consciously yanked down her skirt.

"Jesus, where *are* you? I've been worried sick!" he cried.

"What?" she asked dumbly and stole a quick glimpse of Flynn over her shoulder. He was standing in the middle of the kitchen, hands on hips, looking at her. His hair, she noticed, was all messed up, and she vaguely remembered running her fingers through it.

"I *said* where are you? I've been out of my mind worried!"

"Since when?" she asked in a near hiss as she turned away from Flynn and walked into the other room, gaining a distance of oh, say, six feet.

"Since I came over to make a sandwich and you were gone, that's when! You're *never* out this late, Rachel—it's almost three in the morning!"

Damn, was it that late? "Thanks for the time check, but I happen to be *out* at the moment," she whispered harshly.

"What do you mean, *out*?" Myron demanded just as harshly.

"What do you *think* I mean?" she whispered, and glanced over her shoulder again. Now Flynn was at the sink, cleaning up. Oh *great*. Party over. Thanks, Myron!

She walked deeper into the living area for a little privacy to tell Myron what he could do with his stupid sandwich, but Flynn could still hear everything she was saying.

"You mean . . . you're on a *date*?" Myron's voice, she couldn't help noticing, was full of disbelief.

Rachel sighed to the ceiling. "In a manner of speaking, yes I am," she said coolly.

"Wow," he said, as if trying to wrap his mind around what was obviously a hugely improbable concept. "I mean, I didn't know—"

"Right. So really, thanks for your concern, but—"

"Who is it?" he asked.

"I beg your pardon?"

"Who are you out with? Is it that guy from the bar?" Gawd, he was so irritatingly . . . *incredulous*. Was it that unbelievable? Rachel Lear on a date? Sort of?

"Is it?" he asked again.

"Wait . . . what are you talking about?" she asked, confused now.

"You know, the guy that was in the ladies' room."

"Oh, for Pete's sake, he was *not* in the ladies' room, Myron!"

"It's *that* dude?" he said, skipping right over the ladies' room into incredulity again.

The whole thing was just making her really, really furious. "Yes, *that* dude. Why not that dude?" she hissed.

"Wow."

"Would you please stop saying that?"

"I mean . . . he really didn't seem your type from what I saw of him. Like, at *all*."

She wanted to demand *what* type he saw as being hers, but thought the better of it, seeing as how Flynn was now

at his little table just behind her, tidying everything up.
"Whatever. Look, I really have to go—"

"Hey, did you get any salami this week? I'm standing
here looking, but I don't see any."

If she'd been in a B-movie about the chick who goes off
the deep end, this would be the point she'd take the butcher
knife and chop Myron into teeny-tiny pieces and feed him
to Valicielo's little dog. "Bye," she said indignantly, and
clicked off, over Myron's "what about the sala—"

She fussed with the phone for a moment until she had
figured out how to turn it completely off, then screwed up
her courage and turned around to face Flynn. With a huge
smile plastered on her face, of course. So plastered that it
hurt her cheeks. "Friend," she said, shrugging.

Flynn just gave her a wry smile and walked back into
the kitchen to fetch her bag. "Really, it's quite all right if
you're with someone—"

"No! I'm not with anyone!" she insisted, and really, the
irony was not lost on her that she was, for the first time in
her life, desperate *not* to have a boyfriend. "I don't even
have a dog! That guy is just an old—" The word dick came
to mind. "He's just an old friend, and he was worried that
I wasn't home." She didn't add that he was worried because (a) she apparently had no life and was never unac-
counted for, and (b) she was out of salami.

"Just happened to be driving by, eh?" He smiled again
and glanced none too subtlely at his watch.

All right. She wasn't exactly a girl who had it going on,
that was for sure, but she definitely knew the international
sign for this-is-so-over. She sighed, dropped the phone into
her bag. "Actually, he was *in* my house. I have a couple of
friends who sort of come and go . . . well, more come than
go, actually. Sometimes they need a place to hang out. Or
something to eat," she added with a roll of her eyes, and
realizing, for the first time, maybe, how insane it was for
an ex-boyfriend to have free run of her house. "But it's
really all very platonic, and believe me, even if *he* was interested, I couldn't possibly be *less* interested, and I—"

Flynn put his hand on her arm, stopping her. "It's quite all right, really," he said again. "Like I've told you, it's not as if I expected you were living alone in a hovel just waiting for a chap like me to appear," he said with a charmingly lopsided smile. "And it's certainly not as if I—" Whatever he was about to say, he stopped there, looked briefly but strangely confused, then shook his head, as if to clear it.

But then again, he really didn't need to say anything, because it suddenly dawned on Rachel, and man, she was *so* stupid! All this time she'd been so focused on making sure he knew she didn't have a boyfriend that it hadn't really occurred to her that *he* might be attached. Of course he was! A man like Flynn couldn't be unattached if he tried! What was amazing was that she hadn't thought of it before.

"I see," she said, nodding and smiling as if this sort of thing happened to her all the time. "*You're* the one with the attachment."

"Actually, *I'm* the one who hasn't had a bit of sleep in days, really. I'm quite knackered."

He didn't deny it. Great. Just great.

He picked up his trench and held it open for her. "I think it would be best if we continued this conversation another time. Perhaps over dinner sometime soon."

Fabulous! He was going to dump her before he'd ever really had her, all because Myron was stoned and wanted a salami sandwich and had opened up this can of worms.

"Yeah," she said, and walked into the trench coat, let him put it around her shoulders again.

She leaned over to pick up her bag, but Flynn stopped her with a hand on her shoulder, forcing her around. "Monday I'm all booked up, and then there is the weaving class Tuesday—I'm really looking quite forward to it, you know. I've come round to the whole weaving thing and am thinking of making Mum a little scarf or something fetching like that for Christmas. So would Wednesday be convenient for you? I've heard of a quaint little place on Benefit Street, if you're free."

Rachel blinked. "Are you kidding?"

"Kidding?" he laughed. "Why would I kid about such a thing? What, you thought I'd be put off by the American competition?" he asked, grinning. "Absolutely not. I thought I'd start with dinner, and if that doesn't work, I'll simply challenge him to a duel."

Rachel laughed, decided that she wouldn't be put off by the competition, either. At least not yet.

Flynn smiled fully, his blue-gray eyes warm. "Is Wednesday good for you?"

"Wednesday is great," she said genuinely.

"Smashing," he said, putting his hand on the small of her back and ushering her to the door.

They talked about the party as he drove her to her car. Flynn told her about Marlene and how he'd driven her home and put her on her couch and left her snoring something fierce.

"You've made some impressive friends in your short time here," she said. "How did you meet Mr. Feizel?"

"I did some work for him."

"Computer work?"

"Yes, right. Where's your car? I don't see it."

"Another block," she said, pointing ahead. "But I thought you specialized in bank software."

"Actually, we specialize in anything in which people are willing to pay us gobs of cash."

Rachel laughed at that as he pulled up next to her car. As she gathered her things, he grabbed the trench coat by the collar and pulled her across the car, kissed her once more with passion before getting out and coming around to her side to open her door.

She got out, handed him his coat. "Wednesday, then. You'll promise to keep free, will you?" he asked as he leaned forward to nuzzle her neck.

"I will."

"I'll ring you Monday to make sure you have."

She must have looked doubtful because he laughed and wrapped her in a big bear hug. "I *promise*. You have my permission to cast a spell complete with the eye of the newt if I don't."

"If you don't call me, I just might," she said laughingly, and let him give her one last kiss that was, she was certain, full of his promise.

WHEN she arrived home, Myron was on her couch, remote in hand, his feet encased in dirty socks on the coffee table, and the remains of some sort of sandwich on the table next to his feet. "Hey!" he said brightly as she let herself in.

Rachel walked in, dropped her bag, and glared at Myron. "*What* are you doing, Myron?"

"Watching a movie," he said cheerfully. "*The Matrix.* Dude, it is so . . . so *unreal*," he said with awe.

Stoned again. "Is there a *reason* you are watching it here instead of your own place?" she asked.

He thought about it for a moment. "Not really. Just turned it on when I was eating a sandwich and kind of got caught up." He turned it off, tossed the remote aside, and looked at Rachel. "Hey . . ." he said, as if he was noticing her for the first time. "You look really *hot* tonight."

What was it about a skirt that was at least two sizes too small that made her look hot? She looked like a freaking sausage and she knew it. "Thanks," she said, tossing aside her lavender shawl. "But it's time for you to go, Myron. I want to go to bed."

"Hey, Rach," Myron said, coming to his feet. His corduroy pants, too big as usual, pooled at his ankles. "What's the matter? You seem really uptight."

"I'm not uptight," she lied, but had no idea how to put it. She *was* uptight. Restless. A malcontent. And actually, she'd been uptight for weeks now and all the reasons why were starting to crystallize in her mind. She'd never really broken up with anyone before. Not that there was really anything to break up with Myron, but that's what she wanted to do, wasn't it? The whole scene was getting stale. "I just wish you wouldn't call me in the middle of the night," she blurted.

"Okay," he said, holding up his hands. "That wasn't cool, I get it. But I really was worried, Rach. It's not like you go out, and shit, *I* didn't know you had some guy in the wings." That he said as if he somehow had a right to know.

"So now you do. And you won't call me, right?"

"Yeah," he said. "I get it."

"There's one other thing . . ."

"What's that?"

She looked at Myron standing there, looking concerned and thoughtful and not too terribly stoned at the moment. But she wanted to tell him to quit eating her food, to quit dropping by unannounced and using her stuff. She wanted to tell him that they were through, that they really weren't very good friends, were they? And that she didn't think she wanted to see him anymore. But he looked so vulnerable at the moment, and she considered that part of her feelings about him had to do with a raging case of PMS—this really was the first time these thoughts had broken the surface of her consciousness. Perhaps this wasn't the best time to tell him to get lost. Perhaps she just needed to get out of this skirt and go to bed.

"What is it, Rachel?" he asked, looking all worried now, as if he thought she had committed murder or something. "You can tell me. Whatever it is, I'll help."

That really pissed her off because she really believed Myron meant just that. Whatever was ailing her, he'd help if he could. The only problem was, he never could and she didn't want him to help her. She didn't want him hanging around. She didn't even want to talk to him at the moment.

"Could you just . . . maybe *call* before you drop by?" she asked at last.

Myron looked taken aback. But he nodded after a moment. "Sure," he said, and actually leaned down to pick up his plate. "I'll just clean up a little and go."

"Okay," she said.

Myron walked into the kitchen. She could hear him fumbling around in there as she tried to unfasten the hook on her skirt. When he emerged again, she was already on the stairs, waiting for him to leave.

"Just one last thing. Where's your phone? I programmed a couple of numbers I need."

She sighed, stepped off the stairs, and walked to where she'd put her bag, dug around the junk inside and pulled out the phone. She handed it to Myron on her way back to the stairs. "Will you please lock the door on your way out?"

"Yeah, sure," he muttered, punching the phone on. Rachel walked up the stairs and into her bedroom. A moment later, she heard the front door shut below her.

She peeled off her skirt, leaned up against the wall, seriously contemplated crying.

Damn PMS.

Chapter Twenty

✦ ✦ ✦

RACHEL tracked down Dagne after returning from the gym the next afternoon and told her they had to go shopping. She'd ridden fifteen miles on her stationary bike but was still feeling restless.

"I thought you were broke," Dagne said.

"I *am* broke. But I have a credit card and I made a hundred bucks last night, *and* I need something really, really hip to wear because I have a date."

Dagne gasped. "Get out!" she screeched over the phone. "What happened?"

"I'll tell you when I pick you up," Rachel said, grinning.

"Okay, give me a half hour. I could use something new to wear on my date with Glenn."

"Glenn? I thought you were trying to get rid of Glenn!"

"I was. But he invited me to see a play," she said, as if that explained everything. "I'll see you in a half hour."

AN hour later, Rachel and Dagne were in a Hope Street boutique that Dagne said had the hippest clothes in town.

As they wandered through the racks and the shelves, Rachel told Dagne about the party, about Mike, and then Flynn showing up, and about the blonde, and giving Mike her number after the party was over, then freeing the cat (which Dagne got very excited about, insisting that freeing a "sister" would bring her good karma), and running into Flynn again—literally.

"Ran into him, nothing. He came back for you," Dagne said with much assurance. "He's into you."

"He didn't come back for me," Rachel laughed. But as she picked up a dark red velvet jacket and held it up to her body to check it out in the mirror, she wondered if he had.

"Bullshit, of course he did. Try this," Dagne said, handing Rachel a cobalt blue dress that hit right above her knees.

"God, this is *gorgeous,*" Rachel said as she held it up to her body and looked at herself in the mirror.

"That's a great color on you," Dagne said as she wandered away. "Try it on."

It was a great color for her, but first—Rachel checked the tag and almost gagged when she saw the price of $450 dangling daintily from the sleeve.

She carefully hung it back on the rack.

"So he comes back for you, takes you to his apartment, and then what?" Dagne asked.

Rachel gave her a wink. "He cleaned up the cat scratches," she said, showing Dagne the back of her hands. "And then he kissed me."

"And?"

"And . . . it was fabulous."

"So did you *do* it?" Dagne squealed excitedly.

Rachel's smile faded. "No." She was still disappointed about that.

"Damn it! It's that British thing, I'm telling you!" Dagne said with a disgusted shake of her head.

"Wrong, girlfriend. He was very . . . *ready.* Nothing happened because *Myron* called me on my cell."

"No way!"

"Oh yeah."

"What is *with* that guy?"

"He's an idiot," Rachel said, trying on a hat.

"Never mind. When you go out this week, you'll get lucky."

Rachel sighed, looked at the cobalt blue dress again. "Yeah, I thought about that. The thing is . . . I really *like* this guy, Dagne. He is so hot . . . and he's funny, and he's nice, and he's got that fabulous accent . . . but I don't think it's really a good idea," Rachel said. "He's only here temporarily—"

"Right, which is all the more reason to get you some," Dagne interjected. "No strings attached." She picked up a sheer gold blouse and held it up to her.

"All the more reason not to get involved at all," Rachel corrected her. "I could really fall for this guy, so what's the point?"

"Okay. What if he's here for three months? That's not so temporary. You could be missing a really great life experience. You know how I feel about life experiences—"

"Yes, yes," Rachel said, cutting her off before she launched into her theory that life experiences carried over into your next life and gave you firmer footing in whatever you turned out to be. It was a sort of mystical theory that Rachel didn't fully understand, but she was not foolish enough to admit that because Dagne would want to *make* her understand.

"But look at it the other way. What if he's here for three months?" Rachel asked. "I can't even pay the utility bill. The last thing I need is to get involved with someone and burden them with all that. Besides, I have to finish my dissertation." Either Dagne had something in her eye, or she was rolling her eyes at that one. "I *do*," Rachel insisted.

"So what, you're going to deny yourself *life* because you're a little short on cash and you're in school? Get real! Who knows where this might lead? And if doesn't lead anywhere, at *least* you get laid. When is the last time you had sex, anyway?"

"I think he's involved with someone."

"So?"

"*So?*" Rachel echoed. "That's not right, Dagne. In fact, it's really, really wrong!"

"Oh great, so now you're going to be his conscience?"

Rachel turned away, looked at sweaters and jackets, refusing to debate the issue further. But Dagne was not finished. She marched to where Rachel was standing, picked up the cobalt blue dress again. "This is the one you want. With those killer boots you have, you are one drop-dead gorgeous babe."

Rachel looked longingly at the dress again, shaking her head. "I can't afford it," she said, but took it from Dagne and went behind a curtain to try it on.

"Yes, you can. You have a credit card!" Dagne's disembodied voice reminded her.

"My *maxed* credit card," Rachel muttered. She emerged a few moments later. "And I don't have any jewelry to wear with it," she added as she marched to the mirror to have a look.

Dear God, she looked . . . *hot.* Not fat. Not big-boned. Sort of curvy and . . . *hot.*

"You don't have jewelry, but I do. I got something off eBay that's perfect for this. You'll love it," Dagne said, standing behind Rachel.

"I can't afford it," Rachel said again as she turned every which way, checking it out. Damn, even her *butt* looked good!

"*Charge* it. And don't worry about the money. I'm working that out."

Rachel laughed at Dagne's reflection in the mirror. "What do you mean? What, are you going to cast a spell for a money tree?"

"Maybe," she grinned. "You'll see later."

Rachel laughed and looked at her reflection one last time. She looked good. Really good. And it was sort of amazing, seeing as how she hadn't lost any weight, but her body *did* seem different—sort of rearranged.

"Wow," a salesclerk said, her reflection appearing over the opposite shoulder from Dagne. "That looks *great* on you. Not many women can really carry that off."

"Really?" Rachel squeaked.

"Oh yeah," the girl said, nodding emphatically. "You really need curves for this. You *make* that dress."

Impossibly pleased, Rachel beamed at herself. But then she remembered her little finance problem, and her smile faded, and she shook her head. "God, this is stupid," she said, walking, dejected, back to the curtain to change out of it. "I don't even know if I'm going to have another temp job from one day to the next! The last thing I need to do is spend this much money on something like this!"

"Will you just trust me?" Dagne yelled through the curtain, and the moment Rachel emerged, she grabbed the dress from her hand. Before Rachel could speak, Dagne took the dress, plus the gold blouse and winter-white skirt she'd picked for herself, and marched to the counter, held them out to the salesclerk. "We'll take them!"

A brand-new charge and no way to pay it later, Rachel and Dagne drove to an obscure side street and a little shop called Makin' Magick! to buy oils and candles for Dagne's witchcraft.

They also had some amulets marked down 50 percent, and Rachel, never one to pass up a bargain, was all over that.

Then they went to Rachel's, because Dagne had bought the necessary items to put a sex spell on Flynn and would not be deterred, as she was very worried about his being British. They went outside to commune with Mother Nature while they cast it.

"I'm freezing my balls off," Rachel hissed as she stood on the other side of her detached garage from the last spell casting, hugging herself, checking every few seconds to see if Mr. Valicielo was going to call the cops.

"This is perfect," Dagne said. "Stop whining." She had Mexican vanilla, honey, and ground almonds, which she had mixed inside. She held up the bowl to Rachel. "Spit in it three times."

"I will not spit into that bowl!" Rachel cried.

"Spit!" Dagne said, waving the thing beneath her nose. "The sooner you spit, the sooner we can go inside."

Rachel spit. Dagne grinned maniacally. "Now you have to stir it with your finger, counterclockwise. Just three times. No more, no less."

With a grimace, Rachel pulled her hands from her mittens and stirred. "You're really freaking me out," she said, but she stirred three times exactly, no more, no less.

Dagne gave a little laugh and went down on her knees, lit the fat candle she'd brought for atmosphere, and handed Rachel an apple and a knife. "Cut it in half, then carve a triangle."

Rachel did as she was told, shaking her head.

Dagne gestured for her to give the apple halves back when she was done and carefully set them aside. "Okay, lift your sweater," she said, picking up the bowl and holding it up to Rachel. "Then dip three fingers into the mixture and make a triangle on your belly, point up. Make *sure* the point is up!"

"Are you nuts?" Rachel demanded. "Why do I let you talk me into these things?"

"If you don't hurry up, Mr. Valicielo is going to come out here," Dagne warned her.

Rachel lifted her sweater, dipped in three fingers, and made a triangle. Point *up*.

"Now, dip more," Dagne instructed in hushed tones, "and repeat it. But this time, look at the moon and repeat this while you trace the triangle over and over: Scents of the goddess I put in me, to bring my special night irresistibility."

Rachel frowned. "How many times must I make that ridiculous statement?"

"Until you *feel* it," Dagne said with a huge smile as she clasped her hands to her breast.

Honestly. Okay, well, the night air was frigid on her belly, so Rachel dipped her fingers into the mixture, looked at the moon, and began to chant, "Scents of the goddess I put in me, to bring my special night irresistibility."

This, she repeated, over and over until her vision began to blur and she thought she was getting frostbite—but then suddenly, Rachel felt a shot of warmth down her spine, from her neck to her tailbone, and lowered her head, blinking. "I *felt* it!" she whispered. "At least I think I did!" She paused, rubbed her shoulder, wondered if maybe it wasn't from leaning her head back like that for too long.

Whatever it was, Dagne was on her feet, the two apple halves in her hand. "That's it, that's it!" she shrieked and grabbed Rachel's hand, jerked her to run behind her.

Into the house they ran, to one of Rachel's big potted ferns. "Bury it," Dagne said so excited she could hardly transfer the apple to Rachel.

"*Bury* it?" Rachel exclaimed, looking at the big pot.

"Don't wait! Bury it, bury it!"

Rachel dug into the soil until she'd made a hole, then quickly put the apple inside and covered it with dirt. She and Dagne stood there for a moment, staring at the pot.

"That's it. My work here is done," Dagne said and put her hands on her hips.

"Thank God," Rachel said and turned, headed to the kitchen to wash her belly and her hands, but she noticed her message light was blinking. "Hey, it worked!" She laughed and punched the button on her way by.

"Ah . . . hi, Rachel. This is Mike. You know, from last night?" He paused, chuckled a little. "Listen, I tried to call your cell, but some guy answered . . ."

"Ohmigod, it *did* work," a wide-eyed Dagne whispered reverently.

"You weren't doing the old wrong number routine, were you?" Mike chuckled again as Rachel ran to her bag and dug through it with her clean hand best she could. No cell. God*dammit*, Myron!

"So if this is really your crib, will you give me a call? I was hoping we could get together sometime over Thanksgiving if you're around." He rattled off his phone number, made some joke about giving her the right number, and said he'd be in later.

The message clicked off. Rachel glared at Dagne. "Myron took my phone again, that asshole!"

"So are you going to call him?" Dagne asked excitedly, blowing right past Myron.

"No! I'm going out with Flynn, remember?"

"Don't be an idiot, Rachel! Go out with *both* of them! Be in *charge* of your life! Don't let opportunities pass you up! Don't let men dictate who you will see! *You* decide which one suits you!"

She was so adamant that Rachel almost expected her to pull out some *Women of the World Unite!* banner and march down the street. Nevertheless, she thought about it. It seemed weird, especially for her, who wasn't exactly experienced in dating at all. Much less two guys. At once.

Dagne must have read her thoughts because she followed her into the kitchen and made her case while Rachel cleaned up. "Look at it this way. What if you go out with Flynn and discover it is true what they say about English guys—that they can't fuck to save their lives? Then what? Mike could be the best lay in town, and you've missed it! There's no law that says you can't see more than one guy at once! The smart, *chic* women see as many guys as they can."

"They do?" Rachel asked timidly.

"Of course they do! Call him!" she insisted, waving her hand at the phone.

Dagne was right. Not that this was about getting laid, really, although that would be very nice. But she really had no reason to hold back. For the first time in her life, a couple of guys were interested in Miss Fortune. Why not take advantage of it? It sure wasn't like she had anything to lose, was it? Hell, she deserved it! She had spent her entire life being the chubby, doll-faced little sister of the two most beautiful women in Houston, and watched them go on date after date while she sat home and read romance novels.

For once in her life, she had guys after her, and by God, she wasn't going to pass it up. She picked up the phone, punched in the number Mike had left, felt her heart beating like a drum in her chest as it rang once, then twice, then three—

"Yo," he said when he picked up the phone.

"Ah . . . Mike?"

"Rachel?" he said and sounded genuinely glad to hear from her. "Great! You called!"

Rachel looked at Dagne, gave her a thumbs-up. Dagne grinned, waved her hands in a way that said Rachel was to talk. "I'm really sorry about the cell phone thing. I wasn't trying to ditch you, I swear it."

"Oh that," he said, laughing. "Well, I'm glad you called all the same. So what are you doing?"

Well, I've shopped for another date, and then I cast a spell, whataboutyou . . . "Hanging out with a friend. And you?"

"Football. The Pats are beating the shit out of the Jets. So listen, what do you say we get together over the Thanksgiving holiday? I mean, are you going to be around?"

"Yes," Rachel said. "I'd like that."

"Great." He sounded relieved. "I'm really glad we met, Rachel. I never expected to meet someone as hot as you at those catered things."

Hot. He thought she was *hot*.

"So, why don't we plan on hooking up the Friday after Thanksgiving? I've got a gig down at the shore to work for a couple of weeks, and then see the folks on Thanksgiving Day. But I'm coming back that Friday. Think you'll be free?"

"Yeah, I think so."

"Fantastic. There's a club I go to you might like—great food, great music."

It sounded wonderful. Mike sounded wonderful. "That sounds wonderful," she said, beaming.

"All right. I'll give you a call late in the week and we'll firm it up."

Now she was positively levitating. "Thanks, Mike. I'm looking forward to it." She hung up, looked up at Dagne.

"I have to go shopping again!" she said with a squeal of laughter.

FLYNN woke to the sound of a trumpeting phone on Sunday and groped his way out of bed, found the phone, then noticed he had an erection the size of a skyscraper. That would be due to one very erotic dream of a girl named Rachel, thank you.

"Hello," he croaked into the phone.

"Flynn darling!" Iris fawned.

Oh *God.* "Iris."

"I should be very cross with you, Flynn Oliver! You promised to ring me yesterday, do you recall?"

"Sorry—I had to work."

"They sound like monsters there, always making you work," she said petulantly. "When are you coming home, Flynnie?"

"I can't say," he told her truthfully. Both projects were taking more time than he'd anticipated. "It may be a while yet."

Iris sighed her displeasure. "Oh, Flynn," she said softly. "I do believe you'll never forgive me."

He rolled his eyes, sat on the couch, arms braced on his knees. "Iris, please, couldn't this all possibly wait until I've returned to jolly old England?"

"No, it can't. I don't think you understand how crushed I am by the whole thing, and I've scarcely slept a wink since you've been gone, darling. I think about the wonderful times we had together, and how foolish it was of me to jeopardize everything simply because I was lonely."

"Iris—"

"The thing is, lambkins, that I never meant to harm *us*. I really rather thought of it as nothing more than a silly little tryst. It meant absolutely nothing."

"Yes, so you've said several times now. But really, how am I to trust you, Iris? How can I know that when I'm off on assignment, you aren't shagging the neighbor?"

"Because I am swearing on my life that I won't do it again," she said, her voice pleading. "I am giving you my solemn vow to be ever faithful."

Flynn suppressed a groan.

"Oh darling, you *know* how much I love you! Remember that afternoon we drove to Windsor and took the little boat out onto the river?"

He remembered it; of course he remembered it. He'd been terribly happy then—it was a couple of months before he'd gone off so terribly sentimental and asked her to marry him.

That day at Windsor, she'd been in the front of the boat, lounging against several pillows, a parasol over her head, looking quite delectable as they floated along to a picnic spot she knew about. He had adored that day—they had laughed and talked about a number of things, as comfortable together as an old pair of slippers, and he'd seen his future stretch before him—a beautiful wife, happy children, a dog or two.

"Remember the spot where we picnicked?" she asked, her voice suddenly husky.

He recalled that as well and leaned back against the couch. In a secluded area, on a thick quilt, she had seduced him, had enticed him, with the help of strawberries and cream, to eat her as if she were a luscious dessert. Just the memory of it aroused him, and he put his hand on top of his boxers, felt his dick growing thick again.

"Think of it, darling," she said softly. "Remember it with me. I'm thinking of it, too, touching myself precisely where you *licked* me," she whispered. "Do you remember? Wouldn't you like to lick me again like you did that day? *Wouldn't you like to feel me come again?*"

His dick was beginning to pulse, and he slipped his hand inside his boxers, stroked it. "Go on," he said hoarsely, as his fingers curled tightly around it.

"It was delicious," she purred. "I was quite wet, just as I am now, and insatiable. I couldn't get enough of you. I came so hard, but I only wanted more. I said, 'Flynn, darling, *shag* me,' " She moaned into the phone.

But Flynn's hand stilled. This was all a lot of fun, but Iris had skipped one small detail he could never skip. That same day, he had asked her to return the favor, but she had wrinkled her nose with disgust and vowed that her lips would never go near "that thing."

"And I remember how it felt when you slid inside me—"

"You're forgetting something, aren't you, Iris?" he said, withdrawing his hand from his boxers and sitting up. "You're forgetting that I wanted something from you, too."

She said nothing for a moment, but he noticed her breathing stilled. "Oh Flynn, why must you bring that up now?" she asked softly. "I thought we were having a spot of fun."

"Because it's important to me. Now let's play another game of recall, shall we?"

"Flynn—"

"Let's start with the day I discovered you and Paul. You tried to brush it off by saying that you had only—and these were your precise words—*blown* him on occasion."

Iris wisely said nothing.

"I actually loved you, Iris. But I'm not certain you ever loved me."

"Of course I did, Flynn! What a horrid thing to say! And I still *do* love you! Desperately so! Why do you think I keep ringing you? I am quite despondent and quite frantic to salvage what we had!" she cried.

"I'm hardly convinced," he said calmly.

"What other possible motive could I have?" she demanded, her voice going shrill.

"Actually, that's an excellent question, and one I haven't quite put my finger on. But I suspect it has something to do with my family's ties to the Duke of Alnwick and your esteem of the aristocracy."

"That's horrid!"

"Perhaps it is. As I said, I haven't quite worked it all through. But I don't think I want to work it through, Iris. I think I'm quite done with you, really. It's over. Really very much over. And now, if you will excuse me, I must run along, for I've got quite a lot to do here."

"Flynn!" she cried. "Please don't hang up! Don't toss everything we had into the rubbish bin!"

"I haven't tossed a bloody thing—that was you, love," he said, and hung up, tossed the phone aside, dragged his hands through his hair.

That was the first time she'd said she loved him since he had discovered her infidelity. He wondered if even Iris realized it. It mattered little now, for he really felt as if he was completely and irrevocably through with Iris Willow-Throckmorton.

He sighed, stood to go shower, and walked past the little table where he kept his laptop and files.

Something caught his eye as he walked past, though, and he paused, leaned down to look at the table.

It was glitter. She'd left a bit of her sparkle behind.

With a smile, Flynn headed for the shower.

Chapter Twenty-one

* ✦ ✦

Subject: RE: RE: RE: RE: RE: [FWD: Re: What's going on?]
From: <earthangel@hotmail.com>
To: <reparrish72@aol.com>
CC: <rmanning70@houston.rr.com>

Rmanning70@houston.rr.com wrote:

. . . So where have you been, you little witch? Ha haaa. I'm figuring no news is no news. I'm guessing the guy you "conjured" up didn't work out, right? Well, don't worry about it, kid. Your time will come, and like you said, you really don't have time for dating right now with all that's on your plate. And besides, half the time it's not all it's cracked up to be, believe me—remember Evan?

P.S. Don't forget the book.

P.S.S. You don't have to explain white magic, duh. It's all stupid.

What's that supposed to mean, don't worry about it? I'm not worried. Why should I be worried? Do you think I have something to be worried about? Like what? Like always a bridesmaid, never a bride worried? Is that what you mean? Like if a woman isn't married or significantly involved in her 30s then there must be something wrong with her? There is nothing wrong with me! I just said it wasn't that spectacular, like don't write home to Mom and Dad, I'm not going to reach the exalted status of married Lear girl anytime soon. But I'm still going to SEE him. Actually, I'm seeing him and another guy. So let's see . . . that's one guy—white magic; one guy—just my good looks and charm. See? Nothing to be worried about! I'm still playing the field that's all. And I won't forget the stinkin' book!

Subject: Imodium AD contest
From: Lillian Stanton <lilandel@aol.com>
To: Rachel Ellen Lear <earthangel@hotmail.com>

Hi honey. Thanks for the name of the stuff you gave Grandpa at Blue Cross. He still ain't 100% but he's better you know how he is has to discuss each detail till he's just blue in the face or you are. But a funny thing happened. Imodium AD had a little thing on the back of the box that said they'd pay five hundred dollars for a funny Imodium story well El just got up and typed them an e-mail about one day when he was playing golf and had an attack. Let's just say he wasn't in the pond looking for lost balls. But I had put a thimble full of Imodium in his golf bag and sure enough it cleared his problem right up. I'll let you know if Grandpa wins the contest. He says if he does he's going to share it with every one of you girls. What's the weather in Providence it is still too warm here and the holidays right around the corner. Well gotta go fix his supper because if he don't eat at five I'm gonna hear about it. By the way I found this diet in Good Housekeeping. I hope you like grapefruit as much as I do because you really need to eat a lot of it according to the article but I'm sending it to you see for yourself. Luv U. Grandma

When Rachel hit the gym Monday morning, Lori, the desk jockey, said, "*Wow!* I mean, you've been coming almost a whole *month* now!" as Rachel signed in. And judging by her half-sneer, she was losing the office pool on that one.

Rachel did twenty miles on the bike and even a few weights before heading off for Turbo Temps with a pay slip and the caterer's black skirt in hand. An hour later, she left Turbo Temps without the skirt and ten dollars lighter, but with a paycheck and a three-day job. Yessir, as of 7:30 in the morning, she was entering the heady world of fishing industry's processing and production phases.

Her next stop was the Brown University library so that she could continue her search for a dissertation topic. By the time she arrived home, her head was hurting and her sight was blurred from reading such tiny print all afternoon, but she believed she was very close to settling on a topic.

Fortunately, her sight wasn't so blurred that she couldn't see the red light blinking on her answering machine. She put down her bag and checked the display. There were three messages; she punched the playback button.

"Hey. Call me," Dagne said into the phone. In the background, Rachel could hear the familiar sound of a computer keyboard being tapped at warp speed and figured Dagne was buying off eBay again. "See you," she said, and hung up.

Rachel took off her coat and kicked off her shoes as the answering machine moved to the second message. "Ah . . .

Rachel, this is Flynn. You know—the chap who saved you from certain incarceration?"

Rachel immediately turned around to beam happily at the answering machine.

"As it happens, I've been thinking quite a lot about you, and frankly, I'm rather disappointed you're not in. In the future, I'd request that you might better anticipate when I might ring you," he said, and she turned her beaming up a notch. "We're still on for Wednesday, are we? If it's not a bother, could you possibly ring me and let me know for certain? There's a love." He rattled off the number. Rachel memorized it, etched it into her conscious thoughts for all of time. "Cheers, then," he said, and clicked off.

She was still smiling when the machine moved to the last message. "This is Mr. Donald Gregory calling for Miss Rachel Lear."

Surprised, Rachel looked at the machine. "I regret to bother you at home, but I must reluctantly inform you that I will not be attending class tomorrow evening," he said evenly. "My wife passed away today after a lengthy illness."

He said it as if he was announcing he'd had a gall bladder attack.

Rachel didn't know if she should be more startled by his apathy at having lost his wife or the fact that he *had* a wife. She would have sworn he had a boy toy or an ancient queen stashed away in a tiny apartment.

"While this is very sad news, it is also a blessing," he continued stoically. "She has really . . . suffered . . . for a very long time," he said, his voice catching just a little. "In any event, I shall be absent from class. Thank you, and have a good day." The answering machine clicked off.

That poor, poor man! Regardless of how ill his wife had been, or for how long, it had to be excruciatingly painful to lose her so close to the holidays. It reminded Rachel of her father's cancer, and she felt the burn of tears in her throat just thinking about the awful possibility of his death.

She shook off the morbid thought, glanced at the clock,

picked up the phone and dialed Myron's number. His answering machine picked up. *"I'm not in. Please leave your name, a brief message, and a number where I may reach you."*

"Myron, my cell?" she said to the machine, wondering if that was brief enough for him. "Did you *borrow* it again? If you did, I'd really like it back." She clicked off, dialed her cell phone, but got her own voice mail and hung up. She next dialed Flynn's number.

He wasn't in, either, and more was the pity. *"Hi,* Flynn," she said, trying to sound sexy, and wincing at her lack of finesse. "We're definitely on for Wednesday. I'm really looking forward to it. And of course, there is class tomorrow evening. I think you'll find my loom techniques are very . . . *good,"* she said, unable to think of a sexy word, and said a quick good-bye, then hung up and moaned, *"Loom* techniques? *Gawd,* Rachel!" And with that, she stomped away from the phone, headed upstairs, determined to pay a visit to Mr. Gregory, poor thing.

After successfully locating the class papers and Mr. Gregory's address, she dressed in a long denim skirt, a ruby sweater, and Doc Martens, then donned a denim jacket and scarf and walked out onto her drive. She was fitting her key in the car lock when Mr. Valicielo stepped out of the shadows to the fender of her Beetle. "Judas Priest!" she cried with alarm. "Mr. Valicielo, you scared me!"

"Sorry," he said, ducking his little head. She took a breath, noticed he was wearing a giant parka that swallowed him, and a fishing hat that was barely on his head, which gave her the impression that he had slapped it on in a hurry. "I'm sorry to bother you, but I can't ever seem to find you at home. You, ah . . . you said you'd have money to remove the tree?" he reminded her, glancing uneasily at said tree.

Right. She had said that. But that was before she'd gone and spent her money on a new dress for her first date in eons. "Yeah, I did," she said, nodding thoughtfully, and looked at the tree. What was the big deal, anyway? It didn't look like the fence was any more damaged than when the tree first fell. "The thing is, I didn't make as much as I hoped," she explained.

Mr. Valicielo pressed his lips together so hard that they almost disappeared. "Your father has money, doesn't he? Maybe he'll loan you the money."

"Well, there's just a little bit of a problem there," she said, holding up her fingers to show him just how little a problem, which of course he could not see through her mittens. "My dad doesn't support me—"

"I meant, just ask him for a loan."

"*Riiiight* . . . but not even that. He's, ah . . . well . . . here's the thing, Mr. Valicielo," she said, studying the angle of her sideview mirror intently. "The long and short of it is, he has sort of cut me off."

She peeked at him. Even in the dim glow of her porch light, she could see the color drain from his face. He looked at the tree, put his hands on his bony hips (sort of— his jacket was far too big), and turned a pretty hellacious glare on her. "I don't know if I can be any plainer, Miss Lear," he said, going all formal on her. "*Your* tree is ruining *my* fence. If you don't have it removed, I am prepared to take you to small claims court!"

"*What?*" she sputtered. She had visions of Judge Judy and cameras and a rooting section filled with dozens of Valicielo clones. "Mr. Valicielo!" she cried. "Please don't do that! I promise I'm saving money as fast as I can to have it removed! You just have to give me a little time!"

Now he tried to fold his arms in that huge parka, but could only manage to grab each elbow as he shifted his weight, still glaring at her from beneath his stupid fishing hat. "I'm sorry, Miss Lear, but you are running out of time!" he declared. "I have tried to be patient, I have tried to give you time, but the fact is, you have made no effort to dispose of that tree, and it is ruining my fence!" he said sharply, and pivoted about, marching back into the dark and toward his house.

"Miserable old coot," she said.

"I can hear you!" he shouted from the edge of darkness. Rachel quickly got in her car and drove off.

This was the last thing she needed. But for the moment, she was refusing to let Mr. Valicielo ruin her good spirits. She had Mr. Gregory to worry about after all, and besides, SHE HAD A DATE THIS WEEK, THANK YOU! Right, like some stupid tree was going to mess *that* up.

But a teeny-tiny voice kept whispering *small claims court* in the back of her mind.

SHE found Mr. Gregory's house easily enough—it was in Mount Pleasant, an older, established neighborhood where neat bungalows and cottages lined the streets. A porch light was on, but there was no light coming from the windows, save a sliver that peeked out between a crack in the curtains.

Rachel hoisted her bag onto her shoulder, walked up the old steps and across the wooden porch, and rapped sharply on the door. She heard a floor creak somewhere, then footsteps, steady and slow. The footfall stopped just on the other side of the door, and although she couldn't see anyone, she smiled and waved at the peephole.

One lock bolt slid open. Then a deadbolt. Then two more bolts and maybe even a chain lock before the door creaked open a couple of inches. "*Ra*chel?" Mr. Gregory said.

"Hi, Mr. Gregory." He did not open the door farther, nor did he speak. "I, ah . . . I got your message," she said uncertainly, "and I came to see if I could do anything for you."

He said nothing.

"In Texas, when someone suffers the loss of a loved one, friends and neighbors come to pay their respects and help if they can," she explained.

"You're an instructor, not a friend or neighbor," he informed her.

"Right. Okay. Well . . . I guess I'll just go," she said, gesturing lamely toward her car.

"Don't be ridiculous," he said sternly. "Of course you should come in now that you've come all this way," he said, pushing the screen door open.

She was having some serious second thoughts about this altogether and very reluctantly stepped inside the dark interior. She was immediately hit with the strong smell of antiseptic spray and had the very morbid thought that maybe his wife died days ago, and he'd kept her here until he could come to terms with it. *Eeew!*

But one glance at Mr. Gregory and she changed her mind. He looked a lot like Mr. Rogers in his button-up sweater and his house slippers as he led her through a very narrow and dark hallway and into a small kitchen that was spotless. Rachel expected lots of different dishes to be lying around, mail and phone messages—something to indicate his life had been turned upside down. But it looked like no one had eaten or cooked in that kitchen in years.

Mr. Gregory shuffled toward the refrigerator.

"I'm very sorry to hear about your wife, Mr. Gregory," Rachel said as he opened the fridge and looked inside.

"Don't be." He bent over, peered into the empty racks. The man had no groceries at all—unless you called a tub of butter and a half pint of buttermilk groceries. "She was sick for a long, long time," he said, straightening up again. "Bedridden and lacking most of her faculties. She's in a much better place now," he added, and carefully shut the door. "I'd offer you something, but I haven't been able to get to the market. I'll bury Clara Wednesday."

The look on his face belied his casual tone, and Rachel's heart wrenched. "Do you have any family? Children?"

Mr. Gregory shook his head.

"Siblings? Cousins?"

He gestured for her to follow him. "No sibling or cousins, either," he said as they entered the living room, which contained one Barcalounger, a positively ancient TV on which

CNN was broadcasting with no sound, and a couch covered in plastic. On one wall was a cross-stitched picture of a wolf. That was the only ornament besides an end table, a lamp, and a remote control. On the end table was a newspaper, neatly folded. "What few friends we had drifted away over the years with Clara's illness," Mr. Gregory added as he slid into the Barcalounger and hiked the foot rest. "Please sit down," he said, motioning to the couch.

Rachel sat on the very edge of the plastic. "I beg your pardon for asking this . . . but surely you aren't going to bury your wife alone, are you?"

"A pastor will be there to officiate."

"I mean," she said gently, "anyone besides the pastor."

He thought for a moment and shook his head. "Might be a neighbor or two will show up, but I really don't expect so. Clara's been bedridden for so many years," he said, and it looked, from where Rachel was sitting, as if he was tearing up.

Her heart went out to him—she could not imagine how awful it must be to be so totally alone at the last stage of one's life. A cold shiver ran down her spine, and she put a hand to her gut, wondered if this could be her someday, sitting in an empty house, living an empty life, being an empty shell of a person.

"Mr. Gregory, is there anything I can do?" she asked. "Is there someone I can call? Make you some tea?"

He shook his head. "I'm all right. Just haven't had a chance to get to the market," he said again, and stared blankly at the silent TV.

"Let me do that for you," Rachel said eagerly, glad to have a way to help, and began digging in her purse for a piece of paper.

"I couldn't—"

"Of course you could! Really, it's no imposition. I was going to stop by the market on my way home anyway," she lied. "Just tell me what you need."

Mr. Gregory eyed her suspiciously. "You'd do that for me?"

"I'd be more than happy to do it for you," she said, smiling as warmly as she could.

After a moment, he shrugged. "All right," he said. "I really don't need much. Maybe some bread and milk. And prunes. A big jar. You know, the one they have on the bottom shelf . . ."

SHE found a Shaw's Supermarket nearby, and with basket in hand, gathered up some staples, and then went in search of prunes. Not prune juice, but the actual black and squishy prunes in a jar. And no cans. Only a jar. Mr. Gregory was very adamant about that.

On the prune aisle, there were more varieties and brands than one could possibly imagine would be available for the lowly prune, so she picked up two competing brands, one jar in each hand, to figure out why that was.

So naturally, Flynn would choose that moment to appear out of nowhere and startle her out of her wits again. "Mind, you're blocking the prunes," he said from behind her.

Rachel jerked around, clutching the two jars of prunes to her chest. "What are you doing here?" she exclaimed breathlessly.

He grinned, held up a package of razors.

With a laugh, Rachel relaxed. "You know, I could really begin to believe you are following me around Providence."

"Actually, I was going to accuse you of the same," he said, and glanced at the jars she was holding, lifted one thick brow above the other.

Rachel looked down at the jars and felt her face flame. "Okay," she said quickly, "they aren't for me—"

"That's quite a lot of prunes, isn't it? I can only hope they are for a spell of some sort."

"Oh *no*," she said with exaggerated seriousness. "We prefer bird shit for spells."

Flynn laughed. "Who wouldn't?"

"Actually, these are for Mr. Gregory."

"Who?" he asked as his smiling gaze roamed her face.

"Mr. Gregory. You know, the elderly gentleman from weaving class?"

"Ah." Flynn nodded. "How could I have possibly forgotten?" He glanced at the prunes again, and lifted that brow once more. "It's really none of my affair, but do you and Mr. Gregory have some sort of relationship I should know about?"

Rachel laughed, put one of the prune jars in her basket and the other on the shelf. "No! I hardly know the man. But his wife died—"

"His wife?" Flynn interrupted, looking just as confused as she had been earlier.

"I know . . . a *wife*," she whispered. "I was really surprised," she continued, looking around. "I thought he sort of swung the other way," she added in a very soft whisper. "Apparently, she'd been ill for a long time and finally died. And he hasn't had a chance to get to the market, what with all the stuff he had to do, so I told him I'd come for him."

Flynn's cheerful smile faded to a lopsided and soft smile, and he casually reached up to push a curl behind her ear that had fallen over her eye.

Rachel's blood immediately began to rush warm—the man really had that effect on her. "A-and," she continued unsteadily, "he's apparently a huge fan of prunes. Jarred prunes. No cans. And definitely no fresh prunes, as they are, you know . . . too tangy."

"You're quite amazing, Rachel Lear."

"I know, amazingly easy?" she said laughingly, looking down at her prunes.

"No . . . just amazing. I don't believe I've ever known anyone quite like you."

His gaze was actually very intense, as if he was seeing her in a different light all of a sudden, and unused to that sort of acute attention, Rachel shyly glanced down, made a show of rearranging the things in her basket and turned toward the head of the aisle. "You mean anyone quite as weird," she said with another self-conscious laugh.

"I mean anyone as captivating," he said.

Damn, he was good! Rachel glanced up at him; he was just looking at her, his gray eyes holding her gaze, the warmth in them filtering down to the tips of her toes so that she felt all sparkly inside. "Do you say that to all the girls?" she asked with a smile.

"I've never said it before this very moment," he said, and put his hand on her arm, sort of stroked it fondly. It seemed to Rachel that in that moment, there was a weird lavender glow around them.

But then a woman turned onto the aisle with an overflowing cart, one child hanging on to the handle, and another in the baby seat, and the lavender glow disappeared.

Rachel laughed sheepishly, adjusted the heavy basket in her hands. "So what are you doing in this part of town? More local homicide investigations?" she asked with a wink. "Interviewing chaps, that sort of thing?"

Flynn's cheerful countenance returned and he took the basket from her hand, put his free hand on the small of her back as they began to walk to the front of the aisle. "Actually, no. Someone threw a spanner in the works on that front, unfortunately, so tonight I've been investigating another sort of crime."

"*Do* tell," Rachel said with a laugh.

"Oh, I couldn't possibly bore you with the details of it—just a bloke who nicked a few things, that's all."

"What things?"

"The Eiffel Tower. The *Mona Lisa.* And we're not entirely certain, but we think perhaps that Staten Island ferry, of all things."

Rachel laughed as they reached the cashier stand. "And how is it that a computer guy gets involved in all these crimes?" she asked as she began to unload the basket and put the items in front of the cashier.

"The usual way," Flynn said with a shrug. "Hard work and perseverance."

"You're funny."

Flynn put down the pack of razors on the cashier's conveyor and pulled out his wallet.

"And you came all the way to Mount Pleasant to buy razors? The last time I checked, it's clear across town from your apartment."

"What's a few miles? I've heard they have spectacular razors here," he said with a wink. "And for a chap who's a bit lost driving about on the wrong side of the road, it seemed the perfect place to pull in and have a look at a map."

She was about to ask him what he was lost from, but the guy behind the stand said, "Thirty-two seventeen, lady." She paid for the groceries, Flynn paid for his razors, and he accompanied her to the door, where he paused to pull the collar of his trench coat up around his ears. "Rather cold out tonight," he said idly.

"Yeah," she sighed, and glanced out the glass doors, thinking of Mr. Gregory. "It's sort of poignant, isn't it? That feeling of being all alone is so cold anyway, but to feel it on such a frigid night . . ."

Flynn glanced down at her with a strange expression. "Are you cold, Rachel?"

The question startled her; he was looking at her very seriously, and she realized he was asking if she was lonely. "Who, me? *Nah,*" she said, waving a hand at him.

He nodded, looked toward the parking lot. "I can't think of ever a time that it's particularly good to be alone."

Of course not. She figured a man like him would hardly ever be alone, would have all sorts of hangers-on and women surrounding him. But then again, the man was constantly surprising her. And at the moment, he was looking impossibly gorgeous, and was holding the door open for her.

On the sidewalk, he kissed her cheek, pressing his lips to cheek for a long moment, then pushed the errant curl from her eye again before letting his hand drift down her arm. "Wednesday, is it?"

"Wednesday," she said, giving him a mittened thumbs-up.

He winked, shoved his hands in his pocket, and strode down the sidewalk. But he paused a few feet from her, turning partway. "My condolences to Mr. Gregory."

"Thank you. I'll pass them along." Flynn walked on, turned the corner, to where, she presumed, he had parked his car.

Rachel turned in the other direction, toward her car.

She stayed on with Mr. Gregory for a little while after that, watching him eat an entire bowl of prunes and trying not to gag while they watched an episode of *Trading Spaces*. Mr. Gregory, she discovered, was just as hooked on the show as were she and Dagne.

When she finally left, Mr. Gregory walked her to the door and opened it. Before Rachel could step through, he stuck out his hand.

"Thank you," he said, shaking her hand vigorously. "Thank you very much."

That night, Rachel tried to read about her knight, but soon put it aside and thought of Mr. Gregory. And when she slipped into sleep, she dreamed of Flynn and his gray eyes. He was trying to tell her something, but she couldn't hear him, and when she tried to move closer to him, a giant spoon fell on her car and smashed it, and then Mr. Valicielo was chasing her with the spoon.

BACK at his flat, Flynn pulled out his mobile and hit the speed dial. "Yeah," a sleepy Joe said.

In the background, Flynn could hear the sound of some sort of sport blaring out of a telly. "Once again, you owe me," he said pleasantly as he loosened his tie.

"Oh, yeah?"

"One of the weavers had a death in his family and she'd gone to pay her respects."

"No kidding," Joe said thoughtfully.

"I wouldn't kid about something as dreadfully serious as ten quid, mate," Flynn said with a grin, reminding him of a little wager they'd made earlier.

"Yeah, yeah, you'll get your ten quid."

"Just so we're clear, that's about fourteen dollars American," Flynn reminded him.

Joe snorted at that. "Did you get anything else?" he asked.

"Nothing, really. Except that earlier, before she arrived home, the friend—the tall one with the blondish-red hair?"

"Yeah," Joe said appreciatively.

"She stopped by and left with two paper bags that appeared to be quite heavy."

"Oh, yeah?"

"I thought it a bit odd . . . seemed rather like she was filching it."

"That whole damn crew is odd if you ask me," Joe said, and yawned. "Okay, pal. See you bright and early in the A.M."

"With my ten quid, if you please. Cheers," Flynn said, and hung up over Joe's grousing.

He walked into the tiny bedroom, removed his coat and tie, then sat on the edge of the bed for a moment, staring out over the parking lot of the Corporate Suites. He did not see the concrete below him, but rather Rachel's smiling face, the flush of cold in her cheeks, the tiny little curls that framed her face, and the fullness of her lips. He was quite looking forward to their evening on Wednesday. Quite. So much so, that he was beginning to worry a bit about himself. These feelings were starting to approach Richter levels, and he wasn't entirely certain what to do about that.

This was quite bothersome, really, as there was a bit of reality gnawing a hole through him, and as of late, it felt as if that hole was becoming unmanageably large.

Chapter Twenty-two

✦ ✦
✦

FLYNN and Joe caught up with Mr. Castaneda, the Wassermans' yardman, on Tuesday, who assured them he had not seen anyone come or go from the Wasserman house the day Mrs. Wasserman was murdered.

"I left around two," he told them at the burger joint where they had convinced him to meet. "Didn't see no one."

"Did you have anyone helping you that day, Mr. Castaneda?"

"No, no one. It's too cold for anything to grow, so I just go by and rake leaves."

"You gonna eat those fries?" Joe asked Flynn.

Flynn turned his head and gave Joe a look. "Please. Help yourself."

"Thanks," he said, and picked up a handful.

Flynn turned his attention back to Mr. Castaneda. "Did you happen to note if Mr. and Mrs. Wasserman were home that afternoon?"

"I know she was. I saw her walking her dog," he said.

"And did you happen to see Mr. Wasserman that morning?"

"No. I think he was already gone when I got there," Mr. Castaneda said as he watched Joe take another handful of Flynn's fries. Joe noticed him looking at him and offered him one. Mr. Castaneda shook his head.

"And you saw no one else come or go from the house but Mrs. Wasserman. Is that likewise correct?"

"Yeah," he said, nodding.

"What about that pickle? You gonna eat that pickle?" Joe asked Flynn.

Flynn abruptly pushed his plate in front of Joe, who smiled and picked up the pickle.

"And again, how long would you say you were there, sir?" Flynn asked.

"Got there around eleven and left at two."

"Smashing, thanks. Just one more thing, if you'll indulge me—has anyone lent you a hand at the Wassermans' house prior to that morning?"

"Sure!" Mr. Castaneda said. "In the summer, there's too much work to be done. I use my nephew."

"His name?"

"Joaquin Castaneda," he said readily. "But he didn't do it, Mr. Oliver. He's in the army now."

"Anyone in addition to Joaquin?" he asked as Joe polished off the pickles and the last of the fries.

Mr. Castaneda squinted his eyes as he thought about that. "Maybe once or twice."

"This summer?" Flynn pressed.

Mr. Castaneda shrugged. "Maybe. I don't remember. If I did, it was in the spring, I think. One of Joaquin's friends." He glanced at his watch. "Are we about done here? I have to get back to work. I got two yards this afternoon."

"All done," Flynn said, withdrawing his wallet and tossing a few bills on the table. "We appreciate your help, sir," he said, coming to his feet. Joe did, too, but not before reaching for a toothpick. "Thank you kindly for your time."

Mr. Castaneda nodded and got up to go. But before he got too far, Flynn said, "I do beg your pardon, Mr.

Castaneda, but there is one more little thing." He casually put his wallet in his trousers. "Did you like the Wassermans' dogs?"

"Their *dogs?*" he asked, confused. "I'm not really a dog man—my wife's got cats, and you know—"

"Did they bark?"

He thought about that for a moment and shook his head. "Not at me. I don't know, I didn't see them too much. They were always inside."

Flynn smiled, extended his hand to the yard man. "Thank you again," he said, shaking the old man's hand.

Mr. Castaneda beat a hasty exit out the door. Joe chuckled as the door closed behind him and clapped Flynn on the back. "Hate to say I told you so, but I told you so. It was Wasserman."

"And exactly how do you come round to that stunning conclusion?" Flynn asked as he picked up the check and started for the counter.

"Easy. Listen to a pro, pal. The yard man doesn't see anyone coming or going all day. The lady is dead since late morning—"

"Or early afternoon, after Mr. Castaneda's departure. The coroner did give quite a long range to time of death. You might recall reading that fact in the coroner's report," he said as he handed the pretty girl behind the register a twenty-dollar bill.

"Just like you to read all the crap. Me? I just called up the doc and asked him straight up to save myself some time. So anyway, Mom and Mom's dog are already dead when Castaneda arrives. Pop has already left for work. No one hears or sees a thing that morning. It's pretty clear cut, I'd say. Pop killed Mom and Mom's dog, made it look like some sort of break-in, and skipped off to work. Just need to wrap up a motive and there you have it."

The girl gave Flynn change, let her middle finger slide suggestively across his palm. He gave her a slight wink and pocketed the change. "Ah, but therein lies the rub, eh?" he remarked as he turned and motioned for Joe to proceed him. "You haven't got the slightest bit of a motive, have you?"

"Like I said," Joe announced as they walked into the bright sunshine of a brilliant fall day. "Watch a pro at work. Bet I've got a motive before Thanksgiving."

"I'll bet I've got the killer before then," Flynn said, and grinned. "One hundred of your American dollars says I do."

"You're on, pal," Joe said with a snort, and punched the automatic lock on his key chain. "So what have you got going on the other deal?" he asked as he opened the driver's door.

"I've a weaving class this evening," Flynn said as they got into the car.

Joe laughed. "Dude, you have *got* to be the first guy in the history of the world to take a fucking weaving class just to get inside some chick's pants!"

"Rather effective, wouldn't you say?" Flynn asked with a grin. "At least more so than rubbing against her to show her *what I'm working with,*" he said, mimicking Joe's earlier advice in an American accent.

"Hey, whatever floats your boat. I happen to like the direct approach. Sounds like you prefer the . . . what do you call it? The *nancy-boy* approach."

He started the car over Flynn's objections to the use of the term *nancy-boy,* and he was hardly done with it. At the precinct, he told the chaps he worked with that Flynn was off to a weaving class, and before Flynn could escape, they were asking after personalized pot holders. Not to be outdone, and to their considerable and collective amusement, he'd called them a fat lot of uncultured plebeians as he had taken his leave.

FLYNN arrived late to class, and quite on purpose, hoping that he'd be dismissed from it altogether for his tardiness. But as luck would have it, no one seemed to notice his tardiness.

So much for being expelled.

The other students were already paired off at one of four looms; Chantal and Tiffinnae, obviously, David and Lucy (David insisting that Lucy stay on his right so that he could get a proper feel for the loom, the nesh wimp), and Jason and Rachel were working together. Rather, Rachel was stringing the loom while Jason was watching her with the expression of a young man desperately in love.

That left Flynn to share a loom with Sandy, who, he couldn't help noticing, was on crutches this week.

"Twisted my ankle," she said cheerfully as Flynn pulled up a chair.

"Put a bit of ice on it?" he asked absently as Rachel turned and smiled at him, her eyes lighting up.

"Oh, I did everything, trust me," Sandy quickly assured him. "I probably should have stayed off of it, 'cause I'm pretty sure I tore some ligaments, and if that's the case, then I might as well get used to getting around on these things!" she said brightly, and pulled a giant plastic bottle of Gatorade from her bag. "You ever jack up your ankle, Finn?" she asked as she began to stack a variety of pharmaceutical bottles on the small table next to her.

"I broke my leg playing football," he said.

"Whew!" Sandy laughed, waving her hand at him. "Don't *even* get me started on broken limbs!"

Flynn rather thought he'd take her advice on that score. "So what have we here?" he asked, looking at the giant loom. As Sandy began to explain, he felt Rachel come up behind him. He knew, because he caught the faint scent of vanilla, and because he felt her energy. That rattled him a bit—Flynn was not the sort of man to "feel" energy—but when he turned around, Rachel was smiling down at him, and the radiance of that smile filled the room.

It was little wonder Jason was such a besotted bloke, he thought absently as he returned her brilliant smile. She wore a white turtleneck sweater and a long gray knit skirt that hugged her curvaceous frame. She wore her dark curly hair in a rather remarkable and complex knot at her nape, and a pair of dangling crystal earrings.

"Hello," she said, smiling softly.

"Hello," he said, returning the smile.

"Miss Lear!" Chantal suddenly shouted across the room. "Tiffinnae done jammed this thing!"

"Uh-uh, *she* jammed it, Miss Lear!" Tiffinnae quickly shot back.

Rachel's smile did not hide the glimmer of exasperation in her eyes, and with a sigh, she said, "I'll check back with you guys later." With a subtle wink, she went off to see what could be done for the loom.

Flynn looked at Sandy. "Mr. Gregory's wife died," she announced.

"Oh dear."

"I know what you're thinking," she said. "I sure didn't think he was straight. And *married?* Uh-uh, I would never have guessed that. Well anyway, the funeral is tomorrow, and we're all going."

"Are you?" he asked as he reached to touch some of the yarn already strung through the loom.

"Don't touch that!" Sandy said sharply, then quickly smiled. "I'll show you how to do it," she said, and resumed her explanation of how the loom worked.

And just as Flynn was about to doze off, Rachel reappeared at his side and he'd never been quite so happy to see her. "Everything all right?"

"Yes, of course," he said. "Sandy was telling me all about the loom."

Rachel's sympathetic smile indicated she knew his agony.

"I told him about the funeral tomorrow, and how we're all going," Sandy added.

"Oh. Well." Rachel glanced uneasily at Flynn. "We just thought . . . not that *you* should think this, but . . . it's just that poor Mr. Gregory has no family or friends. And we thought, how horrible to lose someone as precious as your spouse, then face that final good-bye alone," she said, and for a moment, she lowered her head, touched a hand to her eyes.

That puzzled Flynn greatly—yes, of course it was sad and all that, but to be so distraught for a man she couldn't possibly know? He felt a little embarrassed and pushed a hand through his hair. "I, ah . . . I really am very sorry."

"Uh . . . Rachel?" Jason had turned around, was eyeing Flynn suspiciously. "I did what you said."

"Yes, right. Okay," she said, and walked away to help Jason. Flynn watched her intently, fascinated by her sorrow.

"Hello? We're doing a project here, remember?" Sandy testily reminded Flynn.

"Righto, that we are."

"Sorry if I seem a little mean, but I think I'm getting a migraine," Sandy informed him, and picked up a pharmaceutical bottle. "I hope I brought the right medicine."

God in heaven, so did Flynn.

FLYNN managed to endure the entire class without actually being allowed to touch anything, but was uncommonly bored for the two-hour duration. As Sandy worked and talked, he found himself watching Rachel move from loom to loom. She had a way about her that put everyone at ease, an ability to relate to people from all walks, the sort of person that most people were instantly drawn to.

Certainly he was.

But when the class thankfully came to an end, the others packed up their things and left—Chantal and Tiffinnae helping Sandy, who could not possibly negotiate her very large bag and her crutches—which left Flynn and, predictably, Jason, who seemed determined to wait Flynn out.

Flynn obliged him. He got up, walked to the door, and looked back at Rachel. "Ah, Rachel, there was something I meant to inquire."

"Sure," she said, and walked to where he stood.

Flynn smiled, glanced over her head at Jason, who was pretending to examine the loom. "I'd rather hoped to have a chance to chat, but I think Jason won't allow it," he whispered.

She smiled sadly as she glanced over her shoulder. "He's a very lonely kid. I think he sees me as some sort of big sister," she whispered back.

"Actually, I think it's possible he sees you as the love of his life." He smiled. "But I'm the lucky chap who has the date."

"You do! And I'm really looking forward to it."

"So am I." He glanced over her shoulder, to where Jason was still hunched down over the loom, waiting for him to leave. Flynn took a step closer to Rachel and leaned over, whispered in her ear, "Frankly, since you left that rather provocative message on my telephone, I've been imagining what it is, exactly, you do with your loom," he said, and laughed low at her blush. "Shall I come round at eight?"

"That would be great."

He gave her a subtle wink, opened the door, and walked out.

"Ah, Flynn?" she asked, poking her head out the door as he began to walk down the corridor.

"Yes?" he asked, glancing over his shoulder.

"Umm . . . don't you want to know where I live?" she asked, her expression curious.

Bloody hell—her blue eyes had knocked him off balance again, but he quickly recovered with a laugh. "That would indeed be helpful." And he withdrew a small notebook from his coat pocket to take note of the direction he already knew quite well.

Chapter Twenty-three

* * *

THE next morning, Rachel began her fish-packing stint and decided she had finally reached rock bottom. The fish were disgusting and the stench was enough to turn the most iron-clad of stomachs.

That afternoon, after a long hot bath that still hadn't quite removed the stench from her nostrils, Rachel attended Mrs. Gregory's funeral and, thanks to Chantal and Tiffinnae, the impromptu reception of sorts that occurred thereafter.

It was at the reception that one of them came up with the bright idea to have Thanksgiving together, and before Rachel could stop it, they had agreed to have it at her house.

When she arrived home, with hardly enough time to prepare for her date, her answering machine was blinking with five messages.

The first one was from Dad. "Rachel, call me when you get in, please," he said in a voice that sounded more impatient than anything else. So she made a mental note to call him someday and went on to the next four.

They were all from Dagne. Her first message was to re-

port on her date with Glenn, which, she said, had been surprisingly *hot*. And then she had called wanting her spell
book for another date with Glenn. Her third message was
to inform Rachel she had come by and picked up the spell
book, and her fourth message was her explanation that she
had returned the spell book, along with a cream Rachel
was to use in conjunction with spell number forty-two before *her* date tonight, because that combination had apparently worked wonders for Dagne. She ended the call with
a plea to call her first thing in the morning, and oh yes,
she'd left a little gift for her on the dining room table.

Rachel found the cream on the dining room table, along
with the spell book, and a lovely moonstone necklace. The
accompanying note from Dagne explained she had picked
it up off eBay for her and she was to wear it, as it was her
stone and had been blessed, naturally, by Dagne, Goddess
of Kitsch.

Rachel was not above kitsch.

She took the cream, moonstone, and spell book upstairs
to her bedroom and master bath with the idea of having
one last try at ridding herself of the fish smell, please God.

By the time Flynn arrived, she had donned her new
dress and boots, had her hair artfully arranged at the nape
of her neck with delicate sliver filigree wending through it,
and was wearing the moonstone necklace that went very
well with her crystal earrings, a combination that, according to the spell book, would bring her harmony.

She didn't know if she had any harmony, but for the
first time in a very long time, Rachel felt pretty.

When she opened the door, Flynn smiled broadly and
stood back to admire the full length of her. "God," he said.
"You're bloody gorgeous!"

That remark earned him a smile that was at least the
wattage of two million candles. Rachel moved aside so he
could come in, and as he stepped across the threshold,
he leaned forward as if to kiss her lightly, but then thought
the better of it and wrapped his arms around her, kissed her
more fully as Rachel giggled against his mouth.

"Beg your pardon, but you do have that effect on me," he said with a lopsided grin as she laughingly wiped the lipstick from his lips. "You look smashing, Rachel."

She laughed, grabbed up her coat. Flynn took it from her hands, held it open for her to slip into, and as she straightened the sleeves of her dress, he nuzzled her neck. "That perfume you are wearing . . . it smells a bit different," he murmured against her skin.

"Fish?" she asked weakly.

"More like . . . *cake*. Whatever is, it certainly has my full attention."

"That's the intent," she said, relieved that it was not fish and appreciative of just how powerful a little bit of vanilla and a scent spell could be. She belted her coat, turned around, and noticed Flynn was looking around the living area of her bungalow. "I know, I know, it's really cluttered," she said apologetically. "You're probably the neat type, right?"

"Not exactly," he said. "I'm never in one place long enough to be one sort or the other."

Why that should make her feel strangely insecure, Rachel wasn't certain, other than the fact that he had used the words *never* and *in one place* all in one sentence. But never mind that—she glanced around, winced a little as she realized what he was seeing—books and plants were everywhere, dozens of strange knickknacks, a stagnant, half-completed project on a large loom, and crystals hanging in each window to ensure positive energy flow.

It occurred to her that it might be better if they got out of there before he could see the witchcraft stuff in the dining room that might, to the casual observer, make her seem totally wacked.

"Ready?" she asked, opening the door. She picked up her big bag, slung it over her shoulder. Not exactly a look, but in a previous era of eschewing anything that wasn't made from natural plant fibers, she had given away all her really cool purses.

"Ah—yes!" Flynn said, dragging his gaze from the

room to her, and caught the door, held it open for her. He waited for her to lock the door, then took her hand and escorted her to his car.

On the drive to the restaurant, Flynn asked her about Mrs. Gregory's funeral.

"Not particularly remarkable as far as those things go," she said. "No one came except some of the weaving class—Sandy, Chantal, Tiffinnae, and Jason and me."

"I'm sure the old chap was quite touched," Flynn said.

"Actually, no," Rachel said with a snort. "He seemed more annoyed than thankful, particularly when the pastor began to speak of the afterlife, and Chantal and Tiffinnae answered every point with a *hallelujah,* or a *praise Jesus,* or a more generic, *mmm-hmm.*"

"I can picture it all quite clearly," Flynn said with a grin.

"And then, after the service, the church ladies set up a buffet, and Chantal and Tiffinnae decided we must all stay so that Mr. Gregory wouldn't have to eat alone. We all agreed it was pretty good," she said, but looked at Flynn from the corner of her eye. "Everyone except Sandy, of course. Acid reflux, you know. But I had some Tums in my bag just in case, so she managed to choke down two plateloads."

He laughed heartily at that, and Rachel continued to regale him with the very long list of maladies that had afflicted Sandy, until they reached the restaurant.

The restaurant was in one of the old historic homes that had been turned into an establishment for cozy couples dining with fancy tablecloths and real candles. Rachel had been in lots of places like this, usually as the third wheel in her parents' night out. This was the first time, however, she had been invited to such a restaurant by a man who was not related to her, and it gave her a whole new sort of thrill.

They were seated at a small bay window, and Flynn ordered a bottle of wine (a very *expensive* bottle of wine, ooh-la-la), and when the steward had poured the wine and left, Flynn lifted his glass. "A toast. To an intriguingly beautiful woman with brains and compassion for cats and old men and witches."

Rachel beamed, touched her glass to his.

"It was really quite nice of you to do that for Mr. Gregory." Flynn nodded sincerely. "He didn't strike me as an endearing chap."

"Oh, he's not the least bit endearing." Rachel smiled—actually, as the afternoon had worn on, she'd been rather irritated with the old coot. "I didn't intend to have a whole caravan attend her funeral . . . but when he called and left a message, there had been something in his voice . . ." (And there *had* been something in his voice—the pitch of loneliness, maybe. Or desperation. Who knew?) "And he wasn't very glad to see me when I went to his house. He wasn't going to let me in. He said I was just an instructor, not a friend or neighbor."

"Sodding bastard," Flynn said cheerfully.

Rachel laughed. "But he finally let me in, and once he did, I think he was glad that I had come." She paused again, looked at the candle flame. "I can't imagine just how . . . deep that ache must reach, you know? It must feel as if an organ has been wrenched right out of you," she said, and damn it all to hell if she didn't feel herself tearing up for the thousandth time that day as an image of her father flashed across her mind. Talk about sodding bastards . . . and now he was really going to piss her off by dying.

Before she could hide the sorrow, Flynn reached across the table and covered her hand with his. "Yes, I would think it must," he said softly, and squeezed her hand. "But I can't imagine this distress is just for Mr. Gregory, is it?"

"No . . ." she said, shaking her head with a self-conscious smile. "You're on to me." She drew a deep breath, gained her composure as Flynn laced her fingers through his. "My dad has colon cancer, and it keeps coming back. We never know from one month to the next what the prognosis is because it seems to change all the time. And when Mr. Gregory's wife died . . . I just can't seem to stop thinking about how it all might end for my parents, or how devastating it would be to lose someone who has been part of your entire life, from start to finish." She bit her lower lip to keep tears in the back of her eyes, told herself to get a goddamn grip.

But Flynn smiled sympathetically and said, "For what it's worth, I rather think that real love between two people is, by its very nature, quite devastating. And I rather suspect that when it's time to face that long good night, if one hasn't felt love's devastation in one form or another, then perhaps one hasn't known true love at all. That's the payoff, I suppose."

The profundity of that statement and the elegance with which he had said it astounded her. Rachel swallowed back any tears. "That was . . . beautiful," she said sincerely. "And you're *right*."

He flashed that lopsided grin at her.

"It sounds as if you speak from personal experience," she added, which was the wrong thing to say, apparently, because a strange look clouded Flynn's face. His smile faded as he looked at her, and it almost seemed as if he was seeing someone else altogether.

"Actually, no," he said, after an awkward moment. "I've certainly had my share of love affairs, I suppose, but I can honestly say I've never been devastated." He sat back, seemed to consider that a moment more.

She thought she'd just leave that alone for the time being. "What about your folks? Are they well?" she asked before sipping her wine.

"Oh, quite," he said with a chuckle. "They operate a small B and B in Butler Cropwell. A Scottish B and B, mind you."

"Scottish?"

"Mmm. It's all the rage, you know. Mum has a sign hanging out front—*Cead mile failte*—"

"A hundred thousand welcomes," Rachel said.

Flynn blinked. "You knew that, did you?"

"Let's just say I've been to the U.K. a few times."

"An Anglophile, eh? Then perhaps you'd like my parents' little B and B. Glen Farley, it's called, yet another name fabricated for the Scots-loving Americans. In fact," he said, his eyes shining with amusement, "I should take you there to test their theory—to see if you, by sole virtue of being American, are so charmed that you actually believe yourself to be in Scotland, and therefore are so filled with delight that you dance a jig. Scottish jigs, of course, are performed Thursday evenings. Uncle Harry dabbles in bagpipes, and my father fancies himself quite the dancer—or jig artist, as he prefers."

"You're joking!" Rachel exclaimed gleefully.

"Why in God's name would I joke about something as very painful as that?" he deadpanned, and casually sipped his wine.

With a laugh, Rachel asked, "What of your siblings? Where are they?"

"Ah, my siblings," he said, and told her about his family as they dined on shrimp-stuffed mushrooms for their first course. His sister was married and had two "perfectly horrid" children. His brother was a banker, which, Flynn said, his parents considered a proper occupation.

"Don't they consider a computer programmer to be a proper occupation?"

Flynn smiled enigmatically. "It's not quite as grand as they had hoped. In truth, I always wanted to be a homicide investigator, the sort portrayed in the old Humphrey Bogart movies. But alas, that was not on my parents' list of suitable occupations and I was steered in another direction."

"So what would they consider a suitable occupation?"

"Prince consort," he said. "And what about your family?"

Rachel gave him the usual, well-rehearsed rundown. Her father and mother had been together since they were teens, but were currently in marriage therapy as they tried to sort through years of stuff.

"Sounds perfectly awful," Flynn said as the waiter cleared the appetizers.

"You cannot begin to even imagine," Rachel quipped with a roll of her eyes, and explained to Flynn how her father was a self-made man, had built a fortune in freight, but how that fortune came with a price for their family.

Flynn listened intently, nodding thoughtfully as she spoke, offering insights here and there, but without sounding superior or patronizing.

"Siblings?" he asked as the main course of mahi-mahi was served.

Rachel laughed. "Two older sisters." She told him about Robin and Rebecca, and a little about their lives, but leaving out, at least for the time being, the part about them being beautiful and successful and nothing at all like their baby sister, Miss Fortune.

They talked easily and openly over dinner, like a pair of old friends. They had both traveled a good deal. And they were both prolific readers and had, on their bookshelves, some of the same authors, although Flynn liked thrillers and Rachel had a definite taste for character literature.

Their conversation was so easy that Rachel even talked a little about her interest in metaphysics, astrology, Buddhism, and a host of other things she typically reserved for several months out when meeting someone new. But Flynn took it all in stride, and while he did not subscribe to the same theories, he was open about them, asking honest questions and listening to her with interest. When the subject rolled around to astrology, and Flynn said he was born under the Pisces sign with Cancer rising, Rachel thought she'd died and gone to heaven. There could not be a better match for her than that, and she should know—she'd studied her birth chart enough times to know.

That evening felt nothing short of magical, either the conjured type or pure coincidence. Rachel could count on one hand the number of times she'd made such a connection with another person, so quickly, and so strongly. Not once did she feel self-conscious, or inelegant. Not once did she have that feeling that he thought she was a wacky broad tilting at windmills.

And Flynn—wow. She had a growing and abiding sense of respect for Flynn. He was witty, and unerringly cheerful. He was respectful and thoughtful and considerate and very smart, and really just delicious to look at.

He asked her how she had landed on ancient British history in her schooling, and she confessed a fascination with kings and queens and knights and romance. "The medieval period was such a brutal time, yet such a romantic time, too."

"As to romance," Flynn said, "how are you on that?"

She laughed. "I'm definitely okay with it."

He smiled, propped his elbows on the table and leaned forward, his gaze intent. "Do you prefer the subtle approach? Such as candlelight dinners, and flowers, and vintage wine?"

"*Ooh* . . . that sounds excellent," she murmured. "What other romance is there?"

"Well, there is the purely Neanderthal approach, of course—a bit rougher in the wooing, but in terms of instant gratification, it can't be beat."

She laughed a little, leaned forward to match his intent gaze, and said, "With a good bottle of wine, I could be persuaded."

Flynn's brows lifted in surprise. "Smashing!" he said with a deep smile. "All right, how about the metrosexual romance?"

"The *what?*" she asked, wrinkling her nose with a laugh.

"Clearly you are not versed on the metrosexual option. This romance encompasses the finer points of both your subtle and Neanderthal romances. For example, a suave, debonair chap such as myself may begin his romance with dinner and wine. But in the course of it, he begins to notice things," he said, his gaze falling to her mouth. "Like how her lips look as if they were carved from coral, or how her eyes are the exact color of the Pacific Ocean. Or perhaps," he said, reaching across the table to take her hand, "he can't help notice the curve of her waist into her hip, and that curve makes him think of the little hollow just above her bum that he longs to kiss, or how she might arch her back when she enjoys lovemaking."

"Wow," Rachel murmured, feeling a stirring deep down.

"Wow," he echoed, lacing his fingers with hers. "And perhaps, by the time the dessert is served, this chap says no thank you to the flan, for he's thinking of something infinitely more delectable." His gaze casually drifted to her chest. "So he asks the object of his desire if she might enjoy a nightcap," he said as he caressed her hand with his thumb, "but he's not thinking of brandy, exactly."

Oh Christ, her knees were weak and her belly was fluttering. *Fluttering.*

"How would you find that sort of romance?" he asked, looking at her from the cloak of thick lashes.

"Perfect," she managed to whisper.

Flynn's gaze darkened; he let go of her fingers, leaned forward, his hand sliding up her arm to her elbow. "Rachel . . . would you like a nightcap?"

"Yes," she murmured. "Yes, I would *love* a nightcap." And with Flynn's smile, she felt herself light up like a Christmas tree inside. She suddenly lifted her wineglass. "A toast," she said. "To a man who is handsome and charming and kind to strangers, all rolled up in one, but best of all, terribly romantic."

"You forgot frightfully attracted to blue eyes," he said, lifting his glass.

"And frightfully attracted to blue eyes," she added. "Just like I am attracted to gray eyes."

Flynn grinned, signaled the waiter and quickly paid the check as Rachel finished her wine, feeling it sluice through her, warming her.

They walked outside, bundled up together against the cold as they waited for the valet to bring his car around, and from there, Flynn drove to the Corporate Suites parking lot. "I just happen to have an excellent brandy," he said as he helped her out of the car.

"Thank God."

That earned an appreciative chuckle from Flynn. "Why, Miss Lear, I do believe you might be a saucy little minx beneath all that glitter," he said, pushing open the door to the lobby and ushering her inside.

"Thank you. That's the nicest thing anyone has ever said to me."

They strode past the reception desk; Flynn saluted the guy behind the counter, punched the up button on the elevator, and fairly pushed her inside the small compartment.

The moment the doors closed, he turned to her, put his hands on her shoulders, and gently pushed her up against the wall. "I have a confession to make," he said, his breath warm on her lips. "I lied." He kissed her. "Horribly," he added as Rachel caught her breath and kissed her again. "And not very imaginatively. I've got an interior boom box, a lousy jazz CD that a friend loaned me, and a bottle of cheap Scotch that might begin to taste like brandy after a tot or two."

"Why, you silver-tongued devil," she said, lifting her face, brushing her lips against his.

The elevator doors opened. Flynn grabbed her hand and pulled her behind him, off the elevator and down the hall to his door. He put his key in the lock, pushed the door open, and stood aside, letting Rachel through first. When the door shut and locked behind him, he caught her hand, pulled her into his arms, and said, "I don't know how you do it, but I find you utterly irresistible."

Rachel laughed. "The spell is working, then."

Flynn chuckled low in his throat, guided her up against the wall. One hand slipped inside her coat and went around her waist as he edged his knee between her legs. With his other hand, he caught hers and dragged it up the wall, holding it above her head. Rachel's enormous bag slipped from her shoulder and landed with a thud at their feet.

Laughing, they both looked down, and much to Rachel's chagrin, the little illustrated book she had intended to send to Robin for several days now, had landed, faceup, on his foot—*The Art of Making Tantric Love, with Illustrations and Notes.*

Chapter Twenty-four

* ✳ *

RACHEL moved quickly, but not quickly enough. Flynn picked up the book as Rachel shoved several questionable items back into her bag and tried frantically to think of a good reason why she might be on a lovely date with a sex book in her bag.

She popped up with her bag. "Oh hey, there's that silly thing!" she said, laughing a little like a hyena. "I know what you must be thinking about *that!*" She tried to snatch it from him, but Flynn moved it just out of her reach and cocked one inquisitive brow.

"That," she said, shaking a finger at the book, "that is a . . . very . . . funny . . . *story*. Yessir, a funny story. Not what *you're* thinking."

Flynn looked at the book again. "I think I've heard of this." He opened the book—and his eyes went a little round.

Rachel leaned in, peeked at what he had turned to, saw it was one of the many getting-in-touch-with-your-lover's-sexual-being positions explained. This was *so* just her luck! And things were going so great up until this!

"Okay. Here's the thing," she started, but Flynn had

turned away, was walking into the tiny little living area with the book, studying it.

"Frankly, I'm rather certain this is impossible," he said, more to himself than to her as he pointed at something.

Rachel was instantly behind him, straining to see over his shoulder. "See, the whole thing about Tantra is getting in touch with the universe, which I was *trying* to explain to my sisters one night, but they have a very rude habit of not actually ever listening to me, and all *they* heard was—"

"Look here," Flynn said, pointing to the next page and turning it sideways. "What do you make of it?" He turned the book upside down, shook his head. "Really, if one was to contort oneself in such a manner, I can't imagine that an injury wouldn't result from it, can you? Nor can I think it would be particularly enjoyable." He looked at Rachel. "But perhaps I'm missing something. Do *you* think it would be enjoyable?"

"I, ah . . . I'm not really, ah . . . sure."

"Really? Well, speaking strictly from the male point of view, this one looks rather painful."

"Pain is definitely not part of Tantra," Rachel said, waving her hand dismissively at that particular picture, wishing to God he'd put it down. "Which is what I was trying to explain to my sisters, and I finally said, look, you'll just have to see for yourself, and I'll send you—"

"Now *that*," Flynn said, ignoring her as he went on to the next page, "is *infinitely* doable." And he flashed a smile—not the charming, boyish smile she was accustomed to, but a very wolfish, sensual smile that definitely made her curious about the picture.

She stopped trying to explain it and pulled his arm so she could see the picture. "Oh. *That*," she said, nodding appreciatively. "It does seem . . . doable," she said, and tilted her head a bit. "With the right foot gear."

Flynn laughed, turned his wolfish grin to her again. "Full of surprises, aren't you?" he said, holding up the book. "Honestly, you leave me gobsmacked more times than not," he added, and tossed the book carelessly onto the couch.

He put his hands on his hips, looked at her in a way that made her heart suddenly wing a thousand beats a minute. "I really had in mind a sort of quiet evening. A little music, a little Scotch, chatting up our favorite movies—"

"Braveheart," she muttered.

"Lord of the Rings: The Two Towers. But now I fear I can't possibly do anything but imagine you . . . like *that,"* he said, nodding toward the book.

"I, ah . . . I think I have the same problem."

"Then there is only one thing to be done for it," he said, advancing toward her, head down, that sexy lock of hair hanging across his brow. "We simply must explore what we've both wanted to explore all evening. What do you think?" he asked, reaching for her, pulling her to him.

She thought that she was seething with desire, literally boiling with it, and said, "I think you are a genius."

"Granted." He pushed a curl from her forehead, cupped her face in his hand, and kissed the corner of her mouth. "But where exactly might a genius begin," he asked as he kissed her brow, "if he wanted to experience the full monty of tantric sex?"

"Touch," she answered in a whisper, and unthinkingly, her hands went to his shoulders. With his mouth on her cheek, Flynn shrugged out of his suit coat and dropped it, then pushed the coat from her shoulders, too.

"Touch," he repeated, slipping his arm around her waist, drawing her into him. "Any sort of touch? One touch? A series of touches? A slap, a bump, or hopefully, a poke?"

"Ah, well," she said, bending her neck a little to accommodate his roaming mouth. "There are many types of touches. For example, the blind man's touch, you know, where one or the other closes their eyes and sees their partner through the fingertips," she said, her voice faltering a little as he slid a hand up her rib cage to the side of her breast.

"Sounds fabulous," he muttered against her skin. "Go on."

"And massage," she said as she impulsively buried her face in his neck, inhaling the spicy scent of his aftershave, the clean smell of soap and shampoo from his collar.

"Ah, the *massage*," he said in a very seductive voice as his hand wandered down her side, to her hip and squeezed it.

"And then, there is, the ah . . . *oh*," she whispered as he filled his free hand with her breast.

"The what?"

"The use of the, ah . . . mouth," she said, and felt the desire percolating beneath her skin as she motioned vaguely to her lips. "You know, the mouth can be a very nice tool for, ah . . . touching."

"Indeed?" His laugh was a throaty chuckle as he slid his hand down her arm until he caught her hand. "Then I opt for the mouth . . . and tongue . . . and every inch of your lovely flesh," he murmured.

Oh, oh, *oh*, so did *she*. Rachel sighed dreamily as he artfully moved her into the darkened bedroom and leaned her up against the wall. He braced his arms on either side of her, leaned in to kiss her, his tongue sweeping fully into her mouth, his lips firm and pliant on hers.

And just when she thought she would melt all over the carpet, he lifted his head. "Stay right where you are, will you?" He pushed away from the wall, walked to somewhere near the bed, and after a moment of fumbling about, the soothing sound of a piano filled the small room. He turned toward her, and in the light that spilled in from the adjoining room, she could see his face as he walked back to her, loosening his tie. It was an expression that sent the deepest of shivers of anticipation through her.

As he reached her, he casually put a finger under her chin, tilted her face up to his, and tenderly kissed her lips, soft and long, carefully shaping them, and desire began to pool in her groin. "I should very much like to explore a bit of the Tantra with you, Rachel," he murmured. "You inspire that sort of thing in me. In fact, I'm rather amazed by all that you inspire in me."

The sentiment was so unexpected and sweet that Rachel caught a breath in her throat as he stood there, admiring her body. It was the sort of sentiment she had heard expressed on the silver screen, on those nights she would sit alone in the family's little theater, watching romance movies alone while her sisters were out with their dates, leaving her to dream of someone to say those things to her.

This time, it was really happening to her. She had the gorgeous guy, and he had the words, and she had never in her life felt more emboldened or sexy or just plain horny as she did then.

And Rachel suddenly kissed him for it, flinging her arms around his neck, crushing up against him. Flynn caught her, put his arms around her, and held her tightly. She was vaguely aware that something in her had snapped; all the inhibitions, all the insecurities, went floating away on a cloud of lavender, and she no longer worried how she appeared, because she felt beautiful and desirable and sexy. She could think of nothing but Flynn, could see nothing, taste nothing, feel nothing but him. Her hands went to his face, her fingers light on the five o'clock shadow, then spreading, to his ears, and the hair brushing his collar.

Flynn grabbed her wrist, pulled her hand from his face and pressed his lips to her palm, then began to pull her, while he walked backward, to the bed in the middle of the room. Rachel followed mindlessly, moving carelessly across the carpet, not really conscious of anything but Flynn, and hardly even noticing when she bumped up against the bed.

She laughed, lifted her face again, and touched her lips to the corner of his mouth.

Flynn's hands were at her back, fumbling with the zipper of her dress. Rachel laughed against his mouth as he released her zipper. It was a strange sensation, to feel the cold air on her back at the very same time something had detonated white hot inside her.

His hands slipped inside her dress, big hands on the smooth skin of her back, a finger tracing the path of her spine. "I think I rather like the Tantra thing," he said into her hair.

Tantra, witchcraft—whatever it was, Rachel liked it too. She felt impossibly alive; the energy surging through her was not of this earth. She lifted her hand to his silk shirt, deftly unbuttoning it. "If you really want to know about Tantra, you must be completely naked, knickers and all."

"That can definitely be arranged," he said as he lazily caressed her bare back. "But what of you? If it is to work properly, mustn't you be naked, too?"

"As a jaybird," she emphatically assured him.

Flynn groaned, pressed his forehead to hers for a moment. "You've no idea how I've longed for that," he said, and quickly shed his shirt.

He was beautiful, absolutely beautiful. His shoulders were broad, his arms thickly muscled, and his abdomen flat and trim.

Rachel closed her eyes; Flynn kissed her deeply as she blindly sought to unbuckle his belt and pull it free, then yanked the top of his trousers free. She unzipped his pants, felt the hard evidence of his lust for her beneath the fabric, and slipped two fingers inside his silk boxers, touching the tip of his penis.

Flynn's body shuddered at her touch; he was suddenly working feverishly to have the dress off of her, alternately pulling it off and stroking every inch of her flesh, every curve, his mouth following closely, inhaling her skin.

Rachel realized she was working just as feverishly, her hands inside his shirt, feeling the rock-hard body of a strong man, and then clawing the garment off of him, desperate to feel his skin as he felt hers. When she had at last freed him of the shirt, her hands were everywhere, caressing him, gliding over his chest, stroking the soft down of hair trailing to his groin. She reveled in the feel of a man, a grown man, a man with substance to him, hard planes and ridges and softness all at once.

But it was not enough just to feel him; an unworldly energy was pulsing alive and deep within her, demanding more, demanding satisfaction.

Flynn caught an audible breath in his throat when she fumbled with his trousers to free his arousal, caught her shoulders, and tossed her down on the bed and fell on top of her, catching himself on his arms so that he didn't crush her, and with a dangerous smile, yanked the dress down her legs, leaving her to lie there wearing a bra and her only pair of thong panties.

Quickly and expertly, he sought the fastenings of her bra and released her breasts from it, caressed the flesh of them, groaning with pleasure when they began to swell in his hands. With a kick, he was free of his trousers, and lowered his head, took one breast in his mouth, sucked the hardened peak onto his tongue.

Rachel gasped, then moaned, closing her eyes, letting herself sink deeply into the sensation of it. Every fiber of her was burning with the fire that licked at the deepest part of her; she felt Flynn's body against her as she had never felt a man before, his hardness pressed against her softness. His hands were in her hair now, grasping at the curls, pulling it free of its ties, then from behind her head, so that it covered her shoulders, draped one breast.

"Fantastic," he said hoarsely.

Then he dipped to nibble at the string of her panties. She felt them sliding down her thigh, and when she raised up on her elbows, she saw his bare thigh next to hers. She looked smaller and feminine next to him. He glanced up from his devouring of her panties, and the dark, sensual look in his eye made her feel like a sex goddess, very alluring . . . and a little like she was falling off a precipice into a warm pool of vanilla.

"You're beautiful," Flynn said softly as his hands traced languid patterns on her skin. His hand slipped between her legs, into the folds of her wet sex. He stroked her, watching her eyes. "I want to touch every inch of you, feel you and taste you, every bit," he said, and lowered his head to her belly. "Would you like that?"

Was he nuts? Rachel moaned her reply, moved against his hand.

Flynn chuckled, his breath hot on her skin, then mouthed a warm, wet line to her leg, to her thigh, nibbling there for a moment. Rachel's back arched; her body was beginning to quiver with the anticipation of a smashing release, and when his breath glanced the apex of her thighs, and then his tongue, she gasped and unthinkingly grabbed his hair.

Flynn made a small laugh in his throat and thrust his tongue deeper, pushing her legs farther apart, his mouth working around the core of her desire.

Rachel was lost, riding a shimmering wave, up and down and around and to the crest, tumbling off the other side too fast and too hard. "Ohmigod," she breathed. "That's wicked, absolutely *wicked*," she said breathlessly.

Suddenly, she came up on her elbow, startling him from his ministrations to the valley between her legs, and sat up, tugging him to her. With a laugh, Flynn came up; she pushed him down, onto the bed, and he lay back, a Cheshire cat grin on his face, and stacked his hands behind his head.

"You're really bloody gorgeous, Rachel," he said, his gaze freely roaming her nude body. "Very sexy what with the curves and delightful tastes."

She smiled as she straddled him, slid up his shaft. "I love your curves, too," she said with a sly wink, and put her hands on his shoulders, began to knead his flesh lightly. He settled back, smiling as he watched her, moving lightly beneath her as she traced soft lines down his chest with her fingertips, swirling around his nipples, then leaning forward in a curtain of curly hair to nibble them. She continued down his body, her tongue flicking into the crevice of his navel, her hands on his hips.

When her lips touched the velvet head of his penis, Flynn released his breath and shifted beneath her. His response prompted her to trace the length of him with her tongue.

"Bloody *hell*," he groaned above her; his hands clasped the edge of the bed as he tried to restrain himself from writhing against her mouth as she tasted him as thoroughly as he had tasted her. But it was pointless to hold back, for Rachel had lost all self-control, and was gleefully pushing him to the brink of orgasm.

But Flynn wouldn't have it so easily, and suddenly sat up, grabbed her beneath her shoulders, and pulled her up like she was nothing more than a doll. He swung his legs off the side of the bed, guided Rachel to his lap, and then his cock to her wet folds, teasing her.

"Don't make me beg," she said above him.

Flynn grabbed a fistful of her hair and wrapped it around his hand, pulled her face to his. "Tell me what you want, Rachel," he muttered.

"I want you," she said hoarsely. "I want you inside me." Flynn thrust his tongue wildly into her mouth at the same moment he slid deep inside her, and began to move.

It was sensual overload; Rachel was wet and throbbing, aroused like a long-buried dinosaur, ravenous for physical pleasure.

When Flynn slipped his hand between her legs, Rachel's head fell back; she was precariously close to ecstasy. But Flynn taunted her with his fingers, stroking her mindlessly, bringing her to the point of desperation, then easing off again, until Rachel could stand it no more and cried out for him to fuck her.

He made a guttural sound and thrust hard inside her, again and again, taking her breasts into his mouth, nibbling the hard peaks of them as her body took him in. Over and over again he thrust into her, and she rode each wave with great anticipation, harder and faster than the one before, her fingers digging into his shoulders, reaching for the earth-shattering climax she could feel pressing down on her until it rained in around her, pushing her off the precipice into that warm pool again.

Her body went limp; she fell onto his shoulder. With

one last powerful thrust, Flynn gave a strangled sob of release as he pulled out of her, spilling hot on her belly.

They sat that way for a moment, Rachel hanging limply over his shoulder, until Flynn somberly put his arms around her, slowly leaned back until she could stretch out her legs and lay beside him.

The heat at last ebbed from their bodies, and he reached over the bed, pulled a blanket of some sort over them. "I think I should tell you before I announce it to my mum, but I've converted, here and now, to Tantra," he said, and kissed the crown of her hair. "Just tell me where to enlist."

Rachel laughed into his chest and shifted, propping herself up on her elbows so she could look at him. "I have some bad news," she said with a smile. "I'm not sure if we did it right. We might need to do further study."

Flynn laughed low, tapped her nose with his finger. "You'll never meet a more willing study partner," he said. "That was fantastic."

Fantastic. He had no idea how fantastic. And as Rachel was mulling over in her mind how she'd break the news to Dagne that at least one British guy knew what he was doing in the boudoir, Flynn said, "How odd . . . I have the strongest hankering for my mother's rum cake. Do you smell something like cake?"

Rachel buried her face in his chest, laughing uncontrollably.

Chapter Twenty-five

✦ ✦ ✦

THEY lay in bed laughing at inconsequential things, playing a little game of naming their favorite things and marveling at how much they had in common.

"Favorite city," Rachel said.

"New York," Flynn answered instantly.

"Me, too!" she cried.

The favorite country was France. They both preferred alternative rock to rock and roll, and they both loved the circus.

It amazed Flynn that he could have so much in common with a woman so far removed from his little circle of almost-aristocracy friends. As she talked about a dog she'd had as a child (he, too, was a dog lover), he idly wondered how he had ever become so imbued in Iris's way of life to have believed he loved her. How could he possibly have done so? Iris was nothing like Rachel, not nearly so engaging, or frankly, so pretty.

He was, he realized, accustomed to a whole different breed of animal—the sort of woman who never left her flat unless she was wearing strappy high-heeled shoes and was perfectly made up, the sort who worked to snag a wealthy partner in marriage, then spent the remainder of her days dreaming up the next soiree and sending children off to boarding school.

And while Rachel could seem a bit strange what with all the eastern philosophies and witchcraft and tapestry weaving, she was uncommonly stimulating. She had an immutable and charming personality, was compassionate and free.

Frankly, when he'd begun this little journey, he had not been prepared for her charm; he had believed her to be just one part of another job, like dozens of jobs he'd done around the world. Yet Rachel had surprised him from the beginning—she had begun to grow on him in a way that now he could think of little else.

First, there were her all-American looks. Rachel was beyond pretty; she had that fresh look of a woman who actually lived life and did not require cosmetics to give the illusion that she lived. And she was healthy—not so very thin that a man would worry about snapping a bone here or there. There was that gorgeous mane of wavy hair that any man would desire to touch, and she laughed so fully and easily that it was quite obvious it came from somewhere deep inside her, someplace genuine and never contrived.

What was most remarkable was that in spite of coming from a very wealthy background, she was the most down-to-earth person he'd ever had occasion to meet. Certainly if she'd come from that sort of wealth in England, she'd be quite impressed by it. But Rachel seemed to dismiss it somehow. Her family's fortune seemed to be the least important thing in her life, as if she could take it or leave it.

Looking at her now, measuring their hands against each other, Flynn thought that he'd never meant for things to come to this.

But they had, and he was feeling very peculiar about it all. After that extraordinary romp in the sack, he was terribly curious about her, wanted to know every little thing about her, how her mind worked, what she liked to eat for breakfast, and what the little scar was on her arm and the significance of the tiny little tattoo on her ankle. And he thought, lying there that night, having named his favorite pet to be the penguin, to which she had frowned prettily and informed him in all seriousness that a penguin was not a pet, that he could imagine himself looking into those beautiful blue eyes for a very long time to come.

Therein lied the source of the peculiar feeling, for that was a bit of a problem, wasn't it? He couldn't quite sort out how he might possibly be falling in love with a woman he'd end up, in all probability, having arrested.

But at the moment, she was playing a little footsy game with him, and he could feel his wanker nudging him again, and thought he'd have a bit of a think about it tomorrow.

Subject: R U mad or what??
From: <rmanning70@houston.rr.com>
To: Rach <earthangel@hotmail.com>
CC: <reparrish72@aol.com>

I'm sorry if I offended you but I wasn't implying ANYTHING about bridesmaids or otherwise all right? I know you probably date, at least I think I do, but you never really talk about it so I am assuming. Gawd, never mind what I thought. I am trying to say I am sorry, so if you are mad, quit being mad and e-mail me back. This is like the fifteenth e-mail I've sent you. Don't make me call the cops up there, because I will, I swear I will. P.S. Dad said he's been calling you and you're never home but he wants to talk to you. I think he is planning to come see you Thanksgiving, so you better call him back.

Subject: Thanksgiving Plans
From: Lillian Stanton <lilandel@aol.com>
To: Rachel Ellen Lear <earthangel@hotmail.com>

Rachel honey, I just want you to know that you are invited to our house for Thanksgiving. Your sister Robin and Jake and Cole and baby Madeline are coming and I think so are Rebecca and Matt and Gray and that sweet pea baby Jeff. They are not going to the ranch this year because your dad is not leaving New York altho I hope Bonnie will come because I haven't seen my girl in awhile. I sure hope you can come too and you can bring your friend whatever his name is I'm sorry honey I forgot it. But you just write me back and tell me when your getting in and I'll make sure El comes to pick you up at the airport. XOXOX Grandma P.S. What did you think of the grapefruit diet—they are on sale here five for a dollar.

Subject: Re: R U mad or what?
From: Rebecca Parrish <reparrish72@aol.com>
To: Rach <earthangel@hotmail.com>
CC: Robbie <rmanning70@houston.rr.com>

Rmanning70@houston.rr.com wrote:

This is like the fifteenth e-mail I've sent you. Don't make me call the cops up there, because I will, I swear I will.

Rachel, seriously, I tried to call the other day and your friend Dagne answered the phone and said you hadn't been around in a while, and she kind of laughed when she said it, and frankly, I think she's pretty weird and I am worried for your safety. I would not put it past a real witch to have done something like boil you in some spell soup or something horrible like that. Matt is laughing as I write this because he says you are the smartest of all of us (please) and that you wouldn't be stupid enough to get yourself boiled in a spell soup and to quit worrying about it, but I can't. It's not like you to be off e-mail for days on end and not answer your phone. I know you better than Matt does, and I can remember all the bone-headed things you've done, and getting yourself into some weird situation you can't get yourself out of is not outside the realm of possibility. I also know how sensitive you are about the boyfriend situation, so if you are just being mad at least write us and tell us you are not dead! If you're NOT being mad and you ARE dead, we will know when we don't get an e-mail from you or the cops arrive on your door and find your body sacrificed on some altar. So call me!

Subject: RE: RE: R U mad or what?
From: <earthangel@hotmail.com>
To: <reparrish72@aol.com>
CC: <rmanning70@houston.rr.com>,
<lilandel@aol.com>

I am not dead. But I am very busy. Will write soon love Rachel.

P.S. Grandma, I cannot come for Thanksgiving, but thanks anyway.

FLYNN and Rachel were spending every day together, working around his consulting schedule and her thankfully short-lived job of packing fish. At present, she was answering phones for a paint company and working up an outline for her dissertation. In the mornings, she'd pop off to the gym to ride a few miles while Flynn went off and did whatever he did with his computer job, and then in the evenings, they'd go out for dinner, or bundle up and walk down to the water to watch the boats go by, or wander around and look at the old and stately historic homes.

But mostly, they talked. About everything. Flynn asked lots of questions about her, which Rachel liked, because he seemed genuinely interested in her. That was definitely a new experience and she discovered, as she answered his questions, that there was more to her life than she'd given herself credit for.

He asked about her school, her travels. And about Dagne and witchcraft.

"I'm not really very good at it," she had said with a laugh.

"Perhaps you could cast a spell to make yourself better at it," he had quipped.

He asked about Myron, too, about his dual professions of professor and assistant curator, which Rachel thought was a little weird, but then again, she figured he wasn't entirely convinced that there was nothing between her and Myron. The fact that Myron still had her phone and occasionally left messages advising her "they" were out of salami or sodas did not help that impression.

Honestly, Rachel was wondering more and more why she hadn't cut ties to Myron a long time ago. All right, he'd morphed into a security blanket, she could admit it. She hadn't believed another guy would be interested—so why not hang on to Myron? At least he was someone to hang out with.

Dagne had been so right—who hung on to ex-boyfriends after the affair was over? Fat chicks who were afraid of never having another boyfriend, that was who.

Just mentioning Myron reminded her of how sad she was, and she always changed the subject when he came up, usually by asking about Flynn's life.

He talked a lot about his family, rolled his eyes when he told her his mother was obsessed with their connection to the Duke of Alnwick.

"Really? You're part of the aristocracy?" she had asked, suitably impressed.

"Hardly," he had replied with a snort of laughter. "I worked it out once. We're several hundred steps removed from the mayor of Butler Cropwell, and many, many more from the unfortunate Duke of Alnwick."

"Unfortunate?"

"Tragically so, for my mother believes there is some connection and therefore writes him rather frequently, including the obligatory Christmas letter about all the goings-on in our branch of the 'family.'"

Rachel laughed, looked at the plate of Lebanese food they had ordered at a local restaurant. "Is it your mother who calls in the middle of the night?" she asked slyly.

His first reaction had been to wave a dismissive hand at her and claim it was just an old friend. But when she reminded him that he'd actually raised his voice on one of the calls, he sighed. "All right . . . the fact is, I was recently engaged to a woman in England."

At Rachel's look of surprise, he quickly added, "But I ended it with her. It really wasn't meant to be, and I told her so, but she's been rather gormless about the whole thing and has had a rather difficult time coming to terms, as it were."

"Oh," Rachel said.

"More importantly, how do you find the tabouleh? I think it's rather too tart, don't you?" he asked, quickly changing the subject, and leaving Rachel feeling strangely unsettled.

The other thing Flynn was vague about was his work. This stood in stark contrast to her, of course, who went on like a Chatty Cathy with her many tales of temporary assignments—fish packing, receptionist, theater usher, mailroom clerk, check-out girl at the local craft store. But Flynn preferred not to speak of his work. "It's frightfully boring, really," he told her.

"But you work such long hours. There must be *something* interesting."

"No, really," he would insist, and silence any more questions from her with a kiss.

Rachel didn't mind. She chalked it up to his obvious boredom with his job, and when he couldn't answer some of her questions about her laptop, she figured he was trying to keep his work from their relationship.

So the only question Rachel was left with was the one that needed asking before she went any further, but the one question she couldn't scrounge up the guts to ask: How long was he in America?

That question dogged her through endless hours of temp work—she was so torn between *dying* to know the answer and refusing to acknowledge the inevitable ending to the sweetest thing she'd ever known. Of course, she wanted there to be more to their relationship, to see it go on and on . . .

But she couldn't possibly see how it would ever work.

First of all, there was her, Miss Fortune, an heiress who had been cut off from her fortune and couldn't get a real job for love or money. Several applications for teaching positions had gone unanswered. As far as she knew, she'd be working temp jobs to pay the utility bill for the rest of her life, and Flynn was not the sort of guy to be attracted to that sort of poverty—she could tell by the cut of his clothes and his penchant for the finer things in life. He was a man who could have any woman he wanted—why would he saddle himself with someone who packed fish? Even if it was a temporary job.

And then there was the prospect of explaining Miss Fortune to him, and how she'd ended up like this. Every time she tried to think of how to say it, the words just sounded ridiculously stupid. *"I've been cut off because I couldn't seem to get out of school,"* she could imagine saying, or *"Honestly, my dad is a prick, and that's why he cut me off, to be mean and spiteful."* Or how about: *"I lived off my dad for the first thirty years of my life, but I've turned over a new leaf. I swear."*

Nevertheless, there was *something* between them that

could not be denied, and if Rachel ever had any doubt of it, Flynn put that doubt to rest over and over again, and especially at night, when they would invariably end up in his little apartment, in his bed, making wild and passionate tantric love, complete with strangely shaped pillows and arousing creams, both fiercely determined to explore each and every chapter of the tantric sex book before she mailed it off to her sisters.

So it was, for the time being, anyway, her heaven on earth, and at the very least, a few moments in time she could cherish as long as she lived.

When it was over, she fully intended to write *Cosmo* and tell them that their research on the British men had been so far off base as to be laughable. Honestly, where did they think James Bond got his swagger?

RACHEL wasn't the only one caught up in their time together—it wasn't something Flynn would bloody likely well forget, either. And, like Rachel, he couldn't have been more surprised. Not because she wasn't his type—surprisingly, she was more his type than any woman he'd ever met. But he'd never expected to get so caught up as he had. He'd half expected to go back to Iris once the sting of her betrayal had left him, and naturally, he'd assumed the sting would leave him—affairs among his crowd were not exactly news, as almost everyone seemed to have them now and again.

But Iris's affair had not left him. In fact, the more he had thought of it in those days and weeks after it had happened, the angrier he became. What infuriated him was that *Iris* believed it to be something he should overlook. She was never sorry for it, not really, and that said more about her as a person than he'd ever really seen before. It was plainly evident that he did not really know the woman he almost married.

Moreover, that circle of people who thought occasional affairs were quite all right was not a circle he'd ever aspired to. In truth, it was a circle that had annoyed him for far too long.

So here he was, caught up in a real love affair, one he was grateful to have found and experienced. And he would have been perfectly content to have gone on with it, but then reality would seep in.

It did not help matters that Joe thought he was quite off his trolley. *"Dude,"* he'd said with great exasperation, arms rather akimbo, "You can't be banging the perps!"

"There is no evidence she is a perp," Flynn had calmly informed him, "and I am not *banging* her. I'm really rather fond of her."

"That chick is *wacked*. WACKED!"

"She's unique. She's really quite witty and very smart, and more compassionate than you and I," Flynn argued.

Joe looked at him as if he'd lost his mind, his mouth gaping open to his lap, his eyes bulging out quite horribly. He managed to poke his eyes back in his head and ask, "Are you *serious?*"

"Quite," Flynn said evenly, and moreover, of late, he was a firm believer in the power of witchcraft, too, because the chemistry between him and Rachel was sizzling. He liked the woman very much—bloody hell, who was he kidding? He adored her.

It was a first for him to adore someone, to truly adore them, and was as unexpected as it was unwanted. Really, he wasn't certain what to do with it, particularly since this was more than a transatlantic fling—Rachel was not just an American girl to whom he'd formed an almost instant and an increasing attraction.

She was also a suspect in a major crime.

That was the problem that kept Flynn awake at nights. He couldn't conceive of her being involved in the nutty professor's scheme, but nor could he prove otherwise, not yet.

All that being said, his involvement with her, undercover notwithstanding, was reaching a point where Flynn was teetering precariously on the edge of a serious and career-ending lack of professionalism.

At some point, he had to confront what was happening to him and come to terms with the realities of this particular case. And if he didn't do it soon, he had the distinct feeling Joe would do it for him, if he wasn't already, with remarks such as, "What, they don't have any ass in England?"

"I'll kindly ignore that," Flynn had said, quietly seething. "But really, Joe, are you so bloody macho that you haven't been smitten once or twice in your life?"

His partner had blushed fiercely at that, and he'd looked out the window, muttered something that sounded a bit like *maybe.* "Well, whatever," he said, a little louder. "You're nuts, pal. That chick is so in on this deal she's drowning in it."

Flynn had smiled darkly at that. Until he'd been in her bungalow and determined what she did indeed have in her possession, he couldn't say one way or the other, but he knew Rachel. He *knew* Rachel. "Would you care to place a gentleman's wager on it?"

"Sure," Joe said, grinning like a man quite sure of himself. "What would you like to wager?"

"One thousand American dollars . . . or is that too rich for your blood?"

That made Joe chuckle. "You're on, little Lord Fauntleroy. You're *on.*"

They had dropped the subject in favor of wrapping up the homicide they were working, and drove down to the shore to have one last chat with a young man who had served a little time for breaking and entering a few years ago.

BACK in New York, Aaron noticed that Daniel had new office furniture. Giant butterfly chairs and a big, sixties-type cubed ottoman between the clients and the master manipulator, which is how Aaron had begun to think of the idiot therapist, because damn him if he couldn't get him and Bonnie to do the most ridiculous things. This week had been their at-home experiment in touching. Fingertip to fingertip, hand to hand, elbow to elbow, and so on.

Daniel seemed pretty pleased with his furniture and himself, and was beaming at Bonnie as she talked about the touching exercise. "It was really . . ." She paused; cast her gaze heavenward as she tried to think of the right word. "Something close to . . . *magical*. Not sexual, really," she said, lowering her gaze and trying to find a comfortable position in the new butterfly chair, "but I was cognizant of the connection, you know? I was struck with how long it had been since Aaron and I had been *aware* of each other on a purely physical level. I didn't remember Aaron's skin was so smooth."

Aaron moaned.

"Aaron?" Daniel asked, smiling at him. "Was there something you wanted to say?"

"My skin is *smooth* because I live in hospitals and they are turning me into an old man," he said gruffly, and tried to sit up in that fucking chair.

Daniel was still smiling. "Is there something wrong with smooth skin?"

"No."

"Good, *good*. So what did you take from the exercise, Aaron?" he asked, leaning forward and looking concerned and interested.

"Well, *Daniel,* I learned that I can't get it up anymore. When a beautiful woman touches me, there ain't nothing going on downstairs. Not even a whimper. Might as well lop the damn thing off."

"Oh, honey . . . you think I'm beautiful?"

Aaron looked at Bonnie like she was nuts, which she certainly was if she didn't know that he thought she was beautiful. "Hell yes I think you're beautiful, Bonnie! What do you think?"

"I haven't heard you say it in so *long,*" she said, with a girly sigh.

"And how does it make you feel to hear him say it now, Bonnie?" Daniel asked, shifting that concerned look to her.

"It makes me feel beautiful. And loved."

Judas H. Priest, what was it with women? Of *course* he thought she was beautiful, the most beautiful woman in the entire fucking world!

"Aaron? Do you understand that Bonnie needs that sort of reinforcement from you?" Daniel asked carefully, as if he were speaking to a moron.

"Yes. I understand that I have to tell her five thousand times over that I think she's beautiful, because I cannot trust her to remember it or believe it from one day to the next," he groused, but his tone did not douse Bonnie's pleased-as-punch smile in the least.

"As we have discussed, women respond to aural stimulation," Daniel said, gesturing to his ears. "Talking and sharing feelings are important to them. When you have thoughts about Bonnie, they may not seem important to you, but they are very important to her. It's just as I've suggested to Bonnie that for most men, *doing* is the preferred verb."

"The preferred *verb?*"

"In other words," Daniel said patiently, "Bonnie should *show* you more than *tell* you how she feels, because men respond to visual stimulation," he said, gesturing to his eyes with two fingers. "But you should tell her, because women respond to aural stimulation."

"The same is true for our daughters, honey," Bonnie said.

"She's right," Daniel quickly added. "Your daughters will respond to a more sensitive, aural approach."

"Whatever," Aaron said.

Bonnie exchanged a look with Daniel. "So . . . for example, when you go and see Rachel over Thanksgiving, I think it would be very good for you to explain to her that you love her and you think she's beautiful and you really care what she thinks. You know, have an exchange with her."

"That's an excellent suggestion, Bonnie," Daniel the ass-kisser said. "What we're saying here, Aaron, is that your daughters will really respond to *conversation* as opposed to *dictation*. They don't necessarily like to be *told* what to do, but like most women, prefer to have a discussion and reach a consensus. The challenge for you, of course, is to take off your CEO hat and put on your daddy hat. Instead of issuing orders for the good of the company . . . or the daughter, as the case may be . . . try having a conversation and gently guide your daughter to reach a reasonable conclusion."

No, the challenge for Aaron was not to punch the man's lights out, a struggle that was becoming increasingly difficult with each session. But Bonnie was nodding so hard that she almost levitated out of her butterfly chair, and he wondered, like he always did in these situations, if he hadn't been living on another planet all these years while the rest of the world was spinning around somewhere else to a completely different set of rules.

"Aaron?" Daniel said softly. "Do you think you can do that?"

"Hell yes I can *do* it," he said irritably.

"Oh God, it's a breakthrough!" Bonnie said dramatically, and looked to Daniel for confirmation.

Chapter Twenty-six

✴

Subject: Thanksgiving
From: Aaron Lear <Aaron.Lear@leartransind.com>
To: Rachel <earthangel@hotmail.com>

Hello Rachel. This is your father. I have tried to contact you by phone but you have not returned my calls. I am using this method to inform you that I intend to come to Providence on the morning of Thanksgiving. You are my daughter and you cannot shut me out of your life, no matter what you might think, and therefore, avoiding me seems pretty futile. I am coming, and if you lock the door, remember that I have a key. If you disappear, I will wait until you come home. So instead of avoidance, let's try to work together to resolve our differences. I look forward to seeing you. Love, Dad

Subject: FWD: [Thanksgiving]
From: <earthangel@hotmail.com>
To: Mom <10sNE1@nyc.rr.com>

Mom is this your idea???? This marriage counseling is making you guys crazy! Hell, it's making ME crazy!! Please don't let Dad come here, I am begging you. We never do anything but fight and I do not want to fight with him. I'M NOT MAD! I AM BUSY! I really don't want Dad to come. I am sorry if I am being a bad daughter but I'm sooo busy right now that I really don't have time for all his bullshit. Please call him off!

Subject: RE: FWD: [Thanksgiving]
From: BonLear <10sNE1@nyc.rr.com>
To: <earthangel@hotmail.com>

This is an automated message from BonLear 10sne1@nyc.rr.com:

I will be out of town from November 18 through November 30. If you need to contact me, please call my cell phone, 212-555-9035, and leave a message. Thank you, Bonnie Lear

Subject: Re: Thanksgiving
From: Rachel <earthangel@hotmail.com>
To: Aaron Lear <Aaron.Lear@leartransind.com>

Hi Dad. That's great that you want to come to Providence! You will get to meet all my friends. I am having several people over Thanksgiving Day, mostly from my weaving class. You remember that I teach "a bunch of losers" how to weave medieval tapestries, right? Anyway, this is great, because hopefully, you will get a chance to meet and talk with "Byron" and I know you've really wanted to do that. And oh yeah, I almost forgot. My best friend Dagne is a witch! She wants to try a couple of spells on you and see if she can cure the cancer

so you won't have to have surgery. They won't hurt but they might smell a little. Okay, see you next week! And listen, if I'm not home, just let yourself in with your key. Yes, I remember you have it, and honestly, I'd never forget that in a million trillion years. Rachel

Rachel was convinced her dad's determination to come to Providence was a full-fledged, goddamned disaster and figured this was some sort of cosmic punishment, seeing as how she'd been dabbling in witchcraft and enjoying it.

But Dagne was optimistic about it. "He'll love your class, he'll love Flynn—I mean, I am assuming he will, just as I will, if I ever get to meet him. But keeping him such a top secret might work against you," she said with a sniff, still miffed that Rachel hadn't found time to introduce them. "And then your dad will say, I was so *wrong* about you, Rachel, you've really got it going on, so I am going to restore your entire bazillion-dollar fortune this very minute!" And with that, she lifted her third glass of wine in a toast.

"Have you been smoking incense again?" Rachel asked suspiciously, then rolled onto her back so that she could stare up at the ten-foot ceiling and crown molding of her living room. "Do you know how ballistic Dad is going to go when he sees that tree and finds out Mr. Valicielo is suing me? Or that window upstairs that's been broken for over a year? Or that the garage is leaning to the right and the cable has been cut off?"

"Pretty mad, huh?" Dagne asked as she examined a spot on her arm.

"Yep. Pretty mad. From the beginning, he told me I had to keep the place up, and if I didn't, he was going to sell it. And then he told me if I didn't get out of school he was cutting me off, as in permanently. I don't really care, I swear I don't, but I just need some time to get on my feet before he yanks the rug out."

"It'll work out. Trust me. I've got your back," Dagne said with a wink.

Rachel half laughed, half moaned.

"I'm not kidding," Dagne said, frowning at Rachel's smile of disbelief. "All right, you don't believe me? I'll show you," she said, and suddenly stood, marched to where her purse was lying on the dining room table. She pulled out an envelope, turned and marched back to the living room, and tossed it onto Rachel's tummy.

"What's this?" Rachel asked, sitting up.

"You know that figurine of a dancer Myron gave you that you thought was so stupid? It got thirty dollars on eBay."

"What?" Rachel cried, and looked in the envelope. It was full of money.

"And the torch thingies, they brought sixty," Dagne said proudly. "There's three hundred bucks in there."

Rachel stared at the money, then at Dagne.

"I wanted to wait another week. You remember that tea set he gave you? The bidding is up to one hundred and twenty-five dollars, but it won't close for another three days."

"You mean you sold those things on eBay?" Rachel asked, just to say it out loud.

"Yes," Dagne said, beaming. "I mean, you were in a bind, and the stuff was just stuck around places. You haven't even noticed they're missing!" she said proudly.

"Dagne! You did that for me?" Rachel squealed.

"I just wanted to help. You've always helped me out when I needed it, and I just wanted to do something."

"I think I'm going to cry," Rachel said, clutching the envelope to her chest.

"Please don't," Dagne said, blushing now. "Come on, forget that and tell me about Flynn. I wanna *meeeeeeet* him!"

Rachel sighed dreamily and set the envelope aside. "God, Dagne, what can I say? He's perfect. Absolutely perfect."

"So did you figure out if there is anyone waiting for him in England?"

That one caused her to wince a little. "There *was* someone. And now I think she doesn't want to let go, and who can blame her? He told me he'd ended it, but that she's not accepting the end." She pushed herself up on her elbows and looked at Dagne. "I won't be able to accept it, either."

"Accept what?"

"The end."

Dagne snorted and gave her a dismissive flick of her wrist. "Don't be ridiculous. It's not going to end! From everything you've told me, he's just as crazy about you as you are him!"

"Right . . . but he doesn't know the whole story. He doesn't know about Lear Transport Industries, or that I've been cut off and can't pay my bills and my neighbor is suing me for all I am worth, which as of this moment, is about $410. He knows I am doing temp jobs, but I think he thinks that is just me having a little fun until I land on a dissertation topic. At least *that's* partially true," she said miserably.

"Hey, money is not everything," Dagne said, with a bit of a spark. "*Lots* of people don't have your kind of money and they manage to make a happy life!"

"I'm not saying it's all about money, but . . ." She stopped there. There was no polite way to explain that a lot of money really did make a difference in the way people perceived a person. She should know—she'd been Miss Fortune long enough.

"He's not going to hold it against you," Dagne continued. "Anyway, we are going to *solve* that problem. You may not be an heiress anymore, but you won't be a pauper, either. At least until you find a real job. Actually, I was thinking of asking Glenn if there might be something in his company you could do."

"Glenn?" Rachel said, coming to a full sitting position. "You're still seeing him, aren't you?"

Dagne shrugged, sipped her wine.

"Are you kidding?" Rachel shouted, laughing. "I thought you couldn't stand him!"

"I didn't think I could," Dagne said defensively. "But he is a nice guy and he's got a really great job. He probably pulls down seventy-five grand a year."

"Really? Doing what?"

"Boat sales. I was going to ask him if maybe you could be the boat girl."

"Boat girl?"

"You know, the one who stands on the boat and points to things." She glanced at her watch. "Oh geez, I really have to go soon," she said and stood up. "I'm meeting him at Fratangelo's later."

"Oh God, you're actually letting him into the 'hood?" Rachel cried, surprised.

"Shut up," Dagne said. But she was smiling. "Come on; let's do that spell for your dad."

"Did you have one in mind?" Rachel asked, gaining her feet.

"Of course. The one that instills kindness in meanies," she said, walking over to a mirror next to the door to check herself out. "That's the beauty of being a witch, you know. You can trot the spells out when you need them. So okay!" she said, turning away from the mirror. "This should go real quick as long as you have some dried wisteria and cow dung."

"Cow dung," Rachel said thoughtfully. "I think I left it in the basement."

Dagne was halfway down the basement stairs before Rachel told her she was kidding.

A half hour later, they were standing under the eaves of the garage, shivering from a bone-chilling rain, preparing to do an "anti-misfortune spell," which Rachel thought was hilarious. So hilarious, she kept giggling as Dagne tried to get the balsam wood to light. But it was too wet.

After several tries, Dagne tossed the match aside. "Never mind. We probably don't really need to burn balsam anyway. So okay, all we have to do is wrap these stones in the ribbon and stack them. Five separate bundles," she said, thrusting the stones and the ribbon to Rachel.

"Why do *I* always have to do it?" Rachel whined, snatching the stones and ribbon from Dagne.

"Because you are the one with all the problems, Miss Fortune," Dagne testily reminded her.

"I can't even see what I'm doing," Rachel groused as she stacked the five stones they had taken from her water garden and tried to wrap them in the ribbon.

"Would you please hurry up? I'm going to be late for my date."

Rachel fumbled in the dark with the stones, and finally, freezing and exasperated, she tied them as best she could. "Okay. There they are."

"Great," Dagne said. "Give me your hands."

Rachel put her hands out; Dagne grabbed them and they stood, facing each other, holding hands.

"Turn your face to the moon," she instructed Rachel.

"The moon? There is no moon! It's raining!"

"God, just look up!" Dagne snapped. "Okay, here we go. *Goddess moon, shine your light and show us the path away from the many misfortunes that surround us. Goddess moon, shine your light and lead us away from the misfortunes that will come. Goddess moon, shine your light, and fill us with your strength to avoid mi—*"

The sound of the stacked stones falling over startled them both.

"Toavoidmisfortunes," Dagne muttered quickly, and they both looked down. The stones had fallen out of the ribbon and scattered around their feet.

"That can't be good," Rachel said.

"It can't be that bad—we got most of the spell in." Dagne glanced at her watch. "Shit! I really gotta go," she said, letting Rachel's hands go, and she stooped to pick up the wet balsam.

Rachel grabbed the red ribbon but left the stones behind in her haste to follow Dagne inside. She followed her all the way to the front door. "You're coming Thanksgiving, right?" she called as Dagne ran across the porch and down the steps.

"Wouldn't miss it!" Dagne shouted as she reached her car, and quickly dove inside to get out of the rain.

Rachel stood there, watched her pull out of the drive. And as Dagne started down the street, an old Geo Metro pulled into the drive. Oh, *fabulous*. Myron. She was supposed to be spared misfortune!

She stepped inside, went to pick up the wineglasses.

"Yo!" Myron called from the front door as she washed the wineglasses. "Anyone home?"

"Back here!"

He came striding through the kitchen door, planted a big kiss on her cheek. "I was beginning to think you didn't live here anymore," he said, moving instantly to the fridge. "I've been by a half-dozen times and you aren't home. So I guess you're working hard, huh?"

Rachel glanced over her shoulder at him to see if he was kidding. Apparently, he wasn't.

"Man, your cupboard is like, *bare,*" he said, shaking his head. "Can't even get a decent sandwich out of here."

"I'm having a little financial crisis, remember?"

"What about the temp thing?" he asked.

"I can't really make enough to pay all the bills," she said.

Myron turned and looked at her. "You really need to call up the old man, Rachel. You're wasting away to skin and bones."

Hello, what did he say? "I *am?*" Rachel asked, looking down.

Myron laughed. "You could fit another you in those jeans, haven't you noticed?"

She stepped back a little farther from the sink and looked down, then behind. They did seem a little baggier than usual. But according to her scale, she hadn't lost more than a few pounds at most.

"Anyway," Myron said, "your old man is not going to cut you off, no matter what he says. I bet if you call him up and tell him you're starving, he'll come through. He's just trying to scare you into finishing school, that's all. So how's that going, by the way?"

"Pretty good," she said, perking up, for school was, at last, going well. "I think I settled on a dissertation topic. I'm going to write up the prospectus over the holidays."

"Hey, that's great!" Myron said, and his smile was, Rachel knew, genuine. "You know, I've been doing some thinking about my situation," he said.

There was a huge shock, Myron thinking about himself.

"I'm not sure teaching college-level courses is my thing."

Whoa, that was *really* a shock. Rachel stopped what she was doing and turned around to look at him again. Not high, not kidding . . . "What do you mean?" she demanded. "You've been a college professor for, like, *ever!*"

"I know," Myron said with a laugh, and shut the fridge door, sauntered over to the pantry. "I just feel like it's time for a change. You remember that place my folks have on Hilton Head?"

How could she forget? It was the one decent place he'd ever taken her, and even then she'd had to pay for half of the trip.

"I was thinking of going down there and doing some surfing. Just spend some time getting my head on straight, maybe smoke a joint or two and sort of mull over what life is all about, you know what I'm saying?"

No, she didn't know what he was saying. This could not be the same, tenure-starved man she'd known for the last few years. "Are you all right, Myron?" she asked. "This doesn't sound like you at all. I thought academia was your life."

He laughed again, pulled out some bread and peanut butter and proceeded to make a sandwich. "I guess you aren't the only one who's been changing, Rach."

"Have I been changing?"

"Are you kidding? Look at you. Working, finding a dissertation topic, going to the gym . . . that's not the Rachel I know."

It wasn't really the Rachel she knew, either.

The phone rang. "Ah . . . I need to get that," she said, and ducked out of the kitchen, feeling his eyes on her back.

"Hallo, might I please speak with the gorgeous woman who refuses to believe that penguins make marvelous pets?" the distinctive British voice asked when she answered.

A warm flush went right through her. "Speaking," she said, smiling softly, and pushed her hair behind her ear.

"What are you about, Rachel? I've missed your laughter today."

"I've been holed up in the library."

"How exciting for you. I hope it was at least productive."

"It was. I've got enough to write a prospectus, I think."

"Fantastic news!" Flynn said happily. "I've absolutely no idea what a prospectus is, but I'm chuffed to bits for you, love. Perhaps we might celebrate your blinding success—I'll grab some takeaway Chinese and stop by, eh?"

"Well . . ." She glanced over her shoulder. Myron was standing in the kitchen, eating his sandwich, staring at her. "I could just come there."

"Here? But we're always here, aren't we? And besides, your place is much roomier. After a thorough study of chapter fourteen of the tantric manual, I'm rather convinced we'll need all the room we can get."

Rachel laughed, but she could feel the heat in her face and stole another glimpse of Myron. "But my house is really a mess. Honestly, there's not that much room," she said low. "I promise, I'll have it all cleaned up in time for Thanksgiving. You're coming, aren't you?"

"Wild horses couldn't keep me away," he said. "But can't we have a preview—"

"Tonight's really not good," she said quickly.

He said nothing for a moment, then laughed low. "Are you, by chance, hiding anything?"

"Hiding?" She laughed nervously.

"Bodies, perhaps? Gold bouillon? Brownies?"

Rachel smiled. "Wouldn't you like to know."

"Yes, actually, I would. You treat that charming little bungalow like Fort Knox."

She detected a little irritation in his voice. "Flynn—"

"Right, come here, then. I'll order up the Chinese, if that's all right."

"Thanks. I'll see you in an hour, okay?"

"Yes and do be quick, will you? Chapter fourteen will take a bit of time."

"What about special shoes?"

"Couldn't possibly hurt."

"See you soon," she said, and clicked off, stood there for a moment, then finally turned around. Myron had finished his sandwich. But he was still staring at her.

He brushed his hands together, removing the crumbs. "So! I guess then, from the sound of it, you're still seeing that guy."

She nodded.

He looked down at his shoes and sighed. "That's great, Rachel. I'm happy if you're happy. Really. I am. I'm probably going to move to Hilton Head anyway, so it's not as if we were going anywhere, right?"

"*Going* anywhere?" she echoed loudly. "We haven't *gone* anywhere since I can't remember when, Myron."

With a sheepish laugh, he folded his arms. "Yeah, you're right, I know you're right. I guess I've just been thinking about us lately and I thought maybe . . . well, you know. Maybe we could hook up again."

Okay, so now the world had really spun right off its axis. She put the phone on the dining table, next to a pair of porcelain candlesticks Myron had left last week. "Hook up? You and me? You dumped me, remember? Honestly, Myron, sometimes I don't get you at all."

"Hey, it's just a thought! No big deal," Myron said laughingly. "Listen, I gotta run. So what's the deal with Thanksgiving?" he asked as he strolled past her, as if he'd never mentioned hooking up.

"Nothing," she said, still perplexed by his last statement. "Just a few friends."

"Great. I'm not doing anything, so I'll stop by. Maybe I can check out this dude you're so hot about," he said with a laugh. "Okay, see you. Thanks for the sandwich." He reached for the door.

"Myron!" Rachel called.

He turned, and shook his head with a smile. "Don't worry, Rach—I'm not going to come back into the picture and screw things up for you."

Who *was* this guy? She didn't know if she should be more appalled that he thought he could actually screw anything up for her, or that he was even contemplating renewing a long-dead relationship. But at any rate, she had something more pressing on her mind. "Actually, I was going to ask about my phone—you know, the T-Mobile?"

"Oh yeah," he said, nodding thoughtfully. "I still have that, don't I?"

"Yes. You still have it, you've had it forever, and I'd really like it back. I haven't paid the phone bill, and that may be the only phone I have—"

"Not to worry," he said, lifting his hand and cutting her off. "I'll bring it Thanksgiving. Okay, gotta jet. See you," he said, and with a wink, he sauntered out the door.

Chapter Twenty-seven

✦ ✦ ✦

CHAPTER fourteen began with a mutual bath and cleansing, and was supposed to progress to something a bit more athletic, but thanks to some yin-and-yang techniques Flynn had perfected on his own, they never got past the bubble bath and champagne.

Afterward, they lounged in the bath, lying at opposite ends. Flynn's toes were doing a little postcoital exploration on their own, but Rachel's were on either side of his head, and wiggled when she talked.

He was admiring her, scarcely hearing her discourse on the intricacies of successful sidewalk pamphlet distribution, or whatever odd job she'd done recently, because he was thinking of their lovemaking and how terribly pleased he was that she was a lustful lover, a woman who was as emboldened to seek her own pleasure as she was to give it.

Iris—he didn't really like thinking of Iris—but while Iris thought nothing, apparently, of blowing Paul, she had been a fragile lover with him, always making little sounds to signal her fear of being broken in two, or her displeasure with particular positions.

Rachel, on the other hand, was eager to try almost anything, reveling in the most intimate of acts, encouraging him with her voice and her body. His orgasms were seismic, like a meteorite crashing to earth, and that just made him want her all the more.

So when she asked him what he was thinking, he felt himself get a bit red-faced. "What, wasn't I listening with proper discernment?" he asked with a lopsided smile.

"No, you weren't listening at all," she said, playfully splashing him. "I asked you how you liked America, and you just grinned," she said as she pushed herself up and reached over the edge of the tub for the champagne bottle.

"I adore America," he said.

"Really?" she asked as she hoisted the champagne over the side of the tub and refreshed one of the four glass tumblers the corporate flat boasted. "I've known some Europeans who don't care for it."

"That's what they say," Flynn said, holding his glass out to be refilled. "They like to hate America, when really, this is where they'd like to be. As for myself, I'm not afraid to say it—I like America, and I adore at least one American."

Rachel smiled prettily and leaned up again. Flynn languidly watched her breasts rise from the water and float there as she put the bottle away. "And I like the U.K.," she said thoughtfully. "It's funny, isn't it? We're so compatible in so many ways."

"It's refreshing," Flynn agreed, and chuckled when he stuck his big toe in between her legs and Rachel gave a little squeal. But her eyes lit up with pleasure, and she shifted slightly, forcing his toe to slip deeper between her legs.

"You're a shameless tart, you know that," he said, grinning wickedly.

"It's all your fault, Mr. Oliver. A man is not supposed to know about toes . . . So if you like it, do you think you'll stay?"

"If the rest of me is permitted to join the toe."

"I meant," Rachel giggled, "do you think you'll stay in America?"

That stopped his toe's exploration cold. Of course he'd

thought of it, but he'd come to no satisfactory conclusion for a variety of reasons, not the least of which was his uncertainty of how Rachel fit into the museum scheme.

But he forced a smile to his face and shrugged his shoulders behind a sip of champagne. "I couldn't rightly say, love. Why, have you an offer for me?"

She laughed as she idly made a mountain of bubbles between them. "Maybe," she said diffidently. "I just wondered. Not that I am *expecting* anything, you know, but . . ."

As her voice trailed off, Flynn sensed something, and put his glass aside, sat up, leaning forward to see her over the mountain of bubbles. "But . . . ?"

She looked up; the intense expression in her blue-green eyes pierced him clean through, so much that he almost reared back. An uneasiness cropped up in the pit of his belly, a certain signal of danger, but he held her gaze nonetheless—

"But . . . I am falling . . . *have* fallen . . . in love with you."

The pronouncement so stunned Flynn that for a moment, he could not move, could not so much as draw a breath. He felt like a sodding idiot, an inexperienced fool. How could he have not seen this coming?

"Rachel," he started calmly and quietly, but saw instantly that it was too late to salvage the moment, for she had seen and heard his hesitation and took it to mean her feelings were unrequited. Only nothing could have been further from the truth, really, and he was desperate to know how to say so without giving everything away, months worth of work, as she sank back against the edge of the tub, sliding down and down until the water was up to her chin, her face almost crimson.

"But hey, don't let *that* get to you," she said with a very uneasy laugh before he could muddle his way through this excruciatingly unpleasant moment. "I'm the type to fall in love with just about anyone," she said, and he could hear the anxiety in her chuckle. "People, animals, plants," she added with another panicked laugh. "I even had a bike once that I fell in love with. I named him Arthur—after King Arthur, of course—and I rode him around the grounds, round and round. But I was like, twelve or something, way too old to be in love with a bike. Ha ha, right?"

When Flynn didn't laugh, she suddenly shot up out of the water, sent some of it slopping over the sides in her haste to get up. Flynn tried to reach for her, but she backed away from him, stood there naked with dozens of rivulets of soapy water running down her body. "Food, too. Remember chocolate? Now *that's* love. And movies. I've seen *Braveheart* about ten times, did I tell you that? I just *love* that movie!"

"Rachel, please listen, will you?" Flynn tried as she stepped over the tub and onto the small bathmat.

"Oh no, I've made you feel awkward! I'm sorry, Flynn, I was really just sort of kidding around!" she said, her hand flailing helplessly. "Honestly! I don't expect you to say anything in return, and really, I thought you'd just laugh," she said gaily, and reached for a towel, hurriedly wrapped herself in it, then struggled with the wet mane of hair down her back.

"It's not that I don't have feelings," he tried in desperation, but thought it sounded terribly hollow. He stood up.

Rachel thrust a towel at him without looking at him, and honestly, for the first time, she seemed afraid to look at him. "Oh, I know," she said. "It's obvious you like me well enough, or we wouldn't be doing this, right?" she said, and stepped to the sink and mirror, and focused on her hair, watching herself comb it . . . except that the mirror was fogged over and she couldn't possibly see a thing.

Flynn wrapped the towel around his waist as he stepped out of the tub, then stepped behind her, wrapped his arms around her. "I do adore you, Rachel. I *do*," he insisted. "There are just some things I cannot explain, at least not yet," he said, feeling fantastically phony for it.

"You don't have to explain anything, Flynn," she said, and leaned forward to the mirror again at the same time she pulled her hair over her shoulder, forcing him to let go of her. She began to braid it.

"I've hurt you." Stating the obvious made him feel like an ass.

"You haven't!" she insisted in a high voice. "Like I said, I didn't expect anything in return. I was just . . . talking."

"Rachel. Dear God, there is so much I want to say—"

"Oh stop, will you? You're making this into a much bigger deal than it is, really!" she insisted with a laugh, and turned around, leaned up against the sink, smiling. A smile that came nowhere near her eyes. There was no masking the distress and humiliation he saw in her eyes, and he'd never felt like such a cad as he did at that very moment.

"Come *on*, Flynn!" she said, laughing again. "It's not as if I thought this was *going* anywhere," she said, motioning vaguely to the bathroom. "I mean obviously, you're British, I'm American, we live thousands of miles from each other, our lives are very different—"

"But I thought we were entirely compatible. You said so yourself."

"*Phhht*," she snorted with a roll of her eyes. "Yeah, I did. But you know, the fact that we both like Coldplay does not mean that we are going to be a couple. I was just talking!" she said, and stepped around him. "You took it too seriously. You know me, I like to talk. Chatter chatter chatter." She opened the bathroom door; a rush of cold air hit him square in the face, sobered him even more. "Speaking of chatter, I'm going to have to run. I have to call some people tonight and make sure they're bringing stuff to Thanksgiving. And a turkey. I really need to get a turkey."

Flynn followed helplessly behind her, padding out into the bedroom and standing there like an idiot as Rachel found her clothes and began to dress, wishing he could think, could find a way to tell her everything. But his professional self convinced him not to say anything, not yet.

She chatted on about the turkey, but he was silently and

fiercely debating what he should tell her—if he told her she was part of an investigation, he would tip his hand, and they might lose a very valuable link to solving it. He could not forget the job he was sworn to do, or the fact that he was breaking every law enforcement convention that he knew by falling in love with her. But that was the rub— he *wanted* to be with her, because he, too, had fallen in love, and God, he desperately wanted to say so.

Which left him standing there, wondering exactly what he intended to begin with—where had he thought this would all lead? Did he think he'd never have to face the truth? It was inevitable, and he was wholly unprepared to deal with it, bloody fool that he was.

He'd fucked it all up, and it was not something that could be easily rectified. Certainly not while he was standing bare-arsed wearing nothing but a towel.

So he just stood watching miserably as Rachel dressed and stuffed her big bag full of her things that were scattered about, and when she turned to face him with that blindingly false smile, he opened his arms, wrapped her in an embrace. Rachel responded by pressing her face to his shoulder, and her body sagged against him.

"Rachel—"

But she suddenly lifted her head, stepped out of his embrace. "So you're coming Thursday, right?" she asked.

"Yes, of course," he said, trying to sound reassuring.

The bird did not bite. *"Great!"* she exclaimed. "And now, I've really got to run." She gave him a peck on the cheek and quickly proceeded to the door, her wet braid swinging above her hips.

He shoved both hands through his wet hair in despair. "I'll ring you later, all right?" he called after her as she reached the door.

"Okay!" she said, and with a cheery wave, she walked out the door. "One o'clock! Don't be late!" And the door closed.

Flynn stood there for what felt like hours, staring at that

closed door, his hands on his hips, his mind racing badly, until he realized he was freezing quite to death.

OKAY, so now she had finally reached that pinnacle of achievement, had performed that singular, crowning act that would forever label her a giant loser. It was unwritten rule numero uno, the *one* thing a girl *never* did unless she was a certified imbecile—never tell a guy you love him first. *Augh!*

She raced away from the Corporate Suites and into the oblivion of night, trying to outrun her humiliation. Naturally, she was stopped in her escape by a red light.

With a moan, Rachel laid her head against the steering wheel. "Idiot," she muttered beneath her breath. "Did you really believe all that witchcraft stuff could change the universe? You're still Miss Fortune."

A honk behind her brought her head up—the light was green, and she threw the car into first gear, hit the gas, and hurtled through the intersection, made a sharp right, and turned into the lot of a small market. The sign said they closed at midnight—it was ten to. She grabbed her bag, dashed inside with the thing banging against her leg, then race-walked the aisles until she found what she was looking for.

Yes, the baking aisle, with every type of brownie mix known to man. With a box of extra-moist and fudgy Duncan Hines and a carton of eggs, she ran to the checkout, dug in her purse until she came up with the required $3.37, and slipped outside just before midnight.

At one-thirty, she was sitting in the floor of her living room, a freshly-baked pan of brownies in her lap and a fork in her hand. She was methodically eating the brownies between gulps and sobs of bitter, bitter disappointment.

In the middle of one particularly big bite, however, she spied the stupid spell book on a little occasional table in the dining room, and felt a hot rage wash over her. Damn Dagne and her witchcraft! No, no, that wasn't fair. If

Dagne jumped off a bridge, she wouldn't necessarily follow—wait. Scratch that. She might. But the point was that *Dagne* hadn't given her this false sense of confidence, she had given that to herself.

Witchcraft! What was *up* with that?

Incensed by her own stupidity, Rachel shoved the half-eaten pan of brownies aside, came to her feet, marched across the room to that ridiculous and *pink* spell book (who the hell put spells in pink leather?), and knocked it off the occasional table with an angry swipe of her hand. The book fell off and landed open.

"Oh please, I'm not falling for that again," she said defiantly, but bent over nonetheless and peered down. It had fallen open to a spell designed to rid yourself of negative energy.

"Idiots. Whoever writes this stuff is an idiot," she muttered, and hatefully kicked the spell book. It skid across the wooden floors, beneath the dining table and out the other side and came to a rest next to the hutch. It was, she could see, still open.

Cautiously, folding her arms defensively against her, Rachel walked around the table and went down on her haunches in front of the spell book.

Escaping Negative Energy and Reviving the Chakra with Positive Energy

Rachel squinted again, read the instructions. All she needed was a piece of lavender cloth—had that, hanging around her neck. And the herb anise, which she knew she had plenty of, thanks to Dagne's spell shopping. Green tea, a bowl made of silver (she stood up, looked at the hutch. Yep, still had the bowl Myron had given her), and an amulet.

Well, hell.

Okay, she didn't believe in witchcraft, and she would *not* be sucked into believing that it actually worked, thank you. But on the other hand, she had all the stuff, and she was wide awake, thanks to half a pan of double fudge chocolate brownies. It was just something to do until she was ready to go to bed, that was all.

Rachel picked up the spell book with two fingers and marched back to the living room to prepare the last spell she would ever, *ever* do.

That night, Rachel went to bed with a tummyache, having devoured the rest of the brownies, but having also swallowed down most of her humiliation. She fell asleep quickly, and was soon dreaming of a field of yellow flowers.

In her dream, she was wearing a long, flowing silk white gown like the damsels in distress always seemed to wear. As she walked through the field, every flower grew taller and taller, and as she touched them, they gave her positive energy. Rachel touched so many flowers, she was practically floating above earth, and was laughing as she went.

Then at the end of the field, she noticed a figure, and as she drew closer, she realized it was Flynn. Still wearing nothing but a cheap, flimsy towel.

Chapter Twenty-eight

✦ ✦ ✦

RACHEL awoke with a start Thanksgiving morning with the sick realization that in the time it took to make a gigantic faux pas with Flynn, she hadn't heard a word from Dad since sending him that e-mail. Was he coming? Oh God, she'd been so freaked out by what she'd done that she hadn't remembered to call him.

Of course, there was no answer at either his penthouse apartment or his cell.

Dagne was the first to arrive with her so-called famous Brussels sprout and cauliflower casserole and found Rachel frantically picking up the clutter in the living room when she came in. But Dagne walked straight through to the living room and into the kitchen without a single word.

As it was unlike Dagne to do anything without speaking, Rachel followed her.

Dagne was standing in front of the fridge, a beer in hand.

"Hey," Rachel said.

"Hey." She took a big long swig of her beer, then put it down on the breakfast bar with a huge bang.

"What's the matter?"

"Glenn."

"What—did something happen? Is he bugging you?"

Dagne rolled her eyes, swiped up the beer, and took another long swig of it before answering, "Hardly." She wiped her mouth with the back of her hand. "Remember that date we had? You know, the night we did the spell? I thought it went great. I met him at Fratangelo's, we had a couple of drinks, we went back to my place . . . and I haven't heard from him since. Not a peep."

"But that was only two or three days ago," Rachel reminded her.

"It was *four,* thank you very much. I think he dumped me. And don't try and talk me out of it. That asshole dumped me, I can feel it."

"But what about the spell?" Rachel tried, in spite of having decided yesterday that it was, at least in her case, a bunch of hocus-pocus crap.

"I don't know," Dagne said, staring thoughtfully at the peeling wallpaper above the window. "I just have this really funny feeling that something isn't right . . . Where's Flynn? Is he coming?"

Rachel had not told Dagne about her brush with stupidity yet, and quickly turned her attention to the potatoes on the stove. "Supposed to," she muttered.

"Great. At least *one* of us is going to have a good time. I can't wait to—"

"Hel-lo-oh!"

Dagne looked at Rachel. "Chantal," Rachel said.

Chantal and Tiffinnae had come along with their five children in tow. Rachel never did get which child belonged to which woman, but after a lot of standing around in the living room, they began to disappear, one by one, out the front door. Neither Chantal nor Tiffinnae seemed to notice, as they were too caught up walking around and admiring Rachel's things while Rachel pulled their very large and heavy cooler into the kitchen.

"Mind if we go upstairs?" Chantal shouted from the top stair.

Dagne opened the cooler, started sorting through. "Oooh, pumpkin pies. And look at this, a green bean casserole," she said, her eyes getting wider. "Where's the turkey? Who's got the turkey?"

Someone was knocking at the door. *Flynn!* Please let it be Flynn! "I do. It's in the oven," Rachel said, tripping over Dagne in her haste to get to the front door. Nervously, she threw it open with a huge smile . . . but no one was there.

There was, however, the distinct sound of children giggling around the side of the house.

Rachel closed the door, returned to the kitchen to check the turkey while Dagne tried to fit all the food Chantal and Tiffinnae had brought into the fridge. Another knock at the door, and Rachel told Dagne to ignore it. "The kids," she said.

But when Chantal and Tiffinnae finally came downstairs again, she heard Tiffinnae say, "Well, come on in, Jason. Was you just going to stand out there and wait for someone to figure out you was here?"

Rachel instantly came out of the kitchen. "Jason, I'm so sorry—I thought it was the kids again."

"*Whose* kids?" Chantal instantly demanded with a dark and defensive frown.

"Come in, Jason," Rachel said, taking his hand and ignoring Chantal.

She led him to the couch; he sat cautiously on the edge. "Was I supposed to bring something? I didn't bring anything."

"That's all right, there's plenty," Rachel said over Chantal's snort of disapproval. "Just come in and make yourself at home."

"Well, I certainly didn't come empty-handed," an effeminate male voice sniffed. Mr. Gregory had arrived.

"Look what Mr. Gregory done brought!" Chantal cried, holding up a box with several bottles of wine. "Mmmmmm, we gonna have us a *fine* time!" she informed Tiffinnae.

"Clara was rather fond of her wine," Mr. Gregory said. "But I have no use for it. By the bye, I was viciously attacked with small mud pellets on my way in," he added as he shrugged out of his coat and handed it to Dagne without so much as a glance.

Chantal marched to the door and flung it open, stuck her head out the screen. "RAY. SHON. *DRA!*" she hollered. "YOU BETTER NOT BE DOING THEM MUD BALLS OR I WILL SKIN YOUR BLACK HIDE, YOU HEAR ME?"

Whether Rayshondra heard her or not, they would not know, for Chantal instantly slammed the door shut, then turned and walked into the living room. "That a new shirt, Jason?" she asked pleasantly.

Rachel took the opportunity to introduce everyone to Dagne.

Everyone said hi, except for Jason, who sort of muttered at his toes. Then Chantal suggested Rachel needed help in the kitchen, but Rachel insisted she didn't, as she was scared to let Chantal anywhere near her kitchen unsupervised, but the woman was determined. So Rachel, Chantal, Tiffinnae, and Dagne all tromped to the kitchen together, leaving Mr. Gregory and Jason to stare at each other.

It wasn't long before they heard Sandy shout, "Happy Thanksgiving!"

"Happy Thanksgiving," Rachel responded, coming out to greet her. Mr. Gregory was holding the door so she could maneuver in with her two grocery bags and her crutches.

"Hiiiii-iiiii!" Sandy sang out to Rachel.

"Jason, maybe you could give Sandy a hand with the bags?" Rachel asked. Jason came to his feet, slunk over to Sandy, and looked down at her foot.

"I thought the other one was hurt," he said. Rachel had to agree with Jason—two weeks ago, it had been the other foot bandaged up.

"Oh it *was,*" Sandy cheerfully confirmed. "But would you believe I twisted this ankle so bad I can't even walk?"

She laughed. "Just as I was getting off these darn things! But then one night, I had one of my attacks, you know, and I got up in the middle of the night to go to the bathroom—this medicine I'm on makes you pee every ten minutes and that's *so* annoying—well anyway, I get up, but my sinuses were acting up so bad I could hardly think, and it was dark, and I was trying to find the wall switch, and I hit a stool, which made me sort of stagger back," she said, now re-enacting the tragic accident, "and wouldn't you know it, my *right* ankle wasn't strong enough to recover since I had hurt it so bad, so I twisted my *left* ankle trying to compensate for the right!"

No one said a word for a moment, just stood there, blinking at her in disbelief. "Girl, you a mess," Chantal said from the dining room, shaking her head.

"I *know*," Sandy said gleefully.

Chantal snorted, walked back to the kitchen with Sandy hobbling after her.

Jason looked at Rachel, still holding the bags. "What am I supposed to do with these?" he asked, holding the bags out to Rachel.

"I'll take them," she said, wondering what in the hell had possessed her to host Thanksgiving. At the moment, she couldn't think of a worse idea, and glanced at the clock on the mantel. Half past one. *Where is Flynn?*

As she worked to prepare the meal, she kept one eye on the window for any sign of Flynn. The later the hour became, the clearer it became to her that he was not coming.

He was not coming because she had gone and blurted the *L* word, and had scared the shit out of him. That was so like her, to ruin everything by doing something stupid. And it didn't help that Dagne sidled up to her more than once with a hushed, *"Where's Flynn?"*

Rachel's distraction caused her to forget the bread, and it wasn't until Tiffinnae asked if anyone else noticed something burning that she remembered it—with a screech, she ran to the oven, pulled out two burned loaves of French bread.

The smell filled the kitchen, and the women set about opening windows, as Sandy directed them from her perch at the breakfast bar, and during the melee, Chantal's gravy went bad and lumpy, and Dagne dropped her casserole, and Brussels sprouts went shooting across the floor.

The meal was quickly turning into a disaster. But then someone was knocking on the door, and Dagne beamed at her. "There he is!" she sang.

Yes, yes, it had to be him, he was just running late!

"Who?" Tiffinnae demanded.

Rachel was already on her way to the door and did not answer. She flung it open, all smiles, certain it was Flynn.

But it was not Flynn. "Happy Thanksgiving, Mr. Valicielo," Rachel said warily, noticing that his face was unusually red.

"Do you see what they did?" he demanded, dispensing with any greeting and gesturing wildly toward his house.

"Who did?"

"Those *kids!*" he spat.

With great reluctance, Rachel stepped through the screen door and out onto the porch and looked at his yard. Oh, man. His little herd of deer and his frog had all been turned upside down and the pinwheels were missing altogether. The only thing that had survived the assault was the concrete rabbit. "Yikes," Rachel said, wincing. "What happened?"

"What *happened?*" he echoed in a roar. "Your *kids!* I'm calling the cops!"

"No, Mr. Valicielo, please don't do that!" Rachel cried. "They're children of my guests and I'm certain they don't know any better, but we'll make them come inside—"

"What's going on here?" Chantal demanded behind her, and Rachel groaned as she stomped out onto the porch.

"Those kids attacked my yard!" Mr. Valicielo shouted, pointing to his yard.

"*Whose* kids?"

"I don't know! Kids! Kids from here!"

"If you be implying that *my* kids did that, you better

step off, little man," Chantal said, waving her head back and forth to match the finger she was waving at Mr. Valicielo.

"I don't know whose kids they are!" Mr. Valicielo shot back. "I just know they were *kids. Black* kids!" he added.

"Oh gee, I wish you hadn't said that," Rachel said, but no one heard her on account of Chantal's primal roar.

"You think just 'cuz some *black* kids in this neighborhood that *they* do that?" she asked, punching her fists to her enormous hips.

Mr. Valicielo at least had the good sense to look scared, but it did not stop him from speaking. The next thing Rachel knew, she was standing between Chantal and Mr. Valicielo, arms outwardly extended to keep them apart, begging Tiffinnae to stop baiting Chantal, and thoroughly disgusted with Jason and Mr. Gregory, who remained behind the screen door, peering out like scared little rabbits.

Rachel begged Mr. Valicielo to please go home and she'd make sure all the kids at her house were inside, and then she would come and clean his yard up when they were finished with the Thanksgiving meal. Then she begged Chantal to please get her kids inside before he actually called the cops and ruined Thanksgiving.

When they finally turned away from each other, both fuming, Rachel sagged against the porch railing, wondering what in the hell was going on here.

"Rachel."

His voice startled her almost to her knees, and now Rachel was certain—something had gone terribly awry in the spell department, for now her nightmare was complete.

She turned slowly, pushed her hair over her shoulder, and tried to smile. "H-hey, Dad. I didn't think you were going to make it."

He sort of frowned, reached for the railing, as if he needed to prop himself up. "Did you honestly think I'd stay away?" he asked. "Well, I didn't. I'm here. So are you going to invite me in?"

Oh man, this was the last thing she needed, the very *last*

thing she needed. But Dad was standing there in his cashmere coat and scarf, a fedora on his head, and a suit beneath that, judging by the trousers and shoes peeking out from beneath the coat. But even under the bulk of his coat and suit, she could tell he was thinner, and his face, she noticed, was more gaunt than it had been a couple of months ago.

Yet . . . given what he had apparently witnessed so far, he didn't seem particularly unhappy. Not particularly happy, either. More . . . confused than anything else. *Confused?* That was weird—her father was many things, but confused was never one of them.

"Hello?"

She snapped out of it. "Of course, Dad," she said, and reached out to him to hug him. "I have to warn you, my weaving class is here—"

"I gathered—you said so in that smarty e-mail."

"Right," she said weakly. "But . . . they aren't . . . they're not exactly the sort . . ."

And then Dad, in an uncharacteristic display of affection, put his arm around her shoulders and squeezed her into his side. "I got a pretty good picture a minute ago, baby girl," he said with a crooked smile. "You don't need to worry about me; I'm neither shocked nor appalled. I'm just glad to see you. You look great, you know it?"

"W-what?" she stammered. "What?"

He chuckled, kissed her temple. "I said, you look *great.*"

She could not remember the last time Dad had said anything kind about her appearance, and Rachel blinked up at him in complete astonishment.

And Dad laughed. He *laughed.*

AARON had argued with Bonnie about making this trip. After Rachel's sarcastic response to his e-mail, he could not see that anything would be gained from it until she had a major attitude adjustment. But Bonnie had convinced him a quiet Thanksgiving with his daughter was just the thing—they could relax, they could talk, and he could listen.

He really did want to make things right with Rachel, he really did. She was his baby girl. So he'd geared himself up for it—a day of listening and struggling to keep his mouth shut.

But naturally, he and Bonnie had misunderstood Rachel again—her sarcasm had been the truth, and as he looked around, he wondered, God in heaven, who *were* these people?

He sat at the end of the table he had bought for Rachel at some tony furniture shop in New York, gazing at them all, as the meal was hardly edible (the turkey terribly dry, the dressing missing some major ingredient, the gravy lumpy. The only thing that was any good was the wine).

There were the two black women, who, while highly entertaining, were really not who he pictured bent over the looms he imagined Rachel used when she was doing her earth angel thing, instructing people how to weave tapestries or whatever.

And the old dude. Jesus, who'd *died?* He was as morose as he could possibly be, and every expression, every gesture, telegraphed his desire to be elsewhere. And Sandy, the hypochondriac. Whoa, what a nut job that one was. If she laid one more ailment on him, Aaron was going to call her bluff, ask her if she'd ever had cancer, then match her chemo for chemo, surgery for surgery. There was a name for that, the need to be sick all the time, he was pretty sure. What was the name of it?

Her friend Dagne had to be the nuttiest of them all, what with all the crap about witchcraft, then getting upset when everyone laughed at her.

The kid dressed in black sort of fascinated him, for Aaron couldn't make what he was supposed to be. From where he was sitting, it looked like the kid was wearing eye makeup. But it was clear the kid was crazy about Rachel, and who could blame him?

Aaron was not surprised by how engaging she was; he'd always suspected it. She had an uncanny ability to relate to each and every one of these fruitcakes. She was the bright spot at the table, the one to whom everyone naturally gravitated. Nothing at all like the meek girl she was around him, preferring the shadows and leaving Becky and Robbie up front. Here, she was the sunlight.

What did surprise him was how uncommonly talented she was. The nut job Sandy had shown him a tapestry she was doing on the loom, apparently one she had taken from a picture in a magazine and calculated onto her loom. She was an artist.

Wow. It was amazing how many things he'd been wrong about in his sixty years.

His good mood was dampened, however, when The Professor strolled in halfway through the meal, all smug-looking, and carrying a single six-pack of beer.

He first stopped to bless the children, all five of whom were eating off paper plates in front of a movie. The ass-hole bent down to speak to each one of them. Like he cared. Like *they* cared. The oldest kid, a girl, looked at him with the complete disdain he deserved.

So did Aaron.

"Hello, everyone, I'm Professor Tidwell," he announced with a smile and a bow.

Mostly, they just eyed him curiously. But then he strolled down the length of the table and kissed Rachel on the top of her head. Aaron did not miss her grimace at that, or Dagne's roll of her eyes.

The Professor continued on into the kitchen, during which time Rachel hastily explained he was a friend. He returned a few moments later with a plate and a chair, which he put next to Rachel and asked for a variety of things to be passed to him, filled his plate, cracked open a beer, then looked around the table. "So," he said, interrupting another conversation, "you're all Rachel's students, are you? I once oversaw her on a teaching internship, and I know she's an excellent teacher. I am sure you all agree."

"Myron—" Rachel started, her self-conscious blush evident to Aaron at the other end of the table.

"It's okay, Rach," The Professor said with a laugh. "They won't say anything disparaging while you're sitting here." He laughed again. No one else did, but Professor Tidwell didn't notice, as he was diving headfirst into that turkey like he hadn't eaten in days. "No, I'm serious," he continued with his mouth full. "Rachel's got a gift for teaching."

"Hey Myron, did you bring beer for anyone else?" Dagne asked, and Aaron thought perhaps he'd misjudged her—that little fruitcake might have more sense than he'd originally thought.

"I brought a six-pack. I figured you'd have plenty."

"That was very thoughtful," Dagne said coolly, earning herself another brownie point with Aaron. "Can I get anyone anything? I'm going to the kitchen."

"I'd like one of those beers, if you don't mind, Dagne," Aaron said, his gaze on The Professor.

"Sure thing, Mr. Lear," she said, and The Professor jerked his head up, wide-eyed, and looked at Aaron.

"Hello, Byron," Aaron said. "I'm Rachel's father, Aaron Lear."

"Ooh, girl, this is gonna be *good*," one of the black women said with a snicker.

"Mr. Lear?" he said, and suddenly didn't seem quite so full of himself. "I, ah . . . I didn't know you'd be here," he said, and came to his feet, wiped his hands on his cords, and hurried down the length of the table to shake Aaron's hand.

"I just couldn't stay away," he drawled, looking the ass straight in the eye.

The ass quickly dropped his hand, returned to his plate of food, and was, thankfully, silent, allowing one of the black women to wonder why her dressing had dried out so.

"Probably the moon," Dagne opined with a sigh.

Everyone looked at her blankly; and then one of the other women stood with her plate.

"At least we got dessert," she said, and began to clear the table.

The rest of the afternoon was excruciatingly boring for Aaron. Rachel's guests milled about the living room, some staring at a muted football game, the kid in black trying to play a game with the kids (but from the sound of it, they were constantly correcting his understanding of the game), one of the black women—Chantal—lounging after trooping over to the neighbor's house to right his deer.

The Professor tried to make small talk with Aaron, but he was too bored with the man to make conversation, and answered his silly questions ("Are you a history fan, too?" "Rachel is going to make a great professor, don't you think?" "I like the St. Louis Cardinals . . . oh, when did they move to Arizona?") with one- or two-syllable answers.

Aaron tried to watch football, but he couldn't help noticing that Rachel seemed terribly distracted, kept walking to the window and peering out, then disappearing into the kitchen again.

There was no one more grateful than Aaron when at last everyone began to leave, trickling out until there was no one left but The Professor, Dagne, and Rachel.

The Professor was the first to take his leave. "Okay! I better get going. I have to work tomorrow." He glanced nervously at Aaron, then went and kissed Rachel on the cheek. "Thanks for the meal."

"Sure," she said, looking at her feet. "By the way . . . did you bring my phone?"

The ass winced, snapped his fingers. "I *knew* I was forgetting something," he said. "I'll bring it tomorrow. I've got a couple of things I want to give you."

Aaron could only imagine what they were. As The Professor slunk out the door, Dagne gathered her things. "Nice meeting you, Mr. Lear."

"You, too, Dagne. Now don't get yourself in trouble with that witchcraft," he said with a wink.

Dagne sighed, shook her head. "It's too late for that, I'm afraid," she said, and looked at Rachel. "Remember that thing we did the other day? I think we screwed it up. I think we might have made it work in reverse—"

"Okay, well listen, I'll call you later," Rachel quickly interrupted, ushering her friend to the door. They stepped outside; Aaron could hear a rather heated discussion taking place, and then finally, Rachel called good-bye and came back in, looking more distressed than before.

"Something wrong?"

"No," she said quickly, shaking her head. "It's just—" The telephone interrupted whatever she was going to say, and she practically dove for the thing. "Just a minute, Dad," she said, grabbing up the receiver. "Hello?" she answered breathlessly, but instantly, her face fell. "Oh. Yes, hi, Mike . . . I'm sorry, I'm just sort of rattled. I had a lot of people over today," she said, and turned from Aaron, walked into the kitchen.

A guy. That's what all the nervousness was about. Aaron hadn't raised three daughters and not learned all the signs of guy anxiety. But hey, it wasn't that idiot professor, so he was happy.

Actually, he was pretty damn happy in general. Rachel was a-okay in his book. A little on the weird side, but nevertheless, he was beginning to appreciate how special she was.

Yep, he thought he'd stay overnight and have a nice chat with his daughter. And *listen*. He could not forget that part; Bonnie would kill him.

Chapter Twenty-nine

✦ ✦ ✦

AARON might have been happy, but Rachel was one step away from a nervous breakdown, no thanks to Dagne, who had very heatedly insisted in a whisper, on the porch while they froze, that she'd worked through it over the course of the afternoon, and figured out that they had cursed themselves the other night when they had cast their goddess moon spell.

"Think about it, Rachel. No moon to shine, no fire . . . we did everything the opposite of what the spell said, and now we are getting just the opposite of what we wanted. Haven't you noticed that everything is *haywire?*" she insisted with a punch to Rachel's shoulder. "Glenn has dumped me, Flynn's dumped you, the meal was awful . . ."

Rachel didn't really hear the rest of the list, because yes, thank you, she'd noticed that everything was upside down and inside out today, most notably in the Flynn category.

And now there was the Mike factor. How in the hell could she have *possibly* forgotten the astounding fact that she had another date with a different guy? But she had, until the very moment she picked up the phone, and holy shit, there was her Friday night date, sounding very cheerful on his drive back from the shore.

After the usual exchange of Thanksgiving pleasantries, he asked, "Want me to pick you up tomorrow?"

Oh God, nononono. "How about we meet at Fratangelo's?" she asked, trying her damnedest to sound enthusiastic.

"Seven-thirty? I was hoping we could catch the Freemason Mothers," he said. "They're playing down the street."

She had no idea what a Freemason Mother was, but agreed nonetheless.

"Great!" Mike said. "I'm really looking forward to it."

"Me, too," she lied, and they chatted a little longer before hanging up. She stood in the kitchen, staring at the phone, thinking not of Mike, but of Flynn.

She had, of course, been through all the standard emotions during the day, as she could hardly think of anything else. She'd run down the full gamut: He was just a little late, to unavoidably detained. Dead on the side of the road where no one could see him or call her to say he wouldn't make it.

Or maybe, she had scared the shit out of him with her declaration of love. Maybe she had never been anything more than a casual fling to him. Maybe he'd gotten laid, and now he hated her for being such a pathetic little sap and not understanding grown-up flings and she would never see him again, because, at this very moment, he was on a plane back to London to get as far away from her as he possibly could.

Okay, maybe she was overdoing it a little. It wasn't as if he'd behaved as if he *hated* her, hated her. But then why didn't he come today like he said he would? Or at least *call?* Even if he was dumping her, she was pretty sure he'd at least call.

Back to dead on the side of the road again. And she couldn't very well go sit in a bathtub with a gallon of ice cream and sort it all out with Dad here, so reluctantly, she returned to the living room, a very thin and very false smile already hurting her face.

Dad had taken off his suit jacket and his shoes, had his feet propped up on the coffee table, a glass of wine dangling from one hand.

"Who was that?" he asked. "That moron who calls himself a professor?"

"No, Dad," she said with a sigh as she took the chair next to the couch. "Just a friend."

"Uh-huh," he said. And then he winked at her. *Winked* at her. Like they shared some little secret.

Jesus, who was this man in her living room? Honestly, he'd been remarkably composed all day, had not made even the slightest joke about her students or Dagne or even Myron for that matter, and kept winking and smiling and acting like they were big buds.

Being on the edge of a nervous breakdown as she was, it was about all she could endure. "Okay," she said, in all seriousness, "where's my dad?"

"Right here, baby girl."

"No, you're not him. You've been far too calm today. You haven't said a word about my students, or my friends—"

"Nice people," he interjected with a grin. She gasped with surprise. Dad chuckled. "Ah, Rachel," he said, pausing momentarily to sip his wine, "why don't you have a drink with your old man and relax a bit? You did a lot of work today. Take a load off; tell me what's going on in your life. You know, a little chat among friends."

Now she gaped at him. "I will definitely have some wine, because I can't cope with this weird change in you," she said resolutely.

"Great. So tell me about your life," he said as she came to her feet.

"Dad!" she exclaimed, disconcerted. "There is nothing going on in my life. It's exactly the same as it has been for years now. And let's please not forget that you haven't been a big fan of my life," she said, and walked into the dining room and an open bottle of wine there.

"I don't care if there's nothing new. I still want to hear about you," he sunnily insisted.

Fat chance of *that* happening, a thought she broadcast to him with a look of pure tedium. The last time they'd had a little chat, she'd gone running back to Providence.

"Hey, it's not what you think," he gaily continued. "I've turned over a new leaf. No, really! See, I've been doing some work with your mother, and I have come to a couple of conclusions about you and me."

Oh great, just great. She already knew what his conclusions were, and this was really not the day she wanted to hear it—she was a tubby with a dead-end degree and a dead-end life and a dead-end boyfriend who wasn't even her boyfriend.

She poured wine to the very rim of the wineglass, pounded the cork back in with her fist, then returned to the living room and glared down at her father on the couch. "I thought you and Mom were in marriage counseling, not father counseling."

"We are in marriage counseling," he said, completely undaunted by her glare. "But part of marriage counseling covers our joint parenting, and before you tune me out," he said in response to her groan, "at least *hear* me out."

"I don't want to hear—"

"Sure you do. Like I said—a new leaf."

Rachel sighed, sat down, looked at him skeptically.

"I promise, no fighting," he added.

"Do I have a choice?"

"Sure! If you don't want to hear me out now, I'll just stay on indefinitely until you're ready."

Rachel took a big gulp of wine and said, "Okay, shoot."

Dad chuckled. "Let me start with your professor. He's a dead-end—"

"Da-ad!" she cried. "I *knew* you were going to do this!"

"Rachel, please let me finish," he said calmly.

She bit her tongue. Literally—almost clean in two.

"Believe me, there is no one on the face of this earth who is happier to see there isn't much between you and that jerk. But today I saw that there isn't, and I'm happy. Do you understand why that's important to me?"

"Yes. He's not good enough for you."

"Wrong. He's not good enough for *you*. And I think maybe I never made it very clear that you are too damn good for a man like him."

Rachel snorted into her wineglass. "No, you never made that clear. Maybe because you were too busy getting across that I was too heavy and too long in school, and too whatever."

"Yeah," he said, and sighed heavily. "I know I did that and I'm really sorry."

He could not have shocked her more if he had socked her in the mouth. She peered closely at him, had the unsettling idea that perhaps his prognosis had worsened and now he was going to try and make amends for all the things he'd ever said to her over the years. Ye old deathbed amends.

But Dad sighed with enough exasperation for her to know that wasn't it, then suddenly sat up, bracing his arms on his legs so that he could focus on her, his eyes narrowing as he studied her. "Let me get something off my chest, will you? The thing is, Rachel, of my three girls, you are the one who has always had the biggest heart and the biggest dreams. You were always taking in stray animals and lonely little kids, and you're so damned creative. I'd give my right arm to have a tenth of your natural talent. I've always thought that of all my daughters, you had the greatest potential to really *be* someone."

Drugs. He was obviously taking some sort of drug cocktail for cancer that was making him crazy. "You're kidding," she said flatly.

"Nope. Not kidding," he said, looking pretty serious. "I have never—*never*—wanted anything but the very best for you, Rachel. That is the God's honest truth. Now I know sometimes it didn't seem that way. I know I harped on you about your weight, but not because I thought you were any less beautiful than your sisters. Because I thought—and I think now—that you are far more beautiful than they are. You have that glow that comes from somewhere inside you. But over the years, I've seen you on a path of self-destruction that I couldn't abide."

"Oh *Dad,*" she said, disbelieving, shaking her head at this bizarre conversation.

"And I harped on you about school," he said, undeterred, "not because I think you don't deserve to achieve the highest levels of education, but because you were letting that idiot guide your thinking."

That, unfortunately, was something she could hardly argue, given that she had come to the same conclusion herself several months ago.

"I want you out of school because I know your future is bright and I don't want you to squander it. You have to *seize* it, Rachel, and you can't be afraid to do it. I don't know why you are—maybe I made you afraid, but if you will just step out into the world, it is yours for the taking," he said, sweeping his arms wide. "You have everything going for you—looks, brains, sense of humor, a huge heart, an ability to connect with the people most of us can't tolerate, as you proved to me today—"

"Dad, what has *happened* to you?" she cried. "You're like someone else entirely!"

"I don't know," he said, shrugging lightly. "Maybe I should have gone to therapy a long time ago. Maybe I should have gotten cancer a long time ago, because that sure has made me smarter about some things. But enough of that," he said, waving his hand dismissively. "What about you? What's going on in your life? I really, truly want to know," he said, and looked so sincere that Rachel almost had to pinch herself to see if she wasn't having one of her very vivid dreams.

"Well," she said cautiously, "you're right that I'm not seeing Myron and I haven't in a long time."

"Good news." Dad grinned.

"But he's remained my friend. Sort of. He was," she said, feeling terribly confused, and pressed her palm to her forehead. "Actually, I don't know what he is anymore," she said truthfully, and considered there had been some sort of cosmic rift in the universe, because she was talking to her dad about *Myron*.

"I really don't want him around, but I don't know how to say it. And then there's Dagne. I know she's out there, but she's also genuine," she said, and went on to talk about Dagne, and school, and the things she had considered for her dissertation, and the topic she thought she might have settled on.

As the night progressed and they drank more wine, Rachel told her father about her financial situation, how she had loaned money to her friends, then waived fees and class costs for people who really wanted to learn weaving, and how Mr. Valicielo wanted to sue her, how she hadn't been able to find a teaching job like she wanted, so she had to take a job with a temp agency that was sending her on some really bizarre assignments.

Dad took it all in stride, she had to admit. There had been an initial burst of fatherly outrage about her finances, but then he'd laughed at some of her jobs, nodded his agreement that she was doing the right thing.

"I don't mind the struggle," she said, voicing aloud a feeling she'd had for a while. "All my life I've had whatever I wanted—I never had to really think about it. But most people I know go through life like I am right now, working to make ends meet. I'm really learning a lot," she said, realizing just how much for the first time.

"Yeah," Dad responded with a world-weary sigh. "It's a different world than you girls were raised in. But I know what you're talking about. There was a time your mother was pregnant and I worried about putting food on the table. Jesus, it's been so long I hardly remember what it's like anymore." He paused, looked into space, seeing something in the distant past, she thought.

"So, good for you, Rachel," he at last said with a smile. "Good for you for willing to learn that important lesson. Most kids who come from your kind of money couldn't be bothered."

She hadn't set out to learn a lesson. But she'd set out to crawl out from beneath her father's long shadow, she realized.

Dad asked about the phone call and she told him about Mike, how they'd met, about their date tomorrow. "Good, good. But he's not the one on your mind."

His rare perception on that front completely unnerved her. "What? There's no one on my mind," she started, but Dad's chuckling silenced her.

"So all those trips to the window and staring off into space and not hearing people talk to you was just . . . what?"

Rachel cleared her throat, tried to think of a good excuse. Flynn seemed too huge, too important to share just yet. But Dad was smiling kindly, and she couldn't help herself. She started with a bit of a stammering, "Ah . . . well, now that you m-mention it," and proceeded to tell him, in spite of an inner voice screaming at her to stop, about Flynn. How they'd first met, how she kept running into him, how he had enrolled in her class, and how she hadn't believed a guy like him would be interested in a woman like her (that made Dad mad, and she had to endure his lecture on how she was really too good for *any* guy). She even told him, in a moment of sheer madness, how she'd said some things to Flynn she shouldn't have and sent him running.

"What things?" Dad asked.

"Things," she said, staring into her wineglass.

"Well, if they are the things I think they are, then maybe this is the point you should take the bull by the horns."

"Meaning what?"

"Meaning, call him up and tell him to get over it."

She laughed. "Seriously?"

"Are you kidding? Yes, *seriously.* He needs to know you haven't already built the house with the picket fence and picked out the names of your children, but that you are a mature woman who wants to explore what's between the two of you. And if that's too uncomfortable for him, then better to know it now, right?"

Wow. A mature woman.

"You've got a good head on your shoulders, Rachel—the business with the witchcraft notwithstanding, of course. If this guy has half a brain, he'll understand. And he'll know what a gem he has in you."

A *gem?* What a funky dream this was turning out to be!

They talked for a long time until it was obvious Dad was tiring. Before he said good night, Dad grabbed her in a big bear hug, embraced her with a strength he did not look to have, and kissed her on top of her head. "I love you, baby girl. More than you'll probably ever know," he said.

Her vision was misty, but Rachel smiled. "I love you, too, Dad. I always have." She waved her fingers at him as he started upstairs and wished he'd hurry before she started bawling. When he'd made it upstairs, she decided maybe he was right. Maybe she should grab the bull by the horns.

Maybe . . . very slowly and prudently, she picked up the phone. Then instantly put it down. And picked it up again and dialed his number as quickly as she could so that she wouldn't chicken out. And then she stood there, listening to each ring, her heart pounding harder and harder and harder until at last his answering machine picked up.

Answering machine! Crap!

She closed her eyes, tried to think, but the beep rattled her. "Ah . . . hi. It's me," she said, and punched herself in the leg for her timidity. "Me, Rachel. Ah . . . well, I am calling to say I missed you today," she said, remembering what Dad had said. *Mature woman, too good for him.* "And I'm sorry you didn't come," she added, opening her eyes and lifting her head. "I was wondering if perhaps you didn't come because you were scared off by what I said. If that is the case, I would like to set your mind at ease. You have nothing to worry about, Flynn. I am all grown up and can handle it. I just hope that we can continue to see each other until you have to go or I have to go or whatever, because I enjoy your company, and . . . well, and *that,* too . . . so if you could please call me, I would appreciate it. If not . . . I would like to say I really enjoyed meeting you."

She clicked off, and shook the phone to the ceiling. "I enjoyed *meeting* you?" she complained. But she was feeling a little lighter when she put down the phone.

Subject: Un. Bee. Leevable.
From: <earthangel@hotmail.com>
To: <rmanning70@houston.rr.com>,
      <reparrish72@aol.com>

Hey. Happy Thanksgiving. So you will not BELIEVE what happened. Dad came for Thanksgiving even though I sort of begged him not to, and guess what. He was NICE. I mean nice, as in very pleasant, very nice to my guests, and he did not criticize me even once in front of them or at all! PLUS he did not insult anyone! What is happening to the world as I know it? I've been through some pretty strange full moons, but this one, like, takes the cake! Not only was he NICE, but he said he thought I was pretty and smart and had the world at my fingertips. And then he told me—GET THIS—that he loved me. I AM NOT MAKING THIS UP. Apparently he and Mom are getting more than just marriage counseling. So be on the lookout for a person who looks like Dad but isn't really him. All kidding aside, the new Dad is way better than the old. It's un-freakin'-believable.

P.S. Thanksgiving was . . . eventful. Did Grandpa make his fried turkey again? That always makes me sick.

P.S.S. I don't think I'll be really busy anymore, so write me! Love you guys, Rachel.

Subject: RE: Un. Bee. Leevable.
From: Rebecca Parrish <reparrish72@aol.com>
To: Rach <earthangel@hotmail.com>

Hi Rach. We knew Dad was there—Mom had said he was really starting to come around after weeks and weeks of therapy and that he was going to Providence whether you liked it or not. So we were wondering how it went.

Dad's going to have to go in for surgery whenever they can schedule this one surgeon, and I can tell Mom's really worried about it. Did he say anything?

Anyway, Rachel, you ARE pretty and smart and have the world at your fingertips and you are a colossal moron because you don't see that. So I am sure Dad was relieved when you told him that Myron is just a friend. Did you mention anyone else to him? Rebecca.

Hey, Robin here on Bec's mail. Can you believe she still uses AOL? Anyhoo . . . first of all, yes, Grandpa made his fried turkey again and almost sent all of us to the hospital. I think he must use all the oil in Texas to fry that damn thing. And he made his world-famous fried okra, too, only the okra were the size of baseball bats. Jake says I am paranoid, but I will not let my baby anywhere near his garden, because I am certain there is something very illegal going on out there. How can okra possibly get that big? Okay, so, about you not

being busy anymore—what happened? I thought
things were going pretty well with you and mystery
guy 1 and 2, or however many there are, seeing as
how you never write and you STILL haven't sent the
book. Tell Dad we said hi and we love him, too, especially the new and improved him, although I will have
to see it to believe it. And then write back and tell us
what happened with the guy(s). Bec and I are sneaking
out to get some vodka and a pack of smokes. She's all
nervous about the kids seeing us and thinks we're
going to hell for it, like that's news or something.
Happy Thanksgiving, kiddo. We miss you!! TTFN . . . .
Robbie.

Rachel made Dad a gourmet breakfast the next morning, thanks to the last of Dagne's eBay money. They talked
about the house—he said he intended to sell it as soon as
she finished her dissertation and surprisingly, Rachel was
okay with that.

She finally found the nerve to ask about his surgery.
"What sort of surgery is it?"

"They need to remove part of my colon. And maybe
some other stuff, who knows. But I don't want you to
worry about me. I've come to terms with it, I think."

"Don't say that, Dad," she pleaded. "That sounds like
you've given up!"

"I haven't given up," he said with a reassuring pat. "But
it's strange . . . somehow, eventually, you do come to terms
with it." He smiled, picked up his fork. "This is damn good
bacon," he said, changing the subject.

A half hour later, Rachel watched Dad get into the backseat of the car he had ordered up. He rolled down the window and waved. "I love you, baby girl. You remember
what I told you now," he said to her.

Like she could possibly forget this extraordinary
Thanksgiving Day. "I love you, too, Dad," she said, and
waited until his car had turned onto Laurel before she
wiped the tears from her eyes.

Subject: Thanksgiving
From: Aaron Lear <Aaron.Lear@leartransind.com>
To: BonBon <10sNE1@nyc.rr.com>

Hi honey. When are you coming back to New York?
I've been doing some thinking, and I think you should
sell the place in L.A. I know you probably won't like
that idea, but the truth is, I just ache when you are
away because I love you so much, BonBon. I know
you're busy with the girls and the folks (glad to hear El
hasn't killed anyone in the RV yet), but I wanted to let
you know that the trip to Providence went really well.
Our Rachel is a good girl—no, she's better than that.
She's excellent. I am so proud, and honestly, I don't
know why I've been such a dick to her. But seeing her
there in Providence and the way all those people love
her, well . . . I haven't been fair to her. I think everything
is fine now, Bonnie. I think I have mended that fence.
And I think I'm finally ready for the surgery. Love you.
Call me. Better yet, just come home. Aaron.

Chapter Thirty

✦ ✳ ✦

WHEN Myron showed up for work at the RIHPS curator offices Friday morning, the head curator, Darwin Richter, poked his head out of his office and cheerfully called out to him, asking him to step inside his office.

Myron walked into the office with a smile . . . that quickly faded when he saw the man sitting in the chair across from Darwin. "Ah, hey . . . what's up?" he asked Darwin as he eyed Detective Keating, the senior investigator he'd met with the Rhode Island State Police a few weeks ago.

"Myron, you remember Detective Keating, don't you?" Darwin asked as he eased his two-hundred-fifty-pound frame into his executive chair.

Myron cocked his head to one side, nodded thoughtfully. "Sure, sure . . . the thefts down at Newport. Did you ever find anything out?" he asked, looking very concerned.

"Not a lot," the detective said, coming halfway out of his seat to extend a hand to Myron. "We're still nosing around, trying to get a handle on this catalog listing," he said, waving his hand at some imaginary catalog. "This preservation business is a lot of work! But of course you know that, right?" he asked with a chuckle. "I mean, you're the one who gave us the catalog listing, remember?"

"Yes, that's right," Myron said, nodding eagerly as he came deeper into the room and took the seat that Darwin gestured to. "That was a lot of work going through that list, huh? So do you have any clues?"

Detective Keating smiled. "Not yet. But you've been such a great help—we're going to need a little more of your help, if that's okay with you."

"Sure!" Myron said, leaning forward a little. "Anything! Just tell me what you want me to do and I will make it a top priority. By the way, did we get you the names of the people who work in our properties?"

"Yeah, I think you got us all their names, thanks," Detective Keating said, and leaned over, pulled a file out of his briefcase and put it on his lap, then pulled a pair of reading glasses from his breast pocket and perched them on the end of his nose. He opened the file, looked at it very carefully. "There were a couple of items on here that we weren't able to locate," he said thoughtfully, squinting down at the file. "Probably mislabeled, something like that. But I figured, if anyone knows where to find them, it's Professor Tidwell." He looked up, smiled at Myron. "You really seem to know your stuff!"

Myron shrugged with a lopsided grin. "What can I say? I'm a history professor, so I *ought* to know my stuff!" He laughed a little, exchanged a proud smile with Darwin.

"And there are so many properties to keep track of! I could never be that organized," Detective Keating said with a shake of his head.

"I guess anyone in the history business will tell you that's a prerequisite. You have to be able to organize a lot of information to make any sense of it. You learn that right off the bat in my field."

"Right," the detective said, and smiled, Myron thought, a little smugly. "So anyway, so far, we've been unable to locate a few of the items you had listed in the catalog as being present and accounted for. So we're assuming they are around somewhere since they haven't been reported stolen or damaged."

"Probably misplaced," Myron said.

The detective looked up at him and laughed. "So much for organization, huh?"

Myron did not laugh, just stole a glimpse of Darwin from the corner of his eye. "Too bad I can't be everywhere, or that everyone can't be as organized as I am, right?"

"Riiight," the detective drawled. "So our first item is a pair of torchères—am I saying that right? Torchères. Anyway, the catalog says these are circa eighteenth century French, bronze and partly gilt, approximately thirty-five inches tall."

"Torchères?" Darwin echoed, and turned a puzzled look to Myron. "Would those be the Gilles Joubert pair? From the Hamblen collection?"

"The catalog says Potter collection," the detective clarified.

Myron rubbed his palms on the knees of his cords as he thought about it. "Must be Joubert," he said to Darwin, then to the detective, "You should find them at the Lindsey House in Newport. These things get moved around from time to time, depending upon the exhibits."

"I'll make a note of that," the detective said, and squinted at the paper again and shook his head. "But they weren't in the Lindsey House, either."

"No?" Myron asked, and looked at Darwin, shrugging. "Maybe they were stolen. I'd have to go back and check my records, but you know we've had the thefts down on the shore. I suppose I could have overlooked them."

"Would you mind checking?" the detective asked, his smile completely gone now.

"Sure, no problem." Myron pulled a little notebook from his back pocket, made a quick note, and cleared his throat.

"The second item," the detective continued, "is a circa sixteenth century Venetian enameled and gilt-edged hand-painted fruit bowl."

"Oh, yes," Myron said. "From the Botwick House."

"Except that it's not at the Botwick House," the detective responded, and lifted his gaze to look directly at Myron. "Amazing memory you have."

"Not really. I just remember it from the forklift incident," Myron said, rubbing his palms on his knees again. "It was one of the items we moved after the crash. It's probably just in a cabinet. I'll have a look tomorrow."

"Thanks," Detective Keating said. "Oh yeah, here's another . . . a Joseph Badger portrait. The catalog says it is a ten-by-ten inch portrait entitled *Colonial Woman*."

"Oh *yes*," Darwin said proudly. "That is one of our very best examples of early American art, donated by the Pierpont family. It's in the Pierpont House, isn't it, Professor?"

"The Pierpont House?" Myron asked, shifting his gaze from the detective to Darwin. "I don't think so," he said, and winced inwardly at the sight of Darwin's brows raising nearly to his hair.

"It's *not?*" Darwin echoed incredulously.

"There was a corner of it," Myron said, "a smidge of the painting that needed restoration. Just a smidge—nothing to diminish the value. So I sent it out for restoration."

"Could you get it back?" Detective Keating asked.

"Of course. It usually takes about six weeks—"

"I meant today," the detective said with a deceptively soft smile.

Myron laughed as if that was the most ridiculous thing he had ever heard. "*Today?* I . . . I, ah, I don't think— The thing is, I had another assistant curator handle it. I will have to ask him. And you know it's really hard to get these things back in the middle of a restoration process."

"So . . . how soon could you get it back?" the detective pressed.

"Well, restoration takes time, Detective," Myron said, rubbing his palms on his pants again. "I'm not really sure. I'll have to ask about it."

"Could you let me know when you know?" the detective asked, and Myron nodded. Detective Keating smiled and closed his file. "Thanks so much. That would be a great help." He put the file in his briefcase and came to his feet, then stood up, leaning over the desk to shake Darwin's hand. "I really appreciate your assistance in this," he said, and turned to shake Myron's clammy hand. "And yours, Professor. I don't think we could do this job without you."

"No problem."

"I'm sure we'll be talking," he said, and walked to the door, but paused there for a moment and glanced at Myron over his shoulder. "By the way, who did you say the assistant curator was who sent the Badger painting to be restored?"

"Ah . . ." Myron scratched his head for a moment. "I didn't. I'll have to look in the files in my office."

"So much for that memory, too, then, huh?" Detective Keating laughed.

"Right," Myron said, forcing a laugh. "I'll look it up and give you a buzz, how's that?"

"That would be *great*," the detective said, and with a half salute, half wave, he strolled out of Darwin's office.

Myron slowly sank into the chair across from Darwin. Then made the mistake of looking at his boss. Darwin's face was ashen as he suddenly lurched forward, landing on pudgy hands atop his desk, bracing so far over that for a moment Myron feared he would come clear across and grab his throat. "*When* did that painting go out and why wasn't I informed?" he demanded.

"Didn't we tell you?" Myron asked weakly, and rubbed his hands on his knees again.

DETECTIVE Keating walked out to his car in the parking lot, lost the coat and the briefcase and tossed them in the backseat, then climbed in behind the wheel and grinned at Flynn. "We got him."

"Smashing," Flynn said, looking up from a file he'd been studying.

Joe looked at the file on his lap and groaned. "Are you ever going to get over yourself?"

Flynn chuckled cheerfully and carefully closed the file. "Naturally, I am required to report to my superiors about my involvement in other law enforcement matters, particularly when I am abroad," he said.

"Oh, naturally," Joe said, assuming a really bad British accent. " 'To the attention of Snuff and Snuff, I should be pleased to report that I've solved a homicide for the bloody Americans, in which I proved that the husband could not have possibly done it, and with a bit of tramping about, I coerced a confession from the scoundrel who did.' " He shook his head and laughed. "Jesus, your head's so big it's a wonder you can fit it into the car at all."

"You're jealous of my keen intuition, admit it."

Joe snorted, looked out the window. Then he looked at Flynn again. "So really, how'd you know it wasn't him? I mean, lookit—an extramarital affair, no forced entry, his dog alive and walking around, her dog dead along with her."

"It was the dog, really," Flynn said with a very self-satisfied smile. "I've owned Labrador retrievers. Lovely dogs, but frighteningly useless. Once I noticed that the male dog—*his* dog—had been neutered, I was quite confident that he could be easily silenced with a generous chew bone. The female, on the other hand, was a little more curious, and, like most bitches, a little more territorial. She was not so easily swayed by a bone."

"There was no evidence of any bones!" Joe protested.

"That's because a neutered male Labrador retriever is also a rather ubiquitous chow hound of anything edible and many things not so edible. They're terribly friendly and good companions and all that, but I would imagine he trotted up and helped himself to the female's chew bone without the slightest twinge of conscience."

Joe laughed, peered at the front entry of the RIHPS. "So how'd you figure out Reyes?"

"Another very simple fact—the gardener told us that his son had brought help. I asked your department to run some files, and there you are, pretty as you please, a connection between Reyes, who happens to be a paroled robber—not the one we originally thought, mind you—but a paroled robber, and the gardener's son. Granted, the connection was established when the two of them were juveniles, but it was a connection all the same, so it seemed worth a bit of a chat. And then, as you know, his suspicions were raised, and he called his friend, who called his father the gardener, who, fortunately, called you yesterday morning, and the rest, as they say, is history."

Joe smiled sardonically. "I've been a detective fifteen years, and I'm here to tell you, pal, that you are one lucky shit. But if you ever want to come back and work a homicide with me again, that'd be cool—I enjoyed it, you lucky bastard. If you're interested, I know of an international exchange program. Basically, we send a cop to your side of the pond to learn a few things about insurance fraud, and your folks send you over here for a six-month tour of duty to learn a few things about law enforcement. Might be worth talking to your people about. I'd sort of like it if you stuck around a while longer."

"Careful, mate," Flynn said with a grin, "or you'll have me tearing up."

"Shut up."

"I'm really quite touched—"

"I mean it, shut up or I'll shut you up," Joe said, but he was grinning. "And before you get too full of yourself, remember, we have a little bet riding on the *real* reason you're here. What do those Lloyd's boys think of you dabbling in homicides when you're supposed to be doing insurance fraud?"

"Naturally, they would prefer I stick to fraud. Speak of the devil—here we are," he said, motioning with his head toward the front of the building.

It was Professor Tidwell, all right, walking quickly and purposefully out into the fading light of the afternoon, headed for his car. Joe and Flynn watched him start up, then waited for him to pull up to the exit before easing behind him, pulling onto the street and keeping a distance of a car length between them.

They followed him to a corner market and pulled over on the street as the professor got out of his car and jogged to a pay phone and made a call. Whatever his conversation, it was said with a great deal of animation, his hands punctuating what looked like an angry exchange. After a few minutes of that, he slammed the receiver down, got back into his car, and drove to a bar.

They waited outside for two hours—Joe walked down the block to get a couple of slices of pizza—until the professor emerged again, this time in the company of a man. The two of them walked around to the tiny little parking lot, and stopped at the passenger side of an old Buick.

"He's making a buy," Joe said. "Weed would be my guess."

Joe's hunch proved right, as the two men remained in the parking lot, eventually walking around to the back of the other man's car, where they shared a joint. When they'd finished, they talked a little more, and the man returned to the bar. The professor got in his car.

This time, they followed him down Blackstone Avenue, to Laurel, and then Slater, the street on which Rachel lived, at which point, Flynn's heart began to sink.

"He's going for the painting, you know," Joe said, his voice a little softer than normal, knowing full well how important it was to Flynn that she not be involved.

"We don't know that," Flynn insisted.

Joe said nothing, just pulled up behind another parked car a couple of houses down from Rachel's. From their vantage point, they saw the professor get out of his car and go inside. Joe looked at Flynn. "Free access to her house?"

Flynn was not going to sit back and feel Joe's pity. "I

think I'll just have a quick look about," he said, and got out of the car before Joe could stop him.

Hands in his coat pockets, he pulled his collar up around his face and walked down the sidewalk to Rachel's house. Once he was in front, he paused, squatted down, and pretended to tie his shoe as he glanced at the house.

He noticed straightaway that Rachel's car was not in the drive. So what, then, was the professor doing? With a glance back at Joe, Flynn stood, walked calmly into the drive, could almost hear Joe screaming at him to come back before he blew his cover. To hell with his cover—things had progressed far beyond a mere professional interest.

He walked the length of the drive, eyeing the long bank of windows. There were lights on, but no sign of the professor. It was, therefore, a bit of a shock when the professor suddenly emerged from the garage, and looked at Flynn strangely as he quickly shut the garage door behind him.

"Ah—hello," Flynn said.

"Oh. It's you," the professor said, and stood, hands on hips, squinting at Flynn. His eyes were bloodshot and glassy—he looked quite stoned. "Did we meet?" he asked. "I don't remember."

"Ah, no. Charlie Windsor's the name."

"Windsor . . . that sounds familiar," the idiot said, and Flynn certainly hoped that it might, given the arse's esteemed status as a college history professor. But the professor shrugged, turned back to the house before thinking it through. "She's not here, dude," he said.

"Isn't she?"

"No." He paused, looked at the house as if he was trying to remember what he was doing here himself, and put a hand to his nape, then looked at Flynn again. "Okay, so you want me to tell her you came by?"

"Will you see her?"

"Ah . . . I don't know. I thought she was with you. Maybe she's at school. Look, I'll leave her a note, but I really need to get going."

"That would be lovely, thanks," Flynn said. Yet he stood firmly rooted, waiting to see what the professor did next.

The professor looked at him, terribly confused. "Right, right, so I'll let her know."

"Fabulous. Thank you."

Eyeing Flynn, the professor very tentatively went back inside the house. Flynn smiled, turned on his heel, and calmly walked back to Joe's car.

"Are you *nuts?*" Joe shouted before he could even get in the car. "You want to blow cover or what?"

"My cover is quite intact. I actually spoke with our man."

"Ah, *fuck,*" Joe said, slapping his hand against his forehead.

"It's quite all right, Detective Keating. He remembers me from the bar and thinks I came to call on Rachel. She's not at home, he's no idea where she might be, and promised to leave a note that I dropped by."

"You are so kidding," Joe said with a laugh. "The guy cannot be that stupid."

"Apparently, he can and he is," Flynn said, and slid down, watching the house.

The professor left a short time later, empty-handed, and drove to his apartment.

Joe and Flynn watched him stagger inside as if he carried some invisible weight on his shoulders.

"I'll put a couple of uniforms on him tonight," Joe said. "But I need to get some sleep." He looked at Flynn. "And *you* need to get in that house."

"Right," Flynn agreed, but did not offer that given the events of yesterday, that might be easier said than done.

Chapter Thirty-one

✦ ✦ ✦

FLYNN arrived at the corporate flat around ten that evening. There were four messages on his phone, left since yesterday morning when he'd gotten the call from Joe that the homicide case had broke.

The first was from Iris. "Flynn, darling, do ring me, please. I've got some important news." *Good try, Iris, old girl.* She was wising up, devising new techniques to harass him.

The second message was from his mother. "Oh Flynn, darling, I was so hoping you'd be in," she said. "Your father wants to speak with you. Please ring us, will you, so that your father might have a word. Hugs, darling!"

Dear God, now Mum had roped Dad into the whole sordid affair. He felt sorry for the old man, could imagine him fighting tooth and nail to be left out of the gruesome details of Flynn's love life, but nevertheless being dragged in, bit by bit with Mum's shrill harping, at last giving in for just a moment's peace, a whimpering shell of the man he was.

The third message was, as he had guessed, from Rachel, and he winced with each breath she took in her rather long message to him. Christ, he'd really made a mess of it, hadn't he?

And the last message, the big surprise, was from his brother Ian. "Hello, mate, calling from Paris. Mum's been a pain in the arse and hounding me a bit, so I thought I'd at least ring you up and see what's gone on between you and the dragon lady," he said, referring to Iris—Ian had never been shy about his dislike of her. "Give me a ring when you've a moment. Cheers," he said, and clicked off.

Flynn picked up the phone and dialed Rachel's number, and got the answering machine. "Ah . . . Flynn here. Rachel, I'm terribly sorry about yesterday. Something rather important came up, and I was called away. Please do ring me," he said, and hung up, unable to think of how to convey how sorry he was to a blasted answering machine.

And then Flynn lay on the cheap plastic leather couch waiting for the phone to ring, not unlike he had done in his eighth school year when he had waited for Mary Elizabeth to ring up. Just like that night a thousand years ago, he had stared at the ceiling. Except it had been at a poster of Duran Duran then, not a water stain as it was now.

And he was discovering that the wait was, unfortunately, just as excruciating at thirty-four years old as it was at thirteen.

Twice, Flynn sat up and reached for the phone, determined to ring again. And twice he lay down again, debating. It was too late, well past midnight, and moreover, he didn't want to come across as some sort of adolescent stalker. It hadn't worked particularly well for him the first time.

He did, however, call again Saturday morning, when he awoke stiff and freezing on that bloody couch. Bugger, he got her answering machine again, and he was not inclined to leave another groveling message.

He was not inclined to do much of anything but mope around and feel rather sorry for himself, which he did until early afternoon.

•   •   •

RACHEL arrived home Saturday afternoon after her temporary stint in a very small glassed-in booth of a gas station which was really suitable for only one person, not two, but nevertheless, she had stood behind Mabel Forrester and run credit cards through the machine.

"Don't know why they sent you down here," Mabel said more than once. "I don't usually got no one here with me."

"Maybe because of the holiday traffic," Rachel offered.

Mabel gave a *harrumph* at that. "It ain't as if I can't turn around and run them cards myself," she muttered.

The woman had a point. Seated in the only chair in the booth, Mabel could swivel around and do just about anything, including stare at Rachel during the few lulls that they had.

It had been a long, exhausting day, both physically and emotionally. As she explained to Mabel (when they had bonded a little later in the day), her date with Mike last evening had been a good one. They had had a couple of drinks, had gone to listen to a rock band that was too loud for her tastes. And then he had returned her to her car and kissed her like any guy would do, and it had been perfectly nice. Just . . . *nice*. No sizzle, no spark, no desire to hop in the sack with him.

"So? Don't see him again," Mabel had said.

"I know . . . but the thing is, Mike is the more practical choice," Rachel had argued earnestly. "I mean, he's a nice guy, he likes me, he's local. But Flynn . . ." She moaned, looked out the murky glass windows at the cars lined up at the pump. "Flynn is like . . . a dream guy. Someone you would never imagine meeting in a million years, you know?"

Mabel snorted. "Girl, why would you want to be living practical when you can be living the *dream?*" she'd asked, and snorted again. "I'd live the dream my damn self," she muttered, and swiveled around again to accept money from two guys with dreadlocks.

Live the dream my damn self. How lyrical that had sounded.

It only depressed her more, because (and she had failed to mention this to Mabel), Flynn wasn't living his dream. He'd obviously been appalled by her declaration of love. And now there was a nice, normal guy who liked her, and all she could think of was Flynn.

It was enough to make even the most practical of people insane, and by the time Rachel arrived home, she wanted nothing more than to devour a giant pan of warm brownies and take a hot soaking bath.

Unfortunately, Myron was there. She groaned as she got out of her car, as he was definitely the last person she wanted to see today. But as she entered her house through the kitchen door—the quickest route to avoid any encounter with Mr. Valicielo—she gasped, dropped her bag.

Her house was a *wreck*. Drawers were pulled out, crap was stacked on the breakfast bar, and the refrigerator door was standing wide open.

She dropped her bag, marched into the dining room where she found more of the same—stuff stacked everywhere, drawers and cabinets open and the contents jumbled. And as she stood there, her mouth agape, trying to make sense of it all, Myron came trudging up the stairs from the basement. "Oh. Hey," he said when he saw her.

"*Hey?* That's all you're going to say?"

"What?"

"God, Myron!" she exclaimed angrily. "Look at my house! Look what you've done to my *house!*"

Myron looked around. "Oh, man. I didn't realize," he said stupidly, and she realized he was stoned again.

"*Augh!*" she shrieked. "This is unreal, Myron!" she cried, and whirled around, went into the kitchen, slammed the fridge door shut. "I asked you to please call before dropping by! Do you think I exist to feed you and clean up after you? What sort of friend are you?"

Myron followed her. "Look, I'm sorry! I didn't realize

I was making a mess!" he shouted at her. "But you *have* something of mine and I can't find it!"

"I *have* something of yours? And that's a reason to trash my house?"

"It's a painting of a colonial woman. Small, like an eight by ten. *What did you do with it?*" he roared.

Now she was pissed. Huge, steam-out-of-the-ears pissed. "Don't shout at me," she said through gritted teeth. "I don't know where your stupid painting is. I don't *care* about your stupid paintings! I've let you store them here because I thought we were friends, but you have taken advantage of my friendship long enough! I want my key back, right now."

"Listen, Rachel, you *have* to remember," he said, sounding a little desperate now. "I *have* to find it!"

There was a look in his eyes she didn't like, and she turned away, slammed a knickknack drawer shut. "I don't know where it is. *You* have to remember."

"Fuck," Myron muttered, and stared at the floor for a minute. "FUCK!"

"All right, it's time for you to go," Rachel said, and pointed toward the door.

"I have to find that goddamn painting!" he roared. "Do you not understand? I HAVE TO FIND THAT PAINTING!"

"You're stoned," she said disgustedly. "Look around you! It's obviously not here! You've turned my house upside down and it's not here! I want you to go, Myron. I want you to give me the key and leave my house and not come back. You're stoned and you're rude, and you're—"

"Shut up, Rachel," he said nastily, tossed her key onto the breakfast bar and stalked to the door. "Just shut the fuck up," he said again, and kicked the door open, stepped outside.

Her instincts told her to lock the door, and she raced behind him, locking the kitchen door, then ran to the front to lock that one, too. The phone began to ring as she watched Myron back out of her driveway at breakneck speed, almost colliding with her car as he did.

She grabbed the phone up without looking at the caller ID, her eyes still on Myron. "Hello," she said, walking to the window again.

"Rachel?"

His voice was an injection of calm into chaos, and she closed her eyes, drew a breath. *"Flynn,"* she whispered.

"I . . . I hadn't thought I'd get you. I've been trying to reach you without much luck. Have . . . have you the time to chat a bit?"

"Ah . . ." She paused, looked out the window. Myron was definitely gone.

"Bollocks," he muttered low, and before she could explain, he said, "At least allow me to say a couple of things, will you? Beginning with how dreadfully sorry I am for yesterday. Something cropped up that I couldn't extract myself from, and I—"

"I know, so your message said," she responded, forgetting Myron. "Could you not find a phone?"

"Yes, I could find a phone . . . but for reasons I cannot fully explain as of yet, I could not call you—"

"Flynn—"

"Rachel, please listen to me. I had to do something yesterday that I cannot discuss with you. Not yet, at least, and I know that sounds rather cloak and daggerish, but it's the truth. And the other truth is I *wanted* to come. I was not the least bit turned off by what you said, and in fact, I was rather encouraged by it. I suppose I should have said so straightaway, but the problem is, there are a few things you don't understand that make it rather difficult—"

"What things?" she asked. "Another woman?" she blurted, the idea tumbling out from the dark corners of her mind, where all devastating notions lurked, ready to pounce at the first sign of insecurity.

"No, not . . . That is to say, not . . . just . . ."

"It *is* another woman!"

"God no, Rachel. No." He sighed into the phone, and she could picture him dragging his hand through his hair like he often did. "You know what I did today?" he suddenly asked. "I had a long walk along the river where you and I have walked and talked, and . . . and I worried because I couldn't reach you. I thought perhaps you were avoiding me, which I might have well deserved, but nevertheless, I couldn't stop thinking about you, and I realized that I haven't stopped thinking of you since nearly the moment we met in the coffeehouse. Jesus, I can't seem to think straight at all, really, but I know one thing—we really must talk. I have to ask you some things, I have to *tell* you some things. We can't possibly go on like this."

Could they go on at all? "Yes, I think we need to talk," she said low.

"Then . . . then you'll agree? When might we meet?"

"Tomorrow. Around five," she said, because she couldn't see him now, not after what Myron had done to her house, not as exhausted as she was. At the moment, she had no energy to hear whatever it was he had to tell her. Whatever it was, it could not possibly be good.

"That's the earliest, is it?" he asked, clearly disappointed.

"Yes," she said firmly. "Can you come here?"

"Yes," he said. "I'll come round tomorrow, then. And thank you, Rachel, for giving me a chance to explain."

Right. Explain some things that were going to devastate her. "Okay. See you tomorrow," she said, and clicked off.

THAT night, Rachel dreamed that she was trying to find Flynn in the mess of her house, uncertain if he was real or just a painting. But in each pile she looked, it seemed to get bigger and bigger.

The next morning, Rachel went to the gym. Lori cracked her gum as she gave her the once-over, and said, "You're looking *good,* girl! How much you lost?"

"Three pounds," Rachel said as she signed in.

"No way! More like fifteen or twenty, right?"

"Three," Rachel said, holding up her hand and wiggling three fingers at Lori, then walked on, into the gym, where she rode until her legs were rubber and she couldn't feel her arms.

She did, however, feel remarkably calmer and much more placid about things. Whatever Flynn had to say, she was ready to hear. It wasn't the first time she'd been dumped, that was for sure, but it was certainly the first time she'd been dumped with kid gloves. She fully expected something along a range of "Could we be friends" to "I have a wretched disease" to "I really never expected it to go so far, and I have this thing at home." *Thing* being, of course, a woman.

She had managed to put her house together by mid-afternoon by pushing stuff under furniture and forcing it into drawers, and even avoided two calls from Mike ("Hey, Rachel, you doing anything tonight?"), even though it made her feel extremely guilty. She even tried to find Dagne with no luck to tell her to come get her witchcraft stuff, because she was *not* doing that anymore. No doubt she and Glenn had patched things up. That was always the way it went. Dagne got the guy, Rachel didn't.

So Rachel put the witchcraft paraphernalia away without ceremony . . . except to stand and stare at the cabinet for a moment and marvel at her silly diversion into it.

Well, no more. She would be meeting life head on from here on out, and she went upstairs to check her astrological chart to make sure that was a good approach.

Chapter Thirty-two

✦ ✦ ✦

FLYNN arrived with a full bouquet of flowers, a bottle of pricey champagne, and a bag of gourmet brownies. He might not be able to talk his way back into her good graces, but he was not above trying to charm his way in.

The last twenty-four hours had been excruciatingly slow and surprisingly painful. For years, Flynn had considered himself a rather worldly chap, what with all the traveling and consorting with the very wealthy that he did. It wasn't until he had been charmed by Iris that he began to realize that what he wanted most from life was a woman who loved him completely, with all his bloody faults, and a family to come home to.

That, and a career as a homicide detective, but that was another long and convoluted tale.

When Iris had betrayed him, he had managed to convince himself that it was better this way, that his expectations had been too high—he couldn't *really* expect a woman to love him and him alone, completely and forever. It was too easy for people to move from lover, wife or husband, to the next thing. It seemed that those sort of long-term, loving relationships were few and far between, really.

Even his parents, who had been married for ages, didn't seem to really *like* each other. He supposed the best he could hope for was several jolly good flings in his lifetime.

But then he'd met Rachel, and a belief had sprouted within him. A belief so foreign to him that he couldn't even name it—but he felt rather desperate not to lose it and knew, instinctively, that if he did lose it, it might possibly be lost forever.

So he screwed up his courage and bounded up the steps of her porch, rapping with great determination on her door.

He heard her coming down the stairs, heard the locks being undone. The door slowly opened, and there she stood, as gorgeous and curvy as ever. Her hair was long and unbound, curling with abandon around her face. She was wearing a long black skirt and slippers that had been fashioned to look like Holstein cows. She wore a simple, figure-hugging black sweater and the lavender shawl about her shoulders and a crystal pendant around her neck.

He had never seen a more attractive sight in his life, and he was rather surprised by how quickly his heart lifted in his chest when she smiled timidly. "Are those for me?" she asked, looking at the flowers in his hand.

"They are."

She pushed open the door, stood aside to let him in. Flynn offered her the flowers, and when she took them from him, he couldn't help himself; he caught her by the waist, and kissed her, like a man who'd been marooned on a deserted island for years. When he at last lifted his head, she was looking at him with such brilliance that every ounce of testosterone boiled up in him demanding more.

He kissed her again. A full, deep kiss, one that conveyed how much he hungered for her. Rachel responded warmly by curving into him, pressing her body against his.

When she pulled away, her smile was dazzling. "I'll just put these in water," she said, and turned and walked to the back of the house.

Flynn set the champagne aside, shut the door, and shrugged out of his overcoat. With his hands in his pockets, he stood just beyond the archway that led to the dining room. Rachel returned a moment later, carrying a large crystal vase, and with a smile, set the flowers on the table and began to arrange them, leaning over the table, her long curls falling over her shoulder.

Everything that happened then was a blur of white hot emotion. She was like a magnet, drawing him to her, and he could not resist. He moved behind her, put his hand on her hair, stroking it, deliberately moving it aside, so that he could kiss her neck.

Rachel sighed softly when his lips touched her flesh.

"I missed you terribly, Rachel," he whispered.

She responded by leaning her head to one side. "You missed Thanksgiving," she murmured.

"I'm a sodding bastard," Flynn said into the fistful of hair he had grabbed up in his hand. "I deserve to be beaten mercilessly and fed to lions."

"It so happens I have a pair in the backyard," she said, and turned around, put her hands to his chest. "But weren't you going to 'tell' me something?"

"Tell you?" he muttered absently, and pressed his lips to her forehead.

"That . . . you can't see me, or you're leaving, or you're sorry, but you just don't feel the same—"

"What?" He laughed incredulously, laid his palm against her cheek and smiled down at her. "You've got it all wrong, love."

"You said you needed to tell me some things," she said, folding her arms across her middle.

Nothing was ever easy, was it? "Right you are," he said, sighing. "I needed to tell you that I'm daft. That I made a horrible mistake—not once, but twice. First, in that I should have told you that I feel quite strongly about you—"

"Here we go," she muttered, dropping her gaze.

Flynn slipped a finger under her chin and forced her gaze up. "I *do*," he said in all seriousness. "Look at me now, will you, all atwitter, bearing gifts, begging for mercy. Why would I do that if I weren't absolutely mad for you?"

"Really?" she asked, trying to look skeptical, but looking more hopeful.

"*Really.* Fantastically so. And the second thing I had to tell you was that my work crisis was a horrid fate of timing, but I should have called."

She smiled timidly, punched him playfully in the chest. "You *should* have."

She was forgiving him too easily. "There are more things I am certain I should tell you, really . . . such as my grades were absolutely abominable in history."

Rachel laughed.

"I'm quite serious. My mother used to cry huge crocodile tears when I couldn't name the order of the monarchy. And when I was a small boy, I was a bit chubby, and the other lads called me Sir Fatalot."

That earned him a gay laugh, and Flynn kissed her neck, put his hands on her waist, sliding them up beneath her sweater, tugging her camisole from her skirt, so that he could touch her skin.

"That can't be all," she murmured, her hands dropping to the table, bracing herself against it.

"I can't abide sushi."

"No?"

"Not in the least," he said, and pressed his mouth to her neck, let his hands travel up to her breasts. "And I cannot," he said, filling his hands with her heavy breasts, "resist you. I adore you completely. . . ." He buried his face in the crook of her neck as his hands splayed across her breasts, pinching the nipples between his fingers, feeling them grow and harden in his hands.

Rachel sighed softly and dropped her head against his shoulder as he continued to knead her breasts.

"I have thought of little else but you these last two days. I want to be inside you again, Rachel. I want to be deep inside you, fill you up completely." With a gentle push, he spread her legs apart with his knee and pushed her sweater and camisole higher, stooping down to take her breasts in his mouth, nibbling their peaks.

"I want you inside me," she whispered above him, and her fingers sank into his hair, pulling his head into her breasts.

Flynn rose up and kissed her mouth, pulled her sweater above her head, carelessly tossing it onto the table as he stood back to admire her. They were perfect, those breasts, and he could not resist taking them in hand again, feeling their dense weight in his palm. But then he slowly turned her around, so that she was facing the table away from him, and let his hands slide over the silky skin of her back, then around her waist, to her belly, and slipped into the waistband of her skirt, to inside her panties.

Rachel sighed again; her head dropped forward. She was wet, and the feel of it kicked him into male overdrive. His body was on fire now, desperate to make love to her, to feel her squeeze around him.

She leaned across the table, her arms spreading along the table to steady herself, and she moved her legs farther apart. Somehow, Flynn managed to undo his pants, dropping them to his knees. He snaked an arm around Rachel, pulling her to him, and leaned over, his mouth on her ear, her neck. "You drive me mad with desire," he muttered as he pulled her skirt up with his free hand. "I can't see you without wanting to shag you."

"*Oh,*" she moaned as his hand slipped deeper into her panties. "Keep going, keep on."

It was all the invitation he needed. He pushed her panties down and lifted her skirt. She was bent over the table now, her hips soft and inviting. Flynn positioned himself between her legs, stroked her again until she was slick, and guided himself into her. Rachel instantly arched her back, threw her head back with a long, breathy sigh, and then groaned again, grasping at the table as he began to move in her, his cock sliding in and out, his hand caressing her sex.

It was not a long encounter—she was soon bucking

against him, urging him faster, rubbing against his hand—
and Flynn could hardly contain himself. She was hot and
tight around him, squeezing against him with each thrust,
and her hand, which now covered his, was urging him
harder. He could feel her body tensing beneath his, could
see the arch of her neck and the thrust of her hips into his,
and felt himself sliding down the slippery slope to an astounding orgasm.

By some miracle, they slid together, landing in that pool
of ecstasy at almost the very same moment, each gasping
and crying out as their bodies shuddered against each
other.

They remained bent over the dining table for a moment,
spent and gasping for breath, their clothing in disarray. It
was Rachel who started to laugh first, giggling beneath
him, then turning her head to smile at him. "I accept your
apology," she said, and Flynn laughed, too, pressed his
face against her nape, inhaled the sweet scent of her hair,
his hands warm and tight around her until she moved, to
get up.

They resumed their dress; Rachel shook out her skirt,
smiling at him so happily that he had a pang of conscience
as she slipped the camisole over her head.

He couldn't resist her; he kissed her again as she pulled
the camisole down. "There are some things I'd like to explain," he said, zipping his pants.

"Right," she said, gathering up her sweater to put it
on. "And I want to hear it all. But at the moment, I'm *ravenous*," she said, kissing the corner of his mouth. "I've
got some leftover turkey and dressing," she said, pulling
the sweater over her head, then fishing her hair from the
collar. "But the dressing burned," she said with a laugh.
She put her arms around his waist, hugged him tight for
a moment, then let go. "I'm just going to get it out and
heat it up," she said, and disappeared once more into the
kitchen.

Flynn arranged his clothing, combed his hair with his
fingers, and glanced at the table.

It took only a fraction of a second to spot the thing he most dreaded—a museum piece. He supposed he hadn't noticed it earlier, as her sweater had covered it, but there was no mistake—there, next to the flowers, was a hand-blown glass bowl, gilded and hand painted. Venetian, about three hundred years old. Worth, he'd guess, about fifteen hundred dollars. *"Fuck,"* he whispered.

The phone began to ring; Rachel came through the kitchen door, her smile luminous as she passed him to get to the phone, her eyes bright and full of emotion that he understood explicitly, for he felt it deeply.

Only his heart was in his throat.

She grabbed up the phone. "Hello? Hey, Dagne!" she said brightly. "Listen, I—" Her smile disappeared; her eyes went wide, and she suddenly looked at Flynn. "Get out! What station? Are you serious? I mean, are you . . . okay, okay, I'll do it right now," she said, and laughing, clicked off the phone and grabbed up the remote to the telly.

"My friend Dagne," she explained. "That nut is on the news!" The telly flickered on; Rachel changed the channel to a local news program and gasped. "It *is* Dagne!" she cried excitedly, and pointed.

Flynn walked into the living room and looked at the newscast. A local news reporter was in some cavernous coliseum, where all sorts of people were milling about.

Rachel laughed. "It's that *show*—you know, the one where they travel around and people bring their antique heirlooms and find out if they are valuable or not," she said excitedly.

The newscaster was saying that several local people had come down with family heirlooms and would be featured in a future program of the antique show. And then he stepped aside, and Flynn recognized Dagne Delaney . . . but more importantly, he recognized the thing that made his heart seize—the valuable Joseph Badger portrait, *Colonial Woman.*

He could not believe what he was seeing—it was impossible that they would think to bring that prized portrait to some antique show! Apparently, the host thought the same, because he looked at Dagne with some shock, then took the picture from her—whatever he said was lost in the drone of the newscaster—but Flynn watched as he rubbed a corner of the portrait with his finger. At last the newscaster shut up and turned around to listen.

"Where did you say you came across this painting?" the man asked Dagne.

"A friend of mine has a lot of stuff like this in her house," she said proudly.

"Then she is one lucky woman, Miss Delaney. This would need to authenticated, but if you will look at the lines, here, and the particular style, and here again, the use of monochromatic colors, and the type of oil paint ... well, it's obvious that this is a piece that is quite old."

"Really?" Dagne asked, looking horribly confused.

"Right," Rachel said laughingly. "Really old—like 2001."

"And do you see the name here that I've uncovered?" the host asked, and Dagne leaned forward, so far forward as to obscure the camera's view, then leaned back, nodding like a child.

"The name is Joseph Badger. Joseph Badger is one of America's most treasured artists. He painted in the pre-Revolutionary era."

"Okay," Dagne said, still looking perplexed. A crowd had begun to gather around, and the announcer held up the portrait.

"If this is an authentic Joseph Badger portrait," the man said, "it is likely quite valuable."

"Valuable?" Dagne asked, clearly shocked. "Like ... how many valuable?"

"I'm not an art dealer, but I'd guess upward of a million or more," he said, and pandemonium broke out in the coliseum.

"A million?" Rachel echoed, and with a sudden shriek,

she fell onto the edge of the couch, one hand over her mouth.

Flynn's thoughts were rattling his brain, but the one thought he was able to grasp was that he had to recover that painting. "Has she a phone?" he asked quickly, motioning vaguely to a beaming Dagne, whose face now filled the screen.

Rachel did not immediately answer; Flynn grabbed her elbow. "Has she a *phone?*"

"Yes!" she said, and looked at him strangely before leaping to her feet and lunging for her bag. Maniacally, she began to sift through it.

Flynn grabbed up the phone, dialed Joe.

"Yo," Joe said lazily on the third ring.

"Meet me at the Delaney flat," he said. "And don't let her out of your sight." He hung up, whirled around; Rachel was dumping the contents of her enormous bag onto the dining table. He strode into the dining room and grabbed the Venetian bowl, dumping the apples carelessly onto the table.

"Hey!" she cried.

Flynn put his hand on her shoulder; she looked up at him with a mixture of confusion and anxiety. "You must do precisely as I say, Rachel. You must call Dagne and tell her to stay put. Tell her she mustn't leave her flat! And Rachel . . . you mustn't leave this house. Do you quite understand me? I'll be back later, but you cannot leave until I've spoken with you again." Rachel blinked up at him with big blue eyes clouded with bewilderment.

He did not wait for an answer, but was out the door, determined to retrieve that priceless painting before anything happened to it.

Chapter Thirty-three

* ✳ *

FLYNN'S sudden phone call and departure hardly registered with Rachel, because Myron's monstrous deceit had slapped her hard the moment she heard the man say the painting was a Joseph Badger original.

How could she have been so stupid? So goddamn *blind?*

The glass bowl, the torchères, the figurine, the god-damn tea service, for Chrissakes! How long had it been going on? How long had he been *using* her?

A rage, potent and powerful, was building in her chest. She ransacked her bag, looking for the number to her cell, a number she had forgotten because Myron had kept her phone for so long now. She found it in her PDA and quickly dialed, getting *her,* Rachel Lear, accomplice-to-a-huge-crime, on the voice mail. Furious, Rachel banged the phone down, then picked it up and dialed his house. Nothing.

Bastard! She threw the phone across the room. Her mind was a whirl, her heart on fire. She was reliving every conversation she'd ever had with Myron, recalling every little thing he had ever "given" her. *Given,* her ass! He'd

stolen those things from the RIHPS! Fury prevented her
from working through how he'd done it, or how much he'd
taken—at the moment, she wanted nothing more than to
kick him square in the nuts, then drive the point of her new
Donald Pilner boots up his ass.

In a rage, she picked up the phone and dialed her cell
again. By some miracle, Myron answered. "Yo."

"Myron! You goddamn bastard, I know what you've
done!" she cried, aware of a cacophony of sound behind
Myron somewhere.

"What have I done?" he responded angrily.

"You *stole* those things, Myron!" she cried, tears suddenly leaking from her eyes. "And you used me to hide
them!"

"Oh *fuck*," he muttered. "Look, Rachel. Don't worry
about it. They are never going to figure out where the shit
is—how'd *you* figure it out?"

"How? *How?* Dagne took a Joseph Badger portrait to
the Antique Road Show—"

"Goddammit, *that* is the painting I was looking for, you
idiot!"

She choked on her own rage. "You're going to call *me*
names, you lying, thieving *prick?*"

"Shut up! It's not that big of a deal! I used your place to
stash some stuff, so what?"

"*So what?*" she screeched, incredulous, as tears
streamed down her face. "You have made me an accessory
to your crime! A criminal! Don't you even care?"

"Your dad has truckloads of money—he'll buy you out
of any trouble this causes. But there's not going to be any
trouble, Rachel. Look, I don't have time to argue with you.
I gotta go."

"I'm calling the cops," she tearfully informed him.

"*What?* You do that, and I'll tell them you've been in on
it from the beginning," he said, his voice full of venom
now. "Think where all the shit is! Who are they going to
believe? Me? Or your fat ass?"

That did it. That *so* did it. She was seething now, barely

able to contain her full-scale, nuclear fury. "My God," she breathed into the phone. "You're nothing more than a thieving son of a bitch."

Myron snorted at that. "Maybe. But a rich one now. And you made it easy—Jesus, you're getting a doctorate in history and you can't even tell a *real* piece of art from a fucking replica? How stupid are you? All I can say is, don't be stupid now. Be a good girl and carry all that shit down to the basement just in case the cops show up. I gotta go," he said, and clicked off.

But not before she heard the announcement that the flight to Savannah was boarding.

Well then. She was stupid enough to have trusted him, but she wasn't so stupid that she didn't know Savannah was next to Hilton Head Island, where his parents had a condo, and where he was going to get stoned, lie on the beach, and contemplate his sorry life. "Asshole!" she shouted as she slammed the phone down.

She paced her living room trying to think what to do, and at last came to a couple of hard conclusions. She *had* been an idiot. But she was not about to take this lying down.

Rachel picked up the phone again, dialed Dagne. "Hey," Dagne began brightly, but Rachel quickly cut her off. "It's real, Dagne. That painting is *real*. The bastard has been stealing stuff from the museums. I don't know what his scam is, but he's been using me."

"W-what?" Dagne stammered. "You can't be serious!"

"Oh, I'm dead serious," Rachel said, choking back a sob. "He said if I called the cops, he'll tell them I was in on it. Dagne, that stuff is all over my house! And worse, you sold some of it on eBay!"

"Oh, Jesus," Dagne uttered. "Oh, Jesus. What do we do?"

"I don't know for sure. But I know one thing—Myron's on his way to Hilton Head Island—remember the year we went and stayed a week? His parents have a condo down by the lighthouse somewhere. I know he's going there, I could hear them boarding in the background while he was talking on *my* phone. I'm going after him." And honestly, Rachel had never felt as fiercely determined as she did in that moment. That asshole had her phone, and she was going to go get it back. And maybe kill him in the process, too.

"*No,* Rachel!" Dagne cried. "Don't do that! They'll think you are running away. God knows what else he's got in your house!"

"I have to," Rachel said, her determination growing in leaps and bounds.

"Jesus, no you don't! What do you think—you're Charlie's Angel or something? You can't go chasing after a . . . a . . ."

"Lying sack of shit!"

"Exactly!"

"Yes I can, and I am," Rachel said. "Don't come around here, okay? Who knows what's here or who will be looking for me. Once it gets out you have that painting, the RIHPS is going to figure it out and start looking for the jackass. And they can damn well have him—just as long as I get my hands on him first."

"*Rachel!*" Dagne shrieked. "You *can't*—"

"Yes I can, Dagne!" Rachel cried, on the verge of hysteria. "Dad is right! It's about time I quit hiding and just step off the ledge and fall into life! I'll call you, I promise, but I'm going," she said, and hung up before Dagne could argue.

She glanced at the clock. A little past six. She snatched up her PDA, pulled up the number for Lear Transport Industries in New York and hastily dialed the number.

"Hello?" she said, getting Dad's secretary on the line. "Oh hi, Belinda. How are you?" she said, trying to keep her voice calm. "Listen; is Dad in New York for a while? Great . . . I need the plane . . . No, wait! No, really, it's okay, I don't need to talk to—" *Damn!* "Ah, hi, Dad," she said brightly, frantic now.

"What's this about you needing a plane?" he asked calmly.

"Dad." She took a deep breath. "Remember our talk? About how it was time for me to get out and face life and not be afraid of it?"

"Of course I do."

"There is something I need to face. And I need you to trust me. I just need to go do it and I don't have time to talk, because I have to get to Hilton Head fast."

"*Hilton* Head—"

"Dad, please! I am going to go down there to take that asshole Myron Tidwell down, but I need to do it in a hurry! I'll explain everything later . . . but could I use the plane, please?"

Dad didn't say anything for a moment, and she squeezed her eyes shut, her mind already racing ahead to how she'd get there if he said no. A train. Trains left all night. But for the second time that week, Dad surprised the shit out of her. "I guess it needs to pick you up in Providence?"

She opened her eyes, feeling, remarkably, stronger than she ever had in her life. "Yes," she said, and worked out when to meet the pilot.

FLYNN arrived at Dagne's apartment complex and parked next to Joe, who was waiting for him. "She's inside," he said as Flynn slipped into the passenger seat. "So what's up?"

"You'll not believe it. This one," Flynn said, jerking his thumb in the direction of Dagne's apartment, "took the Badger portrait to some televised show where people bring their heirlooms to have them appraised."

Joe's jaw dropped. *"Antiques Roadshow?"* he exclaimed in disbelief. "Christ Almighty." He shook his head. "I guess I shouldn't be too surprised," he added, and reached behind him, grabbed a pair of silver candlesticks wrapped in plastic and showed them to Flynn. "Some guy in Michigan bought this off eBay. When he received them, he suspected they were authentic and had them checked out. They were authentic, all right, so he turned them over to the police, who traced them back to a seller here in Providence. One Dagne Delaney."

"Bloody hell," Flynn said.

"So . . . what about Rachel Lear?"

What about Rachel Lear . . . Flynn glanced out the window into the dark. "She's got quite a number of items lying around and seems unconcerned in general."

Joe said nothing for a moment, but finally said, "Dude. I'm sorry."

Flynn wasn't sorry. At least not yet he wasn't—in his heart of hearts, he didn't believe for a moment that Rachel was involved in this scheme. That would go against everything he knew about her. And he was, generally, a bloody good judge of character. Actually, he was usually spot on when sizing people up.

But then again, he couldn't come up with a plausible explanation for how those items had landed in her home without her having some part in it.

He couldn't think about that now. At the moment, he was more interested in retrieving that priceless portrait of *Colonial Woman* and said, "I suppose we should have a chat with Miss Delaney to start, eh?"

At the door of 4A, Flynn knocked. Dagne answered a moment later, but the instant she saw them, her eyes went wide and she tried to slam the door shut.

"One moment, if you please," Flynn said, stopping her from shutting the door with a stiff-arm to the door. "I'm Rachel's friend Flynn Oliver."

"Flynn?" she said, her eyes getting wider. "*You're* Flynn Oliver?" She suddenly smiled. "*Wow.* Rachel wasn't lying when she said you were a hunk—"

"Might we have a word?" Flynn asked, pushing a little on the door.

She looked at Joe then, and her eyes narrowed into suspicion again. "Wait. How do I know you're Flynn Oliver?" she said, pushing back. "And who's this bozo?"

"I'm really Flynn Oliver, and this . . . bozo . . . is my

American partner," Flynn said, digging in his back pocket. He retrieved a small case and flipped it open.

Dagne squinted at it. "Lloyds of London . . . Flynn Oliver. Okay," she said, glancing up at him. "You're Flynn. So where is Rachel?"

"At home," Flynn said, smiling charmingly now. "She's quite all right, and in fact, was preparing dinner when last we spoke." That earned him a look of surprise from Joe, but Dagne folded her arms across her middle.

"No she's not. I just talked to her."

"That's great. And now we want to talk to you," Joe said, stepping up. "Take a closer look at Mr. Oliver's credentials. He's an *investigator* with Lloyds of London. And I," he said, pulling out his badge, "am a detective with the Rhode Island State Police. So do you want to let us in, or do you want us to haul you downtown?"

Dagne glared at the badge, then at Joe, and she held on to the door tighter, bracing herself against it. "Listen, pal, you can't just come in here like that. I watch *Law & Order*! You have to have a search warrant!"

"A warrant just to talk to you?" He laughed. "You need to watch a few more episodes, because I don't need a warrant just to talk. And I can talk to you here, or I can take you downtown. Right now I'm giving you a choice. But if you don't let us in, I might stop being so magnanimous."

"I'm calling the cops," Dagne said.

"I *am* the cops, kid. If you call more, they're going to come out here and tell you the same thing I just told you. And then they are going to ask, just like I'm about to ask, what your problem is. Do you have something to hide in there? *Should* we go get a search warrant?"

"I don't have anything to hide!" she said angrily. "I just don't like being pushed around—"

"No one's pushing, Miss Delaney," Flynn said calmly. "This is really about Rachel. She might be in a spot of trouble, and I, for one, would like to help her."

That softened her up. She blinked at Flynn, glowered at Joe, but seemed to think the better of it and stepped back, letting them inside. "I smell vanilla," she said as Flynn passed her. *"Vanilla!"* she said again, only louder.

Flynn ignored her.

Joe assumed a fairly aggressive stance—legs apart, hands on hips and coat flared back so that she couldn't miss his gun, and that backed the poor girl up against the wall. "All right, Delaney. How is it you came to be in possession of the Joseph Badger painting?" he demanded as Flynn walked to where it was perched on the couch and picked it up.

The blood literally bled from the girl's face. "I ah . . . I d-didn't . . . Can you ask that question?"

"I can ask any question I want. Why wouldn't you answer? Afraid of something?"

"No! Look, pal, you are not going to bully me. I was just helping Rachel out—"

"Helping Rachel do what? Fence stolen property?"

"NO!" she cried, aghast. "What are you *saying*? Do you even *know* Rachel?"

"Do *you?*" Joe pressed.

"Yes, I do, better than anyone, and she'd *never* do that! She didn't even know—" Dagne squealed then, clamped a hand over her mouth, and big fat tears welled in her eyes.

Joe eased up on her. "I think you better sit down and tell us what you know."

She nodded slowly, lowered her hand. "It's my fault. I should have done a spell to ward off the evil," she said, gulping down a sob.

"What?" Joe asked, confused.

"I'll explain later," Flynn said, and with the priceless portrait under his arm, he put a hand to Dagne's elbow, guided her to sit at her little dining table.

With some prodding, Dagne told them what she knew. Professor Tidwell, or Myron, as she called him, had been bringing Rachel presents from time to time, all of them, ostensibly, from the museum gift shops. "I always thought he was trying to make up for borrowing her money and eating her food," she said, staring morosely at that table.

"So how did you end up selling the stuff on eBay?" Joe asked.

She explained that Rachel's father, Aaron Lear of the huge Lear Transport Industries, had recently cut her off, which came as something of a surprise to Flynn. "He thought she'd been in school too long and was running around with the wrong people. Which," she said, stabbing the air to point at herself, "she *was,* hello!"

Another loud sob, a comforting pat on the back from Flynn, and she continued.

"So anyway, she was having a hard time finding a job and paying her bills, and I thought I'd help her out! That's all! She didn't like the stuff Myron brought her anyway, and she'd put it in the dining room or in the guest room and say she was going to decide what to do with it later, but she didn't want to throw it out because she was afraid of hurting his feelings or something . . . she's just really *nice* like that. So I started taking things. One at a time, you know, so she or Myron wouldn't notice. And I . . . I sold them on *eBay!*" she cried out in a flood of tears. "But I gave all the money to Rachel!"

"How many items?" Flynn asked.

"Am I going to jail?" she sobbed into her hands.

"Not right this minute," Joe said, casually leaning back, his feet propped on an empty chair as he watched her.

"Perhaps not at all if you can help us," Flynn said. "How many items did you auction?"

"I don't know," she said, lifting a very red, tear-streaked face. "Maybe six or seven things. Enough to pay the utility bill. Except she used the money to have that stupid Thanksgiving party for her weaving class because she'd already *promised* them. God, sometimes I just want to slap her!"

Joe rolled his eyes, drummed his fingers impatiently against the tabletop. Dagne reached for a paper towel and blew her nose, sounding a bit like an old bleating sheep.

"And how many items do you think the professor brought her?" Flynn continued.

"Oh hell, I don't know. There was something all the time."

"Were you ever present when he gave something to Rachel and claimed it was a replica?"

"Yes. The torch thingies. I remember because I thought it was weird they'd have those in a gift shop. I mean, who would buy them, right? And then I thought, well duh, Myron the idiot, who else?"

Joe looked at Flynn. "Let's go pay a visit to Professor Tidwell."

"Righto," Flynn said. "Have you any more items here, Dagne?" he asked. She shook her head.

Joe stood and looked down at Dagne, then suddenly bent down, so that his face was just inches from hers. "You leave this apartment without calling me," he said, flicking a card at her, "you're definitely going to jail for a long, long time."

Dagne wailed, motioned for him to go away.

"Look at me," Joe said sternly, and when she looked up, he said, "Do you think I'm kidding?"

"No," she said, sniffing. "I think you're a jerk."

Joe smiled, came to his feet. She buried her face in her hands again. Flynn patted her on the back, followed Joe out.

Myron was not in his apartment. Nor was he at the RIHPS offices, or the bar he frequented. Their last stop was Rachel's; it was almost eleven o'clock, but there were several lights on in the house, and her car was in the drive. There was no sign of the professor.

Joe and Flynn jogged up the steps to Rachel's house, knocked loudly, then stood there, waiting for her to open. Several seconds passed; Joe walked down the steps, looked at the upstairs lights. "I'll check around back," Flynn said, and withdrawing a small pocket flashlight, walked around the porch, down the steps to the drive, and along the bank of windows that framed the dining room. The garage was closed and locked, but the kitchen light was on and the back screen door was slightly ajar. Flynn tried it, but the door was locked. He knocked, waited for a time, but heard nothing from within.

After checking the back of the house, Flynn walked up the east side and around to the front, where Joe was still banging on the door, and was about to speak when someone behind him asked, "Who *are* you?"

Startled, both Flynn and Joe turned toward the male voice. A short man with a knitted cap that stuck up on his head like Cat in the Hat was standing there with a rake in his hands, despite it being quite dark out.

"One might ask the same of you, mate," Flynn said, turning around fully and shining his light in the man's face. "We're looking for Miss Lear."

"Well, you're frightening my wife with all this noise!"

There was no noise, and the man's attitude did not set well with Flynn. He took several steps forward, until the man had to bend his neck back to look at him. "Sorry if we've been a nuisance, but it's very imperative that we find Miss Lear. Have you seen her?"

"Yeah, I seen her," he said testily. "I keep an eye out for that one—I've called the cops on her before, you know, because they do all sorts of weird stuff back there. And that tree—she don't care at all about that tree!"

Flynn had no idea what he was talking about, but closed in on him, leaning down so that his face was inches from the little man's face. "When did you last see her?"

"A while ago! She took a taxi."

"And what do you mean, a *while* ago? Within the last hour? Two hours? Longer?"

"She left sometime after seven," he muttered, fearfully clutching the rake.

"Thank you," Flynn said, let his gaze slowly flick the length of the man, then turned and walked back to Joe. "She's gone," he said. "A cab, more than three hours ago."

"Shit!"

"I suspect," Flynn said, shooting a glare at the neighbor, who was sneaking up to eavesdrop, "that if she's about, her friend will know exactly where she is."

"Let's go," Joe said, and came off the steps, pausing in front of the neighbor. "Go back home before I punt you there."

The man scurried away.

"What is it about people with plastic yard art?" Joe muttered, and shaking his head, walked briskly with Flynn to the car.

UNLIKE Rachel, Dagne hadn't appeared to have left the table, much less her flat. She opened the door timidly when Joe pounded loudly, and offered no resistance when he pushed inside. The girl had been crying; it was plainly obvious, what with the red face, swollen, bloodshot eyes, and clogged nose.

"Now what's the matter?" Joe demanded impatiently.

"Oh, right, like you care!"

"You're right, I don't. So where'd your little friend run off to?"

Dagne responded by blowing her nose.

"Dagne," Flynn said, before Joe could scare her out of her wits. "You know that Rachel's in trouble. I want to help her—but I can't help her unless you tell me where she's gone."

Dagne sniffed loudly and glanced at Flynn from the corner of her eye. "Do you honestly believe she had something to do with it?"

Flynn instantly shook his head. "I honestly believe quite the opposite. But I must speak with her to prove it, eh?"

With a sigh, Dagne considered that, and finally cried out, "I don't know what to do!"

"Tell the truth," Flynn softly urged her. "It's always the best course."

Dagne wiped her nose, glanced up at Flynn again. "She's on her way to Hilton Head," she said, and the tears welled up again.

"Oh, that's just *great*," Joe groused, and fell into a chair at her little table.

Chapter Thirty-four

✦ ✦ ✦

THE jet landed at a small air strip on Hilton Head Island just after midnight. Thankfully, Dad had arranged a car for her, and the driver took her to The Inn at Harbor Town in Sea Pines, an exclusive resort.

It was late, and Rachel tried to get some sleep, but she tossed and turned. Her sleep was just below the surface of consciousness, her heart and mind on fire with the enormity of what Myron had done to her.

It was impossible to imagine how someone who was her friend, who had even been a lover, could have so carelessly put her in harm's way. Did he even think of the danger he put her in? The sort of criminal charges something like this could bring, even if she was an innocent, ignorant bystander, made her shudder. She could well be on her way to prison.

What hurt the most was how blind she had been to it all. She'd been so quick to settle for being Myron's "friend;" just something to make her feel worthy of a man's affection, and it had all been a lie. Somehow, she had let her insecurities meander along until even her friendship with Myron was seriously out of balance.

The most frightening thing was that it had all happened

without her even questioning it. She'd been a stupid little goose, waking up in a fresh new world every day, the past blithely forgotten. It had just been so easy to just go on and on, pretending.

But then someone had come into her life who mattered, someone who admired her for being Rachel, and she'd had the baggage that was Myron hanging over her head.

The image of Flynn scudded across her mind's eye, and she buried her face in a pillow with a breath-snatching sob. Just yesterday, her future had seemed so bright—but now it suddenly seemed coldly distant and lonely. Surely God had made a mistake with all of this; surely He would take it all back.

Rachel was up before dawn the next morning, walking along the beach and trying to clear her head. Her fury had resumed in full gale force with the first morning's light, and she wanted to find Myron desperately, to wring his fucking neck until he could not draw a breath.

As soon as the sun had come up above the horizon, she was dressed in jeans, Doc Martens, and a thick sweater. She picked up her bunker bag and marched down to the village area of the harbor, where a smattering of shops and markets lined the walk near the lighthouse.

Fortunately, in spite of the cool temperatures, the winds were calm and the sun was bright overhead. She stopped in a coffee bar, ordered a huge double latte and a brownie, and sat at one of the outside tables. Pulling a book from her bag, she pretended to be reading as she watched people milling about.

When she and Myron had come here two years or so ago, they had stayed at his parents' condominium, and she recalled it being somewhere nearby. Every day, Myron had walked to Harbor Town. If he was on Hilton Head Island, he'd be through sometime today, and all she had to do was wait.

And imagine the many ways to slay him, Wile E. Coyote style, with dynamite to stick in his mouth and giant anvils to drop on his head.

•   •   •

BACK in Providence, Joe had called headquarters from Dagne's flat and arranged for a flight to Savannah, Georgia, for him and Flynn, and by the time he had finished telling his commander what was going on, Dagne had appeared from her bedroom, carrying a very large overnight bag.

Joe hung up the phone, took one look at the bag, and immediately started shaking his head. "Uh-uh," he said. "No way."

"You can't stop me," she said defiantly, raising her chin. "It's a free country, and unless I am under arrest, I am going, too."

"You have to be out of your redheaded mind," Joe said. "The last thing we need is someone like you mucking up the works—"

"Did it ever occur to you that I might be able to *help* you?"

"Not once," he said instantly and adamantly. Not even a freakin' second."

"That's because you're just a big bully whose powers of thinking are extremely limited—"

"Beg your pardon, but we could very well stand here bickering about it all night," Flynn said, anxious to get to the airport. He looked at Joe. "Can we legally or physically stop her from taking the same flight to Georgia?"

Joe frowned. "No," he said with a growl. "Not without rousing a judge and losing time."

Dagne smiled triumphantly at that and hoisted the bag over her shoulder. "Told you so," she said, and proceeded to march out of her flat.

"Someone is going to die before this is all said and done, mark my words," Joe muttered as he marched out after her.

"Frankly, I should be so lucky," Flynn grumbled as he brought up the rear.

There was another argument in the parking lot when Joe refused to let Dagne ride in his state-issued vehicle. "I have a gun in there. I don't need psycho-witch touching anything."

"Very well, then," Flynn said sternly, and forced them both into his rental car, figuring he'd take it up with Lloyds of London when this case was finally put to rest.

He drove to Boston, keeping his eyes on the road as Dagne tried to explain the inherent value of witchcraft to them. It was a given, Flynn thought, that a man like Joe would not buy such an argument, and he was quite right—Joe was so appalled that he and Dagne argued the entire hour or so it took them to reach Boston.

In Boston, they found a cheap hotel near the airport, so that they might catch the first morning flight out to Savannah. As they had only a couple of hours to wait, they took one room. Naturally, Dagne stretched out on the bed while Joe and Flynn sat in ridiculously uncomfortable chairs and tried to catch a kip, but Dagne's snoring made that quite impossible.

Flynn eventually made his way to the car and stretched out on the backseat, and when he awoke the next morning, he found Joe in quite foul humor on the floor of the room. Dagne, however, was feeling quite chipper, judging by the way she talked.

And talked.

And talked.

About absolutely nothing, expounding on her life for the most part, pausing occasionally to philosophize—or proselytize, as the case may be. She had many thoughts about witchcraft, and evolution. And a rather adamant belief in life on other planets.

"You're a certified nut job, you know that?" Joe demanded once she had finished telling them of an encounter she had with a space alien as a teen.

"So I suppose *you* think that anyone with experiences and beliefs that differ from yours is automatically a certified nut job, don't you?"

"No—just you."

"That's such typical ogre behavior. Why can't Neanderthals like you open their minds?"

"Maybe you should cast one of your spells," he said, wiggling his fingers at her.

"Don't tempt me, dude," she said, flouncing petulantly back into her seat.

"What do you think, Flynn? Put much stock in witch-craft or space aliens?" Joe asked through a yawn.

Dagne shot forward again. "And before you answer that, Flynn, remember one thing: *Va-nil-la*," she said, rather mysteriously.

"Actually, all the chatting about witches and witchcraft is really giving me a rather fierce headache," Flynn responded irritably. "So if you don't mind."

Dagne leaned forward so that she was practically in the front seat and looked Flynn straight in the eye. *"VANILLA,"* she whispered loudly.

"Sweet Fanny Adams," Flynn said with a groan.

"Jesus, woman, do you mind?" Joe snapped, and the two of them went right back to arguing again.

It was almost more than a man could endure, and Flynn was entirely grateful when the plane landed in Savannah at long last, and he could at least put some distance—if only a foot or two—between him and his two traveling companions.

Naturally, the arguing continued in the car they hired. Flynn tried to distract himself with the business of actually driving to Hilton Head Island, while Joe and Dagne went round and round about directions, or whether or not she really needed to stop at a loo, or which of them was actually doing the most talking, et cetera . . . Flynn lost track of their nonsense somewhere between Georgia and South Carolina.

When they at last passed over the causeway to Hilton Head, Flynn pulled into a petrol station and went inside, purchased a map of the island. As he handed the woman behind the counter his money, she smiled sympathetically. "Hon, you look like you could use a good belt."

She had absolutely no idea.

In the car again, Flynn opened the map. Joe was instantly leaning over to see it, and Dagne, from her perch in the backseat, was hanging like she was suspended from the car ceiling over his shoulder.

"She said the lighthouse, somewhere near the lighthouse," she repeated helpfully.

"So what, we're supposed to go hang out at some lighthouse?" Joe asked, yawning again.

"Unless you've got a better idea," Flynn said, "we'll just go have a look about and perhaps find a good nosh up."

Both Joe and Dagne looked at him as if he were speaking Greek. "Dude, you must be tired!" Joe said with a grin. "You're not making sense."

Flynn rolled his eyes and drove on, Dagne still hanging over his shoulder like a very chummy mutt.

NOW Rachel was furious with Myron for making her wait so long. It was almost noon. It was so like him, so inconsiderate and selfish—she'd gotten up twice now to walk around and put some circulation in her legs. Between thoughts of disemboweling him to being furious that he might be sleeping somewhere while she stood vigil had turned her into a bundle of very bitchy nerves.

On her second stand up and walk around, she saw someone through a café window that looked an awful lot like Dagne. That at least made her scoff out loud—she was losing her mind if she thought Dagne was on Hilton Head. But it did remind her she should call, and she walked to a pay phone, just on the edge of a row of buildings and the outdoor seating she was using as a stakeout.

She put in all the quarters she had, dialed Dagne's line, but no one answered. Honestly, she wouldn't be the least bit surprised if Dagne had up and gone home to Philadelphia, just in case someone came around asking about the Badger painting, and dear God, she hoped Dagne remembered to take the painting with her rather than leaving it lying around her apartment.

With a sigh, she put the receiver down. She leaned over, picked up her bag and hoisted it onto her shoulder, was starting in the direction of the outdoor seating—and saw Myron waltzing through the main concourse. What the hell . . . he was *whistling!* Strolling through the small crowd, hands in pockets, *whistling!*

That. *Bastard.* Not only was he a thief and a liar and a cheat, he was actually enjoying himself!

She didn't even think; she took a long step forward, prepared to march through the crowd and intercept him, then deck him—but someone caught her arm, and as she tried to shake the hand off and twist around to see who it was, a hand clamped over her mouth, an arm went around her waist, and she felt herself being yanked back into the alley space next to the building like a sack of potatoes.

She knew instantly whose hard chest she was up against—she could smell his cologne. And she began to struggle with him, trying to free herself and turn around at the same time. But Flynn's arm was like a vise around her, and his legs, which she knew to be powerful, thank you, were pinning hers together.

"Hush, love," he whispered, dragging her deeper into the little alley. "I really don't want to hurt you, but I will if you keep this up. Hush now, and listen to—*ouch!*" he exclaimed, sucking his breath in through his teeth at her heel to his instep. He let go just enough for her to twist around, but he quickly caught her and pinned her up against the brick wall. "Jesus, there's no call for that! Listen to me, Rachel—we're going to nab your Myron, you have my word, but you really *must* cooperate!"

"No!" she grunted, and tried to come down on his instep again, but this time managed to snag his toes through his Italian loafers. With a groan of agony, Flynn suddenly shoved up against her, cutting off any movement in her legs, and her breath, for that matter. "That was really quite naff, you know. No more, do you understand? If you kick me once more, I will retaliate," he said, and grabbed her shoulder, squeezing a tendon.

Rachel instantly gave up. "Okay, okay," she cried, trying to move from his hand.

Flynn's face appeared, floating before hers. "Do I have your word?" he demanded.

With a grimace, she nodded. Flynn let go, slowly eased up, watching her carefully to see if she might try something.

Rachel glared at him, was ready to give him a piece of her mind—which piece, she wasn't certain—but it was quickly a moot point as she saw the guy behind him who looked oddly familiar.

And then she saw Dagne, who was peeking out behind the guy, smiling and sheepishly waving her fingers.

Chapter Thirty-five

* * *

THE newspaper accounts that appeared in the days following would erroneously report that the whole thing had begun with an altercation between two law enforcement officers and a woman in the heart of Harbor Town; when in actuality, the altercation happened much later, in the condominiums where Myron was hiding out.

The only thing that happened in Harbor Town that early afternoon was that Rachel was driven all but wild trying to understand how Flynn and Dagne—who had never met, mind you—and *that* man, who turned out to be a cop, could be there in that little alley with her.

In truth, there *was* a bit of shoving, starting with Rachel, who put two hands on Flynn's chest and shoved him away from her, then stood there, her hands on her hips, fuming as she took in the three of them. And then she looked at Dagne and made her wince by staring daggers at her. "*You* did this," she said accusingly, and shoved her. But it was a one-handed shove, and really did not deserve the rebuttal shove she got in return.

"They *made* me!" Dagne cried.

"How could they *make* you? You don't even know Flynn—"

"I know, but he knew *me,* Rachel! He *knew* me! He knew where I lived and my name and they said—"

"Ah, actually," Flynn said, nudging Dagne to shut up, "I was hoping to sort of walk Rachel through all that."

Rachel's first, horrific thought was that Flynn and Dagne were involved—but that seemed entirely impossible, so she shook her head to clear it, and tried to make sense of what was *happening.*

"He's a cop," Dagne said.

"Investigator, actually," Flynn corrected her.

"Investigator," Dagne repeated.

A cop? An *investigator?* Now she gaped at Dagne, then at Flynn, almost believing that Dagne had managed the mother of all spells. Flynn smiled a little. He shrugged. He looked at his shoes. An *investigator!* How could that be? She'd never seen any guns or badges or anything that even remotely—

"There he is. That's Myron," Dagne said disgustedly, and the rest of them jerked their gazes toward the street. Rachel caught just a glimpse of the lying asshole as he went by, and instantly started in that direction, but Flynn caught her by the arm. "We really prefer to follow him, see where he goes."

"*Follow* him? Why do *you* want to follow him? And who is we? What we?"

"We," Flynn said, gesturing to his companions. "Why do you want to follow him?"

"I don't want to follow him," she snapped as Dagne inched her way to the corner of the building, watching Myron. "I want to kill him!"

"*Kill* him?" the stranger asked. "Why?"

"Who are *you?*" she demanded.

"Detective Joe Keating, Rhode Island State Police," he said, and suddenly pushed Dagne out into the sunshine and followed her.

Flynn obviously thought to do the same, as he put his

hand on the small of Rachel's back and shoved her forward.

But Rachel caught herself on the edge of the building. "*Wait!* Who is that guy? How are you *here?* And how in God's name do you know Dagne?"

"It's really quite a long and sort of complicated story, so I'd suggest, if you don't want to lose your chance to kill the professor, that we sort of chivvy along and I'll tell you everything later." And he nudged her again.

She did want to kill Myron. Badly. Rachel started walking. But she didn't like it.

They stepped out from the building, walked a few feet behind Dagne and the other guy up the walk. Several yards ahead, Rachel could see Myron strolling along, a plastic bag swinging from one hand. He turned left onto a street, and so did the four of them, but the guy with Dagne made her pause in front of a shop window while he looked around the corner. And then he grabbed Dagne's arm and yanked her around the corner with him.

Flynn and Rachel followed, marching in silence, side by side, and they continued this absurd game of chase until Myron slipped into a very nice Town Car. That bastard owed her money and was driving a *Town* Car?

Flynn, the detective, and Dagne all stopped beside a Ford Taurus.

The detective got in the driver's seat, Dagne in front, and Flynn pushed Rachel into the back. They backed out of the space so quickly that Rachel feared she'd been whiplashed, but then he threw it into drive so fast that Rachel almost went through the window. Flynn caught her again, pushed her down in the seat. "You might want to buckle up there."

"Will someone *please* tell me what is going on here?" Rachel demanded as she fished around for the seat belt. "Who is *he* for starters?"

"Like I said, Detective Keating," the detective snapped.

"Oh please," Dagne muttered.

But it was all beginning to sink in for Rachel—the police had come for her and Myron, and he'd used Flynn and Dagne to find her. "Oh God," she said, looking at Flynn. "Oh God, I'm so sorry—"

"What are you sorry for?" Detective Keating barked as he made a hard right behind Myron.

"Oh for Chrissakes, will you stop acting like a big bad cop?" Dagne insisted, clearly exasperated.

"You are interfering with official police business, Red," the detective said to Dagne.

"Well, *someone* needs to tell her what is going on!" Dagne shot back.

"Actually, Joe, if you don't mind . . . I'll take this one," Flynn said.

Joe? Rachel looked at Flynn again; he was calmly considering her, as if he knew all this was going to happen.

"Okay, that's *it!*" she cried furiously. "Who are you really? I thought you were a computer guy! How do you know a cop and call him Joe? How do you know Dagne? I didn't introduce you to Dagne! I want to know what is going on here!"

"All right," Flynn said, and put his hand on her leg, rubbing her thigh very gently, calming her. "Take a breath or two, will you? All right, here it is. The truth is . . . I'm not actually a computer guy. I'm actually a fraud investigator for Lloyds of London. Lloyds insures quite a lot of property in the United States, and one of their clients is the Rhode Island Historical Preservation Society."

"Oh, Jesus." Her head was going to explode. Literally. Right off her body and it would be a godsend. An *insurance fraud investigator!* Her house *full* of insurance fraud! But worse, much worse, she realized as her heart sank to her toes . . . "You mean you lied to me?" she asked weakly.

"I'm afraid I did," he said. "But more importantly, Rachel, you must be truthful now. Are you part of Professor Tidwell's scheme?"

"No!" she cried.

"I *told* you!" Dagne said angrily. "Look, you're making her cry. Stop it!"

"Miss Delaney, if you please," Flynn said sharply.

"I mean it, you little wack-job," the detective quickly interjected. "I'm about to pull over and put a gag in your mouth," he added, and Dagne shrieked her indignation.

"Rachel, the items in your house," Flynn continued.

"I know!" she cried, stopping him. "But I thought he bought them at the gift shop," she said, realizing instantly how foolish and ridiculous that sounded. "He . . . he owes me money, and he never pays me back, and I thought he got some huge discount, so that was his lame way of sort of paying me back."

"He had a discount, all right," the detective snorted. "A five-finger discount."

"Oh God, oh God," Rachel said, and began to hyperventilate. "What's happened? What has he done?"

She just barely glimpsed Joe's roll of the eyes, because Flynn shoved her head down between her knees. "Breathe!" he commanded her. "Deep breaths, one, two, three . . . that's right, there's a good girl." He held her head down a moment more until he was certain she was breathing. When he let her up, they had pulled into a parking lot.

"Now then. It seems your Myron has been stealing from the various museum properties—mostly estates in Newport," Flynn explained evenly.

She had guessed as much, but she still couldn't figure out why. "But . . . but to what end? It doesn't make any sense," Rachel said. "If he stole stuff and hid it in my house, what good does it do him?"

"Fraudulent claims," Flynn said, as the detective pulled into a parking spot. "I'll explain later."

The four of them watched Myron jog up the steps to one of the condominiums, fit a key into the lock, and go inside.

"Let's go," Joe said. "We'll take it slow and easy, let her go first," he said, indicating Rachel. "He knows her. He'll see her and open the door.

"What about me?" Dagne whined.

"Sit here and keep your mouth shut and don't touch

anything," he said, stepping out of the car, and leaned down, said to Flynn, "I'm calling for backup."

"Oh *wow*," Dagne exclaimed, and got out of the car, too, in spite of being told not to.

But Rachel was too stunned; her mind was whirling around the improbable and impossible events. As she stared at Flynn, the pieces were coming together, coming to the realization that their chance meeting had been no chance at all. "Did you . . . did you ever see me on campus?" she asked tearfully. "Or was that a lie, too?"

Flynn pressed his lips together and shook his head.

"So . . . it was all a lie? Everything was a lie?"

"No, no, not everything, Rachel. Everything between us, that was real, just as I tried to tell you."

"You were using me to get to Myron," she said, ignoring him.

Flynn didn't deny it.

"But why?" she asked as the detective knocked impatiently on Flynn's window. "Why didn't you just tell me what you were doing? Why did you have to lie about the computers and the homicide—"

"Actually, the homicide was not a lie."

"You could have just *said*—"

"No, I couldn't have, because we thought—at least in the beginning—that you were perhaps involved somehow."

This had to be her worst nightmare—and she was humiliated beyond comprehension. She should have trusted her instincts—guys like Flynn did not fall for chicks like her. "You honestly think that I could *do* something like this?" she demanded, fighting tears.

"Of course not!" he said. "But there are other opinions to consider."

"Oliver! Let's go!" the detective yelled.

He had doubted her. He had wondered if she could be part of this, and Rachel was out of her mind now, because the only person who could clear her was a man who had used their friendship unconscionably.

It was more than she could endure, and abruptly, she was moving with blind emotion, fumbling with the door, practically falling out of the car, racing to Myron's apartment as the detective yelled at her to stop. But she didn't stop, she ran up the steps and banged on the door, and shouted Myron's name.

He opened the door a moment later. He was stoned again, she could tell from the lazy look in his eye and the fact that he laughed when he saw her. *"Rachel!"* he exclaimed. "What a surprise! What are you doing here?"

"I want my goddamn phone back!" she shouted.

Myron blinked. "All *right* already—" And then his eyes bugged out, just like in the cartoons.

As it turned out, that was the last thing Myron would say as a free man, because at that precise moment, Flynn came flying past Rachel to grab Myron by the collar and push him up against the wall.

But Rachel tripped when he shoved past, and fell into Flynn and Myron, which made Myron flounder and try to struggle free, and Dagne shrieked, and there was a flurry of arms and legs and a lot of scuffling around and then Flynn was manhandling Myron as he bellowed like a cow.

Everything seemed to happen in one huge blur. Someone was helping her up; Myron was sitting on the floor with his hands cuffed behind his back. Flynn and Detective Keating and two cops in uniforms were inside the condo, and one of the cops had another man up against the wall, spread eagle as he patted him down.

There were several antiquities inside, too, scattered around the small living room—china, silver candelabra, hand-painted bowls, and gold commodes set into mahogany chests.

The other man, the one against the wall, was a Brit, as it turned out. He handed Flynn his identification as Rachel wandered around stunned. Flynn took one look, said, "Hallo, Geoffrey. Fancied a life of luxury, did you?"

And then more cops came, taking statements from everyone. Flynn and Joe asked Rachel a long list of questions. When did the items first begin to appear, how many of them had she seen, where they were kept, what had she done with them. *Had she ever asked Myron why he continued to bring her gifts, since they were no longer lovers? How long had it been since she and Myron were lovers? How long were they actually lovers? They were lovers, weren't they?*

Rachel went from frightened to humiliated to numb.

Later, after they had taken Myron and the British guy off in handcuffs (and Rachel's phone was given over to evidence), the detective and Flynn drove Dagne and Rachel to the Hilton Head airstrip, and ordered her plane to be readied for the flight back to Providence.

"So what happens next?" Dagne asked the detective.

"We'll stay behind to inventory the stuff and get our reports in order," he said.

"I still don't get it," Dagne said thoughtfully. "What were they going to do with all that stuff?"

"Perhaps sell it on eBay, just as you did," Flynn guessed. "Or dump it in the ocean. It's terribly difficult to move that sort of art and antiquities on the black market."

"But I still don't get it," Dagne insisted.

"It went something like this," Flynn said patiently. "Geoffrey is a claims adjuster for Lloyds. He and Myron met up somewhere along the way and concocted the scheme that would make them rich . . . or so they hoped. Essentially, they took small items from the various RIHPS properties and dumped them in Rachel's basement, or in Geoffrey's car—he brought them here, you see. Apparently, it's only used in the summer months, so they were quite safe here for a time. And at Rachel's, well . . ." He looked at Rachel, smiled a little. "They were lost, or used as fruit bowls or what have you."

"Back at the offices," the detective said, "Myron would make the claim for the loss, and Geoffrey would process it. But the claims were always significantly higher than the property was worth."

"Lloyds took the claim," Flynn continued, "submitted

by their adjuster and substantiated by both the adjuster and a professor from Brown University. Somehow, they arranged for the claim to be paid to Myron at RIHPS. RIHPS got the actual value for the lost property, and these two chaps split the additional claim money—they were skimming the gray area. Quite clever, really."

"So how did they get caught?" Dagne asked.

"As is usually the case with such scams," Flynn said, "they got greedy. Our fraud detection unit noticed an unusually high number of claims were being submitted. Their excuse was, of course, a series of thefts had occurred. But our colleagues in America," he said, looking at Joe, "had determined those thefts to be an inside job."

Dagne let out a long sigh and shook her head. "What a jackass," she said. "I just can't understand why Myron would risk so much," she said. "It wasn't like he didn't have a good job. A professor at Brown?"

"Tenure," Rachel muttered miserably. "He couldn't get tenure. He had another few months and they were going to let him go."

"Ah," the detective said. "That explains a lot."

A man appeared at Rachel's left. "Miss Lear? We're ready for you now."

"Thanks, Ted," she said, and sighed wearily as she came to her feet.

"All right, ladies, don't go anywhere for a couple of weeks, okay? We'll need to talk to you again," the detective said, just like on *Law & Order*.

"Fine," Dagne said, sounding exasperated, but Rachel knew that lilt in her voice meant she'd be more than happy for Detective Keating to question her again.

As for Rachel . . . she couldn't even bring herself to look at Flynn. Between her humiliation at having been duped by Myron for all the world to see, and the pain of having fallen in love with someone who was using her to get to Myron . . . she just wanted out of there.

She got up, put her bag on her shoulder, and started walking without a word, without looking back to anyone,

hardly caring if Dagne followed her or not, not even looking at Ted, who smiled and pointed to the jet on the tarmac.

"Rachel!" Flynn called after her, but she did not turn
around. When her foot hit the tarmac, she began to run, not
caring that she looked like a fool, running across the tarmac. She just wanted to be gone.

She was already strapped into her seat by the time
Dagne managed to get on. "Holy *shit!*" Dagne exclaimed
in awe. "My God, this is your *dad's?*" she said reverently,
gaping in disbelief.

"One, anyway," Rachel muttered miserably, and Dagne
screeched her glee, then prattled on about the gold fixtures,
the bed, and the leather seats and monogrammed towels,
and on and on . . .

Rachel said nothing. She couldn't speak. Tears were
streaming down her face as she stared out the little portal
window at Flynn. He was standing at the edge of the tarmac. His hair was all messed up, and she imagined he had
dragged his fingers through it several times in the course
of the day. With his weight braced on one leg, he had a
hand on his waist and was staring at the Lear plane with an
expression that Rachel could not quite make out.

Chapter Thirty-six

✦ ✦ ✦

BY the time Flynn and Joe arrived back in Providence the next afternoon, the press was all over the breaking story. They picked up the *Providence Journal* on the drive from Boston to Providence. The headline read:

BROWN UNIVERSITY PROFESSOR IS MASTERMIND BEHIND INSURANCE SCAM

"Oh, Christ," Flynn muttered, and read the article aloud to Joe, who beamed like a bloody idiot. There were several quotes in the article. Myron's boss at the RIHPS claimed Myron had been a fringe employee for some time, often missing work or coming in late, and misplacing items in their catalog.

His dean at Brown University called him a "mediocre" professor whose path to tenure had never materialized.

And then, of course, was the paragraph about the "girl-friend," naming Rachel, who, according to the paper, had not yet been charged, but in whose house the stolen goods had been stored.

"It's a bloody circus," Flynn said.

"Yeah." Joe beamed.

They arrived at police headquarters, and a dozen or more reporters were waiting for them, all anxious to have a word with them about their work on the case. They held a joint press conference, speaking on behalf of their respective organizations. Joe was a natural, parading around like a peacock, but Flynn stood back, let Joe have the spotlight, particularly when his higher-ups praised the work he'd done.

They filed their joint reports and spoke with prosecutors, who assured them that while Myron and his accomplice faced extradition hearings from South Carolina, that a full range of theft and fraud charges would be brought against each of them, as well as a charge for possession of a significant amount of marijuana, guaranteeing at least twenty years behind bars before there was any hope of parole.

The media frenzy increased throughout the week as the national news media picked up the story. Images of items being carted out of Rachel's house were broadcast over and over again.

With all the media attention, Flynn didn't want to go to her house and draw more. Nevertheless, he tried to ring Rachel, of course he tried—but she hung up—rather, slammed the phone down each time, refusing to talk to him. And then she had her phone disconnected altogether.

Flynn busied himself with the smaller but important case details that had to be attended, biding his time until he could find a way to reach her.

His superiors hoped he might track down the things Dagne Delaney had sold on eBay, which took a bit of time. And there was the thorough examination of the contents of Rachel's house. While Flynn did not attend the gutting of her house, he did examine the items in an RIHPS warehouse. He believed, as he told his superiors in London, that they would be able to recover most, if not all of the items.

There was the media, too, which had yet to complete their feeding on this particular story. It wasn't until the end of that extraordinary week that Flynn was certain no media was following him around and that things were secure enough to drive to Rachel's house. He arrived on a gray Sunday afternoon, parked in the drive, just behind her car. He walked up the porch steps and knocked on her door.

Before she could possibly answer, her neighbor was instantly at the side of the yard. "Are you a policeman?" he called out to Flynn.

Flynn glanced impatiently at the man. "Why do you ask?"

"*Oh* . . . you're the Englishman!" he said, smiling now. "I hope a policeman comes, because I got more things to tell them."

Now Flynn turned fully and looked at him with all the disgust he felt. "Do you, indeed? What sort of things might those be, mate?"

"Well, I am suing her because she won't move the tree," he said, gesturing wildly toward the back of her house. "And she has this friend, and they do some strange things at night. I've *seen* them."

"Fascinating," Flynn said as he walked down the porch steps to where the man was standing. "Go on."

"I saw her carry some things to the garage, too. I think it's stolen property."

Flynn stopped just inches from the worm. "What's your name?"

"Tony Valicielo."

"Tony Valicielo, let me offer you a bit of friendly advice, if I may," he said pleasantly, then roughly grabbed him by the collar, hauled him up to his tiptoes.

"Hey!" Valicielo yelped.

"I am still quite involved in this case, and if I *hear* you or hear *of* you saying even the slightest thing against Miss Lear, I will personally come to your house and beat the living shit out of you."

Tony Valicielo blinked.

"Just so that we are perfectly clear, I do mean the living *shit* out of you. And furthermore, if you do not cease and desist in your spying on Miss Lear, I shall personally have you arrested and thrown into a jail cell where you will promptly be forgotten for all eternity."

Valicielo swallowed so hard that his Adam's apple dipped almost to his waist.

"There you are, you wretched little nancy boy. Now sod off and go tidy up your plastic zoo, will you?"

Mr. Valicielo opened his mouth, but quickly shut it again and stomped back to his house.

"Ridiculous," Flynn muttered, and turned around, and was startled by the sight of Rachel standing on the porch wrapped in her lavender shawl, her arms tightly around her, looking at him. Staring emptily, rather—he instantly noticed the spark in her eyes was gone. Her gorgeous eyes had been replaced by eyes that were lifeless and dull.

Flynn forced a smile. "Rachel," he said, walking toward her. "I wasn't certain you'd speak to me."

She said nothing, just kept staring at him with those wretched eyes. She looked drawn; there were dark circles under her eyes, and her hair was wound in some sort of haphazard knot and secured with a pencil. She didn't seem to be the same Rachel, and it pained him.

Flynn stopped on the bottom step of the porch. "It's ah . . . it's rather hard to know where to begin."

"Then don't," she said. "I don't want to talk to you."

"I gathered as much," he said, putting his hands on his hips. "But I rather hoped you'd at least give me a chance to explain everything."

She gave a strange bark of laughter that sounded like a wounded dog. "I don't need you to tell me what *happened*," she said. "I know what *happened*. You used me. You suspected me of being part of some horrid insurance scam and you cozied up to me just so you could find out what Myron was doing," she said, her tone bitter. Even worse, a tear slipped from one eye.

That, he couldn't abide, and Flynn moved without thinking, but Rachel instantly shot up an arm. "I don't want you near me," she breathed. "And I don't want you to pretend that what you did doesn't matter, that you were on the side of good, or something asinine like that," she said, her voice shaking. "I've thought about this a lot, Flynn. I hate what Myron did to me! He betrayed me in the worst way, lying and stealing and using me! But that doesn't hurt nearly as much as *your* lies. And I know you will argue you had to do it, that it was your job, but I don't care! You lied to me, you used me, you played me for a fool and it hurts because I loved you! *Your* lies cut so deep that I keep thinking I'm going to bleed to death."

A rash of tears erupted from her eyes, and Rachel gulped down a sob, pulled her shawl more tightly about her. "I really loved you, Flynn. And that makes your cut the deepest."

Christ in heaven. He walked up the steps, reached out and touched her face, but Rachel recoiled, turning her head. "Rachel," he said desperately. "I love you, *too,* Rachel, that's just it, that's why I came here—"

"I don't believe you! I can't believe anything between us was real! That night I told you I was falling in love with you, you might as well have crawled under a table! And there was always something you were going to *tell* me. Were you going to tell me there was another woman? Did you lie about that, too?"

The question, flung out of the blue, startled him so badly that Flynn hesitated, if only for a fraction of a second, but in that fraction of a second, Rachel turned her back to him, walked to the door, and yanked it open. "I don't ever want to speak to you again, I don't ever want to *see* you again—I just want the whole nightmare to go away," she said, and walked through the door, slamming it shut behind her.

Flynn stood on the lawn, his jaw aching with the clench of it.

All right. She was frightfully angry. He had no choice but to give her time to cool off. He'd be in the States a few more weeks, tracking down the last items. And as he hadn't the least bloody idea what to do, he turned away, lost in thought, walked to his car in the drive.

But he sat behind the wheel of that car, emotionally and mentally exhausted. Rachel was hurt, all right. But he felt himself sitting on the edge of a dreadful turmoil, bubbling up beneath the silence that had filled his heart and his mind since Hilton Head, a turmoil that was ready to break the surface and completely demoralize him.

But he could see Rachel at the upstairs window, staring down at him, her expression carved from stone.

Flynn made himself drive.

At the Corporate Suites, he grabbed his coat from the car and walked from the parking lot into the lobby and waved at the desk clerk. "Ah, Mr. Flynn!" the young man called as Flynn punched the button. "I got a message for you."

"That's quite all right—I'll pick it up later," he said, and stepped into the lift, smiled thinly as the clerk tried to speak while the lift doors were shutting, and fell against the wall, waiting for the interminable ride up to the fifth floor.

On the fifth floor, he exited the lift, walked slowly down the hallway to his flat . . . and thought, strangely enough, that he could hear a telly blaring in his flat. As he haltingly neared the door, he was certain he did, and wondered if he'd left it on all day. With a shrug, he unlocked the door, pushed it open, and walked in.

"Flynn, darling!" his mother cried happily, startling him out of his wits. "We thought you'd never return!" she said as she hurried to embrace him. She threw her arms around him, went up on her tiptoes to kiss his cheek, then stood back, smiling. "Oh dear, you look absolutely *knackered*," she exclaimed.

"Mum, what are you doing here?" he asked.

"You missed the Farmington Fall gala, you know," she said. "Your cousins were quite distraught."

"Where's Dad? I can't believe he'd let you bring him all this way without some sort of protest."

"Oh no, your father didn't come," she said with a laugh. "*I* came darling, who else?"

The voice sliced through him; Flynn groaned, turned toward the tiny living room and a smiling, bone-thin, Iris Willow-Throckmorton.

"What *is* it, darling?" she laughingly cried as she pranced toward him, her arms outstretched. "You don't seem very happy to see me at all!" She rose up, air-kissed his cheek. "We've come all this way to see you, and you aren't the least bit happy. You haven't gone and found yourself a new fiancée, have you?" she asked sweetly.

For the first time in his life, Flynn felt the urge to deck a woman. "Hallo, Iris," he said, and loosening his tie, stepped around her, walked into his bedroom, and shut the door.

Chapter Thirty-seven

* ✴ ✦

Subject: RE: RE: RE: Re: [FWD: I'm Okay, Really]
From: <rmanning70@houston.rr.com>
To: <earthangel@hotmail.com>

Earthangel@hotmail.com wrote:

. . . thanks, but there's not that much to say and I really just want to be left alone.

Ah kid, you've been through a lot, but isolating yourself is not healthy. Mom is right, you should come home to the ranch and decompress. Get out of Rhode Island and away from those lunatics and come back to Texas where we'll treat you right—Rebecca knows a great spa in Austin, it's like a two-day thing, and they feed you and pamper you and when you come out, I swear you're ten pounds lighter just from all the wraps. Write me back. Why is your phone disconnected, anyway? We luv u, Rachel. Robbie

Subject: RE: RE: RE: RE: Doing Fine
From: Rebecca Parrish <reparrish72@aol.com>
To: Rachel Lear <earthangel@hotmail.com>

Earthangel@hotmail.com wrote:

*. . . appreciate the advice, but this isn't really the same as
when you and Bud split up. I really don't want to talk
about it anymore, Bec. I'm sick of talking about it. But
thanks for trying. Rachel.*

But see? It is the same because I felt the same way after
Bud left me. I just wanted everyone to leave me alone
and let me wallow in my misery for a while. But Rach,
don't do what I did and wallow too long because it
really screwed me up. I started to believe I was worthless and deserved everything he did to me. It wasn't
until you and Robbie sent me on the transformation re-
treat that I began to snap out of it and realize that what
happened didn't happen TO me, it happened
AROUND me (transformation seminar, track 3). There
is a subtle distinction, you know—if something is done
to you, it's malevolent. If something is done around
you, it's a case of your being in the wrong place at the
wrong time, and the trick is to recognize you're in the
wrong place at the wrong time and get out before anyone notices. Do you know what I mean? Gee, I really
wish I could talk to you, Rachel. Do you need some
money to get your phone reconnected? Please write
me back. I am worried about you. Mom's thinking of
coming to Providence, but she said she wouldn't do
that without talking to you first. Love you, Rebecca

Subject: Your Boyfriend's Crime
From: Lillian Stanton <lilandel@aol.com>
To: Rachel Ellen Lear <earthangel@hotmail.com>

Rachel honey Bonnie told me all what happened
and I just want you to know that your grandpa and I
think it's just awful what he done he deserves to go
to jail and hell. Yes I said hell. Bonnie says your real
depressed and I don't blame you honey because
that is an awful thing to have to go through just ask
your sister Robin because she was arrested once. I
think you ought to come home. If you don't want to
go to the ranch you just come on to Houston and I
will make you some brownies you know the ones with
fudge and nuts you like so well. Just let us know when
your plane gets in and Grandpa will come pick you
up at the airport only be sure to come to Bush
Intercontinental and not Hobby because that is too
far for him to drive on account of that blood clot he
had last year I swan if its not one thing its another
with that old man.

Hey Rachel . . . Old Man here . . . Got me a new
hunting rifle. Want me to come up there and plug
that sorry sonofabee? Lil says that's not funny but I
didn't mean it to be funny, I'm serious as a heart attack. I love you pretty face and if you want me to kill
him I will. Hell, I'm eighty years old. They aren't going
to put me in jail. Let me know. Love, Grandma and
Grandpa

Subject: Hello Baby Girl
From: Aaron Lear <Aaron.Lear@leartransind.com>
To: Rachel <earthangel@hotmail.com>

From everything I've read and heard I guess it's safe to
assume that you went to Hilton Head and did what
you had to do. And I don't suppose you need any
more advice than you've been getting from the rest of
the crew—your mom says you've turned off your

phone, and I can sure understand why—but I want you to know that I am proud of you, Rachel, damn proud. I know it hasn't been easy—no one ever likes to find out they've been the ass of someone's sick joke, especially when it's splashed across the news for all the world to see. But I have every confidence you will come through this stronger and better than before. Call me when you're ready, baby girl. Dad

There was, to Rachel's way of thinking, nothing to be proud of. She had waltzed herself right into the middle of a freakin' nightmare and had not been able to muddle her way out. When she wasn't reliving every single thing Flynn had said or done, she was reviewing, with her perfect hindsight, all the clues that should have told her she was being followed, surveilled, and generally spied upon.

For example, the blue car she had seen on more than one occasion driving past her house was Detective Joe Keating's—she had seen it in enough newscasts now to recognize it.

How about the many times she just *happened* to run into Flynn? Please! At the coffee shop, the gym, the market, her *class,* a supermarket clear across town, hello! And his living arrangement, and his knowing the Feizels, and the fact that he couldn't help her with a computer problem even though he was a computer guy. Why hadn't something registered?

She had known right off that a guy like him would not, out of the clear blue, want to hook up with her, so why hadn't it clicked that something was going on?

Dagne's stupid witchcraft, that was why! She had bought into that ridiculous notion, had believed she had cast spells that would bring love and romance to her. Which, if one laid out all the clues and facts in a nice neat little row, made her even more outrageously pathetic than she originally thought. She was a stupid girl, a real Miss Fortune.

So, all right. It certainly wasn't the first time she'd been a complete idiot, and in the greater scheme of things, she probably could have handled the whole Myron thing, particularly after the *Providence Journal* ran a Sunday feature entitled, *A Professor, a Student, and a Tangled Web of Deceit.* In that article, she came off (no surprise here) as a tubby *(Rachel Lear, a tall, big-boned young woman),* pretty air-headed *(did not, according to authorities, think anything unusual with the number or type of "gifts" she was receiving from Professor Tidwell on a fairly routine basis),* pathetic loser *(A search of university records reveals that Miss Lear has been enrolled in a doctorate program for four years).* Par for the course.

Her friends tried to come to her rescue. The reporter spoke at length with Dagne, who, Rachel was discovering, really liked the media attention. *Dagne Delaney, a close friend of Lear's, had sold a few of the items on eBay and collected around three hundred dollars for priceless artifacts.* Dagne vigorously defended Rachel. "I know it might seem really stupid, but you just have to know Rachel," she told them. "She's the nicest person you would ever meet, and very well mannered, and she just really thought Professor Tidwell was her friend. No, really, she *did.*"

Chantal said, "I don't know nothing about that slimy professor, but he ain't the one she had the hots for. Now Rachel Lear, she be the salt of the earth, you know what I'm saying? She'd take the shirt off her back and give it right to you if you needed it."

Mr. Gregory was, as one would suspect, less sympathetic: "Yes, I would agree that Miss Lear is very kind, yet I can't help but wonder at her atrocious lack of judgment."

Jason was defiant: "I can't stand what everyone is saying about Rachel. She's the *best!* You don't know her! You're saying things that aren't [expletive deletive] true!"

And not to be left out, Sandy: "She's real good with people. She always carried aspirin for me, because I am prone to flare-ups of phlebitis when I sit too long in class. She didn't have to do that. It was real thoughtful."

And what would a Sunday exposé be without a little

something from Mr. Valicielo? "Lots of strange people come and go over there, all times of the day and night," he said. "And she cut that tree down, that one there, to let it ruin my fence. I seen her with an axe." The reporter did note, thankfully, that there was no evidence the tree had been purposely cut down, but appeared to have fallen due to root rot.

Most of the feature was devoted to Myron, how a professor who once had a promising future could mastermind such a scheme, pocketing almost fifty thousand dollars for his troubles. That part infuriated her the most. He had stolen upwards of fifty thousand dollars, had two jobs, and *still* he couldn't pay her back?

The article went on to explain Myron's fall from grace at the university, which she read with great interest as she devoured a sheet of chocolate chip cookies. In the end, she decided that (a) you never knew about some people, and (b) she didn't feel quite as stupid in the end. Myron was, by that account, a master manipulator. She could at least say she had been betrayed by the best.

Which left the one thing that she could *not* get over: Flynn.

Flynn, Flynn, Flynn.

Jesus, how many sleepless nights did she lie there, staring at the ceiling, wondering how much he'd manufactured to get Myron? Had there been any truth between them at all? He said he loved her on the lawn. Why would he say that now? Unless it was still part of his stupid undercover operation? Or was he just doing the British thing and being very polite? *"Yes, of course I loved you, but you do understand that it was all in the course of my work, there's a love."*

It was a question that ate at her, and several times she thought to pick up the phone and call him. But she didn't— her phone had been disconnected. And she didn't feel quite the confident, sexy young thing she had when she was casting ridiculous, meaningless spells left and right. Nope, she felt like a poor wallflower who was desperately clinging to a fantasy and a lot of stupid knight-in-shining-armor dreams. How lame! He was just another cop with a job to do, and she had been the convenient way to do the job. That was it!

Maybe the worst thing about all of it was that Rachel had to admit Dad was right about her all along. She *had* been living in a dream world. For thirty-one years, she'd been living in a stupid little dream world with fucking blinders on that kept her from seeing the truth about everything and everyone.

The whole thing had left her mightily depressed and completely rudderless. She holed up in her home, going out only when absolutely necessary. Even Mike, who might have been a port in the storm, lost patience and quit calling. His last message was very cold: "Look, I've tried to get in touch. You wanna see me again? You call me."

She put Dagne off with the excuse that she was cleaning her house. At least that part was truthful, for she had begun to view her house as a symbol of her life—a lot of junk with no place or purpose, just scattered around to obscure the truth about who she was.

As the days trudged by, Rachel had no choice but to face the truth about who she was and what she had become. She had languished too long, hiding away in Providence, and it was time she got on with her life. For the first time, she wanted to. She really wanted to. She just couldn't seem to find the motivation to get off her couch, which was beginning to show permanent impressions of her butt. A noticeably flabbier butt, as she had stopped going to the gym, too.

Dagne grew more and more impatient with her, but Rachel didn't care. She didn't need friends; she had Ben and Jerry to keep her company. She didn't even need a phone. It was great not to have to actually talk to anyone about what had happened. It was fabulous not to have to hear or say Myron's name. And it was wonderful that she didn't have to wonder each time the phone rang if it might be Flynn on the other end, then the ensuing panic over what to do.

Yep, the life of a hermit was perfect for her. And in fact, she managed to finish her prospectus for her dissertation, which her professors loved: *The Use of Art in Political History: How Medieval Craft Guilds Shaped Future Unions and Pseudo-Governing Bodies in a Commercial World.*

She tried to resume her weaving class, but really didn't have the heart for it. She sort of wandered from loom to loom, with a lot of "That's great," or "Really nice," and the ever popular "Looks good."

Chantal and Tiffinnae tried their best to cheer her up by complimenting her. "Girl, you looking *good,*" Chantal said, even though Rachel had worn her fat jeans.

"Thanks," she said, hardly caring.

"Mmm-hmm, I think that's a new hairdo, ain't it?" Tiffinnae added, peering curiously at the pile of hair on the top of her head.

"No. Same old, same old," Rachel had sighed, and wandered over to where Mr. Gregory was working with Jason. "That's great," she said, and jumped a little when she realized Chantal was behind her.

"Something stuck to the bottom of your shoe, honey." Rachel looked down; saw a neon-green Post-it was protruding from the back heel of her Doc Martens. She stooped over, peeled it off, and looked at it. It was an old reminder to send the Tantra book to Robin that had fallen out of her bag. She felt close to collapse, and canceled the weaving class until mid-January with an excuse of the Christmas holidays.

As the class filed out, Chantal tried once more, putting her arm around Rachel's shoulders and squeezing tightly. "You better than this, Rachel," she said. "You way better than this. Now you need me or Tif, you call us, you hear?" she asked, and scribbled down her number. "I mean it, girl. We be there for you."

Rachel smiled weakly. "Thanks," she said. "But I'm all right."

"Well, if you're feeling a little down, let me know," Sandy said. "I've got some real good antidepressants. You look like you could use a bunch."

"Thanks, but I'm okay."

And of course, Jason shuffled around, waiting until everyone had gone. "If you need someone to help you move the tree, I can do it," he said. "I have an axe."

"Thanks, but that's okay," Rachel said. "I sort of like it there," she muttered, and let Jason walk her to her car.

She did slowly resume her job search, but only half-heartedly, driven by the need to eat, at least occasionally. But she didn't look very hard because she preferred, at least for the moment, the obscurity of a string of odd jobs. Which pretty much left her alone with her self-pity and the occasional pint of Ben and Jerry's Brownie Fudge Ice Cream. Well. Okay, frequent pint.

If only Dagne would leave her alone. Dagne was really beginning to bug her. She was not content to watch Rachel slide into a deep depression, and when Rachel would not return her calls, she forced herself on her, arriving at her house, letting herself in, acting all mad and irritating Rachel to no end.

"Get up!" she cried at Rachel. "You're going to get *huge* lying around like this!"

"Actually, I've lost a couple of pounds," Rachel said, and continued to eat popcorn from a bag the size of a king pillowcase. She'd picked three or four of them up at her last temp job, Kettledrum Popcorn, Inc.

That had made Dagne mad, as usual, and she had stalked off to a very clean dining room and had started going through the hutch while Rachel watched *Joe Millionaire*.

It was the night *Joe Millionaire* was to pick his favorite and lay the news on her that he didn't have eighty million dollars. He didn't even have *eighty* dollars, but he still loved the girl. And for some reason, as he started to break the news to her, Rachel started to sob. "Don't believe him!" she wailed at the television. "He's *lyyyyying!* You can't trust him! You'll never be able to trust a word he says!"

Amazingly, she never even saw Dagne hurtling through space toward her. But she did, snatching the popcorn from Rachel's hand, and the remote, which she used to turn off the television before she hurled it into the dining room and shouted, "SNAP OUT OF IT!"

"You're screaming at me," Rachel said tearfully.

"Yes, I'm screaming at you! I'm screaming at the top of my lungs because I can't take it anymore! You and this little pity party have *got* to *stop!* Okay, okay, he hurt you, he lied to you, he should have told you the truth, but how long are you going to go on like this?" she demanded.

"Oh shut up!" Rachel shot back nastily. "You think you know so much! I've forgotten all about Myron!"

"Jesus, Rach, I'm not talking about *Myron!* I'm talking about Flynn!"

The very mention of his name was like a knife in her heart and with a gasp that surprised even her, Rachel came up off the couch, gathered her robe tightly around her, and marched past Dagne in her Holstein cow slippers to the kitchen.

Naturally, the bitch followed right behind her.

"Leave me alone, Dagne!" Rachel shouted.

"I am so *sick* of this, Rachel! How long can one person feel sorry for themselves?"

"I don't know, and what do you care? You *have* boyfriends! Two at last count, Glenn and Joe!"

"Glenn dumped me, remember? And Joe is *not* my boyfriend," she said, her face turning fireplug red, which, of course, meant that she was gaga for him.

Rachel poured a glass of wine, pushed past Dagne, and stomped into the dining room, feeling, all of a sudden, like a fish out of water, like she couldn't quite catch her breath.

"Joe's just been working with me to retrieve the items I sold on eBay, that's all," Dagne insisted.

"Oh, sure," Rachel snorted. "Christ, Dagne, you don't

even *get* it. At least you don't believe he is there for any other reason, like maybe, for *you!*"

Just admitting it aloud was a sucker punch, and Rachel inadvertently gulped back a terrible sob.

"Flynn *was* there for you," Dagne said, the shout gone from her voice. "He *loves* you!"

"Oh God, Dagne, do me a favor and stop trying to make me believe some stupid spell! Right, right, he loves me so much he's gone back to England," she said, and took a huge gulp of wine.

"No, he hasn't. He's here in Providence!"

The floor seemed to shift a little; Rachel looked at Dagne from the corner of her eye. "What do you mean— he's here?"

Dagne nodded emphatically. "He's been tracking down the stuff I sold on eBay, too."

That news hit Rachel hard—she had convinced herself that he'd left, had flown back to England and had put her out of his mind. To think he'd been in Providence all this time, while she had been mourning him . . . "Great. Just *great!* So he's been here and never bothered to let me know! Oh yeah, that's love all right!" she said angrily.

Dagne looked at her with such exasperation that Rachel cringed. "Well, he *might* have called you if your phone wasn't disconnected! And he *might* have come by if you hadn't told him you never wanted to see him again!"

"Did he say that?"

"It's pretty obvious."

"Oh, God," Rachel moaned.

"Anyway, I don't give a shit what you think," Dagne said with all authority, and picked up her purse, tucked the giant bag of popcorn under her arm. "Because you are incapable of thinking straight. But if I were you, I'd get myself ready, because I put a major spell on you, girl. And when the moon is full, which, for your information, is only days away, true love is going to come hopping back into your life. For good."

"Jesus, will you stop with that crap?" Rachel cried, covering her ears.

"No, I will not," Dagne said pertly, and marched to the door. "Because I believe! That's always been your problem, you know that? You *never* believe, unless it's something negative about yourself! Try believing in the positive for once!" she said, grabbing up her purse. "You're pissing me off now. I'll see you tomorrow," she said.

"I can't wait," Rachel muttered. But when she was sure Dagne was really gone, she picked up her wine and went upstairs, to her laptop. She did too believe, and she believed it was time to leave Providence.

Subject: Re: Hello Baby Girl
From: <earthangel@hotmail.com>
To: Dad <Aaron.Lear@leartransind.com>

Hi Dad. Yes, I'm okay, I really am. I wouldn't say I did what I needed to do in Hilton Head, but I learned a few important things, mostly about me, and how I really have been living in a fantasy. I am really tired now, and I don't know what I want to do with my life anymore. But my dissertation topic has been accepted, which means I will actually graduate with a Ph.D. in the next few months. I know, I know, big surprise, right? Anyway, after that, I think I want to come home to Texas. Everything here is just a reminder and I don't want to be reminded anymore. Rachel

P.S. Thanks for not giving me any advice. I still can't believe it. Kidding. Not really, but you know what I mean.

Chapter Thirty-eight

* * *

THE surprise of finding his ex-fiancée and his mother in his flat was the icing on Flynn's proverbial cake, and candidly, he could not eat another bite of that sodding cake. He'd been turned upside down, and he therefore endured the first night by actually speaking very little, drinking quite a lot, and lying on the couch with a bottle of lager in one hand, his arm slung over his eyes, silently bemoaning the fact that he did not possess a single set of ear plugs.

His mother was quite beside herself at his less than warm reception for Iris—she had chastised, pouted, then begun to harp, but Flynn was immune. He loved his mother, but he had no sympathy for her; he'd been unfailingly honest with her on the phone, had told her more than once his feelings for Iris had changed, and not for the better. But his mother, God bless her, saw in Iris the perfect match for her eldest son—the Willow-Throckmortons were also part of the fringe aristocracy.

As Flynn listened to his mother drone on about the Fall Flingaling, or whatever it was he had missed and thereby had embarrassed her for life, he couldn't help but think that he had, in a roundabout way, stumbled on Iris's motive for wanting him all along.

He had known, of course, that there wasn't a more blatant social climber from the beginning. But he supposed he'd been rather numb to it, as his mother was the queen of social-climbing, whereas Iris was more a princess in training. As he listened to them talk about Buckingham and Alnwick, or where the Prime Minister's children were schooled (Iris brazenly informing them that the children she bore Flynn would also attend that school), at what charity event they had seen the Duchess of York (and what she'd had to eat), he began to realize that the *real* reason she had flirted with him, then had engaged him, had not been because of some attraction to *him*. It had been to his mother's insistence that they were kin to the Duke of Alnwick.

It was all the two of them could talk about, and he wondered idly if it had always been this way, and if he hadn't really noticed until he came to America, where the lives of the aristocracy were not all-consuming to so many people.

And now it was quite clear why his mother was such a bloody fan of Iris's. They were cut from the same cloth, both of them wanting to latch on to something beyond their reach, and dear God, how close had he come to marrying a younger version of his mother?

An image of his father skipped across his mind's eye, and in that image he saw himself, twenty years hence, a man silenced by years of shrill harping, reduced to glorified handyman while his wife flitted about, trying to gain entry to all of *the* events.

Come to think of it, now that he was arse over elbow after a few lagers, it was his *mother* who had balked at his wanting to become a homicide detective all those years ago. Jesus, that had been the only thing he'd ever wanted, and he'd gone along with all the high teas and polo matches they'd put him through. But when it came to his life, they had been adamantly opposed to anything as pedestrian as a mere police officer. The compromise had been his stint at Lloyds, which his father had helped him get.

Flynn could hardly grouse about his occupation. Over the years, he had become one of their best investigators, and he had been to some very posh locales, had rubbed elbows with some very posh and frightfully rich people, and moreover, some very exotic women. Lloyds had paid him handsomely for it, and he really had no right to complain, not at all, but lying there, listening to his mum, he felt a certain indignation. It wasn't *right*. They should have encouraged him to follow his dreams, not theirs.

Now, once again, his mum was pushing her will on him. She wanted him to marry Iris so that she'd have yet another connection to some distant aristocratic line. Iris wanted to marry him for the same reason. Not because she *loved* him, as he had once so foolishly believed, but because she loved his income and his name. Christ, how very Jane Austen of her.

In all honesty, he'd really known this deep in his gut since he first walked in on Iris and Paul. But now it had been birthed into the glaring light of day, bawling and wriggling around like a newborn infant. There was no avoiding it—no matter how much Flynn would have liked to have stepped around it, perhaps tiptoed out and left it in another room, or just fled to another continent to avoid it altogether, he could not.

What tormented him was how he had come to believe he was in love with Iris to begin with. It wasn't that she hadn't been perfectly pleasant—she'd always been polite and very keen to make sure he knew what to wear to what event and who would be attending, and so forth, trying to be helpful. And while she wasn't an exciting lover, she had been a cooperative one for the most part.

Perhaps it was nothing more than that she'd said the right things. The truth was that he'd been quite ready to come home to a house with a wife and perhaps even children one day, and there had been times he'd arrived in

Heathrow after one assignment or another feeling an impossible sadness as he looked around at all the anxious faces of people waiting for their loved ones. There he'd walk through them, nothing but his briefcase and overcoat in hand, as they embraced and cried and laughed all around him. Perhaps she'd filled that void in her own way, and he'd begun to see in her an answer to a dilemma he really didn't know he had.

Whatever it was, it was over. Now he knew what love was, for he had fallen in love with Rachel, improbable though that may have been, and her absence in his life had created a hole in him, one that was growing wider each day that passed without her. Iris had never, not once, created a hole in him.

He was determined to fill his hole. But first, he had to rid himself of Iris once and for all, send his mum home where she belonged, and finish up the investigation into the RIHPS fraud (which was being helped along, interestingly enough, by Joe, who had taken a fancy to Dagne Delaney). And then he was going to check into a certain international exchange program Joe had mentioned.

So lying there that evening, listening to them prattle on about Fergie, he quietly put a plan into place.

The next day, Iris and Mum had rested up, and had gone out to do the requisite shopping. When they arrived late that afternoon, Flynn was waiting for them. He had catered in a lovely dinner and had bought copious amounts of liquor for whoever would need it. When the girls came in, they were extremely pleased with what they obviously thought was his attempt at reconciliation.

"Darling, you shouldn't have!" Iris exclaimed, air-kissing him again.

"Oh, my lovely boy, how marvelous!" Mum had cried, clapping. "But I really must nosh up and run along."

"Run along?" Flynn asked.

"Didn't I tell you? I took a room at the Hilton. I can't sleep very well here, you know, and I am quite desperate for a good night's sleep."

Righto. Nothing like a bit of a conjugal sleepover to patch it all up, eh, Mum? "That's really not necessary," he said calmly.

"Oh darling, I insist," Mum said, checking her hair in a small mirror near the entry. "Very well, then, shall I serve? I'm really quite starved!" she said brightly, and busied herself gathering plates.

The meal passed pleasantly enough, if one could tolerate a review of each shop in Providence and what they could find, or not find. "Frankly, if one is to reside in America, it simply will not do to live anywhere but New York," Iris opined as she lit a cigarette.

"Mmm, I would have to agree," Mum said.

"I rather like Providence," Flynn said. "It's quaint."

"Quaint!" Iris laughed. "Darling, you've got Butler Cropwell for quaint!"

Flynn smiled thinly. "Here's something that's frightfully quaint, Iris—I have always wanted to be a homicide investigator."

That earned both the ladies' attention; Iris looked nervously at Mum, then laughed. "I suppose all little boys dream of being a policeman," she said, waving her hand dismissively.

"Perhaps. But I still dream of it. In fact, I think I shall pursue it."

"Such nonsense!" Mum said with exasperation. "You've an excellent job with Lloyds! Why would you want to do something that involved murder and unsavory characters?" she asked, shivering a little for emphasis.

"Dunno, Mum, but I do. And I'm really rather good at it. Furthermore, I care very little about the aristocracy. In fact, you could take the whole bloody lot of them and ship them off to China or some such place for all I care."

Iris laughed, but his mother looked at him as if he'd insulted her somehow. "Oh really, you shouldn't tease your mother in such a way," Iris said, playfully tapping him on the arm.

"I'm not teasing her," he said, swinging his gaze to Iris.

"I'm being honest. I want to investigate homicides. I put in a call to my boss just this afternoon and asked if Lloyds might participate in an international exchange program. He thought it was a rather grand idea and has gone off to see what can be done. In other words, I am hoping that I might remain in Providence to learn the art of homicide investigation from the Americans. And then, I'm thinking of moving to America permanently."

"But . . . But I don't want to live in America!" Iris protested.

"Then I suggest you not do so," he said pleasantly. "Iris, I was quite honest with you when I told you it was over. The thing is," he said, trying his damnedest to be kind, "I wouldn't marry you if you were the last woman on earth, and quite frankly, I really have no desire to ever lay eyes on you again. I'm terribly sorry if you think that's harsh, but it's, at the very least, honest. You should try it sometime—honesty, that is.

"And Mum," he said, turning to look at his gaping mother. "I really don't give a rat's arse about the Duke of Alnwick, and I'm actually quite brassed off that you thought to come here and try to manipulate me in such a manner. Please don't cry—I do love you, Mum, but I really must finish my work, and my life, without your interference."

"Dear God!" his mother exclaimed. "I can't believe what I'm hearing!"

"I rather thought you wouldn't," he said pleasantly. "So I gave Dad a ring this afternoon, told him to expect you home in the morning. I also told him what I'm thinking of doing, and he thought it was a jolly good plan. He asked me to tell you to keep your knickers on, that it's really not the end of the world as you know it."

"So you intend to toss us out?" Iris cried, looking truly affronted.

"Not toss you out, but escort you to the nearest plane. You'll find your bags are packed for the drive to Boston, where I've got you booked on the eleven P.M. flight to

London." And with that, he stood up, began to clear the table.

Needless to say, the drive to Boston was not particularly pleasant, what with Mum crying in the backseat and Iris reviewing all the disparaging names for the wretched cretin that he was, and insisting she'd ruin him socially in London. In spite of it all, Flynn kissed his mother good-bye, promised her he'd be home early in the new year, and hugged Iris, who then broke down in tears. "I'm sorry if I've hurt you, Iris," he said sincerely.

"Oh, don't be ridiculous!" she snapped. "I'm not *hurt!* I'm upset that I wasted so much time with you!" she cried, and wrenched free of him, running to Mum for comfort.

Flynn stayed to watch their plane take off—one could never be entirely certain those two were completely gone—and satisfied they were on their way to London, he checked into a hotel. Tomorrow, he was flying to Chicago to retrieve the last of the items that Dagne had sold on eBay. When he got back, he was to call his boss and see what progress had been made on his request to participate in a six-month exchange.

And then he would turn his full attention to Rachel.

Chapter Thirty-nine

✦ ✦ ✦

PROVIDENCE was glittering with Christmas lights, which meant all retail outlets had expanded their hours to accommodate holiday shoppers. That was good news for Rachel, who stayed gainfully employed for several days in a row, and then paid her utility bill.

Even the Valicielos had gotten into the spirit of things; their plastic deer had been turned into reindeer, and Santa and his sleigh were atop their house. The best news of all, of course, was that the tree had at last been removed. Rachel had managed to scrape together the five hundred dollars she needed to have the tree cut and removed, and another seventy-five dollars to have the chain-link fence repaired. As a result, Mr. Valicielo had stopped stalking her and had dropped his small claims case.

In fact, everyone seemed to be caught up in the spirit of peace. Life, as they knew it on Slater Avenue, had returned to normal. All the houses on her street were decorated—except hers, of course. Rachel didn't feel much like celebrating. She had promised Dad she'd come to New York for Christmas. His surgery had been scheduled for mid-January, and she wanted to spend some time with him.

Apparently, everyone did—Robin and Jake and the kids were coming, too, as were Rebecca and her family. Even Grandma and Grandpa were thinking of making the trip.

A couple of weeks before Christmas, Rachel parked in the drive, fished her bag and a sack of groceries out of the car, and paused to admire the lights on her street. With a hint of a smile, she trudged up the steps to the kitchen door . . . but she stopped midway up, because lying in front of the door was a single red rose.

How weird. Probably one of Dagne's latest spells to bring her out of the doldrums. She'd have to call Dagne on her newly reconnected phone and tell her to stop; she was coming out of the doldrums alone. She shook her head, continued up the steps, stepped over the rose and went inside, put her things down, then came back to retrieve it. She glanced around as she picked it up, and noticed there was a card with the rose.

She opened it. *My favorite flower: Rose. The color of Rachel's lips.*

Her heart skipped a beat or two. "W-what?" she asked out loud, and suddenly clutched the rose to her chest, peered down the drive. There was no one—no cars, no sounds, nothing. So Rachel slowly backed into her house, looked at the flower again, brought it to her nose and inhaled the scent of it, then read the note once more.

A smile crossed her lips.

She carried the rose around with her the rest of the evening, half expecting him to knock on the door. At midnight, having worked on her dissertation for several hours, she crawled into bed, the rose with her, and slept soundly.

That night, she dreamed she was walking in snow. Each step was harder than the last, and she kept sinking, until she was sinking with each step up to her thigh. But ahead of her was a single red rose, and in her dream, she was struggling to reach the rose before it blew away.

The next day, Rachel put the rose in a vase and went to the gym.

"Hey," Lori said as she walked in. "I didn't think we were going to see you again!"

"Did you think I'd died or something?" Rachel asked wryly.

Lori laughed. "You know how it is. People gain weight, they come to the gym, then they feel pretty good and stop coming, then they gain weight again and here they come." She smiled, popped a bubble.

Rachel rolled her eyes, went on back to the machines. She could only make it five miles that day before her legs gave out and she began to see her life flash before her eyes, and as she wobbled out the door, she was furious with herself for having wallowed in pity so long. She warned Lori she'd be back the next day.

The rest of the day she was at the university library, working diligently. When she left there, she picked up some Chinese and drove home, and once again, the cheerful Christmas lights greeted her as she drove down the street and turned into the one dark house on the entire block.

She walked to the steps leading to her kitchen door and caught her breath. There was a package there, wrapped in silver paper, tied with a red ribbon. With a grin, Rachel scooped it up and quickly went inside.

At her breakfast bar, she untied the red bow, took the paper from the box, and opened the lid. "Oh God," she murmured as she withdrew a crystal pendant made of blue topaz hanging on a long silver chain. "Ohmigod," she said again, lifting the pendant from the box and holding it up to the light. It was gorgeous; exquisite. She fastened it around her neck, eagerly took the card from the box.

My favorite gem: Blue topaz. The exact color of Rachel's eyes.

"Oh Jesus, Flynn," she whispered, and still grinning, held the pendant in her palm, admiring it, then let it drop against her body and ran to the front windows. She peered out into the night, wondering if he was out there somewhere, watching her. But she couldn't see very well, and bounced to the front door, and walked out onto the porch with her arms folded tightly against her as she looked up the street one way, then the other.

Nothing.

The cold forced her back inside.

Rachel decided it was such a lovely cold night that she'd have a fire. And then maybe she'd look around for the Christmas decorations. She remembered seeing them during her furious cleaning, and she was going to be in town another ten days or so. It wouldn't hurt to have a little Christmas spirit, would it?

She could hardly wait to get home from wrapping gifts at the local mall the next day to see if he'd left her anything, and she was, therefore, stunningly disappointed when there was nothing lying at her back door. In fact, she was so disappointed that she stood there shivering, staring at the steps to make sure she hadn't missed something, a *little* something. Anything! But there was nothing. *Nothing.*

Rachel dragged herself up the steps, opened the door, and went inside.

There, on the breakfast bar, was a large silver box wrapped in red ribbon. Next to it, a note from Dagne. *Found this outside. Call me!*

Rachel pushed the note aside, quickly undid the package. In the box was a beautiful cashmere shawl, the color of a rich mahogany, thick and absolutely gorgeous. With a squeal of delight, she threw the shawl around her shoulders and reached for the card.

My favorite fabric: Cashmere. The texture of Rachel's hair.

She laughed, brought the shawl to her face, feeling it, smelling it, and walked to the dining room, where her Christmas decorations were strewn about the table. Wrapping the shawl more tightly around her, she walked to the door and opened it . . . and stumbled backward in surprise.

There was a Christmas tree on her porch! A bare Christmas tree, seven feet tall, just standing there. "What the hell?" she murmured, and gasped with delight as a small white card emerged through the boughs of the tree.

Rachel snatched the card and quickly opened it. *My favorite pastime: Being with Rachel, for when I am with her, I feel quite like a tree—a thousand feet tall and ageless.*

"Oh God," she said aloud. "Oh Flynn."

"Oh Tannenbaum," a disembodied but distinctly British voice said from behind the tree.

Rachel laughed. "A talking tree, how weird!"

"Actually, we trees make excellent emissaries of peace."

Rachel leaned against the doorjamb and folded her arms across her chest, the note against her heart. "So are you an emissary, Tannenbaum?"

"As a matter of fact, I've come on behalf of a chap who is not altogether very bright, and he has, on occasion, done things that would lead some to believe he has shit for brains, but really, his heart is in the right place, and he wants nothing more than to apologize for his abominable behavior, and perhaps explain how, exactly, things got so far off course."

"Ah, I see," she said, nodding. "Well, maybe you should go back and tell this stupid chap that I'm not so angry anymore, and that he really doesn't have to send a tree. I'm actually ready to talk about what happened," she said, pushing away from the doorjamb. She reached into the tree and pushed it aside, revealing a very wary-looking Flynn behind it. "Because I still love him."

Flynn grinned broadly at that. "There's an excellent start!"

"And I'd like to ask him in," she said, reaching for his tie, "to thank him properly for the gifts he's left me, but I have to ask . . . is everything . . . okay?"

Flynn smiled as he reached out and touched her chin, his fingers skimming her jaw. "Everything is okay," he said softly. "There is no one but you in my thoughts and my heart, Rachel, and there hasn't been since almost the moment I laid eyes on you. Honestly, if I had it to do all over again, there are so many things I might have done quite differently. But I've come to the conclusion that we never choose who we will fall in love with or when we fall, and I suspect that true love is never very tidy, is it?"

"It's devastating," she said, and tugged at his tie.

"Devastating and rather an ugly mess, with lots of pieces and parts that come together, but don't really fit with one another, eh? But at the core of it, there is that abiding sort of love that two people have for each other, and that is what holds those pieces and parts together, to be used or discarded as time goes on. So I am here to say that I love you, Rachel Lear, in pieces and parts. I love you long and short, round and flat, big and small. I love you left and right and north and south and in any other untidy way you might imagine."

"Oh Flynn," she said, and grabbed his hand and kissed his palm. "How did you get to be so poetic?" she asked.

"How did you get to be so beautiful?"

"You want to come in?"

"Only if my friend can come, too," he said.

"Of course—we might need him later, who knows? Because I want to know it all, no matter how painful it might be. I want to put it out there so we can smash it to pieces and go on."

"Thank God," Flynn said, and shoved a hand through his hair. "Thank God."

Rachel stepped back, held the door open for him so he could carry the tree inside. Once he was inside, she let the door close and walked to the edge of the porch and looked up at the sky.

It was a full moon and love had hopped back into her life.

"I owe you, Dagne," she whispered, and turned around, walked inside, to Flynn's open arms.

Subject: Merry Christmas!
From: <earthangel@hotmail.com>
To: Dad <Aaron.Lear@leartransind.com>

Hi Dad. The train gets in around noon tomorrow. Do you think we could go to that Italian restaurant I love? I don't know how you're feeling, but Robbie said that with everyone coming up for Christmas, she didn't want you and Mom to have to worry about cooking. What time is everyone getting in? I'm really excited and I have a big surprise for everyone. Don't try and get it out of me, but it's bigger than a breadbox, it has nothing to do with my dissertation, and I think you are going to be very very very pleased. At least I hope you will be and I have my fingers crossed. Merry Christmas, Dad, and I love you!
Rachel

Subject: Re: The Lear Family—Brace Yourself
From: Flynn <FAOliver@earthlink.net>
To: <rmanning70@houston.rr.com>

Rmanning70@houston.rr.com wrote:

Dude, are you certain you want to unveil yourself at Christmas? Do you know the murder and suicide rate is the highest at that time of year and our father is famous for going off at family gatherings? I'm not saying he will kill you or anything, at least I don't think so, and you never know what Grandpa might do, but they could make it really, really . . . hard. Okay, all right, if that's what you want to do, just consider yourself forewarned. Robin, Rachel's extremely protective big sister, but whose other sister Rebecca said I needed to lay off because she talked to you on the phone and you seem like a really great guy. You better be, that's all I have to say! :)

Dear Robin, please let me put your mind at ease. I am an infinitely pleasant sort of chap and I have excellent table manners, thanks to my mum, who had dreams of marrying me off to Diana Spencer's cousin. Unfortunately, that dream ended tragically when it turned out that the Diana Spencer to whom the young girl was cousined was not, in fact, *that* Diana Spencer. And lest you think I am the lamb being driven to slaughter, Rachel has told me all about her father, warts and all, as they say, and . . . well, to be a bit blunt . . . about you, as well, which has inspired me to practice a bit of kung fu should the need arise. I look forward to making your esteemed acquaintance and that of the entire family, whom I hope to call my own one day. Yours, Flynn Oliver

Epilogue

✦ ✦
✦

AN unusually cold north wind was whipping across the Texas landscape with such force that Rachel, Rebecca, and Robin were the first to be driven inside the ranch house at Blue Cross.

"Perfect. Just perfect," Robin groused as she tried to straighten the short, knee-length black skirt she wore. "Is this an omen, or what?"

"Stop it, Robbie. Don't start getting all weird on us," Rebecca said, trying to comb her shoulder-length hair with her fingers.

"You have me confused with Rachel. She's the one with all the weird stuff," Robin reminded her, and pointed at Rachel, who was peering out the front windows at the long drive leading down to the ranch house from the main road.

"Yeah, but I don't believe in omens," Rachel said. "And besides, we're supposed to be thinking positively. Chi, remember? Positive energy flow."

"I got some energy flow for you," Robin muttered.

"Here comes Flynn," Rebecca said.

The front door banged open and Flynn jumped inside, then struggled against the wind to push the door shut behind him. "Rather nasty out, isn't it?" he said, dragging his hands through his hair as he looked around. "Do you think we might kip a pint of lager before we begin?"

"Flynn!" they all cried at once.

"Sorry!" he said, holding up a hand. "But it has been a rather trying day all in all, what with the weather." He sighed, and was suddenly bumped in the back as the door flew open and Jake, Matt, and Grandpa crowded into the front entry.

"I never seen a blue norther this blue," Grandpa said, shaking his head. "Don't know why we all had to troop down to that silly pond in the first place. Anyone with a lick of sense would have known to do it all right here, right by the fire."

"It was my idea. Oh God, this is a disaster!" Rebecca insisted.

"It's all right, Rebecca," Matt said. "You did the best you could under the circumstance. I don't think anyone can fault your event planning when the weather is this bad."

"That's right," Robin adamantly agreed, shaking her fingers through her hair as Jake tried to fix the collar of her coat. "It's *freezing* out there."

"So Flynn, this is your first time to Blue Cross, eh?" Grandpa asked. "What do you think of the place?"

"Fabulous," Flynn said, looking around admiringly at the richly appointed ranch house.

"When you finish up that school you're in, you ought to have your green card. You could come down here and hire on, huh?"

"Perhaps," Flynn said with a wink. "But we haven't quite decided where we might end up."

The door burst open again; Bonnie appeared, one hand clutched at the throat of her coat, the other holding her hat firmly to her head. "I can't stand it another moment. I can't!" she said, marching into their midst. "After all we've been through, we're supposed to endure *this* shit?" she exclaimed.

"Mom!" Rebecca cried.

"I'm sorry, Bonnie, it was my idea," Aaron said at the door as he pulled Grandma in behind him, while the pastor pushed her from behind.

"Oh Dad, I know you wanted a scenic spot," Rebecca said. "But it's freezing!"

"Well, good night, honey, your daddy knows it's freezing! Look at his lips!" Grandma exclaimed as she maneuvered through the hall into the great room and the fire roaring at the hearth.

"I thought the weather was sort of appropriate," Aaron said with a grin. "There was a time your mother said she'd come back to me when hell froze over."

Bonnie laughed, put her arm through his. "I never said that, Aaron Lear. And I will never agree to renew our wedding vows in an ice-cold wind storm."

"The good pastor here is going to perform the ceremony in our great room," Aaron said. "Why don't y'all go on in and find a place to sit?"

"Wait!" Rebecca cried as Grandpa headed in that direction to join Grandma. "At *least* let me set up something to work as an altar! Come on, Robbie, help me."

"Me? What about Rachel?"

"I'm coming, *too*, Robin!" Rachel said with a roll of her eyes, and smiled at the pastor. "Actually, Reverend," she said, holding out her hand to take him to the great room, "I'm surprised you're still here with this group of heathens." The pastor laughed as he joined Rachel.

Behind them, Jake and Matt and Flynn looked at one another. "I don't know about you guys," Matt said, "but when Rebecca gets thrown a curve, it's best to stay out of her way."

"Maybe for *you*," Jake said with a laugh, clapping Matt on the shoulder. "But if I'm not in there, Robbie's likely to hurt someone."

"What say we send the new guy?" Matt said, and he and Jake both grinned at Flynn.

"Bloody hell," Flynn said, and with his hands on his

waist, he leaned to one side and peeked in at the flurry of activity within. "Might I inquire," he asked stoically, "how long a mate's got to put in before he's no longer considered the new guy?"

"Thirty years, pal," Jake laughed, and gave him a friendly shove as the three men walked into the great room to help get it ready for the ceremony reuniting Aaron and Bonnie Lear.

Bonnie put her arm around Aaron's waist.

"I'm glad we're all at Blue Cross," he said, smiling down at her. "Just look at those beautiful girls we managed to make. Best thing we ever did."

"That's right," Bonnie said. "And look at the men who love them. Good, solid men, who will protect and care for them all their days."

Aaron smiled, squeezed Bonnie's shoulders. "That's all I ever really wanted, you know, for those girls to be happy. And once I had that, I thought I could just go ahead and die. But apparently, God wants me to stick around a little longer." He looked down at her. "Whoever would have guessed after that surgery I'd still be around a couple of years later?"

Bonnie laughed, rose up on her tiptoes and kissed him. "And for the foreseeable future. Cancer free, Aaron. It's a miracle." She slipped out from his arm. "I'm going to go lend a hand."

"I'll be right there," Aaron said after her.

Cancer free. *Thank you, God.*

Bonnie didn't know it, but he'd made the guy upstairs a deal. If He let him stick around, he was going to do things right. He was going to be a positive presence in his daughters' lives, not an oppressive one. He was going to be a better husband to Bonnie, too, and had actually graduated Daniel the Jerk's counseling sessions with praise.

He was going to be a better dad. It was too late for his girls, but he had all those grandkids. Even his baby Rachel had a bun in the oven (which, she had gleefully announced, meant that she'd have to take a sabbatical from her endowed chair in the Art and Architecture Department at Brown University).

Yeah, he was going to be a better man, all right, and he was not going to squander a single moment of the days he had left, however many there were. He'd spend the rest of his life making up for the first sixty years of his life.

He heard the girls laugh at something, their laughter rising up like angels around him, and felt tears well in his eyes. Damn, he was getting sentimental these days. He blinked back those silly tears, and with a smile, he walked into the room filled with his loved ones.

He was, he recognized, one lucky sonovabitch.

The glamourous Lear sisters are
about to get a make-over...

From Bestselling Author

Julia London

Material Girl

0-425-19123-0

The Lear sisters lead cushy, exciting lives, going
to parties and spending their father's money.
But as he lays dying, the patriarch of this family
is about to teach his spoiled daughters
a few lessons about what is important
in life—like love.

Also in the Lear sisters trilogy:

Beauty Queen

0-425-19524-4

Available wherever books are sold or at
www.penguin.com

BERKLEY SENSATION
COMING IN DECEMBER 2004

Husband and Lover
by Lynn Erickson
When Deputy DA Julia Innes' husband is arrested for
the twelve-year-old murder of his ex-wife, she will
have to team up with detective Cameron Lazlo to
clear his name.

0-425-19938-8

The Sun Witch
by Linda Winstead Jones
The first novel in the Sisters of the Sun trilogy, which
tells the story of the Fyne women, who inherited
supernatural arts from their mothers—but a long-ago
curse makes true love unattainable for them.

0-425-19940-1

Echoes
by Erin Grady
Tess Carson's sister has disappeared after being
implicated in the murder of her boss. When Tess
begins to have visions, she suspects that she is the key
to finding her sister.

0-425-20073-6

Secret Shadows
by Judie Aitken
Tragedy on the Lakota reservation brings together an
FBI agent and a doctor, who share the same dreams—
and a passion for each other.

0-425-19941-X